"We Are Three Sisters"

"We Are Three Sisters"

Self and Family in the Writing of the Brontës

Drew Lamonica

UNIVERSITY OF MISSOURI PRESS
COLUMBIA AND LONDON

Copyright © 2003 by
The Curators of the University of Missouri
University of Missouri Press, Columbia, Missouri 65201
Printed and bound in the United States of America
All rights reserved
5 4 3 2 1   07 06 05 04 03

Library of Congress Cataloging-in-Publication Data

Lamonica, Drew, 1973–
  "We are three sisters" : self and family in the writing of the Brontës / Drew Lamonica.
    p. cm.
  Includes bibliographical references (p.) and index.
    ISBN 0-8262-1436-3
    1. Brontë, Charlotte, 1816–1855—Criticism and interpretation. 2. Women and literature—England—Yorkshire—History—19th century. 3. Brontë, Emily, 1818–1848—Criticism and interpretation. 4. Brontë, Anne, 1820–1849—Criticism and interpretation. 5. Yorkshire (England)—In literature. 6. Autobiography in literature. 7. Sisters in literature. 8. Family in literature. 9. Self in literature. 10. Brontë family. I. Title.
    PR4169 .L36 2003
    823′ .809—dc21
                                                                              2002015365

∞™ This paper meets the requirements of the
American National Standard for Permanence of Paper
for Printed Library Materials, Z39.48, 1984.

Text design: Stephanie Foley
Jacket design: Susan Ferber
Typesetting: The Composing Room of Michigan, Inc.
Printing and binding: The Maple-Vail Book Manufacturing Group
Typeface: Goudy

*For my mother and father—my supporters,
my brother and sister—my friends.*

CONTENTS

ACKNOWLEDGMENTS ix
ABBREVIATIONS xi

Introduction
Family as Context and Content 1

CHAPTER ONE
The Victorian Context
Self, Family, and Society 10

CHAPTER TWO
The Family Context
Writing as Sibling Relationship 36

CHAPTER THREE
Jane Eyre
The Pilgrimage of the "Poor Orphan Child" 67

CHAPTER FOUR
Wuthering Heights
The Boundless Passion of Catherine Earnshaw 95

CHAPTER FIVE
Agnes Grey and *The Tenant of Wildfell Hall*
Lessons of the Family 118

CHAPTER SIX
The Professor and *Shirley*
Industrial Pollution of Family Relations and Values   147

CHAPTER SEVEN
Villette
Authorial Regeneration and the Death of the Family   179

Conclusion
Life after *Villette*   209

ABBREVIATIONS IN NOTES   213
NOTES   215
BIBLIOGRAPHY   233
INDEX   255

ACKNOWLEDGMENTS

THIS BOOK BEGAN as a doctoral dissertation written during my tenure as a Rhodes Scholar at Oxford University and evolved into its current form during my first years of teaching at the Louisiana State University Honors College. Writing as a scholar, I aimed to present a cogent and compelling argument; rewriting as a teacher, I put particular emphasis on being clear and engaging. My experiences both as a scholar and a teacher have helped to shape the form, style, and content of this book, and it is my hope that *"We Are Three Sisters"* will be of interest and use to seasoned scholars and beginning students alike.

My sincerest gratitude goes to Dr. Dinah Birch of Trinity College, Oxford, for her invaluable supervision and support, for helping to turn a naive American graduate student into a "proper scholar." Her unfailing enthusiasm for this project kept me going on the bleakest days, and her example as a scholar, teacher, wife, and mother continues to inspire me. I was also incredibly fortunate to have the input of Drs. Tom Winnifrith and Lyndall Gordon, who read this work in its dissertation form. They not only offered suggestions for improvement based on their own expertise but also graciously welcomed another Brontë scholar to the fold. I am grateful for their kindness in both regards.

The librarians at the Bodleian and English Faculty Libraries at Oxford University deserve my thanks for their cheerful assistance, as do the librarians at the Brontë Parsonage Museum, who guided me through the Parsonage collections and happily answered numerous random questions.

I would also like to thank Drs. Steve Emmett and Regina Schneider, who offered friendship, encouragement, and welcome distractions during the heaviest going of research and writing.

Back in the United States, Dr. Robert McMahon of LSU read this work at various stages and advised me, as Monsieur Heger did Charlotte Brontë, to "sacrifice, *without pity*, everything that does not contribute to clarity." It has not been an easy lesson but one for which I am grateful and one which, I am sure, was intended not merely as advice for editing a manuscript. I have profited from his shared wisdom. Any lapses in the fulfillment of his and Heger's directives in this book are due entirely to my own shortcomings.

My family, to whom this work is dedicated, has always been my mainstay. I have been blessed with "a *good* home" in the terms in which Charlotte Brontë understood it, and this blessing has both contributed to my interest in the formative role of the family and enabled me to produce something to show for my intellectual pursuits.

And, finally, "as to my husband—my heart is knit to him—."

ABBREVIATIONS

All citations of Brontë novels within the text are taken from the Oxford Clarendon editions and use the following abbreviations:

AG   *Agnes Grey*, ed. Hilda Marsden and Robert Inglesfield (1988)

JE   *Jane Eyre*, ed. Jane Jack and Margaret Smith (1969)

P   *The Professor*, ed. Margaret Smith and Herbert Rosengarten (1987)

S   *Shirley*, ed. Herbert Rosengarten and Margaret Smith (1979)

TWH   *The Tenant of Wildfell Hall*, ed. Herbert Rosengarten (1992)

V   *Villette*, ed. Herbert Rosengarten and Margaret Smith (1984)

WH   *Wuthering Heights*, ed. Hilda Marsden and Ian Jack (1976)

"We Are Three Sisters"

Introduction

Family as Context and Content

"INTELLIGENT COMPANIONSHIP and intense family affection" allowed Charlotte Brontë to thrive as a woman and an author, concluded Ellen Nussey in her 1871 "Reminiscences of Charlotte Brontë." More than a century later, Juliet Barker brought her comprehensive biography of the Brontës to a close with the same assertion: an "intense family relationship" was vital to the writing of the Brontës' fiction.[1] Family underpinned the social, emotional, and imaginative lives of the Brontës. Family provided the supportive network in which they wrote and through which they embarked on publication. Family was the medium through which they saw and interpreted the world.

Biographers have widely recognized the significance of the family relationship to the formation of the Brontë sisters as mid-Victorian writers, and various literary critics have viewed the family as a precondition and motive for their writing.[2] Yet the family was not simply an essential context for the Brontës' writing processes—the family is an essential element of content in the texts themselves. The Brontës were a writing family who wrote about families. Within the ever-expanding corpus of Brontë literary scholarship, this conclusion is, I believe, both strikingly obvious and commonly overlooked. "We Are Three Sisters" examines the role of families in the Brontës' fictions of personal development, exploring the ways in which these fictions consider the family as a "defining community" for selfhood.[3] The Brontë sisters share an interest in the familial influences on self-development and self-understanding, and I trace this interest throughout the children's writing, or juvenilia as they are collectively called, and the published novels.

This work responds generally to two tendencies in reading the Brontës' fiction. The first tendency looks to the juvenilia and novels for insight into the Brontës' lives, asserting that the Brontës wrote principally about their own lives, and that their lives were uniformly isolated and unhappy ones, with an abusive, eccentric father and a self-destructive, drunkard brother keeping the sisters imprisoned in a gloomy parsonage on the desolate moors. The biographical work of Barker and Lyndall Gordon, as well as Lucasta Miller's cultural history of the Brontë myth, has shown this to be a false picture. Much of the biographical evidence contradicts the idea that the parsonage was a prison in which the sisters were constricted and deprived. While Charlotte and Anne certainly documented their own claustrophobic feelings from time to time, both sisters also affirmed their abiding sense of peace within the four walls of the parsonage. By all accounts, Emily Brontë experienced true freedom solely at her childhood home, where alone her nature expanded. Ultimately, the sisters' family experience cannot be called fixed or uniform: Charlotte Brontë, for example, referred to her home in Haworth alternately as "Paradise" and interment. Clearly the parsonage was a place of extraordinary creativity and productivity. While many students of the Brontës maintain that this creative production happened *in spite of* the two men in the house, Patrick and Branwell Brontë provided the educational foundation and literary example for the sisters' achievements. The family environment at Haworth was ultimately an enabling one. Both father and brother helped the sisters know about the world—what it expected, what it offered, what it denied—and the sisters built on these understandings, exceeding expectations, challenging boundaries, revising roles.

The second tendency in reading the Brontës' fiction stems from the scholarship of Sandra M. Gilbert, Susan Gubar, and others with a strong feminist note, which views marriage and the nineteenth-century family as restrictive sexist institutions and attempts to enroll the Brontë sisters as advocates for breaking these patriarchal constraints. These critics have tended to see the sisters as revolutionary feminists, but this view glosses over the complexities, obscurities, and qualifications that characterize the Brontës' depictions of family life. While the sisters contested those "narrow human doctrines" that kept women, particularly unmarried women, confined and idle in the home, they were not so revolutionary as to disavow the notion of "self-sacrificing love" or to renounce the idea that women had specifically domestic responsibilities, both of which were promoted as tenets of "true womanhood."[4] Even the fiery Jane Eyre, who rails against the subjection of her sex and struggles for personal autonomy, praises domestic endearments as "the best things the world has!" and only ultimately finds fulfillment in married union with Rochester (*JE*, 499).

In considering the role of the family in Brontë fiction, feminist scholars have emphasized an overarching theme of female enclosure and entrapment in domestic spaces—Jane Eyre in the red room, Bertha Mason in the attic, Caroline Helstone and Agnes Grey in their parsonage homes, Catherine Earnshaw and her daughter Cathy Linton in Wuthering Heights, Helen Huntingdon in Grassdale Manor. Feelings of containment in domestic spaces correspond to the characters' limiting roles as wards, wives, and daughters. But this generalization, leading many readers to conclude that the Brontë heroines seek freedom from domestic organizations and familial roles, neglects the finer points. The Brontës do not dismiss the family as a viable structure for self-fulfillment; families can indeed be repressive if they deny personal development and actualization, but the novels conclude with the realization or promise of harmonious domestic union: Jane Eyre and Rochester, Cathy Linton and Hareton Earnshaw, Helen Huntingdon and Gilbert Markham, Agnes Grey and Mr. Weston, Caroline Helstone and Robert Moore, Lucy Snowe and M. Paul. For the Brontë heroines, a communion of self *and* family, not self-sufficient autonomy, is the goal of the journey of self-development and the concluding site of personal freedom. Jane Eyre's quest, for example, does not end when she becomes an "independent woman" with the economic and emotional means to be self-reliant. Caroline Helstone's call for wider spheres for female development and employment arises not from a feminist impulse but from her frustrated longing to be a wife and to carry out those domestic duties associated with wifehood. Helen Huntingdon's transgressive escape from her house of bondage is driven by her desire to fulfill her socially promoted motherly duty as the moral educator of her child. Catherine Earnshaw longs to escape from and return to the same place, only to long for escape again, seeing Wuthering Heights as both a prison and a paradise.

This study seeks to make clear the Brontës' complex and many-sided views of family experience, attempting synthesis and resolution when possible, drawing connections between the novels when applicable, but not forcing a verdict or reductive position on the Brontë sisters as authors. The Brontës themselves were attuned to complexities; they were not polemical writers with fixed feminist agendas. Their writing responded to a mid-Victorian world in which the status of the family and of the female in the family were matters of debate. And they did not ignore—indeed, they could not ignore, given the significant role of the family in their own lives—the profound influence of family in shaping self-perception. In attempting a broader and more accurate representation of the Brontës' own home life and their fictional domestic spheres, "We Are Three Sisters" shifts the focus from the family's restrictive potential to its formative power, emphasizing not what the family denies but what it engenders—an original sense of self that sets the tone for the journey of personal development.

In shifting the focus from "restrictive" to "formative," I have sought to place the Brontës' writing in a context of family that extends beyond the Haworth parsonage. The sisters' interest in the formative role of the family was animated by a Victorian discourse that promoted the family as the primary school of subjectivity and viewed the home as the place where children gained individuality. The notion of "individual identity as a product of family experience" has been a recurrent subject of feminist studies of the Brontë novels, most recently in Paula Marantz Cohen's *The Daughter's Dilemma: Family Process and the Nineteenth-Century Domestic Novel* (1991), Marianne Hirsch's *The Mother/Daughter Plot: Narrative, Psychoanalysis, Feminism* (1989), Natalie J. McKnight's *Suffering Mothers in Mid-Victorian Novels* (1997), and Dianne F. Sadoff's *Monsters of Affection: Dickens, Eliot and Brontë on Fatherhood* (1982).[5] While a social context is implied in these studies, they are primarily psychological in focus, and they do not consider the sisters' novels in relation to one another. My interest in the Brontës has led me to change the framework of analysis from psychoanalytic to sociohistorical considerations. It is increasingly acknowledged that the Brontës did not write in a cultural or historical vacuum, and I have read their published fiction as both influenced by and contributing to a pervasive mid-Victorian debate over the nature of family life and its role in the formation of individual character.

The 1830s and 1840s witnessed a proliferation of domestic tracts, household manuals, conduct guides, and inspirational writings that reinforced the structure of the family, shaped its internal dynamics, and imparted significant new responsibilities, particularly the duty to prepare children for their future adult roles in society. Because of this social function, the family claimed ascendancy as an institution. Its importance was manifested in and perpetuated by an ideology that served to situate individuals, particularly females, in relation to the family unit and promoted the domestic environment as a place of harmonious relations and self-fulfillment.

The Brontë novels have yet to be examined as commentaries on mid-Victorian family life, as E. Holly Pike has explored Gaskell's novels in her book *Family and Society in the Works of Elizabeth Gaskell* (1995) and Catherine Waters has explored Dickens's in *Dickens and the Politics of the Family* (1997). These and other scholarly works have shown that, far from merely reproducing a highly publicized domestic ideology, Dickens, Gaskell, and later George Eliot, were interrogating "the moral and psychological adequacy" of the institutions in which the individual was placed, especially the family.[6] Their portraits of dysfunctional and disintegrating families (Dickens's Gradgrinds, Gaskell's Bartons, and Eliot's Tullivers, for example) expose disjunctions between ideology and social practice and reveal an underlying tension between the demands of the family and the desires of the self. Culminating with the posthumous publication of Samuel Butler's *Ernest Pontifex, or the Way of All Flesh* (1903), mid- and late Victorian novelists questioned the extent to which individual identity is determined by family relations. This line of questioning found an early voice in the writing of the Brontës.

Victorian concepts of family had particular significance for the construction of female identity. Charlotte, Emily, and Anne Brontë wrote in a historical moment when family almost universally defined and positioned female identity. The fusing of female and family into "one cultural formation" was at the heart of domestic ideology and was signified in Sarah Ellis's well-known designation of Victorian women as "relative creatures," recognized and valued only through their familial roles as daughters, sisters, wives, and mothers.[7] The Brontës entered into a mid-Victorian ideological tumult, wherein celebrants and critics of domesticity were simultaneously formulating and challenging normative definitions of "family" and "female." In placing the Brontës alongside a selection of contemporary conduct writers who debated the nature of female experience in the family, this book shows that the Brontës were engaging with the debate in fictive form. The Brontë novels display a heightened awareness of the complexities of contemporary female experience and the problems of securing a valued sense of selfhood not wholly dependent on family ties.

In imagining heroines who long, as Agnes Grey does, "to go out into the world" or who, as in the case of Charlotte's orphan-heroines, lack a family to call their own, the Brontës challenged the ideological promotion of the family as the *exclusive* site for female development, morality, and fulfillment, without ever explicitly denying the possibility of domestic contentment or the notion that a domestic setting could be the locus of female desire. As voices in a Victorian discourse, their writings underscored the formative influence of family but resisted the complete familial determination of identity, endorsing the need for wider spheres of selfhood. Personal development in the Brontës' fiction that is restricted to the relational experience as a daughter, ward, and wife is shown to be mentally and physically debilitating: Caroline Helstone and Catherine Earnshaw, for example, suffer in mind and body as a result of a stifling domestic enclosure. The Brontës advocate for their heroines and for women generally the opportunity to move beyond the family in the pursuit of self-formation and self-knowledge. Charlotte, Emily, and Anne Brontë had such opportunities through their schooling, teaching, tutoring, and, finally, through their writing and publishing. Nevertheless, in life and in fiction, the Brontës recognized the family as a "defining community"—a pivotal influence in the course of personal development.

In emphasizing the need to consider the family as both context and content, my examination of the novels is preceded by two chapters that consider in detail the contextual framework of the Brontës' writing. Chapter 1 provides the sociohistorical context of this study, emphasizing the ideological importance of the family to the society in which the Brontës lived and wrote. The Brontë novels are examined against a background of eighteenth- to mid-nineteenth–century domestic "improving" literature, much of which emanated from an Evangelical emphasis on the family's responsibility to train moral subjects, and much of which focused specifically on the personal development of young women. This literature was part of the Brontës' own formative experience and helped to shape their responses to the Victorian discourse on femininity and the family.

Chapter 2 considers the specific family context of the Brontës' writing processes. The Brontës' practice of writing in sibling partnership largely defined their experiences and ideas of family relations. Writing was also the primary means to assert individuality within the complex system of family relationship and family likeness. Chapter 2 focuses on the negotiation of familial and individual identities in the act of writing, from the Brontës' earliest juvenilia through the published novels of the three sisters, who, even in taking the masculine-sounding pseudonyms Currer, Ellis, and Acton Bell to mask their identities, presented themselves to the world as a family, a trio of brothers. The sisters' real-life brother, Branwell, deserves a prominent place in the family writing dynamic, and he is considered in his multifaceted roles as innovator, creative spur, artistic rival, wasted talent, and, importantly for Charlotte, a partner with whom she first reckoned issues of gender and authorship.

In my readings of the Brontë novels, I have understood "family" not merely as a background structure out of which the main action—the journey of self-development—takes place. Nor have I taken "family" to be strictly an association of blood relations. Families in the Brontë novels serve as "defining communities" that take on active roles in casting ideas of selfhood. Heathcliff, for example, although not related to the Earnshaw family by blood, is nevertheless a vital member of the family as defining community that serves to shape Catherine Earnshaw's sense of personal identity. In each of the Brontë novels, the family of origin launches what Susan Fraiman has called "the project of Bildung."[8] With the exception of Shirley, the Brontë novels can be said broadly to follow a nineteenth-century bildungsroman course, in which an innocent youth departs the original domestic environment in search of experience in the larger world.[9] For each of the Brontë protagonists, the desire to quit the original environment arises from a lack of full participation in the family and a realization that the familial projection of his/her character is erroneous or incomplete.[10] The protagonist then undergoes a period (or periods) of physical and/or psychological dislocation, or separation from the family unit, whether by choice or fortune. It is during this period that the self-understanding engendered in the original family community is refined and redefined. The journey of education concludes when the protagonist's newly formed sense of self is fully accommodated and valued within a relationship, and, with the exception of Villette (a significance that I discuss in the final chapter), the protagonist participates fully in a family of his/her own. Thus, the protagonist's need to find and secure a valued field of identity in relation to the original defining community of family forms a common structural directive in the Brontë novels.

In suggesting this common pattern of movement in the novels—from a family that cannot accommodate the self to one that can—I realize that I am being greatly reductive. It is impossible to impose unity on the Brontës. Thus, while I argue for their shared interest in subject formation as conditioned by a family, I do not ignore the fact that the novels, like the sisters themselves, are highly individualized. Reinforcing the modern critical assessment that there is no Brontë "oneness," chapters 3 through 7 survey a diversity of approaches, perspectives, analyses, and emphases through which the Brontës scrutinize the family as a force in character development.[11]

Chapter 3 traces Jane Eyre's progress of self-realization and self-determination through a series of defining communities, beginning with Jane's anomalous status as an unwanted orphan dependent upon the Reed family. Jane Eyre's journey of self-development is characterized by a continual negotiation of the original Reed family pronouncement of who she is and where she belongs. Her movement out of the original family environment is a search for kinship that will accommodate and encourage her developing self-esteem. Her realization of kinship occurs on both earthly and spiritual levels. Chapter 3 proposes an interconnection between Jane's secular pilgrimage to family and her spiritual pilgrimage to communion with God in terms of the novel's three-volume structure. The novel establishes a crucial analogy between Jane and the "poor orphan child" in Bessie's ballad, who, lacking human kin, nevertheless recognizes herself as a child of God. Jane also comes to recognize herself as a beloved and protected child of God, and, through this recognition, she matures and is rewarded with a family of her own.

In chapter 4, the tragedy of Catherine Earnshaw is discussed in terms of her failure to negotiate the marital exchange from her brother's house to her husband's. Catherine Earnshaw's bildung is doomed by her inability to disentangle her idea of self from the original defining community of family. I view Catherine's life and death as a historically specific struggle against her social and familial designation as a "relative creature," forced to exist as a daughter, sister, or wife. Catherine's protest against her condition is carried out through her identification with Heathcliff, which, she believes, offers her a sense of wholeness and control that her family bonds deny. Catherine's vision of male-female relations, however, is never realized in the novel. The socially and legally sanctioned notion of woman as man's possession or derivative dominates female selfhood in the novel and finally allows Heathcliff to secure the properties of the Earnshaw and Linton families.

Chapters 5 and 6 underscore the Brontës' didactic use of families for moral and social criticism through their consideration of the family's power to shape self-perceptions as well as the individual's outlook on society. Anne Brontë's novels are most clearly recognizable as social commentaries on the Victorian family, particularly on the formative influence of the family over its members. In Chapter 5, I examine *Agnes Grey* and *The Tenant of Wildfell Hall* in the context of domestic "improving" literature of the 1830s and 1840s, as well as the religious didacticism exemplified by Patrick Brontë's writings. Anne Brontë is specifically concerned with the moral development of the young as directed by the family. She exposes the misdirected, morally destitute lessons imparted from parent to child through middle-class ideologies of femininity and masculinity. In my discussion of *Agnes Grey*, I focus on the inability of the private governess to "unteach" parentally prescribed behaviors and values. In my consideration of *The Tenant of Wildfell Hall*, I examine the struggles of Helen Huntingdon—herself misguided by the idea of her wifely role as saving angel—to deliver her son from his father's corrupting influence, defying contemporary divorce and child custody laws to do so.

Chapter 6 explores the interrelation between family and self-formation as affected by larger socioeconomic forces. My discussion centers on the disruptive power of the mill and the intruding processes of industrialization on family relations. Whereas, in domestic discourse, the family should have been able to reform a competitive industrialized society by its example of harmonious cooperation, Charlotte Brontë instead presents families corrupted by the conflict-driven marketplace environment. Chapter 6 examines *The Professor* and *Shirley* as part of a corpus of midcentury industrial novels that rest their social criticism on the theme of brotherhood forsaken, a charge against contemporary society made explicit by Thomas Carlyle, whom Charlotte admired and whose ideas she incorporated into her own writing.

Having established the centrality of family relationship to the Brontës' writing processes in chapter 2, I underline this significance in chapter 7 by recognizing the absence of family during the writing of Charlotte Brontë's last novel. I discuss *Villette* in the immediate context of the deaths of Branwell, Emily, and Anne Brontë, and in the broader context of Victorian attitudes to death and the Christian promise of life after death. The composition of *Villette* marked Charlotte Brontë's literary attempt to cope with the death of her siblings and the resulting destabilization of her identity as an author. Chapter 7 considers the effects of the family's demise on the surviving self, both on Charlotte Brontë as a novelist and Lucy Snowe as her literary counterpart. All of the other Brontë novels conclude with the protagonist fully integrated in a family of his/her own: for both Charlotte and Lucy, however, *Villette* is a testimony to writing and living without the family.

CHAPTER ONE

The Victorian Context
Self, Family, and Society

> The free, fair Homes of England!
> Long, long, in hut and hall,
> May hearts of native proof be rear'd,
> To guard each hallow'd wall!
>
> Felicia Hemans, "The Homes of England" (1827)

Roles of the Family in Victorian Society: A Brief Overview

An intensely perceived and experienced family relationship was not unique to the Brontës. The three sisters lived and wrote in a society preoccupied with the network of relationships and responsibilities that constituted family life. Numerous studies have sought to trace the historical and structural evolution of the family in England.[1] Jean-Louis Flandrin has examined the changing definitions of "family" through English and French dictionaries, concluding that, prior to the nineteenth century,

> the concept of the family was divided between the notions of co-residence and kinship, which one finds amalgamated in the definition that has become most current today. In former times, the word "family" more often referred to a set of kinsfolk who did not live together, while it also designated an assemblage of co-residents who were not necessarily linked by ties of blood or marriage.[2]

In the late eighteenth century, the term *family* still was used in England and France to designate resident kinsfolk as well as domestic servants, insofar as both were subject to the same patriarchal head.³ The nineteenth-century family was the first to join elements of kinship and coresidence and generally to exclude servants and other kin beyond the married couple and their offspring. Thus, by 1829, James Mill had narrowed the structural definition, asserting, "The Group, which consists of a Father, Mother, and Children, is called a Family." Lawrence Stone identifies this grouping as the "closed domesticated nuclear family," which assumed predominance "in the key middle and upper sectors of English society."⁴

Naturally, not all families conformed to the nuclear model, and the Brontës were among the deviants. The death of Mrs. Brontë in 1821 removed the maternal presence that was vital to the composition and ideology of the Victorian family. "Aunt Branwell" became a resident addition to the family upon Mrs. Brontë's death, and the Brontës clearly considered their domestic servant Tabitha Aykroyd as "one of our own family."⁵ Thus, while death disrupted the nuclear arrangement of many families, wider applications of family status persisted into the nineteenth century and beyond.⁶ The Brontës' interest in orphans and fractured families, as expressed in their fiction, no doubt sprang from their personal loss. The novels also expose ambiguities in the boundaries between the familial and nonfamilial, challenging the extent to which one's "kin" was determined solely by blood relation. Heathcliff's position in the Earnshaw family and his perceived affinity with Catherine Earnshaw, as well as Jane Eyre's recognition that Rochester is her "kin," serve to test the familial/nonfamilial divide.

The crucial shifts in the history of the family, as Steven Mintz has argued, were not in structure but in concept—the expectations and roles delegated to the family and its individual members. Despite deviations in social practice, the *idea* of family as father, mother, and children dominated domestic ideology, and this trio was overwhelmingly taken to be the household model in discussions of family life. Paula Marantz Cohen attributes the ideological dominance of the nuclear family in the nineteenth century to the support and promotion it received from the middle classes. The middle-class vision of domesticity sanctioned the division of the world into "separate spheres," the public workplace and the private home, and fixed the proper place for men and women according to sexual difference: men had the necessary intellectual and assertive qualities to tolerate "rough work in the open world"; women, by virtue of their moral influence and tender affections, were best suited to raise children and counsel husbands in the home.⁷ Although this arrangement most closely corresponded to middle-class experience, it served as a paradigm for which all families should strive.

With the rise of the factory and mill systems in the late eighteenth century, the family all but lost its role as a productive unit in society. Home was no longer the place of work; consequently, two characteristics of domestic life assumed increased importance: enclosure and emotion. According to Stone, the Victorian family began to insist on a greater degree of privacy for itself, and its members, as a subset of larger society. Unlike in previous generations, marriage was based less on economic interests and more on companionship and mutual affection, though the choice of a spouse was still often limited by the dictates of class endogamy. There was also a greater degree of familial containment of women and children, whose emotional and intellectual development was directed almost entirely within the home.[8]

While the Victorian family was visioned as a self-contained and inward-turning unit, the nineteenth-century home was promoted as a haven in a heartless world, a necessary counterbalance to the increasingly mechanized and dehumanized world of work beyond the home. Such is Wemmick's view of his home, the Castle, in Dickens's *Great Expectations* (1860–1861), and Wemmick maintains a strict policy of separate spheres: "the office is one thing, and private life is another. When I go into the office, I leave the Castle behind me, and when I come into the Castle, I leave the office behind me." In 1884, Friedrich Engels argued that the ideological function of the family was to provide a convalescence for the worker alienated by competition and self-interest in an industrializing society. At home, the heart could be alive, active, expressive, and connected, making the family, unlike the workplace, a site of "intensified affective bonding."[9] The domestic circle provided a refuge not only for the sentiments but also for Christian values—values that were increasingly under threat in the cutthroat world of business and politics. Home was visioned as a secure domain where loyalty, honesty, cooperation, mutual affection, sexual morality, and willing self-sacrifice governed the interactions among individuals. By midcentury, the association of these virtues with the domestic sphere had become so complete that they were often referred to as "home virtues."

Jeffrey Weeks believes the early and mid-nineteenth–century proliferation of domestic propaganda, which reinforced the idea of family as a repository of home virtues, resulted from a large-scale fear of social disintegration in the face of rapid industrialization and social change.[10] The political and economic unrest of the 1830s and 1840s, both in England and abroad, culminated in widespread revolution throughout Europe in 1848. Closest to Haworth and the Brontës, agitation was manifest in controversies with Dissenters, protests against the Poor Law Amendment Act of 1834, contention surrounding factory reform in the 1840s, and Chartist riots in Bradford in May 1848.[11]

Domestic ideologues and social reformers sought to preserve the middle-class vision of familial and sexual order, not only to maintain the home as a buffer against "the anxieties of the outer life," as John Ruskin famously urged in 1865, but also to serve as an example of harmonious relations and stable values on which society should model itself. Ruskin described the "true nature of home" as "the place of Peace; the shelter, not only from all injury, but from all terror, doubt, and division." This claim appears less a characterization of Victorian realities than a reminder of the family's responsibility to be *unlike* society, removed, as Ruskin held, from "the inconsistently-minded, unknown, unloved, or hostile society of the outer world." In her influential study of industrial reform literature of the 1850s and 1860s, Catherine Gallagher has identified a common paradox in Victorian domestic ideology: ideologues simultaneously insisted on the family's protected isolation from society and on its engagement with society, maintaining that the family unit has social obligations and that domestic operations have social consequences. The family was promoted as "society's primary reforming institution" by its example and by its crucial role in shaping individuals who were prepared to enter an industrial world, but who would also retain the values associated with the family.[12]

Family was the medium through which individuals entered society. Ideally, the original home environment was the source of Christian values, but as Louis Aimé-Martin asserted, it was also "from the house of each citizen that the errors and prejudices which prevail in the world, emanate." Aimé-Martin and other domestic educationists expressed the fear that the unabated pursuit of self-interest evident in the marketplace would lead to social chaos "unless such aspirations were counterbalanced by self-restraints internalized in the depths of individual personality." It fell to the family to instill these restraints in children by the governing control of parents.[13]

For good or ill, the family thus occupied "a tremendous place" in Victorian society as a formative agency. In 1871, the social reformer Anthony Ashby, Seventh Earl of Shaftesbury, declared: "There can be no security to society, no honour, no prosperity, no dignity at home, no nobleness of attitude towards foreign nations, unless the strength of the people rests upon the purity and firmness of the domestic system. Schools are but auxiliaries."[14] The "lessons" of the family—those directly imparted from parent to child, as well as those indirectly gleaned from familial example—

assumed tremendous emotional and psychological significance for the formation of subjectivity. These "lessons" became the focus of domestic guides and conduct literature, which were flourishing as the Brontës were writing.

"A Good Home is the Best of Schools": Self-Formation in the Family

With the removal of apprentices and trade assistants from middle-class households, and the increase in time adolescents spent in the parental home, sons and daughters became the focus of family-conducted education. The role of the family was no longer simply to produce economically secure individuals—whether by furnishing inheritances and dowries, arranging marriages, or training children in a family craft—but to create emotional, moral, and social selves. Jacques Donzelot has argued that the advent of the modern bourgeois family centered on "the primacy of the educative function."[15] As middle-class sensibilities came to dominate cultural discussions of the family, the emphasis shifted from nature to nurture: it was less important to be *of* a good family, where "good" signified aristocratic lineage, than *in* a good family, where "good" signified the presence and inculcation of home virtues.[16] Domestic educationists stressed the impact of early home instruction: "The world has much to do, it is true, with the formation of character," Marianne Farningham wrote in 1869, "but after all its power is very little compared with that which is held over us at home." Alexander Scott's *Suggestions on Female Education* (1849), which Charlotte Brontë read and admired, insisted that the foundation of character is laid in childhood, and that "no training is here so efficient as the earliest."[17]

By the nineteenth century, childhood was viewed as a separate, highly impressionable "age of life" and children as fragile beings who needed love and affection, as well as guidance and discipline. Evangelicals rejected the Romantic notion of childhood innocence to insist on a doctrine of original sin, maintaining that children required constant watchfulness and correction to uproot their inherently sinful propensities. Like the Romantics, however, they emphasized the impressionable nature of childhood, taking their credo for childrearing from the words of Solomon: "Train up a child in the way he should go: and when he is old, he will not depart from it." In *Domestic Portraiture* (1834), a collection of letters between the Evangelical Reverend Legh Richmond and his children, which

Charlotte Brontë also read and admired, Richmond reminds his son, "Childhood is the period when the character and habits of the future man are formed. Trifle not, therefore, with your childish days." Such advice recalls the Wordsworthian dictum, "the Child is father of the Man," and stands as an example of the seriousness with which many parents regarded youthful experience and impressions in influencing adult character.[18]

Elisabeth Jay explains that Evangelicals throughout the various Victorian sects were united in the belief that a good Christian home provided the best environment for training up a child. "A good home is the best of schools," noted Richmond.[19] Because early lessons determined a child's destiny, the responsibility of the family to oversee children's education carried the weight of a moral imperative. Simply, the objective of family-conducted education was to prepare a child to go beyond the family. Every individual had a dual destination: the world beyond the "walled garden" of the original home, and the world beyond the mortal world—in other words, society and eternity. Family directed one's entrance into both worlds.

Writing his introduction to *Domestic Portraiture,* the Reverend E. Bickersteth stressed that *"to train and prepare the soul for its eternal destiny is the proper business and end of education,"* and it was the family's role to instill in its members a Christian code of ethics from the earliest age. The pressure to promote children's readiness to meet their Maker was underpinned by the ever-present threat of death in childhood, as well as uncertainties regarding personal salvation, which the Brontës themselves suffered periodically. Benjamin Hershel Babbage's 1850 report to the General Board of Health on sanitary conditions in Haworth confirms that the threat of early death was substantial. Between 1838 and 1849, 41.6 percent of the children in Haworth died before reaching the age of six. Yet the insistence on preparing the soul for the afterlife could become oppressive. The Calvinist Reverend Carus Wilson, founder of the Clergy Daughters' School at Cowan Bridge and author of *The Children's Friend,* for example, displayed in his sermons and writings an "extreme and even unhealthy obsession" with early death and eternal punishment.[20]

Naturally, parents hoped that their children would live to enter adult society, and the family mediated this entrance by giving its young members a sense of their social "place" or role. It was a society in which gender marked the most important difference between individuals and served as the most distinctive indication of one's "place." The family functioned as the original arena for the construction of sexual difference. Boys and girls in middle-class families were treated and dressed similarly until about the age of five or six, when boys were normally breeched. From this point, they followed different courses of development within the family, distinguished by different toys, dress, educational practices and goals, and standards of behavior—all of which emphasized different social destinies.[21] In Victorian fiction, these disparities are nowhere more clearly displayed than by the Tulliver family in George Eliot's *The Mill on the Floss* (1860). Mr. Tulliver's sole aim for his children is to provide his son Tom with "a good eddication; an eddication as'll be a bread to him." Although Mr. Tulliver admits that Maggie is "twice as 'cute as Tom," she is denied this outlet and scorned by her beloved brother for expressing any personal ambition that violates his strict sense of proper moral and intellectual standards for women.[22]

The revered educationist Hannah More advocated differing degrees of restraint for the young based on "the natural cast of character, and the moral distinction between the sexes," insisting that the "bold, independent, enterprising spirit" encouraged in boys should be suppressed in girls. Her idea of femininity was rooted in the Pauline doctrine of women's duties—care of the family, edification of the men, and education of the children—all of which kept women confined in the home.[23] More advocated the singular importance of woman's ability to nurture morality, and writers like Sarah Lewis carried this idea of "woman's mission" into the nineteenth century. In *The Tenant of Wildfell Hall*, Anne Brontë radically refutes More's idea of moral distinction, promoting instead an equality of moral education for boys and girls. Her protagonist, Helen Huntingdon, rejects the belief that female knowledge and experience must be limited because female morality is fragile even as it is influential. Gender-determined restraint is also painfully evident to Catherine Earnshaw in *Wuthering Heights*, as her movement is wholly contained within the two domestic spheres of the Heights and the Grange, while the Earnshaw men travel freely out into the world.

For both boys and girls, the Victorian family, like families throughout the centuries, acted as the original disciplinarian, imposing limits on the self. Within the family, restrictions were set, transgressions punished, restraints internalized, conscience developed, and the principles of subordination implanted according to a hierarchy of power relations—children submit to parents, wives to husbands. Recognizing limits was a vital part of a nineteenth-century child's home education. In *Jane Eyre*, the disciplinary function of the Reed family is clearly manifested in Jane's incarceration in the red room, which serves as punishment for her deviation from the expected childlike and ladylike disposition. Mrs. Reed brings a religious fervor to her educative charge to uproot the bad propensities of a willful and passionate nature. As the Evangelical Reverend Richmond advised, "Self-will is a principal source of mischief to young people; submission and deference to age and experience, a chief virtue to be cultivated by them." Submission and deference made smooth the processes of family government, and they were cultivated as home virtues to be carried into society. Domestic education thus served as an "instrument of social order," instilling civic virtues as well as Christian ones. In 1827, the poet Felicia Hemans accordingly praised the "free, fair Homes of England" as the decisive setting "Where first the child's glad spirit loves / Its country and its God!"[24]

As the primary educator of children, the mother was central to the family's role in shaping the self. She directed the child's earliest and most fundamental lessons, fostering speech acquisition, personal hygiene, manners, and the ability to differentiate "right" from "wrong." She was also the child's earliest model of behavior. Ideally, she provided an example of selfless devotion and service to her family, which helped to condition social identity for her children, especially her daughters, advancing a valuation of communal welfare over self-interest and displaying a cheerful acceptance of gender-determined limits.

The recognition of woman's educative importance within the family led to her popular elevation. Aimé-Martin, among countless others, praised maternal influence as the world's chief civilizing agent: "On the maternal bosom the mind of nations reposes; their manners, prejudices, and virtues,—in a word, the civilization of the human race all depend upon maternal influence. . . . Do we not perceive that the thoughts which occupy the woman at home, are carried into the public assemblies by the man?"[25] Such interpretations of a pervasive domestic influence asserted womanly superiority and command over men but also justified woman's segregation from public spheres of influence. An 1843 review in *Blackwood's Magazine*, the favorite of the young Brontës, maintained:

> Great, indeed, is the task assigned to woman. Who can elevate its dignity? who can exaggerate its importance? Not to make laws, not to lead armies, not to govern empires, but to form those by whom laws are made, and armies led, and empires governed; to guard from the slightest taint of possible infirmity the frail, and as yet spotless creature whose moral, no less than his physical, being must be derived from her; to inspire those principles, to inculcate those doctrines, to animate those sentiments, which generations yet unborn, and na-

tions yet uncivilized, shall learn to bless.... Such is her vocation....
Such is her destiny.[26]

Again, this conventional view of woman's "task" simultaneously served to praise and prohibit, invoking a specifically female moral power and, at the same time, imposing female subordination to men and containment within the home. The reviewer underscores the significance of maternal influence by calling attention to the constructedness of identity: the "as yet spotless" child, the Lockean tabula rasa, derives his physical and moral subjectivity from his mother. This notion of a mother's integral role in character formation advanced women to a position of social importance, but it ultimately burdened them with the responsibility for male behavior.

Anne Brontë's Helen Huntingdon embraces her charge "to inspire... to inculcate... to animate" moral doctrine and religious principle in both her husband and son, but Anne shows that Helen is able to succeed in this charge only as a mother. Her failure to effect any lasting change in the reprehensible Huntingdon reinforces the idea that character is set in childhood (Helen blames Huntingdon's adult behavior on his indulgent upbringing) and strengthens her commitment to educate her son in the habits of restraint and self-respect, in order to counter the example provided by his father. Prominent in eighteenth- and nineteenth-century literature on childrearing was the assertion that children learn by example as much, if not more, as by instruction—a point reiterated in *Agnes Grey*. Domestic advice guides thus pressed parents to scrutinize themselves as well as their children. In her 1849 tract *Household Education*, Harriet Martineau announced, "I will but give one brief rule, namely, 'What you wish a child to be, be that to the child.'"[27]

In the absence of a mother, the responsibility of acting as parental example and instructor in the Brontë household fell to the father. Patrick Brontë is often sidelined in discussions of the Brontës' formative environment, but he played a crucial role in his children's intellectual, moral, and social development. Largely owing to Elizabeth Gaskell's portrait of Patrick Brontë, he has been unjustly misrepresented as coldheartedly distancing himself from his family, abandoning his children to the care of servants under the direction of Aunt Branwell. But Patrick was daily involved in his children's lives, most obviously as their primary educator, and he took his responsibility seriously. He made the two objectives of home-based education—preparation to enter society and eternity—priorities in his practice of childrearing.

The Brontës in Context: Education in the Family

Biographers and literary critics since the late nineteenth century have surveyed the Brontës' lives for clues to their writing. Elizabeth Gaskell thought that a knowledge of Charlotte's home life in Haworth was necessary for a "right understanding" of the author and, therefore, of her novels. Gaskell emphasized the family's eccentricities, particularly the father's, suggesting that Patrick Brontë's "strong, passionate, Irish nature" served to excite Charlotte's "strong mind and vivid imagination." Accounts of the father's "mad fits of austerity"—cutting to shreds a silk gown belonging to his wife and burning colored boots given to his children as gifts—were presented as exhibitions of eccentric violence that made an impression on all his children and were translated into their novels. Gaskell's purpose, as Barker has noted, was to vindicate Charlotte by blaming her family and upbringing in Haworth for the critical condemnations of the language, tone, and content of her writing. In this objective, Gaskell was immensely successful. *Fraser's Magazine*, for example, in one of the many reviews of Gaskell's *Life of Charlotte Brontë*, concluded that the "strange childhood" endured by the Brontës "explains a good deal in their subsequent history." The *Christian Remembrancer* declared, "Whatever extenuation can be found for want of refinement—for grosser outrages on propriety than this expression indicates—the home and the neighbourhood of Charlotte Brontë certainly furnish; she wrote in ignorance of offending public opinion."[28]

In this century, the portrait of the Brontës' father as a family oppressor has been greatly tempered. Helene Moglen, among others, has revised Gaskell's emphasis on the Brontës' "strange" upbringing, arguing that "the Brontë family, with all its eccentricities, was prophetically Victorian in its structures and patterns of interaction." While it did not structurally conform to the nuclear model, the Brontë family displayed many of the internal characteristics that Stone and others have associated with the Victorian family generally. From their correspondence, it seems clear that Patrick Brontë and Maria Branwell enjoyed a companionate marriage based on mutual and open affection. The Brontës were a private family, partly owing to natural reserve and partly resulting from their social isolation as the family of a clergyman whose congregation was made up largely of factory workers. The Brontë children, close in age and interests, were self-sufficient in each other's company and thus did not seek out other relationships in the Haworth community. Within the parsonage itself, there was an obvious concern for personal privacy: Gaskell notes the conscious designation of the "father's study" and the "children's study," whose boundaries were mutually respected.[29]

Interactions within the Brontë family were marked by gender-determined differences in experience and expectations between Patrick Brontë's daughters and only son. Like most Victorian patriarchs, Patrick actively promoted the prospects of the son who would "make the family name" in larger society. To secure Branwell's social success was, in Winifred Gérin's terms, Patrick's "main purpose," and the girls themselves recognized that Branwell's destiny was more important and expansive than their own.[30] They observed the familial duties expected of Victorian daughters and sisters: the respectful loyalty and service owed to the father who provided for their well-being and the sacrifice of personal ambitions in order to foster their brother's. Following the example of their aunt, they performed the daily domestic chores and assisted in the management of the household, while Branwell enjoyed almost unrestrained freedom. Considering these dynamics, the Brontës could indeed be called "prophetically Victorian" but for the unexpected outcome: Branwell's demise and the sisters' rise to literary fame.

Steven Mintz has asserted that the figure of the Victorian father stood as the "embodiment of moral and intellectual authority."[31] For the young Brontës, their father's dual authority was underscored by his position as head of the Anglican church in Haworth and his Cambridge education. His staunch Toryism and Evangelical bent were largely adopted by his children, as was his emphasis on education and self-improvement, evinced in his own rise: the son of a poor Irish farmer, he became a Cambridge scholar and clergyman. Inspiring in his children an appreciation of moral virtue and religious principle was a keystone in his lessons, as was guiding them into the gender-determined roles they would assume as adults.

Patrick was certainly one of the first to advise his daughters on the tenets of conventional femininity. Excerpts from his own writing as well as Charlotte's letters suggest that he largely subscribed to the orthodox view that female nature was inherently domestic and that female vocation was ideally located within the home. In this attitude, he was a follower of St. Paul, with whom he repeatedly identified in his didactic writings. In *Shirley*, Charlotte's heroines Shirley Keeldar and Caroline Helstone specifically reject the Pauline doctrine, which held that women should "learn in silence, with all subjection" to male authority (S, 370). Irene Tayler has interpreted this crucial chapter in *Shirley*, which also criticizes Milton's vision of Eve, as the author's pointed protest against society's sexism and, more personally, that of her own father.[32]

Yet, despite the traditional views articulated in his sermonic writing and reading, in practice Patrick Brontë offered his daughters a highly unconventional education, allowed their reading to go uncensored, promoted a liberty of thought, and, most important, encouraged them toward self-sufficiency. While Charlotte, Emily, and Anne clearly redefined patriarchal visions of femininity in their novels, Patrick Brontë himself was an enabling force behind his daughters' literary achievements, fostering those opportunities for personal development, both inside and outside the parsonage, that they advocated for their female characters.

Elizabeth Gaskell maintains that Patrick Brontë probably formed his opinions on child education from the writings of Jean-Jacques Rousseau and Thomas Day, which highlighted the moral power of education, as well as the necessary discrimination between girls' and boys' education also advocated by Hannah More. The 1819 edition of Hannah More's *Moral Sketches of Prevailing Opinions and Manners, Foreign and Domestic: With Reflections on Prayer* assumed a prominent place in the Brontë library and was filled with Patrick's annotations. With parts of her tract specifically addressed to the family patriarch, More stressed the importance of Christian education in the home as the foundation of "true virtue" and sure preservation from vulgar, worldly vice.[33]

It is clear that much of what the Brontës were encouraged to read and indeed did read was theological. The majority of works owned by the family was either directly related to or inspired by Christian theology, including numerous editions of the Bible in English, Latin, and French; several editions of the Book of Common Prayer; collections of sermons; John Bunyan's *Pilgrim's Progress* (1678); as well as eighteenth-century works of moral instruction in the evangelical mode, like More's *Moral Sketches* and G. Wright's *Thoughts in Younger Life on Interesting Subjects* (1778). The Brontë novels are filled with explicit and implied biblical allusions, indicating that all three sisters were well-versed in their Bibles.[34] The sisters were also exposed to contemporary works of Christian didacticism at school. From Margaret Wooler's school at Roe Head, Charlotte Brontë praised Richmond's *Domestic Portraiture; or, The Successful Application of Religious Principle in the Education of a Family, Exemplified in the Memoirs of Three of the Deceased Children of the Rev. Legh Richmond*. Charlotte confessed that the account of Richmond's zeal in fostering Christian virtues in his children "strongly attracted, and strangely fascinated, my attention," and she advised her friend Ellen Nussey, "Beg, borrow, or steal it without delay." Perhaps she saw in the Evangelical Richmond an extreme version of her own father; in any event, it is apparent that, by age twenty-one, Charlotte appreciated the importance of moral education in the family and its role in the formation of character.[35]

Like Richmond, Patrick Brontë was keen to test the inculcation of Evangelical principles in his children. Gaskell includes a letter written by Patrick in which he recounts his attempt to probe his children's beliefs by placing each of them successively behind a mask, hoping that under cover they would speak with less timidity. But the children give programmed responses, clearly more reflective of their father's teaching than of personal beliefs, particularly because they are so young (the eldest, Maria, was only, according to Patrick, "about ten years of age," the youngest, Anne, was "about four"). When he asked a seven-year-old Charlotte to name the best book in the world, she replied, "The Bible," maintaining that the next best book was the "Book of Nature," both authored by God. When Maria was asked what was the best mode of spending time, she responded with a characteristic Evangelical precept: "by laying it out in preparing for a happy eternity."[36]

The exchange of questions and answers in the mask episode also suggests that from an early age the Brontë children were made aware of gender-determined differences and destinies. At six years old, Branwell adopted the mask and was asked by his father to tell the best way of knowing the difference between the intellects of men and women. He answered, "By considering the difference between them as to their bodies." Also from behind the mask, Elizabeth responded that the best mode of education for a woman was "That which would make her rule her house well."[37] Both children articulated, apparently with their father's approval, the standard view that sexual difference determined capacity for intellectual attainment and that girls' education should be geared toward household management as the proper and natural female vocation.

In *The Maid of Killarney* (1818), one of Patrick's characters, Dr. O'Leary, advances the belief that the female mind was not formed to contend with the classical breadth of boys' education:

> The education of a female ought, most assuredly, to be competent, in order that she might enjoy herself, and be a fit companion for man. But, believe me, lovely, delicate, and sprightly woman, is not formed by nature, to pore over the musty pages of Grecian and Roman liter-

ature, or to plod through the windings of Mathematical Problems, nor has Providence assigned for her sphere of action, either the cabinet or the field. Her forte is softness, tenderness, and grace.[38]

If Patrick also turned to the writings of Rousseau to guide his educational philosophy, as Gaskell maintained, he would have read the directive in *Émile* (1762) that "a woman's education must . . . be planned in relation to man. To be pleasing in his sight, to win his respect and love, to train him in childhood, to tend him in manhood, to counsel and console, to make his life pleasant and happy, these are the duties of woman for all time, and this is what she should be taught while she is young."[39] Patrick's advocacy of these views would suggest that female education in the Brontë family was limited to acquiring the polite accomplishments and domestic skills, with a view toward marriage. Although Charlotte, Emily, and Anne had drawing lessons, and Emily and Anne played the piano, economic necessity made these accomplishments auxiliary, except as useful qualifications for employment as governesses.

Patrick Brontë rightly saw that to educate his daughters solely to win men would not secure their future welfare, and whatever his views on the capabilities of the female mind or the proper place of women, he was not so ideologically committed as to be unpractical. He could hardly support five grown daughters on his clergyman's salary of £170.[40] They would therefore train to be teachers or governesses, then among the few respectable occupations open to middle-class women. With this in mind, he sent Maria, Elizabeth, Charlotte, and Emily to the Clergy Daughter's School at Cowan Bridge, assured by the fact that the revered Hannah More was one of the school's patrons. The school's advertisement in the *Leeds Intelligencer* maintained that its "great Object in View" was the "intellectual and religious improvement" of its pupils, adding that, if a more liberal education was required for those girls wanting to be teachers or governesses, "an extra Charge will probably be made."[41] The cost proved high for the Brontës: Maria and Elizabeth died of consumption, which, according to Charlotte, was the direct result of the deplorable conditions of the school.

At home, the three remaining daughters acquired a thoroughly liberal education under the tutelage of their father. Upon Charlotte's return from Roe Head when she was sixteen years old, Patrick entrusted the instruction of Emily and Anne largely to her, which allowed him to devote more time to concentrated study periods with Branwell. In addition to the lessons in Scripture, reading and writing, history, and geography, the sisters appear to have learned at least some Latin and ancient history alongside Branwell, and perhaps some Greek as well—an atypical course of study for middle-class women and certainly beyond the scope advised by Dr. O'Leary and Rousseau. Emily at some stage learned enough Latin to translate portions of Virgil's *Aeneid* and Horace's *Ars Poetica,* and Anne purchased a Latin *Delectus* in 1843 to assist in teaching her pupil, Edmund Robinson, during her time as a governess at Thorp Green.[42] Reading *Jane Eyre* and noting its numerous classical references prompted William Makepeace Thackeray to write to Charlotte's editor, W. S. Williams, remarking, "Who the author can be I can't guess, if a woman she knows her language better than most ladies do, or has had a 'classical' education."[43]

Despite the family tragedy at Cowan Bridge, Patrick Brontë remained committed to the goal of self-sufficiency for his daughters. Their education continued at Margaret Wooler's school at Roe Head, and in 1842 he approved Charlotte's bold idea that she and Emily further their training in Brussels, with the view to setting up a school in the parsonage. Financially subsidized by Aunt Branwell, Charlotte and Emily became students at the Pensionnat Heger in Brussels, where they were instructed in French, drawing, music, arithmetic, and German.

By contrast, it was Patrick's intention to oversee his son's education personally and exclusively at home. Branwell never suffered under the regimen of public schooling or strict tutorials, as did the literary schoolboys Tom Brown and Tom Tulliver, though Patrick did not treat his son's education lightly. In June 1839, he proposed that he and Branwell undertake a fairly rigorous, systematic course of reading that included the first six books of the *Aeneid,* the four Gospels in Greek, books of Homer's *Iliad,* and Horace's *Ars Poetica* and some of his odes. The purpose of this regimen was to fit Branwell for a position as a tutor, which he secured at the end of 1839. But more important perhaps, as Edward Chitham has suggested, this course of classical studies was intended to act as a "moral stabiliser" for a young man about to make his way in the world.[44]

Winifred Gérin contends that Branwell's adult failings were the direct consequence of this romanticized home education: he was schooled by the heroic examples in literature and history, which had little relevance for his eventual entry into an antiromantic, industrializing society. Patrick's decision to keep Branwell at home, however, was supported, if not influenced, by More's *Moral Sketches,* which presented boys' home education by a Christian father as "England's Best Hope" for personal and social morality. But Branwell's sheltered education did not preserve him from worldly vice: Elisabeth Jay has called Branwell one of the "notable failures of the evangelical system."[45] He succumbed to an adulterous affair with the wife of his employer at Thorp Green, falling into drink, opium addiction, idleness, depression, and, finally, death. *The Tenant of Wildfell Hall*, written in the midst of Branwell's deterioration, features Anne Brontë's criticism of her brother's upbringing. Branwell had been conscientiously tutored in religious principle, but, Anne believed, he was allowed too much license to "test" his virtue by experience.

"Literature Cannot Be the Business of a Woman's Life...."

Long before they were of age to be governesses and teachers, the Brontë sisters were already prolific writers. It was a struggle, especially for Charlotte, to subordinate the desire for vocation—"the will to write"—to established ideas of feminine duties and the demands of teaching and governessing.[46] During her Christmas holiday from Roe Head in 1836, Charlotte sent a selection of poems to the poet laureate, Robert Southey, asking his opinion of them. What he thought of her "faculty of verse" is overshadowed by his now infamous injunction: "Literature cannot be the business of a woman's life: & it ought not to be." Although Southey admitted that the writing of poetry could contribute to personal enjoyment and edification, it could not be part of a woman's "proper duties" to which, he maintained, Charlotte had not yet been called, meaning wifehood and motherhood. This appeal to duty struck a powerful chord in Charlotte. Throughout her life, she displayed a keen sense of her family duty and a commitment to the idea of service and self-sacrifice *"for the sake of those at home"* (Charlotte's emphasis). It was a course she recurrently advocated in her letters and one she herself sought to follow at the expense of her own ambitions.[47]

Vowing to keep his advice forever, Charlotte thanked Southey in a March 1837 letter from Roe Head:

> Following my Father's advice,—who from my childhood has counselled me just in the wise and friendly tone of your letter—I have endeavoured not only attentively to observe all the duties a woman ought to fulfil, but to feel deeply interested in them. I don't always succeed, for sometimes when I'm teaching or sewing I would rather be reading or writing; but I try to deny myself; and my Father's approbation amply rewarded me for the privation.[48]

One cannot help but notice a tone of respectful sarcasm in Charlotte's reply, particularly in her assertion that fatherly approval is ample reward for the drudgery of teaching and sewing. Both Patrick Brontë and Southey served in Charlotte's life as patriarchal reminders that female duty was domestic and that literary ambition was deviant. Charlotte puts these conventionalities into the mouth of Mademoiselle Reuter, who objects to Frances Henri's literary aspirations in Charlotte's first novel, *The Professor*. "Ambition," Reuter remarks, "*literary* ambition especially, is not a feeling to be cherished in the mind of a woman" and far "better for her to retain the character and habits of a respectable, decorous female" (*P*, 150, 151).

By linking respectability with decorum in Reuter's idea of proper female character, Charlotte Brontë makes another ironic commentary, as if an "ambitious" mind is necessarily detrimental to a woman's social repute. It is also significant that this notion of the "proper feminine" is voiced by a woman. In *A Room of One's Own* (1929), Virginia Woolf railed against the popular approbation of the decorous and domestic woman as a patriarchal imposition designed to keep women submissive and nonliterary. But Charlotte Brontë clearly acknowledged that women supported and promoted the female ideal. Arguably, the most influential prescriptive writers of conservative femininity were women. Two seminal texts appeared in 1839—*The Women of England: Their Social Duties, and Domestic Habits*, by Sarah Ellis, and *Woman's Mission*, by Sarah Lewis—both advocating the naturalness of separate spheres, the power of a woman's moral influence over men and children (to exert this power was her "mission"), and the idea that, through service to family, a woman did her social duty and attained personal fulfillment. Ellis's *Women of England* was in its ninth imprint and had been succeeded by the equally popular *Daughters of England* (1842), *Wives of England* (1843), and *Mothers of England* (1843) when *Jane Eyre*, *Wuthering Heights*, and *Agnes Grey* appeared in 1847. The concept of "woman's mission" was so well known by midcentury that Charlotte condemned the phrase as hackneyed.[49]

The Brontë novels emerged in the midst of a burgeoning "woman question," when the conservative definitions promoted and defended by writers like Ellis and Lewis were concurrently being challenged by such critics as Ann Richelieu Lamb and Mrs. Hugo Reid, who insisted on spheres of action and influence for women beyond their domestic one. Lamb's *Can Woman Regenerate Society?* (1844) was one of the earliest tracts to refute Lewis's notion of woman's innate influence over men. Lamb condemned "the magic circle called 'the sphere of woman'" as "a silly phrase, which has done more harm to our sex than can be told." Reid's *Plea for Woman* (1843) argued for women's social equality with men and staunchly denied that "the proposed enlargement of woman's sphere is incompatible with the spirit of self-renunciation" in its Christian sense. Custom, she argued, prescribes to women not self-renunciation but "self-extinction."[50] The Brontës' fictional portrayals of females within and without families ("without" in both senses of "lacking" and "existing outside of") invoke these debates, and, although there is no evidence that the Brontës read Lewis, Lamb, or Reid, they participated in the dialogue over the nature and role of women that was undeniably and unavoidably part of the spirit of the age.

The Brontës and the Woman Question: Family and Female Identity

During the composition of *Shirley* in 1848, Charlotte Brontë admitted to W. S. Williams, "I often wish to say something about the "condition of women" question—but it is one respecting which so much "cant" has been talked, that one feels a sort of repugnance to approach it."[51] Despite this disclaimer, *Shirley* says quite a bit about the condition of women. The "woman question," as it has come to be called, was in fact many complex questions considering the extent to which the family defined and positioned female subjectivity. Was a female inherently domestic? Was the family the natural and ideally exclusive site for female development? Should there be opportunities for personal development and experience beyond the home, broader female education, and more socially approved employment options?

From an early age, the Brontës were aware that these questions were being discussed by the population beyond the parsonage, and this debate filtered to the four siblings—like their impressions of Byron, recent history, and political controversies—through the publications they received and the books they purchased and borrowed. In her youth, Charlotte read copies of the *Lady's Magazine: or Entertaining Companion for the Fair Sex* (1770–1830), which she obtained either from her aunt or her mother's belongings, salvaged from a shipwreck during her mother's journey from Penzance to Liverpool in 1812. In addition to the journal's romantic and supernatural tales, Charlotte no doubt read the advice column written by "The Matron" and reader-response pages devoted to issues of love, marriage, and female education and employment. *Blackwood's Edinburgh Mag-*

azine (1817–1980), which the Brontës emulated in their juvenilia, also had reviews of popular domestic treatises and novels. Prior to 1840, Charlotte, and presumably Emily and Anne, read the novels of Samuel Richardson, whose heroines were paradigms of female morality and self-sacrifice within the domestic sphere.[52]

Charlotte Brontë also became familiar with Sarah Ellis's reputation and her conduct guides for the women of England. In 1850, following the publication of *Jane Eyre* and *Shirley*, she began a letter to Williams, "Mrs. Ellis has made her "Morning call"; I rather relished her chat about "Shirley" and "Jane Eyre"; she praises reluctantly and blames too often affectedly—but whenever a reviewer betrays that he has been thoroughly influenced and stirred by the work he criticises, it is easy to forgive the rest—." This reference is to a review of Charlotte's novels in Ellis's 1850 collection of reviews, articles, and fiction, entitled *The Morning Call*. Ellis betrays a thorough ambivalence toward Charlotte's works, finding it necessary, like many contemporary reviewers, to protest against the author's "coarseness," or unconventionality in language and sentiment. She condemns passages as "unwomanly" but is forced to admit, "Even while the head condemns, the heart is taken by surprise, and compelled, sometimes against its will, both to sympathise, and to respond." Nonetheless, Ellis finds the wholly domestic and self-denying Caroline Helstone a far more exemplary female than the passionate Jane Eyre.[53]

In another of Charlotte's letters, it is evident that her publisher, George Smith, had promised to send a series of excerpts from *Punch* (1841–1992) entitled "Scenes from the Life of an Unprotected Female." From November 3, 1849, to April 20, 1850, the series dramatized the comic misadventures of "Mrs. Martha Struggles," a woman ill-prepared and ill-equipped to handle herself in the larger world. In a tone of playful sarcasm, Charlotte agrees to wait for the parcel's arrival "in all reasonable patience and resignation—looking with docility to that model of active self-helpfulness Punch friendly offers the 'Women of England[']' in his 'Unprotected Female.'" Because Charlotte capitalizes "Women of England" and encloses the phrase in at least one quotation mark (she was not always a careful letter writer), it seems clear that she is alluding to Ellis's famous work. Even if she had not read it, she presumably associates patience, resignation, and docility with the type of femininity that Ellis endorsed.[54]

Following the publication of *Jane Eyre*, the Brontës' chief source of domestic fiction and nonfiction was the publishing house of Smith, Elder, which sent parcels of contemporary works for the family to read and return at their leisure. Charlotte's publishers loaned the Brontë family a wide range of books they otherwise would not have seen: history, biography, political economy, poetry, essays, and fiction, by contemporary figures, including Carlyle, Tennyson, Macaulay, Hunt, Mill, Ruskin, Kingsley, Dickens, as well as contemporary women writers, such as Julia Kavanagh, Elizabeth Lynn Linton, and Fredrika Bremer, a Swedish domestic novelist whose works were translated into English by Mary Howitt.[55]

There is only one extant list of the books included in a Smith, Elder parcel, which is documented by Charlotte and dated March 18, 1850. The list is punctuated by works concerned with "woman's lot" both inside and outside the domestic sphere. This assortment of books provided Charlotte with her introduction to the fiction of Jane Austen, whom Charlotte decried for her lack of passion and force of emotion.[56] The parcel also included Julia Kavanagh's *Woman in France during the Eighteenth Century* (1850), which explores the social and political power of female aristocrats during the regency and reigns of Louis XV and XVI; Lady Sydney Morgan's *Woman and Her Master* (1840), a chronicle of and protest against six centuries of female subjection to man's rule; Grace Aguilar's *Woman's Friendship: A Story of Domestic Life* (1850); and Alexander John Scott's *Suggestions on Female Education: Two Introductory Lectures on English Literature and Moral Philosophy* (1849), delivered in the Ladies' College, Bedford Square, which promoted the named subjects as appropriate study for women.

These selections were clearly sent not only to provide recent publications, but also to stimulate Charlotte's thoughts on female issues. Despite her professed reluctance to address the "condition of women" question, Charlotte Brontë, unlike her sisters, did offer her opinions in personal correspondence. It is, however, difficult to detect a clear line of thought in her letters. Harriet Björk has remarked, "We may trace ambiguities, militant and bitter attitudes as well as attempts at reconciliation and understanding." Charlotte saw both progress in the way men regarded the position of women and problems "deep-rooted in the foundations of the social system" that could not be touched and for which she could not suggest a remedy.[57]

The Brontë sisters were not specifically feminist campaigners or propagandists in the manner of, for example, Charlotte's outspokenly feminist friend Mary Taylor, her former schoolfellow at Roe Head who emigrated to New Zealand in 1845, resolved to achieve an economic and social independence that she felt was denied to women in England. Perhaps Charlotte's most provocatively feminist exchanges were contained in the letters she sent to Mary, or perhaps she curbed Mary's zeal with her own questions and quandaries over the stance of women. Unfortunately, Charlotte's voice is lost to us in this case, as Mary saw fit to destroy her letters. In her own correspondence to Charlotte, Mary repeatedly faulted her friend for not being a strong campaigner for women's rights. Commenting on *Jane Eyre*, she remarked, "You are very different from me in having no doctrine to preach. It is impossible to squeeze a moral out of your production. Has the world gone so well with you that you have no protest to make against its absurdities?"[58]

Between 1865 and 1870, Mary Taylor wrote a series of articles for the *Victoria Magazine* (1863–1878) entitled "The First Duty of Women," which advanced not only the right but the obligation of women to be self-supporting. Mary also launched a sustained and overt protest against the world's absurdities in a novel of her own, *Miss Miles*, written over the course of her adult life. The novel features four female protagonists who, removed from their family environments for various reasons, rise to positions of self-possession and self-sufficiency through active self-help. A woman must improve her own condition, old Miss Everard insists, because patriarchal society responds to women as to corpses, expecting from them only lifeless passivity and undisturbed tranquility. "No one will think of helping [a woman] any more than they would think of taking her up out of her coffin, if they once got her into it," Miss Everard advises the young Maria. Mary charts the struggles of Maria, Dora, Sarah, and Amelia as they rise out of domestic interment, locating self-fulfillment for her protagonists in supportive female communities that enable the quest for independence. Throughout *Miss Miles*, Mary maintained that the means and desire to be self-supporting should be taught in the family, and, like Anne Brontë in *Agnes Grey*, she rails against those mothers who sentence their daughters to dependence on men, under whose guardianship they fade into oblivion: "Women do go out of sight. Yes, it is a mysterious dispensation. Is it their own fault? If so, why are they not taught better? Why, why!"[59]

Although the Brontës cannot be said to have preached a common doctrine on the role and position of women in mid-Victorian Britain, they were nonetheless discerning commentators on specifically female problems. The novels of all three sisters contain clear moments of protest and feminist passages criticizing a contemporary social patriarchy that kept women confined in the home and socially appreciated only in terms of their familial roles. Even Emily, who is the least didactic of the sisters and the least ostensibly concerned to advance a position on the woman question, presents the life and death of Catherine Earnshaw as a critique of the designation of mid-Victorian women as "relative creatures," not valued in their own right. The Brontës' fiction addresses specific contemporary issues that affected the state of the family and, particularly, of females within the family. *The Tenant of Wildfell Hall*, for example, clearly suggests the need for reform in divorce laws, anticipating the late-nineteenth–century Married Women's Property Acts (1870, 1882) and Custody of Infants Act (1886). But the novels focus more generally on the complexities of the domestic sphere and private life from a female perspective.

The authors' protests can be heard largely through the voices of their heroines, who declare themselves stifled by or existing outside the bounds of approved femininity. Caroline Helstone, Catherine Earnshaw, Agnes Grey, and Helen Huntingdon voice their discontent in domestic enclosures and their sense of paralysis and mental deterioration in familial containment. As a female without a family, Lucy Snowe asserts her feelings of alienation and despair in a society that only recognizes a woman as a man's daughter or a man's wife. Helen Huntingdon and Jane Eyre implicitly reject the construction of women as saving angels or divine helpmates by proudly pronouncing themselves to be "no angels" and ultimately refusing to bear personal responsibility for Rochester's and Huntingdon's conduct.

That the Brontë heroines were "unwomanly," displaying questionable morality and latent rebellion against their condition, was a recurrent criticism in the mid-Victorian reviews of their novels. The *Atlas* viewed Catherine Earnshaw as "wayward, impatient, impulsive" and condemned the younger Cathy as having "grave moral defects." Helen Huntingdon was, according to the *North American Review*, "doubtless a strong woman . . . but if there be any lovable or feminine virtues in her composition, the author has managed to conceal them." Elizabeth Rigby famously regarded Jane Eyre as disturbingly revolutionary, "the personification of an unregenerate and undisciplined spirit," and Margaret Oliphant saw Jane Eyre as a precursor to the dissident women of sensation fiction that rose in the 1860s, drawing attention to what critics called "her 'protest' against the conventionalities in which the world clothes itself." It was also, Oliphant maintained, a new "sensation" that an unmarried girl like Caroline Helstone should protest against the circumstances that kept her secluded and inactive and "burst forth into passionate lamentation over her own position and the absence of any man whom she could marry."[60] In 1856, selected passages of Caroline's protest were reprinted to form the substance of an article entitled "Woman's Lot. A Fragment, by the Author of *Jane Eyre*" in *The Englishwoman's Domestic Magazine*; this article was subsequently reprinted in the July 1920 *Times Literary Supplement*.[61] Taking the passages out of their narrative context, the periodical format suggested a direct correlation between the text and the personal opinions of the author. For the generations that followed her, Charlotte Brontë was clearly recognized and promoted as a public voice—a feminist voice—condemning the plight of unmarried women, their aimless existence, their economic and emotional dependency.

Female Dependency: "The Great Curse"

The Brontë novels are concerned with the education of female youth, addressing issues of female development, maintenance, and fulfillment prior to or outside of the conventional course of marriage. Throughout the eighteenth and into the nineteenth century, female development was largely viewed in terms of familial transfer: a daughter departed her family of origin in order to become a wife and mother in a family of her own. Female education, therefore, was directed to ensuring a successful negotiation from the father's house to the husband's, emphasizing those accomplishments that would attract a good husband (i.e., the arts, drawing, piano-playing, knowledge of French, etiquette). It was a relative education for a relative creature. Personal development was understood to be a means, never an end, and this view was dominant throughout much of the nineteenth century. In his famous article on female redundancy, William Rathbone Greg emphasized that "the essentials of woman's being" are that "*they are supported by, and they minister to men.*"[62]

The earliest appeals for more comprehensive female education insisted on the need to improve woman's ability to educate her children. In *A Vindication of the Rights of Woman* (1792), Mary Wollstonecraft argued, "To be a good mother, a woman must have sense, and that independence of mind which few women possess who are taught to depend entirely on their husbands.... I only now mean to insist, that unless the understanding of woman be enlarged, and her character rendered more firm, by being allowed to govern her own conduct, she will never have sufficient sense or command of temper to manage her children properly." More than fifty years later, Harriet Martineau reiterated the notion that the best-educated women were also the best wives and mothers.[63]

But while Martineau's *Household Education* stressed the need for a broader curriculum so that women could better fulfill their domestic charges, she also recognized that an increasing number of women were not making the passage from their fathers' houses to their husbands'. As the realities of female redundancy were becoming evident, the goal of girls' education had to be, in Martineau's view, self-sufficiency:[64]

> In former times, it was understood that every woman, (except domestic servants) was maintained by her father, brother or husband; but it is not so now. The footing of women is changed, and it will change more.... What we have to think of is the necessity,—in all justice, in all honour, in all humanity, in all prudence,—that every girl's faculties should be made the most of, as carefully as boys'. While so many women are no longer sheltered, and protected, and supported, in safety from the world (as people used to say) every woman ought to be fitted to take care of herself. Every woman ought to have that justice done to her faculties that she may possess herself in all the strength and clearness of an exercised and enlightened mind, and may have at command, for her subsistence, as much intellectual power and as many resources as education can furnish her with.[65]

In the same year that Martineau published *Household Education*, Charlotte Brontë privately denounced dependency as the "one great curse of a single female life." Earlier in 1846, when the three sisters were arranging the publication of their book of poems, Charlotte confessed to Margaret Wooler, "I speculate much on the existence of unmarried and never-to-be married women nowadays and I have already got to the point of considering that there is no more respectable character on this earth than an u[n]married woman who makes her own way through life quietly pers[e]veringly—without support of husband or brother."[66] Allowing women the means to achieve an "independency"—this is the thrust of the Brontës' feminist concerns, implicit in all seven novels. For the Brontës, "independency" did not simply mean freedom from economic dependency on a man. More important, it signified an emotional and psychological sense of being whole, of possessing one's self without contingency upon others for confirmation of self-worth.

Female dependency was an inevitable outcome of the limited education and restricted formation afforded young girls, taught, as Helen Huntingdon criticizes, "to cling to others for direction and support" (*TWH*, 30). In *Shirley* and *Agnes Grey*, Charlotte and Anne clearly deemed it the responsibility of parents to encourage self-sufficiency in their daughters. Female education, if not wholly carried out within the home, was nonetheless decided and directed by parental authority; parents were generally the intended audience of domestic advice literature. *Agnes Grey* is addressed to those in charge of children's education, upholding the character of Rosalie Murray as an example of the personal disservice parents inflict on daughters reared only to secure profitable marriages.

In *Shirley*, Charlotte makes a direct appeal to the fathers of England to seek for daughters "an interest and an occupation" that will free their minds from being "narrow and fettered" (S, 444). Charlotte reiterated this exhortation to a father she knew personally, her reader W. S. Williams, who sought her advice on the education and occupation of his own daughters. "Do not wish to keep them at home," she wrote in 1849, "give their existence some object—their time some occupation—or the peevishness of disappointment and the listlessness of idleness will infallibly degrade their nature." Charlotte praised Williams's "excellent sense" when he maintained that girls without fortune should be brought up and accustomed to support themselves: "Most desirable then it is that all, both men and women, should have the power and the will to work for themselves—most advisable that both sons and daughters should early be inured to habits of independence and industry."[67]

Female education, Charlotte maintained, should be geared toward establishing a girl's economic independency, but, even more crucial, her intellectual and emotional freedom. When Williams's daughter was to be presented at Queen's College, London, Charlotte encouraged the undertaking: "Come what may afterwards, an education secured is an advantage gained—a priceless advantage. Come what may it is a step towards independency." She laments the girls who, in the manner of Rosalie Murray and Shirley Keeldar, are "reared on speculation with a view to their making mercenary marriages": a girl is never a self for herself; she always and only exists for others.[68]

In life and in literature, the Brontës defied familially and socially imposed limitations on female self-development. In 1849, Charlotte wrote that she wished for "every woman in England" a "hope and motive" not strictly limited to the domestic sphere and not centered on a husband and family. Jane Eyre rejects the prejudiced assumptions that women should be content in the sphere to which society has relegated them, arguing, "it is narrow-minded in their more privileged fellow-creatures to say that they ought to confine themselves to making puddings and knitting stockings, to playing on the piano and embroidering bags. It is thoughtless to condemn them, or laugh at them, if they seek to do more or learn more than custom has pronounced necessary for their sex" (JE, 133). *Shirley*'s Rose Yorke concisely illustrates this refutation of conventional boundaries when she answers her mother's charge that she engage in domestic pursuits: "I will do that," Rose replies, "and then I will do more" (S, 453). Rose proposes a selfhood that exists in but extends beyond the family. It is through this rejection of boundaries that the Brontës articulate desires beyond the orthodox understanding of female nature, revealing and advocating what Nancy Armstrong has called "new territories" of the female self.[69]

It is important to recognize that, even as their fiction promotes various forms of female autonomy, the Brontës do not degrade or attack domestic duties and endearments, or deny the possibility of self-realization and self-fulfillment within marriage. In their fictions of personal development, the drive for "independency" of self does not preclude the longing for relationship. The educational quest for the Brontë heroines is to acquire self-possession and self-knowledge *within* relationship, and the novels conclude with relationships that accommodate and respect the self.

The Brontës' formative environment points to the complexity of the family as an agent in the construction of individual identity. The family of origin functions as a site where the individual is formed, valued, and promoted, but also where individual will is curbed and made to conform, and self-restraint is inculcated. For the Brontë sisters, home fostered their valuation of self-improvement and self-sufficiency, but it was also a place where the self had to be denied to win the approbation of the father, and where sisters had to put a brother before themselves. Patrick Brontë was clearly a reminder of conventional femininity, but, through his liberal educational practice, he nurtured highly original minds. From their programmed voices behind a mask, the Brontës became public voices, questioning and criticizing their society's established ideas of morality and femininity. The Brontës' fiction values the individual—in a relationship with God and in relationships with others, both in the context of the family and in the larger context of society. All three sisters recognized the importance of the original family environment in establishing one's sense of selfhood. The Brontë family served as the decisive setting and network of relationships that launched each sister's course of personal development, as well as the siblings' collective writing endeavors.

CHAPTER TWO

The Family Context
Writing as Sibling Relationship

> The highest stimulus, as well as the liveliest pleasure we had known from childhood upwards, lay in attempts at literary composition....
>
> Biographical Notice of Ellis and Acton Bell, September 19, 1850

WHILE THE MID-VICTORIAN FAMILY was recognized and promoted as an institution for identity formation, the Brontë family additionally served as "an institution for literary production."[1] The following chapters focus on the defining role of families in the Brontës' fictions of personal development. No study of self and family in the Brontës' writing can ignore the family's formative role in the sisters' own development as authors. From their earliest juvenilia to their published novels, when the Brontës thought of themselves as writers, they thought of themselves as a family of writers.

Although writing has typically been described as solitary work, the Brontës thought of it as a group activity. From the beginning, collaboration was intrinsic to the creative process. Shari Benstock has defined collaboration as "the partners' struggle in search of fulfillment and self-expression within bonds." The Brontës' collaborative bonds were sibling ones, and their initial struggle for self-expression as authors occurred not within a male-dominated publishing world but within the private family world. The Brontës' practice of writing in sibling partnership elicited their "deepest feelings of kinship," as Sandra M. Gilbert and Susan Gubar have argued, but it also brought out disagreements and feelings of dissimilarity, even alienation.[2] Through writing the Brontë siblings established, asserted, and explored individual differences within the "family likeness" determined by their common heritage and upbringing.

This chapter illuminates the family context of the Brontës' writing, wherein the siblings negotiated ideas of family and individual identity through their own experience as writers. In recent years, numerous critics have recognized the Brontë novels as "reciprocal commentaries" on one another—an intertextual dialogue through which the sisters expressed differences of opinion and outlook within the family group. This chapter locates the roots of this dialogue in the juvenilia and early family environment. The first two sections establish the family framework of the writing and consider the ways in which the Brontës used writing to define themselves as a family. The following three sections explore the processes of individuation within the Brontës' joint literary efforts—processes, whereby, according to Barbara Prentis, "each life emerges from the group with its own centre of difference."[3] The discussion centers on Charlotte's and Branwell's juvenilia since there are significantly more extant manuscripts related to their shared imaginary world of Angria; Emily and Anne's Gondal prose is lost or destroyed, and the story is pieced together primarily from Emily's poems and from references to Gondal in Emily's and Anne's diaries. Nevertheless, in manuscripts relating to both Angria and Gondal, there is textual evidence suggesting that each sister consciously used writing to establish artistic and ideological differences from her sibling partner. These processes of individuation seem to challenge the family relationship but were dependent upon it, as the sibling partners influenced and set the terms for each other's responses.

Sibling influence and the need to assert individuality continued in the shift from sibling pairs to a trio of sisters and in the move from a private readership to a public one. The final section of this chapter contemplates how the Brontë sisters negotiated the family framework of their writing in the public sphere. The Brontës' public and private defenses of their separate authorial identities constitute a prominent though underacknowledged aspect of their experience as published authors. As a whole, this chapter establishes, in the Brontës' own communal experience of writing, the theme of discovering self in relation to family, which is exhibited in the novels and explored in the following chapters.

An "Unrestricted and In Artificial Mode of Life": Home and the Freedom to Write

The image of the Victorian home, as well as of the familial relationships within the home, is often generalized as being little more than a female prison. Gilbert and Gubar draw on this generalization when they insist that Emily Brontë was literally imprisoned in her father's house. This claim of confinement is grossly reductive of Emily's experience: not only can it be easily contradicted by biographical facts, but all of the biographical evidence suggests that Emily viewed her home as a place of unparalleled freedom and thought of personal fulfillment in terms of family togetherness. The parsonage in Haworth provided all three sisters with a naturalness of character and freedom of expression that the world beyond the parsonage denied. Reasoning why she had dismissed Ellen Nussey's brother Henry as a suitor in 1839, Charlotte maintained that "it would startle him to see me in my natural home-character[;] he would think I was a wild, romantic enthusiast indeed."[4]

Outside the home, the Brontës were remembered not for their wild enthusiasm but for their extreme reserve and homesickness. Recalling Charlotte's arrival as a pupil at Roe Head, Ellen Nussey characterized her as a "shrinking little figure." Emily never successfully functioned outside the parsonage. Charlotte described her sister's sufferings at Roe Head, where she remained as a student for less than three months, as life-threatening: "Liberty was the breath of Emily's nostrils; without it, she perished. The change from her own home to a school, and from her own very noiseless, very secluded, but unrestricted and in artificial mode of life, to one of disciplined routine (though under the kindliest auspices), was what she failed in enduring." The sisters also described their time as governesses in terms of imprisonment and exile. In her July 30, 1841, diary paper, Emily bids "courage courage! to exiled and harassed Anne" in her post at Thorp Green, which Charlotte labeled "'the land of Egypt and the House of Bondage.'" Charlotte complained of her position at Upperwood House in Rawdon for its forced "estrangement from one's real character" and maintained that a governess was like an "inmate" in a strange family. For the Brontë sisters, home—and no place like home—offered the liberty to be themselves, to be together, and, crucially, to write.[5]

Accordingly, the literary output of all four siblings was greatly reduced in the periods away from Haworth.[6] This decline was due in part to the demands of school or employment on the time and energy normally dedicated to writing at home, but also, as they were removed from the family environment, the young authors lacked the stimulus provided by the sibling group. In an entry of her "Roe Head Journal," Charlotte writes that she hears "still small voices" on the wind, calling of the "far & bright continent" of her imaginary kingdom of Angria: "it is that which wakes my spirit and engrosses all my living feelings all my energies which are not merely mechanical & like Haworth and home wakes sensations that lie dormant elsewhere."[7]

For all four Brontë siblings, the home community woke sensations and stimulated literary activity. "My home is humble and unattractive to strangers," Charlotte wrote in 1841, "but to me it contains what I shall find nowhere else in the world—profound, and intense affection which brothers and sisters feel for each other when their minds are cast in the same mould, their ideas drawn from the same source—when they have clung to each other from childhood and when family disputes have never sprung up to divide them." This fellowship of like minds is what, according to Charlotte, makes "a *good* home."[8] Yet, despite Charlotte's avowal that the siblings were never divided by disputes, their creative and emotional intimacy was not always the harmonious union of like minds. Writing in collaboration reinforced the Brontës' sense of family solidarity but also offered a unique framework in which to carry out sibling rivalries. Within families generally, sibling rivalry is a method for establishing difference in the face of natural and nurtured similarities. The natural rivalry among the Brontë children was ultimately productive, resulting in a mass of creative fictions that comprise the most famous juvenilia in the English language.

The Family Framework of the Early Writings

The early writings served as the defining structure by which the four siblings conceived of themselves as a family. In his correspondence with Elizabeth Gaskell, Patrick Brontë recalled how his children formed "a little society amongst themselves" united by their common efforts in acting and composing "their little plays." The juvenilia took their inspiration from twelve wooden toy soldiers that Patrick Brontë brought home from Leeds on June 5, 1826, for nine-year-old Branwell. Branwell allowed each sister to choose a soldier as her own "chief man." Charlotte claimed the largest as the duke of Wellington, and Branwell designated his soldier Napoleon, thus setting up a series of battles that all four siblings acted out—"an imaginative extension of the recent Napoleonic wars." The cooperative plays were supplemented with "little works of fiction" that the children wrote to document the exploits of their heroes. Charlotte's accounts of the plays' origins show that settings, characters, and elements of plots were discussed collectively.[9] The stories themselves, it would appear, were developed and written individually, and later shared with the group. Glass Town (later renamed Verdopolis) evolved as the common setting for the children's stories, with each child ruling one of four states that made up a confederation. Emily and Anne eventually bowed out of the Glass Town saga to form their own narrative of Gondal.

Patrick Brontë was clearly aware of his children's compositions. His lack of involvement or interference in their joint activities seems planned rather than neglectful, a means to foster sibling solidarity among four children left largely to amuse themselves outside their lessons. The juvenilia, nonetheless, owe much to Patrick's influence, incorporating his interest in politics and current events, his Toryism, and his enthusiasm for Wellington.[10] The communal play was also a psychological resource in the face of the family disintegration prompted by the death of their mother and two eldest siblings: playing and writing together filled a void and forged relationship. Yet the Brontës' dependence on one another and on their imaginary worlds did not emerge from deprivation and sadness. As an adult, Charlotte recalled that their early attempts at literary compositions were "the highest stimulus, as well as the liveliest pleasure we had known from childhood upwards."[11]

Undoubtedly, part of the siblings' enjoyment in their "little fictions" was writing themselves into their imaginary worlds. Influenced by their readings of the *Arabian Nights' Entertainments*, the children make their appearance in the chronicles as the four Chief Genii—Talli, Brani, Emi, and Anni—under whose magical authority the Young Men, or Twelves, as the toy soldiers become known, were subject. In Branwell's *History of the Young Men*, the four genii appear in a flash of light and Chief Genius Brani announces, "we are the Gaurdians [sic] of this land we are the guardians of you all."[12] The genii are the literary manifestations of the children's authorial control over the characters and events of their imaginations, wielding their power to bestow punishments and rewards and resurrect characters killed in the course of the stories.

Active intervention by the genii is curtailed as the fictions become more realistic. Christine Alexander records the last instance of the genii playing an active role in Charlotte's story *The Foundling* (May 31–June 27, 1833). Charlotte's hero, Arthur Wellesley, son of the duke of Wellington, is restored to life by the will of the genii, as are his murderers, Lord Ellrington and Mr. Montmorency, for the genii announce that "it is the mighty Brani's will to revivify both the murderers also." This group revival is apparently the result of a compromise between Charlotte and Branwell: Branwell had clearly stipulated that if Charlotte's hero were restored to life, then his characters had to be "made alive" too. In this instance, sibling conflict over the status of characters and course of events is resolved within the narrative by the device of the genii. As the juvenilia proceeded, Charlotte and Branwell would assume direct control as authors and simply rewrite each other's version of events according to their own designs.[13]

Charlotte found numerous opportunities to write Branwell into her fictions, chiefly to mock him. Through caricatures, she continuously sought to undermine Branwell's sense of self-importance as the male leader of their plays and writings. The most obvious caricature is the ridiculous Patrick Benjamin Wiggins, who is physically likened to Branwell by his carroty red hair, spectacles, and Roman nose. The characters in Charlotte's stories are well acquainted with "Wiggins's style of exaggeration," which he regularly displays to the point of buffoonery. In My Angria and the Angrians (October 14, 1834), Wiggins reluctantly admits to having three sisters, Charlotte, Jane, and Anne, who are, he claims, "honoured by possessing me as a brother, but I deny that they're my sisters." In this allusion to her own family, Charlotte mocks Branwell's opinion of himself and his superior attitude toward his sisters.[14]

Charlotte and Branwell also began the practice of writing under pseudonyms, adopting as their literary voices Glass Town characters who were, to a certain degree, projections of themselves. Charlotte's quick wit, critical eye, and occasionally biting sarcasm found an outlet in her favorite narrator, Lord Charles Wellesley, who is succeeded by Charles Townshend later in the saga. Branwell originally wrote prose as Captain Bud and poetry as Young Soult the Rhymer, a character who exhibits Branwell's enthusiasm for versification and all things French. In adulthood, Branwell signed his letters and his only published poems with the pseudonym "Northangerland," his Byronic hero in the juvenilia. Numerous biographers and literary critics have remarked that Branwell developed an unhealthy identification with his childhood hero, consciously or unconsciously emulating Northangerland's morose self-absorption and debauched lifestyle.[15] Personal involvement and identification with the juvenile characters probably accounts for the saga's continuation into the Brontës' adulthood. On a trip to York in 1845, Emily and Anne, aged almost twenty-seven and twenty-five, respectively, pretended to be various Gondal characters escaping from the palaces of instruction. Emily writes, "we were Ronald Macelgin, Henry Angora, Juliet Augusteena" (rather than "we pretended to be"), suggesting that she, at least, experienced complete identification with the characters.[16]

Sibling Divisions in the Early Writing

Early in their joint writing, it was clear that the four siblings had different emphases and interests. Branwell concentrated on meticulous accounts of battles and political intrigue, while Charlotte focused on the lives of their characters off the battlefield, indulging in tales of romance, adventure, and the supernatural. Emily and Anne's early stories centered around more realistic Yorkshire settings and character types, earning them the ridicule of their elder siblings. By the beginning of 1831, Emily and Anne felt the need to devise another imaginative landscape in order to accommodate their differences, which led to the founding of Gondal.[17] They set Gondal against Charlotte and Branwell's Angria by substituting a Byronic heroine, Queen Augusta Geraldine Almeda, for the virulent king of Angria, Zamorna, and by replacing the moral laxity that permeated personal relationships in Angrian society with a rigorous sense of moral consequences in the interactions of Gondalians. These distinctions suggest that Emily and Anne consciously sought to distinguish their imaginary world from that of their siblings.

Despite the irreparable division of the joint play into Angria and Gondal, the pairs of siblings do not appear to have advanced their dramas in mutual secrecy. As late as June 26, 1837, Emily's diary paper reveals that she and Anne were aware of the events surrounding Northangerland's revolution against Zamorna, for Emily writes, "Northangerland in Monkeys Isle—Zamorna at Eversham." Gondal's general plot development also closely parallels Angria's, which likely indicates a sharing of the present circumstances in the kingdoms and the authors' future plans.[18]

The division of the collective sibling imagination into parallel but contrasting worlds did not abate the individual struggle for self-expression. Rather, for Charlotte and Branwell particularly, the split into pairs intensified their interaction and sparked fierce authorial rivalries that propel the Glass Town saga. Wellington and Napoleon, the two greatest political and military rivals of then-recent history, are succeeded by the two greatest political and military rivals of the siblings' literary imaginations, Zamorna and Northangerland. Charlotte acts as the leading advocate for her hero, Zamorna, and Branwell is the chief spokesman for Northangerland. Texts provide the field of battle, and writing the means to attack and counterattack in the struggle to promote one's "chief man" over the other's.

Charlotte became fascinated with the dynamics of antagonistic relationships between Angrian characters. She repeatedly framed rivalries within male sibling or sibling-type partnerships, beginning with Wellington's sons Lord Charles and Arthur (later Zamorna), whose personal clashes are a component of and motivation behind many of her stories, and continuing through to Edward and William Percy, who serve as prototypes for Edward and William Crimsworth in *The Professor* and whom she revised in various forms to the end of her literary career.[19] The recurrent portrayal of sibling rivals in Charlotte's early writing suggests that, to a limited extent, she employed fictional rivalries to interrogate the nature of her own personal and artistic relationship with Branwell. For Charlotte, the process of individuation, whereby she emerged from her Angrian partnership with her own "centre of difference," was carried out through both fictional and authorial rivalries.

Charlotte and Branwell: Authorial Rivalries

Branwell's influence on the development of his sisters as authors is regularly dismissed and often spurned. In 1897, Margaret Oliphant concluded that Branwell "had as little as possible to do with their development in any way." In much modern criticism, Branwell serves the Brontë genius only as a "creative irritant," whose inability to provide financial support for his family prompted the sisters to try their hand at publishing.[20] In this endeavor, he offered a horrible example of self-destructive, drunken indulgence that his sisters shaped into art, most obviously in Emily's Hindley Earnshaw and in Anne's Arthur Huntingdon and Lord Lowborough.

But to do Branwell full justice in the family writing dynamic, we must, in the words of Charlotte's juvenile heroine Elizabeth Hastings, "remember what he was before he fell." Branwell was far from marginalized in either the Brontë home or the Brontës' early writing endeavors; he was, in many ways, a formative influence. His enthusiasm for the early plays spurred the siblings' literary activity. He was an innovator in plot and genre, experimenting with magazine formats, dramatic poems, historical narratives, and epistolary novellas. His interest in composing verse, first evidenced in his 1829 juvenilia, had a pronounced effect on the course of Charlotte's early writing: Alexander has noted that Charlotte wrote three times as many poems in 1830 as she did in 1829 and increasingly included poems in her prose narratives. Branwell's poetic fervor no doubt made an impression on his younger siblings, who also made poetry a significant part of their juvenilia and mature writing.[21]

Branwell's influence on Charlotte's literary development is the most direct, lasting, and complex. Within their joint literary efforts, Branwell acted as a constant goad, whom Charlotte sought to imitate and outmaneuver. She set herself against Branwell's commanding position in the early plays not by creating strong female characters, as Emily and Anne did in Gondal, but by appropriating "maleness." Her reliance on male narrators throughout her early writings and for her first novel, *The Professor,* can be linked to her artistic partnership with Branwell. Employing a male facade allowed her equal standing in their male-dominated world and in their authorial rivalry. When the sisters entered the male-dominated publishing world, they took ostensibly masculine pseudonyms to veil their identities. Charlotte attributed this decision to their "vague impression that authoresses are liable to be looked on with prejudice."[22] This impression was obtained from their reading of periodical reviews and, it seems likely, from their collective writing experience with a domineering brother.

As the early leader in the collaborative writing, Branwell determined that the Young Men should have a magazine. He brought out the first issue of *Branwell's Blackwood's Magazine* in January 1829, modeled in both layout and content on *Blackwood's Edinburgh Magazine,* which the Brontë household received from 1825 onward. Writing as Lord Charles Wellesley, Charlotte contributed stories of her own and jointly composed pieces with Branwell. In August, Branwell handed over the editorship of the magazine to Charlotte, assuring his readers that he would still write for the magazine "now and then." Exercising her new authority, Charlotte changed the magazine's name to *Blackwood's Young Men's Magazine* and, later, to simply *Young Men's Magazine*. Poems appearing in the magazine are regularly signed "UT" or "WT," generally thought to mean "Us Two" and "We Two," respectively, suggesting continued collaboration by Charlotte and Branwell.[23]

From the magazines to the first novels offered for publication, the family acted as the first readers—and first critics. Charlotte and Branwell kept up a healthy series of jabs and counterjabs at the style and content of each other's compositions, as each developed individualized literary voices. The December 1829 issue of *Blackwood's Young Men's Magazine* features "Lines Spoken by a Lawyer on the Occasion of the Transfer of This Magazine." Although the poem is signed "WT," it clearly presents Branwell's opinion of Charlotte's editorship:

> All soberness is past and gone,
> The reign of gravity is done,
> Frivolity comes in its place,
> Light smiling sits on every face. . . . (ll. 1–4)[24]

This poem is immediately followed by Charlotte's reply, "Lines by One Who Was Tired of Dullness upon the Same Occasion." She expresses her preference for the present lightness over her brother's weighty dullness. In *Characters of the Celebrated Men of the Present Time* (December 12–17, 1829), Charlotte repeats the charge of dullness against Captain Bud, Branwell's pseudonym. Using her own pseudonym of Captain Tree, Charlotte praises Bud as "the ablest political writer of the present time" but complains that he "never condescends to be droll but keeps on in an even course of tiresome gravity, so much so that I have often fallen asleep over his best works." In relating the affairs of Glass Town, Charlotte consciously set her own "foolish romances" against her brother's "tiresome gravity."[25]

The siblings' criticisms of each other as writers continued through the mouthpieces of their rival narrators, Branwell's Captain Bud challenging Charlotte's Captain Tree and Lord Charles Wellesley. In a piece called *The Liar Detected* (June 19, 1830), Captain Bud sets out to discredit a work by Lord Charles, written two days earlier, entitled *An Interesting Passage in the Lives of Some Eminent Men of the Present Time*. Bud begins, "IT [h]as always Been the Fortune of Eminent Men in all ages and every country to have their lives their actions and their works traduced By a set of unprincipled[d] wretches."[26] Bud catalogues the characters maligned by Lord Charles and then recalls the events in Charlotte's narrative in order to enumerate the errors in her realism:

> The Footman who told him [Lord Charles] the budget of Information begins with the interview of Capt Tree and Leiut Brock and in Process of the Narrative states that while he was in the Avenue he slipped over a hedge how could that be? a hedge in a covered avenue! is not this sufficient to set the Book and its author down as a lie and a liar! but to proceed again he Mentions the librarian being dressed in a cloak and a Mask. and he (the footman) directly knew who it was. but, stop young Boy—how could a footman know one dressed in a cloak and mask & that to [sic] in the dark? Impossible![27]

All in all, Bud concludes, Lord Charles's story is "beyond the bounds of probability" and thus should be discredited. Branwell's indictment not only displays his meticulous reading of Charlotte's composition, it also underscores his insistence that their imaginative world should be realistic. By contrast, Charlotte did not feel hampered by the constraints of realism and happily employed all manner of "improbability" to heighten the drama of her stories.

Charlotte was not to be outdone as a literary critic, and she returned Branwell's criticism with a strike on his particular pride in his poetry. In

The Poetaster (July 3–12, 1830), Charlotte's only full-scale play, she satirizes the romantic posturing of a character named Henry Rhymer, who is actually the Glass Town poet Young Soult, Branwell's chosen pseudonym when writing poetry. Thinking himself to have the "inspiration of genius," Rhymer presents his poetry to the marquis of Douro and Lord Charles with the command, "Read and be electrified!" The marquis's response upon reading is to advise Rhymer to "sit quietly down to some honest employment and think no more of writing poetry."[28] With this response, Charlotte clearly means to deflate her brother's ego.

This exchange between Charlotte and Branwell, beginning in December 1829 and continuing throughout 1830, illustrates that sibling rivalry regularly motivated the act of writing. The desire of each sibling to outmaneuver the other allowed both to find distinct literary voices and styles and to distinguish themselves as writers. Authorial rivalry was also clearly part of the fun of their collaboration.

Branwell and the Byronic Incarnation of Zamorna

As the Glass Town saga progressed, Charlotte turned her attention to developing characters, providing background and motives, and introducing increasingly romantic relationships. The eldest son of the duke of Wellington, Arthur Wellesley, marquis of Douro and, later, duke of Zamorna and king of Angria, becomes her dominant hero. His exploits, both political and amorous, fill most of her stories. Charlotte's insistence on the unequivocal supremacy and centrality of her hero, however, did not remain long unchallenged. Branwell envisioned a character who would serve as an antagonist to his sister's noble marquis. The advent of Rogue, who becomes Alexander Percy, Lord Ellrington, and earl of Northangerland, had profound effects on the young authors' partnership: he "was to draw brother and sister together in a single creative fiction." The collaborative efforts between 1833 and 1835 focused intently on developing the relationship between Zamorna and Northangerland, who together were to become the "two great drivers" of the Angrian chronicles.[29] Zamorna and Northangerland played out the rivalry between their creators, the other "two great drivers" of Angria: authorial jabs were transformed into the center-stage conflicts of their heroes, whose opposition to one another had life-or-death consequences. Rivalry was now a function of plot, a motive for action, as the battle for political predominance in Angria governed the play.

Northangerland becomes a singular force in shaping the character of Zamorna: his appearance prompts Charlotte's reinterpretation of her hero. Zamorna's "Byronic incarnation" at this point in the juvenilia has been attributed to Charlotte's and Branwell's eager readings of Byron's works.[30] But it is Branwell who brings a Byronic character into the story in the figure of Rogue, and it is Branwell who begins to ascribe Byronic characteristics to Charlotte's marble-skinned, mild-mannered hero. Charlotte's reaction to this reconception of her "chief man" marks a turning point in the juvenilia, when she begins to question the artistic boundaries of her partnership with Branwell.

Northangerland first emerged in the juvenilia under the name Alexander Rogue, a figure described in Charlotte's *Characters of the Celebrated Men of the Present Time* as a gambler whose manner is "polished and gentlemanly" and whose mind is "deceitful, bloody, and cruel." Branwell turned his full attention to Rogue at the end of January 1833. *The Pirate* (January 30–February 8, 1833) gives a broader portrait of the 1829 character, narrating his history as a pirate and adding a penchant for alcohol and the hint of atheism to his vices. Clearly drawing on Byron's *The Corsair* (1814), Branwell's story marked "the first serious attempt in the Brontë juvenilia to develop the role of one particular figure."[31] Once again, Charlotte was not to be outdone. She gives her own full-scale account of Rogue in *The Green Dwarf* (July 10–September 2, 1833), giving him a villainous past as the aristocrat Alexander Percy.

The advent of Rogue, however, threatened to oust Charlotte's hero, Arthur Wellesley, from his preeminence in the juvenilia. In May 1833, Charlotte returned her hero to the center of Glass Town life in *Something about Arthur*. Yet that something about Arthur is something *different* from his earlier character. In 1829, Arthur is "mild and humane but very courageous, grateful for any favour that is done and ready to forgive injuries, kind to others and disinterested in himself. His mind is of the highest order, elegant and cultivated."[32] This idea of her hero is radically altered following the appearance of Rogue. In Charlotte's story, Arthur is violent and vengeful when he discovers that he has been cheated by Lord Caversham at the horse races. To secure his revenge, he leads a mob of workers that burns Caversham's mill in a scene that foreshadows the raid on Robert Moore's mill in *Shirley*. In this narrative, Charlotte also introduces Mina Laury, a beautiful peasant girl who nurses Arthur back to health after he suffers a gunshot wound during the attack. Mina becomes the most prominent of Arthur's mistresses, one of the many victims of the irresistible magnetism Arthur acquires as Charlotte herself is seduced by the excitement of Byronic romance.

Branwell, meanwhile, continued to corrupt his sister's hero, using Rogue as the agent of his designs. In *Real Life in Verdopolis* (completed September 21, 1833), written by Captain Flower (Branwell's pseudonym from 1831 to mid-1834), Rogue, now Lord Ellrington, introduces Arthur to the Elysium Society, where both indulge shamelessly in gambling, drinking, and fighting. In Branwell's hands, Arthur was becoming another Ellrington. In Charlotte's next piece, *Arthuriana, or Odds and Ends* (September 27–November 20, 1833), she admits that her hero has changed. Lord Charles affirms that he has read "the novel of *Real Life in Verdopolis*": "Till I read this admirable work I was ignorant to what a hopeless depth he [Arthur] had sunk in the black gulphs of sin and dissipation." The statement reflects Charlotte's own sentiments upon reading her brother's work. Yet Charlotte does not take the opportunity in *Arthuriana* to refute Branwell's defilement of her hero. Instead, she has Charles show *Real Life* to Arthur: "I watched him narrowly and I am sorry to say I was soon convinced that all Captain Flower had recorded against him was perfectly true."[33]

Charlotte was clearly intrigued by Arthur's Byronic transformation. Yet her story *The Spell, an Extravaganza* (June 21–July 21, 1834) suggests some anxiety over Arthur's increasing resemblance to her brother's hero. With the ascendancy of Rogue, Branwell was exerting his control not only over plot development, which had always been his forte, but also over character development, particularly of Charlotte's favorite character. He was encroaching on her imaginative space, and she was, perhaps to her own surprise, not making much resistance. Exerting her artistic independence, Charlotte decided to attempt her own explanation of Arthur's sudden transformation from mild, high-minded, generous hero to ruthless soldier and callous womanizer, who had by this point earned the title duke of Zamorna. In *The Spell*, she invents a mysterious twin brother, known as Valdacella, to account for "certain inconsistencies in the Duke's conduct."[34] Yet if it were Charlotte's original intention in writing *The Spell* to attribute Zamorna's recent acts of cruelty and debauchery to a sibling-foil, and thus exonerate her hero from Branwell's perversions, she undermines her own efforts by creating brothers "[s]o altogether alike, so undistinguishably similar" (232). Throughout the story, there is no clear difference between Zamorna and Valdacella: both exhibit cunning ambition, coldness to women, and haughty, vengeful language. Charlotte cannot, it seems, write her hero back to his pristine character.

The Spell is a story of sibling rivalry between Zamorna and Valdacella. The telling of the story is also motivated by sibling rivalry, instigated by Zamorna's younger brother Lord Charles in revenge. Charles opens his preface, "The Duke of Zamorna should not have excluded me from Wellesley House, for the following pages have been the result of that exclusion" (150). As explanation for Zamorna's changed conduct, Lord Charles proposes that his brother is mad, for he has recently displayed "all the strong variableness and versatility which characterize possessed lunatics" and diverged "from the straight road of common use and custom" (150). Charles assures his reader that there are "passages of truth" in his narrative that will make Zamorna "gnash his teeth with grating agony," but Charles also reports that he is "not at liberty to point out what those passages are" (150). The "proof" of Zamorna's insanity must be decided by the reader, "who must gather it from the hints interwoven with the whole surface and progress of the story" (150–51). This narrative strategy anticipates *Villette*, in which the reader must actively participate in the construction of the text, assembling M. Paul's fate from the hints interwoven in the novel. The reader is made to determine the truth of Charles's story in *The Spell*, but the narrative is specifically designed to confound the reader with the apparent "double existence" of Zamorna (210). Is the person speaking and addressed as Zamorna *really* Zamorna? This is precisely the question Charlotte as creator is pondering. Her own confusion over the changed nature of her hero is evoked in the reader's confusion.

The plot of *The Spell* explores blurred boundaries of identity and agency within a relationship of like partners. Using her favorite elements of sorcery, Charlotte reveals that a spell was placed on the twins at birth, dictating that "for a length of time they should in reality be but as one; for that it should henceforth be death to them to be looked upon by mortal eyes at the same time" (234). The spell forces the brothers' identities into a tense unity, and the penalty for individuality is death. Zamorna is privileged as the "one" recognized by society, given his father's title and free rein of expression, but also forced to bear the "penalties consequent on discovery" (234). Valdacella must conceal himself with veil and cloak so as not to be seen in his brother's presence. With no publicly recognized existence except as Zamorna, Valdacella finds his only outlet for self-expression in the guise of his brother. He uses this to his advantage, standing in for Zamorna according to his whim, tormenting Zamorna's wife, Mary Percy, with his coldhearted aloofness, and baffling Zamorna's closest associates.

The action centers on the twins' rivalry for ascendancy within the relational bonds dictated by the spell. Zamorna and Valdacella are, as Sally Shuttleworth has argued, "two identical figures struggling for possession of the same social space."[35] When Zamorna's wife unwittingly discovers the existence of Valdacella, she violates the spell's edict, which sends Zamorna to his deathbed. Zamorna, however, rallies against the curse, spurred by the single-minded desire "to spite *him!*" (185), thus preventing Valdacella's attempt to usurp his identity. By the end of the story, the spell is broken and the struggle for predominance can be abated. Valdacella emerges as a character in his own right—and yet not. Despite his manifestation as a character in the narrative, Valdacella ultimately cannot be distinguished from Zamorna: "Their past lives are inextricably interwoven; the achievements of one cannot now be distinguished from the achievements of the other; their writings, their military actions, their political manouevres are all blended, all twisted into the same cord.... Even the sins, incidents, and adventures of their private life are so confused and mingled that it would require a sharp eye to discover what lies to the charge of Zamorna and what to that of Valdacella" (234–35). The sympathy and similarity between Zamorna and Valdacella are so great that it becomes impossible for the two characters to continue as separate entities beyond the narrow scope of *The Spell*, and they merge into a "new" Zamorna. Valdacella appears in no subsequent stories.

In his concluding nota bene, Lord Charles suggests that the very existence of Valdacella is and has always been a fiction:

> Reader, if there is no Valdacella there ought to be one. If the young King of Angria has no alter ego he ought to have such a convenient representative, for no single man, having one corporeal and one spiritual nature ... should, in right reason and in the ordinance of common sense and decency, speak and act in that capricious, double-dealing, unfathomable, incomprehensible, torturing, sphinx-like manner which he constantly assumes for reasons known only to himself. (237)

Valdacella is, it appears, a willful deception by the narrator, Lord Charles, in an attempt to exasperate his brother. For Charlotte, both the character of Valdacella and the narrative revealing his existence are inventions designed to rationalize Zamorna's new character. Yet, as Valdacella ultimately does not exist, neither does he rationalize. The Angrian saga continues without Valdacella or a rationale for Zamorna's changed character. Later, in 1837 and 1838, Charlotte would write retrospective pieces detailing the early life of Zamorna, establishing Northangerland as a boyhood influence in Zamorna's life, which accounts for his adult behavior.[36] The 1829 portrait of Arthur—the mild, humane, courageous, kind, elegant, and cultivated hero—is completely ignored.

The adult relationship between Zamorna and Northangerland emerges as a successor to Zamorna and Valdacella's affiliation. Although not biological siblings, the two men share a familial bond as father and son-in-law once Zamorna marries Northangerland's daughter Mary Percy, and they display the unstable combination of respect and contempt, fascination and disgust, that Charlotte depicts in Zamorna and Valdacella's bond. But this time, with the assurance of Northangerland's autonomous identity as Branwell's particular hero, the struggle for ascendancy is not abated. It becomes the central drama of the remaining juvenilia.

The Spell marked Charlotte's last resistance to the Byronic Zamorna whom Branwell had initiated. Yet, while she never looked back to the Arthur-that-was, the story suggests she felt some anxiety about the implications of her acceptance. It is significant that *The Spell*, with its theme of the struggle for self-expression within sibling bonds, arose in a period of intense partnership when Branwell was reasserting control over the direction of their Angrian narrative. In a story about the fusion of sibling identities, Charlotte questions the boundaries of selfhood and agency in her own sibling relationship. Valdacella's fate suggests a fear of losing self to sibling within the imaginative space that brother and sister shared. *The Spell* displays Charlotte's early awareness of the problems of maintaining identity within relationship—problems that become specifically female ones in the later juvenilia and published fiction. In Charlotte's penultimate juvenile piece, *Captain Henry Hastings*, the personal identity of the heroine, Elizabeth Hastings, is threatened by both familial and romantic bonds.

Henry and Elizabeth Hastings: Sibling Rivalry and Rescue

The relationships that dominate Charlotte's remaining juvenilia are of two kinds: male rivalry, chiefly between Zamorna and Northangerland, and romantic liaisons, which involve Zamorna and his trail of paramours. The heroine's complete self-surrender to her beloved seems to have struck the principal chord in Charlotte's early romantic imagination. Hence, Zamorna has willing suppliants in every bedchamber and bower, and he is able to cast them off or sweep them up at his leisure. Mina Laury stands as the epitome of assenting selflessness in Charlotte's juvenilia. She is described as "strong-minded beyond her sex," but this only serves to underscore Zamorna's romantic potency, for, with him, "she was as weak as a child—she lost her identity—her very way of life was swallowed up in that of another." Yet Mina does not resist; she wants to be swallowed up. For Zamorna's lovers, selfhood without him is inadequate, isolated, incomplete. "Unconnected with him," Mina asserts, "my mind would be a blank—cold, dead, susceptible only of a sense of despair."[37]

In Charlotte's succession of heroines, only Elizabeth Hastings breaks free of blind devotion, the sort that binds the heroine to Zamorna. Zamorna never appears in Elizabeth's story, and when he is mentioned in connection with a mistress who has died for want of his love, he is confronted with the skepticism of a new heroine. "The Duke of Zamorna is a sort of scoundrel from all that ever I heard of him," Elizabeth remarks.[38] Elizabeth Hastings is generally regarded as a forerunner of Jane Eyre, a plain and undersized governess-heroine who cares for herself both economically and emotionally. Like Jane, Elizabeth is aware of her own moral and intellectual worth and unwilling to give herself to an eager lover at the expense of her self-respect.

What, then, prompts Charlotte to write of Elizabeth as different from her previous heroines, especially as she reverts to the beautiful, love-struck Caroline Vernon only a few months later? Caroline, one of Zamorna's young wards who succumbs to his "fatal sweetness," is cast in the same mold as Mina. Elizabeth's difference can be connected to her primary role in the narrative as a sister. The untitled manuscript known as *Captain Henry Hastings*, or simply *Henry Hastings* (February 24–March 25, 1839), is the only one of Charlotte's early writings to center on a brother/sister relationship. Again, Charlotte creates fictional characters and relationships to ponder the nature of her own sibling relationship with Branwell. Her portraits of male rivalry distanced the exploration of sibling conflict from the "psychologically dangerous arena" of a struggle between a brother and sister. But *Henry Hastings* brings the brother/sister relationship under direct scrutiny. The theme of sibling rivalry persists, though it is carefully, perhaps unconsciously, buried in a story of devotion and rescue.[39]

It is probably not a coincidence that Charlotte began *Henry Hastings* in the month after Branwell's return home from his failed stint as a portrait painter in Bradford. Branwell moved to Bradford some time in the summer of 1838, having failed to present himself as an art student at the Royal Academy in London, as was his intention during the autumn of 1835. He is usually assumed to have given up his studio sometime in May

1839, but it is likely that he returned to Haworth as early as the third week in February.[40] In his first taste of freedom, Branwell had incurred debts from drinking, and he continued to drink and run up debts at home. His disappointment in returning to Haworth without occupation was no doubt evident to Charlotte, but they lacked their former closeness. Their interests in the "infernal world," like their experiences in the outside world, were diverging. Branwell was fixated with reliving the episodes of the Second Angrian War, which he had launched in December 1835 and which Charlotte had ended the following December. In 1837 Charlotte wrote independently of Branwell, largely ignoring his developments and concentrating on the private lives of the Angrians. Branwell turned his attention to the character Henry Hastings, a young captain in the Nineteenth Infantry Regiment of Angria.

Branwell had originally envisaged Hastings as the National Poet of Angria, a successor to Young Soult. By the opening of Charlotte's story, however, Hastings's poetic career—like Branwell's career as a painter—is no more. Throughout 1837, Branwell had turned him into a reckless soldier wanted for desertion, drunken conduct, murder of his commanding officer, and even attempted regicide of Zamorna. In a vignette dated April 25, 1838 ("One morning, the first of April"), Branwell presents the fugitive waking from "the sleep of a debauchee" amidst the "wrecks of gross drunkenness." The vivid description of Hastings's miserable state hints at Branwell's firsthand knowledge of the excesses of drink—"a parching thirst," "a sickly loathing," "that wretched coldness," "an overwhelming confusion of shame." Fannie E. Ratchford, among others, has concluded that Branwell's fallen Hastings is "a new dramatization of himself in his degenerate state."[41]

Charlotte was evidently familiar with Hastings's drunken recklessness and self-despair, and there is much speculation among biographers and critics as to whether she recognized an affinity between creator and creation, writing her story of Henry Hastings as an expression of "faith in her brother despite social misfortune."[42] It seems obvious that Charlotte wrote *Henry Hastings* to ponder Branwell's changed personality and her changed relationship with him, since she deliberately shifted her imaginative focus from lovers to siblings, casting a character she clearly associated with Branwell as a brother (a relational role absent from Branwell's own conception), and introducing a sister-heroine far different from her Angrian beauties but not so different from herself. Elizabeth and Charlotte are similar in appearance, mental qualities, love of their moorland homes, and valued sense of their roles as sisters. Thus, we can account for

Elizabeth's difference, compared with the other Angrian heroines, by a new level of Charlotte's personal identification with a female character in the juvenilia. But it is not indisputably clear what *Henry Hastings* reflects about Charlotte's feelings toward her brother. The story operates on two levels: on one, it reaffirms family bonds through the heroine's self-sacrifice and personal commitment to her sibling; on another, more subversive level, the story provides for the heroine's self-actualization through the dissolution of family bonds.

The dissolution has already occurred by the opening of Charlotte's story. Upon learning of his son's crimes, Mr. Hastings disowns Henry, an act which Elizabeth protests as unnatural and which rouses her to leave her father's house. Elizabeth establishes an independent existence as a governess to the beautiful Jane Moore, next to whom Elizabeth is but "a little shade" (206), anticipating the position Lucy Snowe takes by the side of Paulina Home. Elizabeth is reunited with Henry when he seeks her out, needing refuge from his pursuers. She houses him until he is driven from hiding by Sir William Percy and the police, imprisoned, and sentenced to death. Elizabeth appears before the duchess of Zamorna and, sacrificing her pride for the sake of her brother, begs that his life be spared. Her request is granted: Henry is demoted to the rank of a private soldier and marches out of the story, leaving Elizabeth to comfort herself with the knowledge that she has secured both life and a degree of liberty for her erring brother.

As many critics have noted, the juvenilia were highly imitative. The rescue of Henry Hastings by Elizabeth is patterned closely after the sibling rescue plot of Sir Walter Scott's 1818 novel, *The Heart of Midlothian*. Charlotte's passion for Scott's novels is evident in her often-cited letter of suggested reading to Ellen Nussey; she advises, "For fiction—read Scott alone all novels after his are worthless."[43] While Byron seduced the Brontë children, particularly Charlotte and Branwell, with his figure of the tormented wanderer, worn by earthly cares and beloved of countless women, Scott introduced Charlotte to a heroine closer to home and herself: a sister. In Scott's story, a Scottish milkmaid, Jeanie Deans, travels to London on foot to plead before Queen Caroline for the life of her half-sister Effie, who has been sentenced to death for the murder of her illegitimate child. *Henry Hastings* parallels much in Scott's novel: the plain heroine, her strong sense of personal integrity, her fervent devotion to her sibling, her journey to seek audience with a queen, and her moving supplication for the sibling's pardon, which is granted through the force of her appeal.

Michael Cohen has argued that *The Heart of Midlothian* enabled many Victorian writers to recognize the "heroic possibilities of sisterhood" within a rescue plot. The recovery of a sexually "fallen" sister by her "unfallen" or innocent sister became a prominent theme in Victorian literature, present in Wilkie Collins's *The Woman in White* (1859–1860) and *No Name* (1862), Charles Dickens's *Little Dorrit* (1855–1857), Elizabeth Gaskell's *Wives and Daughters* (1864–1866), and Christina Rossetti's "Goblin Market" (1862). The sister-savior facilitates a rescue for her fallen sister by stressing their natural affinity: difference is only temporary, the result of a momentary lapse of judgment. Helena Michie maintains that sisterly rescue uniquely allowed "for the possibility of the sexual fall and for the reinstatement of the fallen women" within the family and society.[44] In Scott's novel, for instance, Effie Deans marries her lover and becomes Lady Staunton.

Charlotte's story provides a variation on the sibling rescue motif by substituting an outlaw brother in place of the sexually deviant sister. Henry, however, is significantly *not* restored to his former status within the family or society. Charlotte's account of sibling loyalty and rescue ultimately affirms the difference between brother and sister and promotes the sister's fortunes over her brother's. Henry's rebellious misconduct ends in the destruction of his identity within the family, as he is struck from his father's will, and within society, as he is "cursed by every mouth ... denounced in every newspaper" (242). By contrast, Elizabeth's "misconduct" as the "undutiful daughter" (203), defending her prodigal brother in defiance of her father, upsets the balance of power within the patriarchal family and redefines her identity. Henry remains "an unredeemed villain" (242), but Elizabeth rises from her position of dependency and nonentity within the patriarchal family to become a self-supporting teacher.

In Elizabeth Hastings, Charlotte constructs a sister whose willing self-sacrifice and commitment to her brother are sources of personal pride. In the face of Henry's public infamy, she does not "think a pin the worse of him for his Dishonour," beholding "his actions through a medium particular to herself" (242). But Charlotte has also created a female character with a strong sense of moral conscience and self-respect, so both creator and character wrestle with the contradictory needs for union with and separation from a beloved brother who is also "an unredeemed villain" (242). In the end, Charlotte has it both ways: Elizabeth the character defends Henry, but Charlotte the author dismisses him. Charlotte allows her heroine to fulfill her duty as Henry's savior, and Elizabeth thereby validates her sense of self as a sister. But, with Henry's departure, Charlotte also provides Elizabeth with an autonomy entirely unavailable to her within her family ties. Elizabeth affirms family, maintaining that "natural affection is a thing never rooted out" (242), but Charlotte dissolves family, writing the object of that affection out of the story and out of Elizabeth's life. It is Henry, then, not Elizabeth, whose selfhood is ultimately sacrificed.

The sibling rescue plot provides the means through which Charlotte creates difference between the fictional brother-sister pair and their real-life counterparts. The writing of *Henry Hastings* continues and, in a sense, culminates the authorial rivalry between Charlotte and Branwell that had propelled their writings from the earliest magazines. Henry is brought down by Charlotte's pen as Wiggins and Young Soult had been: "How are the mighty fallen!" the narrator Charles Townshend remarks as Henry is escorted out of the story (240). In *Henry Hastings*, Charlotte promotes Elizabeth's ascendancy and individuation, and, through Elizabeth's, her own. Elizabeth's mind, unconnected with her brother's, is not the blank void that Mina Laury fears; it is alive and vibrant. She is able to choose the extent of her sacrifice, to question the worthiness of her idol, to retain and value her identity in a way which Charlotte's heroines have never done.

Following Henry's departure, Elizabeth is empowered by her sense of self-worth, and, fearing the "miseries of self-hatred" (256), she rejects Sir William Percy's offer that she become his mistress, though she acknowledges the strength of her love for him. This scene is played out again in Jane Eyre's rejection of a similar proposal by Rochester, which Jane, like Elizabeth, views as threatening to her self-esteem. Throughout the juvenilia, we see Charlotte's growing concern with the need to maintain a valued field of identity within a relationship of intense bonds. Her focus in this concern becomes a strong-minded, independent, though plain and undersized woman, and *Henry Hastings* affirms her value in both familial and romantic relationships. But the self-respecting Elizabeth Hastings remains solitary, still searching for a relationship that will accommodate her sense of self. Jane Eyre will take up the search.

Henry Hastings serves as the symbolic end to Charlotte and Branwell's writing partnership. Despite her regret and loneliness as she recalls the happiness of her past life with Henry, Elizabeth concludes, "Henry was changed, she was changed, those times were departed for ever" (244). Writing with him, Charlotte had taken Branwell as a model, partner, and rival. He was sometimes a threat to her creative integrity and an obstacle to her Angrian plans. Finally, disillusioned with the direction of his imaginative and real-life course, Charlotte disengaged herself from him. Her disillusionment with Branwell induced a disenchantment with Angria, to which she wrote her farewell at the end of 1839, maintaining "we must change, for the eye is tired of the picture so oft recurring and now so familiar." Still, Charlotte could not cut her ties completely, either from Angria or Branwell. She wrote to him from Brussels in 1843: "It is a curious metaphysical fact that always in the evening when I am in the great Dormitory alone—having no other company than a number of beds with white curtains I always recur as fanatically as ever to the old ideas the old faces & the old scenes in the world below."[45] Charlotte returned to one of Branwell's "old scenes" as the basis for the opening of her first novel, *The Professor*, in which she relied on a male narrator as she had done throughout the juvenilia. She would, however, never write with Branwell again.

Emily and Anne: A Gondal Dialogue?

Because the number of Gondal-related manuscripts is meager compared with those related to Glass Town and Angria, it is difficult to reconstruct and explore the sibling dynamics of Emily and Anne's artistic partnership in the same detail as Charlotte and Branwell's. So far as we can understand the Gondal partnership from the existing poetry and jointly produced diary papers, it lacked much of the direct textual collaboration and narrative rivalry that characterized the Angrian alliance. Gondal is dominated by a female Zamorna, Queen Augusta Geraldine Almeda (regularly abbreviated A. G. A. by Emily), but she has no clear rival comparable to Northangerland, so authorial rivalry could not be expressed through plot and characters as easily. Emily appears to have taken the lead in creating characters and suggesting the course of events, each sister writing more or less independently of the other on the themes and characters that interested them most within the general outline of the story. Nonetheless, it is clear from the diary papers that they kept each other informed of their current projects, and each sister displayed a keen interest in the work of the other.[46]

The Gondal poems do not form a chronological plot but rather highlight atmospheres and episodes that roused the authors' imaginations at particular moments. Because the sisters' poems have no character names in common and because Emily and Anne were frequently separated between 1835 and 1845, Derek Roper has proposed the development of "two parallel Gondals." But like Charlotte and Branwell, who were also frequently separated in the course of their joint writing, Emily and Anne cooperated on Gondal when they were reunited during the Christmas and summer holidays. Despite speculation over Anne's waning interest in the joint play as the two sisters matured, both sisters returned to compose Gondal poetry after writing their first novels. Emily's last extant poem, "Why Ask to Know the Date—the Clime?" dated September 14, 1846, is a long Gondal poem providing an account of the dehumanizing effects of the Republican war on individual Gondalians. Anne wrote a companion piece on the same day about the same subject, suggesting that the sisters were still discussing and planning their Gondal writings together.[47]

It seems reasonable to surmise that the Gondal writings, like the Angrian, contain evidence of a dialogue between the sibling authors. Since scholars lack most of the manuscripts, this is difficult to prove, but I propose that Emily and Anne also experienced their early writings as sibling relationship, through which they engaged with each other's ideas, images, and themes and sought to carve out their own literary voices in relation to each other. Within a relationship recognized by Ellen Nussey as "like twins," writing served as a means by which the sisters could differentiate themselves.[48]

As numerous critics have argued, there is evidence in Anne's autobiographical poetry that the two sisters lost much of their childhood intimacy as they matured, diverging in their religious beliefs and artistic interests. Anne distanced herself from Emily's immersion in Gondal and her increasingly pantheistic convictions. Anne's poem "Self-Communion" is often cited as a record of her recognition that the sisters were no longer "like twins." The speaker recalls the "wondrous joy" she knew "In early friendship's pure delight" (ll. 178–79). But, with the passage of time, the two childhood friends are shown to be divided by a dark stream, and Anne depicts them as sundered trees "that at the root were one /. . . But still the stems must stand alone" (ll. 205, 207). Edward Chitham and others have also viewed Anne's second novel, *The Tenant of Wildfell Hall*, as a "corrective" to *Wuthering Heights*, through which Anne articulates her objections to Emily's amoral universe of undeterred passion, where traditional heaven is shunned as incapable of quelling earthly desires and characters lack any sense of Christian humility.[49]

Gondal offered the earliest context for dialogue and debate between the sibling authors. Two pairs of Gondal poems in particular appear to be part of a sibling exchange. The first pair, Emily's "To a Wreath of Snow by A G Almeda—" and Anne's "The North Wind," shows the sisters' variations on a common theme, the prisoner's lament, which is a recurrent subject of the Gondal poetry. In the second pair, Emily's "AS to GS" acts as a direct rebuttal to Anne's "An Orphan's Lament," commenting upon and modifying the ideas expressed in Anne's earlier poem. Differences in perspectives and emphases in these poems appear to be less motivated by authorial sibling rivalry than were Charlotte's and Branwell's stories; rather, distinctions in Emily's and Anne's poems arise from the earnest need for self-expression.

It is not clear whether Emily wrote "To a Wreath of Snow by A G Almeda—" before or shortly after Anne's return from Roe Head in December 1837. It does seem likely that she showed her poem to Anne, for, on January 26, 1838, Anne wrote a companion piece, "The North Wind." Both poems are spoken by Gondal's queen in captivity, who is reminded of her mountain home by the intrusion of nature into her dungeon cell and who derives comfort from the remembrance.[50] In Emily's poem, the messenger from home is an accumulation, or wreath, of snow, carried by chance on "adverse winds . . . To dungeons where a prisoner lies" (ll. 3–4). The poem is an address to the snow by the imprisoned queen, who expresses her rejuvenation at its coming: "Thy presence waked a thrilling tone / That comforts me while thou art here / And will sustain when thou art gone" (ll. 26–28). The stoicism of Emily's queen is particularly felt in these concluding lines. She does not lament the transience of her messenger but draws lasting strength from it.

Anne's poem bears a marked difference in tone and outlook. While Emily stresses the intensity of feeling brought about by the snow, which allows the queen to forbear her present circumstances, Anne's emphasis falls on the confinement and hopelessness of the queen's situation. "The North Wind" is a dialogue between the queen and an intruding wind. Unlike the "voiceless, souless [sic] messenger" in Emily's poem, Anne's wind is personified and speaks its message:

> "No voice but mine can reach thine ear,
> And Heaven has kindly sent me here,
> To mourn and sigh with thee,
> And tell thee of the cherished land
> Of Thy nativity" (ll. 24–28).

In both poems, the queen's love of her native mountains is highlighted—she is "a mountaineer" in Emily's poem (l. 21) and "a joyous mountain child" in Anne's (l. 19). The messengers of snow and wind contrast the present confinement of the prison cell with a past freedom outdoors.

In Anne's poem, the queen responds to the wind with a plea to "Blow on" in order to alleviate the "gloomy silence" of her imprisonment (ll. 29, 31). The purpose of the wind is not, as in Emily's poem, to wake "a thrilling tone," but to "mourn and sigh with thee." Companionship is the comfort offered, not a charge of feeling. The queen fears the transience of her visitor, needing its physical presence to remind her of a time and place beyond her prison walls. Anne cannot find Emily's optimism in forbearance and presents an alternative vision of the imprisoned queen's emotional state—desolate and discouraged. This outlook is perhaps reflective of Anne's own downcast feelings, having just returned from a period of illness and religious depression at Roe Head.[51] Emily's poem provided the outlet and set the terms for Anne's response: self-expression was thus enabled by the writing-sibling relationship.

Emily's "AS to GS" (December 19, 1841) can be read as a response to the attitude toward a mother's death expressed in Anne's "An Orphan's Lament" (January 1, 1841).[52] Anne's poem was composed during her first Christmas holidays at home following her engagement as a governess at Thorp Green. Emily's poem was written almost a year later, also during the Christmas holidays, when the sisters likely reviewed their past Gondal writings. Emily may have seen Anne's poem at this time and been prompted to write a poem on the same theme. Anne's lament centers on the emotional isolation of an orphan who cannot cease to mourn his/her mother's death:

> She's gone—and twice the summer's sun
> Has gilt Regina's towers,
> And melted wild Angora's snows,
> And warmed Exina's bowers (ll. 1–4)

The orphan's preoccupation with the slow passage of time since the mother's death is prolonged over three more stanzas. The orphan sees in the loss of the mother the loss of all earthly affection:

> Where shall I find a heart like thine
> While life remains to me,

> And where shall I bestow the love
> I ever bore for thee? (ll. 44–47)

The pathos of the poem lies in the orphan's despair over the years ahead without earthly companionship, concluding that the mother's loss can never be repaired.[53]

Emily's poem begins with a rejoinder to the sentiments of Anne's character. Appropriately, and perhaps intentionally, her poem is constructed as one sibling's address to another. The character AS (probably Alfred Sidonia) immediately distinguishes himself from GS (Gerald Sidonia) with a rebuke:

> I do not weep, I would not weep;
> Our Mother needs no tears:
> Dry thine eyes too, 'tis vain to keep
> This causeless greif [sic] for years (ll. 1–4).

AS rejects the idea of perpetual mourning—such grief is "causeless" and indefensible. Instead, AS proposes the question, "What though her brow be changed and cold, / Her sweet eyes closed for ever" (ll. 5–6). The mother still is "not dead" (l. 13) but lifted to "that world of heavenly light" (l. 17) from where she will guard and guide her children. The siblings can mourn "That we are left below / But not that she can ne'er return / To share our earthly woe—" (ll. 22–24). To Emily, the desire for restored companionship with the mother on earth, like that voiced by the speaker of Anne's poem, is a selfish desire. Although Emily's ideas of the afterlife are notoriously shifting and complex, this poem incorporates a traditional view of heaven as a place of personal peace and fulfillment. Furthermore, it suggests that to view death solely through one's sorrow and sense of loss ignores the gain for the departed—a gain that should comfort the mourner.

When Charlotte prepared Emily's poem for publication in 1850, she titled it "Encouragement," and either she or Emily changed its internal Gondalian reference: "Gerald" became "Sister," thus making the poem literally an address to a sister. Perhaps the Gondal writings were filled with "addresses" from one sister to another, beyond the two pairs of poems proposed here. That, however, like much related to Gondal, can only be suggested. Nevertheless, even this small sample shows that Emily and Anne, like Charlotte and Branwell, purposely used writing to establish difference and individuality within their private collaboration.

"We Are Three Sisters": Family and Authorial Identity in the Public Sphere

In the move from the private world of the juvenilia to the public world of the publishing house, the sisters retained their collaborative writing habits and their sense of authorship as a family venture. Family continued as the locus of literary activity, and now it also served as a vehicle for publication. Elfenbein has written, "This insistence on the family perhaps resulted from their collective unfamiliarity with publication and consequent unwillingness to venture upon it alone. Instead, they imported a setting that they knew, the family, into more impersonal relations of publication."[54] The sisters chose the Christian names Currer, Ellis, and Acton to mask their identities as women authors, but their adoption of a common surname publicly professed their loyalty to a shared family identity. The decision to present a unified front as the Bell family did not, however, abate the struggle for individual self-expression within the family unit. The only difference was that now the processes of individuation were played before the public. Speculation abounded that the three Bells were, in fact, one, and the sisters were forced to articulate explicitly their separate authorial identities within their family bond.

Charlotte's discovery of "a MS. volume of verse" in Emily's handwriting in the autumn of 1845 evolved into a joint sisterly project—a literary alternative to the abandoned plan to open a jointly run school in the parsonage. Initially, the undertaking was not without friction: Emily was only gradually brought round to the idea, angered by Charlotte's intrusion into a world she shared exclusively with Anne. She would not be reconciled to the project until Charlotte agreed that they would publish under pseudonyms, and she insisted that both her identity and the Gondalian references in her poetry be masked. The decision to attempt a publishable collection of poems resumed the "habit of communication and consultation" that had been discontinued in recent years and marked a return to Angria and Gondal.[55] For the first time in Charlotte's life, Branwell played no part in her literary endeavors.

Like the school scheme, publication promised "financial stability and maintenance of the family as a social and personal unit." But, also like the school scheme, *Poems* by Currer, Ellis, and Acton Bell made little headway, selling only two copies. Yet, as Charlotte recalled, the mere effort to succeed as published authors "had given a wonderful zest to existence; it must be pursued." The sisters redirected their efforts to prose, continuing to share their writing with one another and to comment on one another's work. In her *Life of Charlotte Brontë*, Gaskell described the collaborative effort: "The sisters retained the old habit, which was begun in their aunt's life-time, of putting away their work at nine-o'clock, and beginning their study, pacing up and down the sitting-room. At this time, they talked over the stories they were engaged upon, and described their plots. Once or twice a week, each read to the others what she had written, and heard what they had to say about it." What ultimately ensued from this practice was *The Professor*, *Wuthering Heights*, and *Agnes Grey*.[56]

Assuming leadership in the publishing efforts, Charlotte informed Aylott and Jones, the publishers of *Poems*, that "C. E & A Bell are now preparing for the Press a work of fiction—consisting of three distinct and unconnected tales which may be published either together as a work of 3 vols. of the ordinary novel-size, or separately as single vols—as deemed most advisable." Presumably, the sisters planned to publish their fiction, like their poems, as a family set. But Charlotte was clearly willing to be advised as to the demands of the market, and her desire to see their names in print ultimately outweighed her wish to see the tales preserved in a joint work. It is not entirely clear when *The Professor* (then titled *The Master*) was separated from *Wuthering Heights* and *Agnes Grey* to make its own way around the publishing houses. Tom Winnifrith and Juliet Barker propose that *Wuthering Heights* was too long to occupy one volume "of the ordinary novel size," thus making the three-volume format for the three tales unfeasible. Edward Chitham offers a fascinating interpretation of the events that led up to the separation of *The Master* from its companion volumes: he suggests that a disheartened Charlotte, repeatedly rejected by the "Trade," removed the book in order to revise it, eventually sending it out on its own (despite its only occupying two volumes), and that Emily revised and expanded *Wuthering Heights* in 1846–1847 to fill two volumes so that the novel could continue to be circulated, with *Agnes Grey*, in the recommended three-volume format.[57] Whatever the circumstances, Charlotte ultimately abandoned *The Master* and offered her second novel, *Jane Eyre*, to the London-based publishing house of Smith, Elder and Company. Published on October 19, 1847, *Jane Eyre* was already a bestseller when *Wuthering Heights* and *Agnes Grey* finally appeared together, published by Thomas Newby in December 1847.

With the publication of *Wuthering Heights* and *Agnes Grey*, the *Athenaeum* remarked, "Here are two tales so nearly related to 'Jane Eyre' in cast of thought, incident, and language as to excite some curiosity." The Brontës' foray into the publishing world as a family secured a predetermined comparative context in which the novels and their authors were considered. Jerome Beaty has asserted that, because the Bells were unknown authors, contemporary readers and reviewers would be "unusually attentive to early signals of kinship claims, curious about just what this new work is, what dialogue it is entering, where it fits, and what it has to offer." Following the publication of Anne's second novel, *The Tenant of Wildfell Hall*, the *Examiner* concluded that the Bells were "evidently children of the same family. They derive their scenes from the same country; their associations are alike; their heroines are for the most part alike, three being thrown upon their own talents for self-support, and two of them being all-enduring governesses; and their heroes also resemble each other, in aspect, and temper, almost in habits. We have, once or twice, entertained a suspicion that all the books . . . might have issued from the same source."[58]

The sisters could not have anticipated the troublesome conflation of their individual identities that came with the immense popular success of *Jane Eyre*. *Wuthering Heights* and *Agnes Grey* were repeatedly taken to be immature productions by the author of *Jane Eyre*. In her "Biographical Notice of Ellis and Acton Bell," Charlotte expressed her particular distress that Emily's novel was thought to be "an earlier and ruder attempt" by the hand that wrote *Jane Eyre*, declaring this belief an "Unjust and grievous error!" In April 1848, hoping to quell public speculation and ensure her sisters' (and her own) authorial integrity, Charlotte wrote a note to the third edition of *Jane Eyre*, assuring the public that her "claim to the title of novelist rests on this one work alone" (*JE*, xxxiii). It was Emily and Anne's publisher, Thomas Newby, who finally brought the sisters to reveal their separateness in person as well as in print. In his advertisements for *The Tenant of Wildfell Hall*, Newby conflated the identities of the Bells with what Charlotte called "a certain tricky turn" in wording, and sold part of Anne's novel to an American publisher as a new work by Currer Bell, clearly hoping to capitalize on the popularity of *Jane Eyre*. Newby's misrepresentation of the Bell novels as the production of one author prompted Charlotte and Anne's July 1848 journey to London, where they went "with the view of proving our separate identity" to Charlotte's publisher, Smith, Elder and Company, who were clearly concerned that their best-selling author appeared to have found "himself" another publisher.[59]

Writing her preface to the second edition of *The Tenant of Wildfell Hall* less than a week after the London "revelation," Anne also intended to make clear to the reading public that the Bells were three: "Respecting the author's identity," she writes, "I would have it to be distinctly understood that Acton Bell is neither Currer nor Ellis Bell."[60] Anne's statement is clearly a response to Newby's maneuvering, but it is also a subtle declaration of her artistic individuality. Emily never defended her separate identity publicly, but privately she insisted upon her personal integrity as *Ellis Bell*, refusing to be identified as one of the Brontë sisters. Upon her return from London, Charlotte wrote to W. S. Williams at Smith, Elder:

> Permit me to caution you not to speak of my sisters when you write to me—I mean do not use the word in the plural. "Ellis Bell" will not endure to be alluded to under any other appellation than the "nom de plume". I committed a grand error in betraying [her] his identity to you and Mr. Smith—it was inadvertent—the words "we are three sisters" escaped me before I was aware—I regretted the avowal the moment I had made it; I regret it bitterly now, for I find it is against every feeling and intention of "Ellis Bell."[61]

Despite their efforts, public skepticism over the separate identities of the Bells outlived both Emily and Anne. In 1850, for example, Sydney Dobell openly professed to disbelieve Charlotte's preface to the third edition of *Jane Eyre*. He wrote in the *Palladium:* "That any hand but that which shaped "Jane Eyre" and "Shirley" cut out the rougher earlier statues, we should require more than the evidence of our senses to believe." Following the deaths of her sisters, Charlotte considered it her "sacred duty" to prove at last that Ellis and Acton Bell existed as separate and distinct persons, not simply as "noms de guerre" of Currer Bell. Thus, she opened the "Biographical Notice of Ellis and Acton Bell" with the intention "distinctly to state how the case really stands."[62]

Charlotte's purpose in writing was not primarily to reveal Currer, Ellis, and Acton Bell as women, but to reveal them as individuals. Nicola Thompson has observed that Charlotte's motives in this revelation were not entirely selfless. Following the critical attacks on *Wuthering Heights* as coarse, immoral, even barbaric, Charlotte was, according to Thompson, actually attempting to distance herself from her sisters' works, particularly Emily's, in order to protect her own reputation as an author. Revealing and insisting on the three sisters' separate identities spared Charlotte the "attacks by association" from critics who sought "family likenesses" between *Wuthering Heights* and *Jane Eyre* and who refused to believe that the works were not by the same hand.[63] While this is a convincing interpretation in light of the critical response to the Bells' novels and the confusion of authorship, I do not think we have to entirely discredit Charlotte or dismiss all noble intentions in her penning of the "Biographical Notice." In asserting, and even apologizing for, her sisters' singularities as authors, she was indeed, consciously or not, protecting her own singularity, but she sought to be the interpreter standing between her sisters and the world in order to defend them against their critics. As their defender, she stressed their uniqueness. In so doing, she attempted to establish the autonomous identities that both Emily and Anne had sought as published authors.

Still, we must not forget that we have come to know Emily and Anne as individuals originally through Charlotte's perspective. It is through Charlotte's interpretation that we have come to regard Emily as "stronger than a man, simpler than a child," not having many records in which Emily speaks for herself. It is through Charlotte's interpretation that we judge Anne to be "milder and more subdued," though her own writing, particularly *The Tenant of Wildfell Hall*, suggests that Anne had a power and a fire of her own.[64] Thus, even as Charlotte found it necessary to characterize her sisters' individualities for the public, her characterizations are testimony to the power of the family to shape perceptions of self.

From the earliest juvenilia to the published novels, the negotiation of individual and family identities mediated the Brontës' relationship to writing. The Brontës' practice of writing in sibling partnership underscored the dual nature of the creative process: a shared experience of family but also an expression of individuality within family bonds. The need to assert one's own field of identity in relation to the family unit emerged as an important aspect of the sisters' experiences as authors, and this need also drives the journeys of self-formation in their novels. Jane Eyre is continually negotiating a family-imposed identity with her own private sense of who she is. Her search is for kinship that accommodates the self.

CHAPTER THREE

Jane Eyre
The Pilgrimage of the "Poor Orphan Child"

But this is not to be a regular autobiography. . . .

IN GENRE STUDIES OF the bildungsroman, *Jane Eyre* has figured prominently as a "distinctly female" novel of development. Of the Brontë protagonists, Jane Eyre most obviously follows the pattern of movement discussed in the introduction: she departs from an original defining community of family (one which she is "in" but not "of"), undertakes a process of refining and redefining her sense of self through her interactions with other defining communities, and, finally, finds a secure and valued place for herself in a family of her own. Jane's personal development in the novel is traced in terms of her physical movement, and that movement, as critics have widely discussed, is structured as a quest or pilgrimage that traverses five powerfully coded locations: Gateshead, Lowood, Thornfield, Moor-House, and Ferndean. Each place brings new challenges, new opportunities for growth, and, thus, new levels of self-awareness.[1]

The nature of the pilgrimage is determined by the nature of the pilgrim. Jane begins her journey as a "poor orphan child," and, accordingly, hers is a search for family—but not a notion of family strictly limited to marriage or blood relationship. More precisely, Jane Eyre searches for kinship, a sense of place in a relationship characterized by "fellow-feeling," a term Jane uses repeatedly throughout the novel. Jane's idea of herself is recurrently dependent on whether or not she feels "akin" to those around her, "at home" in a particular place. The novel plots her course from displacement at Gateshead Hall, where she is "like nobody there" (*JE*, 13), to "full fellow-feeling" (*JE*, 495) with the Rivers family at Moor-House, and finally to symbiosis with Rochester at Ferndean, where she is "ever more absolutely bone of his bone, and flesh of his flesh" (*JE*, 576).

But *Jane Eyre* does not measure its heroine's progress simply in terms of an earthly journey to kinship with the Rivers family and with Rochester. The poor orphan child Jane, who strives toward an earthly home, has a counterpart in the "poor orphan child" of Bessie's ballad, who looks toward her heavenly home and communion with God. Although the child Jane initially rejects this figure as a model for herself, *Jane Eyre* is as much concerned with the "poor orphan child" finding God, as it is with the main character finding a family of her own. The quests for earthly and spiritual kinship are interrelated, and Jane's physical and temporal journeying from house to "home"—from rejection at Gateshead to acceptance at Moor-House and Ferndean—also marks her spiritual progress, from self-reliant skeptic to faithful and thankful believer.

Following the path shaped by such critics as Gilbert and Gubar, Elaine Showalter, and Ellen Moers, whose readings highlight Jane's self-reliance and rebellious self-assertion, contemporary interpretations of *Jane Eyre* have tended to be predominantly secularized and those of Jane herself overwhelmingly feminist. Gilbert and Gubar (whose *Madwoman in the Attic* takes its title from Charlotte's novel) maintain that the "distinctly female" *Jane Eyre* borrows "the mythic quest-plot—but not the devout substance—of Bunyan's male *Pilgrim's Progress*." As Margaret Soenser Breen has recognized, *Pilgrim's Progress* (1678) served as a crucial source text for the English bildungsroman, and Barry Qualls has noted its particular attraction for Charlotte Brontë. It was certainly a text with which she was intimately familiar, as the widespread explicit and implicit allusions throughout her novels attest. To read Jane's story strictly as a feminist journey of self-reliance and self-assertion, then, is to lose some of its depth and originality and, in Charlotte's words, to "doubt the tendency" of *Jane Eyre* (*JE*, xxx). Recently, several critics have argued that *Jane Eyre* does contain the devout substance that permeates Bunyan's work. Margaret Smith, for example, sees *Jane Eyre* as "a moral pilgrimage" that is concerned with "the individual soul's testing, proving, and response." Jerome Beaty locates the novel in a tradition of spiritual autobiography headed by Bunyan's *Pilgrim's Progress* and carried into the nineteenth century by Thomas Carlyle's *Sartor Resartus* (1833–1834) and John Henry Newman's *Apologia pro Vita sua* (1864), in which the "spiritual autobiographer, real or fictional, traces or witnesses to his or her own moral growth, conversion, or deliverance."[2]

As Jane herself attests, hers is no "regular autobiography" (*JE*, 98), fusing as it does the secular domestic life with the spiritual life from a distinctly female perspective. Jane's journey has two "destinations"—a domestic site of kinship and personal fulfillment and a spiritual one (i.e., a home in this world and the next). This chapter offers a new reading of *Jane Eyre* that explores the interconnection between Jane's secular pilgrimage to family and her spiritual pilgrimage to God, specifically in terms of the novel's three-volume structure.

Volumes one and two follow Jane's movement from domestic confinement at Gateshead and exclusion engendered by her hard-hearted Reed relations, to a sense of being "at home" with Rochester at Thornfield. It is a journey made through proud self-faith: in the face of familial deprivation and opposition, Jane progresses from despised and dispossessed orphanhood to the altar of true love and much wealth. Yet in this worldly progress, Helen Burns and the figure of the "poor orphan child" function as providential messengers, encouraging Jane to look beyond her "feeble self" and see the "sovereign hand" at work in her life (JE, 81). But Jane does not see, demanding "Where is God? What is God?" (JE, 96). Helen and the "poor orphan child" testify that a life journey made without personal knowledge of God will be fruitless and unfulfilling, and the first two volumes of *Jane Eyre* bear this out. Thornfield proves unable to accommodate Jane, and she returns to a state of homeless orphanhood.

In volume three, the pattern of movement is repeated as Jane, "a cold, solitary girl again" (JE, 373), journeys from domestic discontent at Thornfield to acceptance at Moor-House. On this journey, Jane makes spiritual as well as worldly progress: she acknowledges an intervening Providence and allows His hand to guide her onward, leading her to family at Moor-House and personal fulfillment at Ferndean. Thus, Jane's progress in volume three repeats, reinterprets, and corrects the journey of the previous two volumes through its incorporation of God. Throughout the novel, the secular and Christian topography work in parallel: Jane begins her journey orphaned both of family and God, "poor" in terms of wealth and faith. By the end, the "poor orphan child" has come into her earthly and spiritual inheritance.

Jane Eyre at Gateshead: Family Identity and the "Poor Orphan Child"

The childhood of Jane Eyre focuses on her emerging sense of who she is and where she belongs. Jane's "place" in the Reed household is designated by a series of confinements and exclusions—both forcibly imposed and at times voluntarily sought. The novel opens with a scene of such confinement: winter wind and rain have prevented the usual afternoon walk, so diversion must be found indoors. But Jane is glad of it, thankful to be spared the "nipped fingers and toes" and the humiliating reminder of her "physical inferiority" to her regular walking companions, Eliza, John, and Georgiana Reed (*JE*, 3). Jane's first self-assessment is made in comparison with this community of kin: she is the self-professed inferior, at least in physical stamina.

Confined to the house, the Reed children cluster around their mother in a classic Victorian family tableau, the mother "reclined on a sofa by the fire-side" with her "darlings about her," looking "perfectly happy" (*JE*, 3). This image captures the domestic ideal, conveying the warmth and insularity of the family unit, tranquil and safe from uncontrollable forces beyond the home. Like the storm, Jane is blocked out. Mrs. Reed extends Jane's "inferiority" beyond the physical, claiming that because Jane lacks the "sociable and child-like disposition" of her own children, she cannot be admitted into their company (*JE*, 3). Jane's protest against her exclusion suggests her yearning to belong and her hurt pride when she is made to be a peripheral onlooker. Her challenge to the adult authority that ostracizes her, however, only further convinces Mrs. Reed that Jane is "unchild-like," a stormy presence that threatens to corrupt her brood of "contented, happy, little children" (*JE*, 3).[3]

As a mature narrator looking back on this exclusion, Jane presents the happy group ironically. She undermines the tranquillity and desirability of the family scene by noting in a parenthetical aside that the Reed children are "for the time neither quarrelling nor crying" as, we are meant to understand, is their habit (*JE*, 3). The tableau does not accurately represent reality at Gateshead, and its falsehood is confirmed by John Reed's hasty departure from the scene in tormenting pursuit of Jane. In suggesting that the family portrait is a "fake," the mature Jane offers a form of narrative consolation to the young "experiencing" Jane: the Reeds are not a family she would want to join anyway. And the child eventually learns this herself, maintaining her difference and distance from them.

Jane's original self-conception at Gateshead is determined expressly by her difference and distance from the family unit. She is, to both herself and her relations, an anomaly, "a heterogeneous thing, opposed to them in temperament, in capacity, in propensities; a useless thing, incapable of serving their interest, or adding to their pleasure; a noxious thing, cherishing the germs of indignation at their treatment, of contempt of their judgment" (*JE*, 13–14). Thus stigmatized, Jane actively seeks separation from her blood kin, removing herself to different nooks and rooms of the house and finally to "an entire separation from Gateshead," which is the primary alluring characteristic of Lowood (*JE*, 25).

Her first retreat is to the breakfast room window seat where, with the curtain drawn around her, she watches as the rain and wind disfigure the lawn. The "double retirement" of the window seat (*JE*, 4) represents the only domestic space that can peacefully accommodate Jane, underscoring what Gayatri Chakravorty Spivak has called her "self-marginalized uniqueness."[4] Yet the enclosure is also a signifier of her displacement. It is a kind of limbo, a space between two worlds—the cold, stormy outdoors and the fire-lit but emotionally cold drawing room—into neither of which Jane wishes to venture. She invokes imagination and the pictures in Bewick's *History of British Birds* (1797–1804) to create other worlds in which she can move.

Jane's imaginary escape behind the crimson curtain is, however, short-lived. Calling her out of hiding, John Reed only seeks to reinforce her marginalization and inferiority by taunting her about her monetary want, claiming, "you are a dependant, mama says; you have no money; your father left you none; you ought to beg, and not to live here with gentlemen's children like us, and eat the same meals we do, and wear clothes at our mama's expense" (*JE*, 7). John is the first to articulate Jane's orphaned status and her role as a family dependent, which, in his mind, warrant her alienation from "gentlemen's children." Being "poor" and an "orphan" thus underlies Jane's difference and persecution. John also clearly understands the socioeconomic power of the family in determining one's place in the world. Membership in a family entitled children to certain "services" that did much to secure their social status as adults, including rights of primogeniture, inheritances, dowries, and arranged marriages. A girl's financial prospects and marriageability "tended to be directly related to the wealth and status of her father" who provided for her dowry or settlement.[5] As John makes clear, Jane's father left her no money, and so Jane must make her journey without this family mediation.

As the "master of the house," John assumes his right to punish Jane for possessing herself of family property to which she has no claim: "Now, I'll teach you to rummage my book-shelves: for they *are* mine; all the house belongs to me, or will do in a few years" (*JE*, 7–8). He then hurls the Bewick book at Jane, not only as an assertion of his patriarchal inheritance, but also as a staggering reminder (causing Jane literally to stagger) that Jane has no rights or natural place within the Reed household, a reiteration of Mrs. Reed's refusal to allow Jane into the family picture. For all his patriarchal bravado, John is merely voicing his mother's hostilities against Jane as an encumbrance on the family's resources, a "burden" left on her hands (*JE*, 290). Her sentiments correspond to those of Mrs. Earnshaw in *Wuthering Heights*, who rails against her husband for adopting Heathcliff "when they had their own bairns to feed, and fend for" (*WH*, 45). Jane occupies a position in the Reed family similar to that which Heathcliff occupies among the Earnshaws: both are orphans taken in by the father against the mother's wishes and persecuted by the family's natural progeny. Mrs. Reed's hatred of Jane as "an uncongenial alien permanently intruded on her own family group" (*JE*, 14) partly derives from her husband's preferential treatment of his niece over his own children; Mr. Earnshaw similarly "pets" Heathcliff up above Hareton and Catherine. Both acts of favoritism breed "bad feeling in the house" (*WH*, 47).

In the manner of Hareton Earnshaw, who rejects Heathcliff as a "beggarly interloper" (*WH*, 49), John Reed denies Jane's claim to the family at the same time as he asserts her dependence upon it. She is, in John's view, a debtor, for without his family's charity, she would be a beggar. Both the nurse, Bessie, and her maid, Abbot, also dependents in the Reed household, confirm Jane's position. Bessie reminds Jane that the alternative to Gateshead is the poorhouse, and Abbot underscores the economic divide that makes Jane inferior to her cousins: "you ought not to think yourself on an equality with the Misses Reed and Master Reed, because Missis kindly allows you to be brought up with them. They will have a great deal of money, and you will have none" (*JE*, 10).

Thus, the Jane Eyre at Gateshead is defined by what she lacks. Gilbert and Gubar have noted that, as her surname suggests, Jane is "the heir to nothing," a condition that elicits her "ire."[6] The servants' scolding recall to Jane the crushing "reproach of my dependence" (*JE*, 10), a burden that prompts her to lash out at the cousin who insists on being her "master." "Master! How is he my master? Am I a servant?" Jane demands of Abbot, to which the maid replies, "No; you are less than a servant, for you do nothing for your keep" (*JE*, 9). Jane's place at Gateshead is ultimately anomalous: she is less than a servant, family and yet not family, an unnatural child, a "kept" orphan, a heterogeneous thing. In her struggles against both John and the servants who carry her upstairs to the red room as punishment for her misbehavior, Jane finally likens herself to a "rebel slave" (*JE*, 9).

Jane's segregation from the family is signified by another crimson-colored enclosure: her self-elected window seat refuge is replaced by a family-enforced red room prison. It is a fitting prison: the shunned child is sent to a room that the family shuns. She is locked up as a "rebel slave"; the storm of passions that threatens family harmony, the "bad animal" that John taunts (*JE*, 6), is contained. Natalie J. McKnight sees the red room as "a physical manifestation of the emotional separation Jane has already undergone. She has already been locked away from the family." The red room also attests to Jane's imprisonment *within* the family: she is a victim of their caprices, forced to accept their charity and humiliated by her role as the "family pariah." The manifold ambiguities of Jane's position—excluded from the family and confined by it, dependent upon it yet longing to leave it—mark the full extent of her imprisonment and isolation.[7]

It is in recalling her red room experience that Jane makes explicit the reasons for her persecution. When the adult narrator remembers her "mental battle" therein, she reflects, "I could not answer the ceaseless inward question—*why* I thus suffered: now, at the distance of—I will not say how many years, I see it clearly. I was a discord in Gateshead-hall: I was like nobody there: I had nothing in harmony with Mrs. Reed or her children, or her chosen vassalage" (*JE*, 13). Again, Jane's lack is her defining feature—she is like nobody; she has nothing in harmony with the established household. Lacking sympathy from every living thing at Gateshead, Jane cannot even take comfort in her own mirror image when she catches a glimpse of herself in the red room's "great looking glass": it too is alien, "unchildlike," a "strange little figure," "like one of the tiny phantoms, half fairy, half imp" (*JE*, 12). Jane sees herself as the heterogeneous *thing* that she believes the Reeds see.

Unloved by the living, Jane imagines herself beloved of the dead, conjuring up the presence of a kindred spirit in her Uncle Reed: "I doubted not—had never doubted—that if Mr. Reed had been alive he would have treated me kindly . . . and I thought Mr. Reed's spirit, harassed by the wrongs of his sister's child, might quit its abode . . . and rise before me in this chamber" (*JE*, 15). In this early stage of Jane's story, it is significant that in her friendlessness she calls upon a masculine protector, but not God. God is first introduced in the novel by Abbot, who says that God will punish Jane for her rebellious behavior: "he might strike her dead in the midst of her tantrums, and then where would she go?" (*JE*, 10). In her imprisonment, Jane specifically does not say prayers of repentance, as Abbot has advised, but instead muses on the injustice of her situation, putting her faith in Uncle Reed's ghostly retribution on her behalf. Yet, while such thoughts are "consolatory in theory" (*JE*, 15), the prospect of an otherworldly communion with her uncle proves too terrible for Jane, and she collapses in fear.

Chapter 3, which depicts Jane's convalescence from her red room trauma, introduces the figure of the "poor orphan child" of Bessie's ballad. In her first ten years at Gateshead, Jane has learned that to be poor and orphaned in the world is to be treated as an inferior and excluded from a community of kin. Bessie's song offers a counterimage, which, as Jane matures, plays a defining role in her idea of self: Bessie's "poor orphan child" is accepted and loved by a heavenly father and welcomed into his heavenly home. The ballad itself previews the solitary wanderings Jane undertakes after leaving Thornfield, and, with its descriptions of bleak landscapes and perilous travels similar to those in Bunyan's *Pilgrim's Progress*, it also serves as Jane's introduction to a benevolent providentialism. Although the orphan child, like the Christian pilgrim, struggles and suffers, the ballad concludes with the promise of kinship with God and a home in heaven:

> There is a thought that for strength should avail me,
> Though both of shelter and kindred despoiled:
> Heaven is a home, and a rest will not fail me;
> God is a friend to the poor orphan child. (*JE*, 21)

Yet the child Jane is not consoled by assurances of God's friendship, focusing only on the "morbid suffering" (*JE*, 21) of the orphan child at the hands of hard-hearted men, which recalls her own self-pitying victimization at the hands of the hard-hearted Reeds. Jane does not embrace a kinship with God, mourning instead the lack of a living "father or mother, brothers or sisters" (*JE*, 23). It is this absence—this "shelter and kindred despoiled"—which makes her miserable and on which she dwells, prompting Helen Burns later to caution Jane that she thinks "too much of the love of human beings" (*JE*, 81). Jerome Beaty has remarked that Jane's inability or reluctance to know and accept God is a recognizable feature of the spiritual autobiography: "the protagonist in the early stages of the narrative must be, or have been, ignorant of God or His ways, if not sinful."[8]

Hearing Jane's avowal that she "should be glad" to leave the Reeds (*JE*, 24), the apothecary Mr. Lloyd suggests the possibility of her joining a new home and new kin in the form of her father's family, the Eyres. But, as Jane remembers, Mrs. Reed has denounced them as "a beggarly set" (*JE*, 24), confirming Jane's belief that the only alternative to Gateshead is a "poor house," as Bessie has indicated, being the beggar that John Reed says she ought to be. Even with the hope of a new family, she rejects this alternative, vowing that she should "not like to belong to poor people": "poverty for me was synonymous with degradation" (*JE*, 24). This reasoning affirms just how deeply ingrained in Jane's mind is the family-imposed equation of money and self-respect.

Jane's emergence from the red room and explicit rejection of the Eyres mark a turning point in her attempts to achieve self-definition within familial parameters. Coming forth from the red room—a chamber the color of blood which encompasses Jane like a womb—Jane is born into a new sense of being. Jane's delivery from the red room, however, does not involve the entry into a family normally associated with a birth; rather, it involves her dispossession of the family by her own choice. After her conversation with Mr. Lloyd, Jane furthers the process of de-identification and dissociation from her blood kin, embracing her orphaned subjectivity completely by distancing herself not only from the wealthy, cruel Reeds but also from the poor, low Eyres. At Gateshead, Jane remakes the Reeds' rejection of her into a rejection of them: "If they did not love me, in fact, as little did I love them" (*JE*, 13). Following her illness, Jane redraws the "more marked line of separation" (*JE*, 27), which Mrs. Reed enforces between Jane and her children, into her own willing segregation. She overturns the familial pronouncement of her unworthiness into her own condemnation that the family is "not fit to associate with me" (*JE*, 28). Her shabby, lifeless doll is deemed a worthier object of affection than her Reed relations.

Yet in this battle of self and family, Mrs. Reed maintains the upper hand, and in summoning Mr. Brocklehurst to remove Jane to Lowood, she succeeds in portraying Jane as "an artful, noxious child," thereby, Jane complains, "obliterating hope from the new phase of existence which she destined me to enter" (*JE*, 36). This defilement of her character prompts Jane's final act of defiance and de-identification: "I am glad you are no relation of mine," she tells Mrs. Reed, "I will never call you aunt again as long as I live" (*JE*, 39). The freedom that Jane embraces as she bids goodbye to Gateshead is also, however, true orphanhood. As Rod Edmond has noted, "Families may be repressive but to live without them is to be adrift, isolated, and vulnerable."[9] Jane is temporarily released from familial constructions of her selfhood, but in this release she becomes a "little roving, solitary thing" (*JE*, 42), more than ever before a "poor orphan child."

Jane's time at Lowood gives her the opportunity to position and define herself within a new, all-female community, a precursor to the sisterly community she shares with Diana and Mary Rivers. Jane enjoys, for the first time, being "treated as an equal by those of my own age, and not molested by any" (*JE*, 79). The character of Helen Burns presents Jane with a living embodiment of Bessie's "poor orphan child," for whom God is both a father and friend, and Eternity a "mighty home" (*JE*, 67).[10] Not only does Helen rightly "live" the message of faith and "doctrine of endurance" (*JE*, 63) contained in Bessie's ballad, she encourages Jane to see herself anew in the song's orphan figure. Helen sees how minutely Jane recalls her sufferings at Gateshead, and she counsels Jane to reevaluate her relationship with the Reeds in accordance with the teachings of Christ. Jane, however, cannot accept Helen's instruction to "Love your enemies" as Christ has taught and exemplified, concluding, "Then I should love Mrs. Reed, which I cannot do; I should bless her son John, which is impossible" (*JE*, 66).

At this point in her journey, Jane is unwilling to endure without complaint or retaliation the wrongs of the "hard-hearted" or be guided and comforted by a caring Father. Harboring her past sufferings, she notes, "I felt that Helen Burns considered things by a light invisible to my eyes. I suspected she might be right and I wrong; but I would not ponder the matter deeply" (*JE*, 63). A reconsideration—or revision—of her relationship to the Reeds would disturb Jane's sense of self: the family must be seen as the enemy, and Jane must maintain her hostility and difference. This sense of self is, in some degree, carried over to her relationship with Helen. Even in their friendship, Jane persists in asserting, "I was no Helen Burns" (*JE*, 75). Jane is not ready to accept the lessons of humility, lowness, and compassion that Helen, Lowood (the name is suggestive), and Christ offer; she is, in her own way, as hard-hearted as the Reeds.

The family-enemy resurfaces in the form of Mr. Brocklehurst, who publicly denounces Jane as the liar of Mrs. Reed's private accusations, reigniting Jane's passionate indignation in "an impulse of fury against Reed, Brocklehurst, and Co." (*JE*, 75). With this mark of shame, Jane is pronounced to be "a little castaway: not a member of the true flock, but evidently an interloper and an alien"—a characterization that echoes her role at Gateshead (*JE*, 76). Brocklehurst threatens to recast Jane as the ostracized outsider not only in the Lowood community of girls and teachers whose good opinion Jane cherishes, but also in the community of "God's own lambs" (*JE*, 76). Brocklehurst warns, as he did in the

Gateshead breakfast room, that heaven will not be Jane's home if she does not mend her ways; God will not claim her as one of His own.[11]

Thus, two versions of God in contrasting guises of patriarchal power dominate Jane's childhood: Brocklehurst embodies Abbot's vengeful God passing judgment over Jane's faults and barring the gates of heaven against her, excluding her from heaven as she was from the company of the Reeds. This image of a stern, unforgiving, and uncaring God is countered by the merciful, protecting, benevolent God worshiped by the "poor orphan child," figured both in Bessie's song and in Helen Burns. Advancing her creed of universal salvation, Helen has faith that heaven is a home for all of God's children.[12] Helen is a "child of God," and at her death she assures Jane of their kinship together as children of God, to be reunited at last under "the same mighty, universal Parent" in "the same region of happiness" (*JE*, 96).

Despite Helen's assurances, there is little indication at this point in the novel that Jane accepts Helen's God over Brocklehurst's. Spiritually, she remains solitary and roving, questioning, "Where is God? What is God?" (*JE*, 96) but maintaining a firm policy of self-reliance. Jane's time at Lowood under the influence of Helen and Miss Temple serves to placate the deep impression of her childhood sufferings, but it does not alter the character of her quest. The departure of Miss Temple and, with her, "every settled feeling" (*JE*, 99) leads Jane to question, "What do I want?" and ultimately to conclude, "A new place, in a new house, amongst new faces, under new circumstances" (*JE*, 102). This resolution marks Jane's continuing desire to secure and define a place for herself within a temporal domestic community. The search continues at Thornfield.

Jane Eyre at Thornfield: Family Secrets and the Politics of Primogeniture

"Hitherto I have recorded in detail the events of my insignificant existence: to the first ten years of my life, I have given almost as many chapters" (*JE*, 98). Despite Jane's claim to an "insignificant" childhood, her authorial intrusion at the beginning of chapter 10 calls the reader's attention expressly to its significance. The young Jane Eyre is shaped by two contrasting "defining communities." The loftiness, pride, and hardheartedness exhibited at Gateshead lead to Jane's humiliation and hardheartedness in turn. She makes the transition from Gateshead to Lowood with a passionate vengeful outburst against Mrs. Reed, which is followed by a "pang of remorse" (*JE*, 40) and a sense of the burden of her "hated and hating position" (*JE*, 41). This penitent denouement is the first step to Lowood, where Jane is "brought low," witnessing and imbibing the examples of humility and composure. Thus, Jane evolves from a "picture of passion" (*JE*, 8) at Gateshead to a picture of self-control at Lowood, where, she acknowledges, "to the eyes of others, usually even to my own, I appeared a disciplined and subdued character" (*JE*, 99).

Jane's relationship with Rochester at Thornfield is governed by the self-images she acquired at Gateshead and Lowood, which she is continually negotiating and evaluating. The various, sometimes conflicting, aspects of her developing selfhood—her passion and her self-control, her desire to live "as an independent being ought to do" and to think well of herself (*JE*, 296), as well as her need to be accepted and thought well of by others—are channeled into her longing for kinship, a bond characterized not by blood but by a "fellow-feeling" (*JE*, 14), which was denied at Gateshead with the Reeds and introduced at Lowood with Helen and Miss Temple. It soon becomes clear, however, that kinship, for Jane, must accommodate the self; it must allow for a meaningful personal identity within the relationship. It is Jane's recognition that Rochester is akin to her, in a way that no one has been previously, that ultimately feeds her love for him. It is her discovery that their bond does not accommodate her idea of herself that ultimately compels her to flee.

The Thornfield section of the novel continues Charlotte Brontë's thematic concern with the "controlling power of the family" over the individual, with the controlling family now the Rochesters, and Jane learns that she is not the only individual to suffer at the hands of hard-hearted, money-conscious kin.[13] As governess at Thornfield, Jane lives in a house of secrets. The function of the house itself is to conceal family history and contain family secrets (specifically, Rochester's wife-in-residence) under lock and key. At Thornfield, family connections are suppressed and denied: the housekeeper, Mrs. Fairfax, would never presume on her connection to the Rochester family; Rochester denies that he is Adèle's father; Jane continues her dissociation from the Reeds, maintaining that she has no living relatives. In effect, Rochester's efforts to suppress Jane's knowledge of Richard and Bertha Mason mark his attempt to exert a form of control over the family that has for many years controlled him. But, like Bertha's laugh, the family will not be silenced. Throughout this section, families surface and resurface, not to be forgotten.

The practice of primogeniture underlies the Thornfield drama, uniting the three main players (Jane, Rochester, and Bertha Mason) and setting up both Rochester's and Bertha's affinities with Jane as "slaves" who rebel against family injustice and imprisonment. Primogeniture was a custom of inheritance by which the whole of a family's estate descended to the eldest son, thereby keeping property intact through the generations. This practice, in addition to the rule of entail, which limited the heir's ability to divide or sell the estate, "governed the structure of the English family at all levels of the propertied classes from the sixteenth century on through the nineteenth century."[14] Because Rochester is the younger son, his father left him no money; like Jane, he is orphaned, denied his claim to the family and yet, without a profession, is dependent on it. Rochester implicitly denounces primogeniture as the underlying source of his personal misfortune, blaming his "avaricious, grasping" father for refusing a partible inheritance of the family estate, and thereby denying Rochester his "fair portion" (*JE*, 388).

Rochester's protest against the injustice of his lot is comparable to Jane's complaint against the constricted "portion" allotted to women, which Jane makes in her walk along the third-story corridor, thereby suggesting that the socially endorsed enslavement of younger sons through primogeniture is in some way equivalent to the subordination of women. Their lack of economic status left women and younger sons vulnerable to family abuse, as both Jane's and Rochester's family experiences demonstrate. Committed to primogeniture to keep the family property intact, Rochester's father is nevertheless anxious to secure Rochester's separate fortune in order to "keep up the consequence" of the family name (*JE*, 156). Rochester is thus bartered for money, his good English blood for the £30,000 dowry of the Creole Bertha Mason. His decision to marry Jane and thereby commit bigamy can be seen as his rebellion against the family that worked to place him in his "painful position" (*JE*, 156).

Jane first hears of Rochester's "family troubles" (*JE*, 155) from Mrs. Fairfax, who presents an evasive, intriguing tale of family-inflicted suffering. "He is not very forgiving," Mrs. Fairfax concludes, "he broke with his family, and now for many years he has led an unsettled kind of life" (*JE*, 156). This portrait of Rochester strikes a note of affinity with Jane. Like her, Rochester is a "rebel slave" whose "spirit could not brook" his domestic confinement (*JE*, 156), and who still harbors his bitterness at family injustice (though, Jane does not yet know what this "injustice" is).

Jane soon becomes aware that she and Rochester share not only a history of family troubles, but also, more important, the "fellow-feeling" she desires. Rochester, in turn, comes to recognize that he and Jane possess "natural sympathies" (*JE*, 187). He is pleased with her candor in his presence and finds it increasingly impossible to maintain the conventional distance between employer and governess, not wishing, he tells Jane, "to treat you like an inferior" (*JE*, 163). Rochester finds that he can proceed in conversation with Jane "almost as freely as if I were writing my thoughts in a diary" (*JE*, 167), going so far as to share the story of his "grande passion" for the French dancer Céline Varens (*JE*, 173). Throughout their interactions, Jane develops a thrilling awareness that her employer is really her "kin": "I felt at times, as if he were my relation, rather than my master.... So happy, so gratified did I become with this new interest added to life, that I ceased to pine after kindred: my thin crescent-destiny seemed to enlarge; the blanks of existence were filled up" (*JE*, 180–81). Jane suggests that blood kindred are not needed if spiritual kin exist; Rochester alone seems to give her wholeness.

In volume two, families repeatedly intrude upon the growing affinity between master and governess at Thornfield, testing Jane's faith in her kinship with Rochester and her own sense of self-worth. The arrival of the Ingram party and Rochester's apparent marital designs on the beautiful and wealthy Blanche Ingram remind Jane that Rochester is "not of your order: keep to your caste" (*JE*, 203). Jane's use of the word *caste* suggests her sense of the exclusiveness of the social strata and, consequently, her estrangement from Rochester. In their gentry airs and family makeup (two sisters, a brother, and a mama who has "a fierce and a hard eye" reminiscent of Mrs. Reed's [*JE*, 215]), the Ingrams are another Reed family. Jane again seeks the window seat to avoid their insinuations against her poverty and inferiority (to both themselves and Rochester) as a member of "the anathematized race" of governesses (*JE*, 221). This family, too, attempts to define Jane by what she lacks, to relegate her to the margins of accepted and acceptable community.

Jane accepts that Rochester will marry Blanche out of class affinity—"for family, perhaps political reasons; because her rank and connexions suited him" (*JE*, 232), but she ultimately reaffirms a bond with Rochester that defies conventionality and bridges the strictures of caste: "'He is not to them what he is to me,' I thought: 'he is not of their kind. I believe he is of mine;—I am sure he is,—I feel akin to him,—I understand the language of his countenance and movements: though rank and wealth sever us widely, I have something in my brain and heart, in my blood and nerves, that assimilates me mentally to him'" (*JE*, 219). As Maurianne Adams has argued, Jane claims "an affinity based on moral and spiritual qualities as a counter to the impoverishment of marital relationships based on status and money."[15] Despite their difference in rank and beauty—which Jane resolutely impresses upon her mind in her contrasting sketches of herself "disconnected, poor, and plain" (*JE*, 201) and Blanche "an accomplished lady of rank" (*JE*, 202)—Jane is able to pronounce Blanche an inferior, lacking originality, goodness, sincerity, and, most important, kinship with Rochester. This pronouncement signals that Jane is rejecting the Gateshead-imposed sense of her own inferiority based on her lack of money and beauty.

Significantly, at this point Jane is called back to Gateshead by the dying Mrs. Reed, and she must confront her childhood memories. Gateshead, the original site of self-formation, reappears, halfway through the novel, as a site of self-evaluation. Approaching the "same hostile roof" of her childhood (*JE*, 285), Jane recalls the feelings of displacement and inferiority enkindled therein, but she acknowledges her changed position with regard to its inhabitants: "I still felt as a wanderer on the face of the earth: but I experienced firmer trust in myself and my own powers, and less withering dread of oppression. The gaping wound of my wrongs, too, was now quite healed; and the flame of resentment extinguished" (*JE*, 285). Back among the Reed family, Jane no longer sees herself in terms of what she lacks, but of what she has gained—a calm self-possession, a "firmer trust in myself and my own powers," which implies a notion of self-worth not imposed from without, but generated within.

In her return to Gateshead, Jane proves that she has indeed been able to "get on whether your relations notice you or not," as Bessie predicted (*JE*, 110). She has incorporated Helen's Christian precepts, no longer viewing the family as her enemy and able to offer Mrs. Reed her "full and free forgiveness" (*JE*, 300) when Mrs. Reed confesses to withholding information about Jane's only other living kin, her uncle Eyre. This gesture marks Jane's spiritual and emotional growth and stands in stark contrast to Mrs. Reed's frozen hostility and resentment, which remains "unchanged, and unchangeable" (*JE*, 289). Jane's growth demonstrates her superiority, both to Jane herself and to her readers. The Reeds—the bitter, unforgiving mother; the self-indulgent, materialistic Georgiana; the ascetic, sermonizing Eliza—are not a family she would have wanted to join after all.

Charlotte Brontë also fulfills our sense of poetic justice in the Reed family's demise. Jane's childhood tormentor, John Reed, who condemned Jane for her economic dependence, has, in the end, ruined his family financially and committed suicide, prompting his adoring mother to take to her deathbed and bringing his own sisters to economic dependence, which Eliza relieves by joining a religious order and Georgiana by marrying a "wealthy worn-out man of fashion" (*JE*, 303). Jane leaves Gateshead this time not a disowned charity child, but an heiress with the hope of earthly kin and a human home figured in her uncle Eyre, who proves to be "as much gentry as the Reeds are" (*JE*, 110).

Jane's thoughts of home at this point, however, are connected with Thornfield and Rochester—she wholly forgets her uncle's letter until after her engagement. "Wherever you are is my home," she tells Rochester upon her return from Gateshead, "my only home" (*JE*, 308). Jane's presence also makes Thornfield "home" to Rochester, transforming it from a "great plague-house" that he abhors and avoids (*JE*, 175). Jane's uncontrollable grief at the prospect of leaving Thornfield upon Rochester's marriage to Blanche reflects her despair at losing her kin—her *only* kin—in him: "I grieve to leave Thornfield: I love Thornfield:—I love it, because I have lived in it a full and delightful life. . . . I have not been trampled on. I have not been petrified. I have not been buried with inferior minds, and excluded from every glimpse of communion with what is bright, and energetic, and high" (*JE*, 317). Jane's feelings of personal freedom and fulfillment in the domestic space of Thornfield correspond to her feelings of kinship with Rochester. In contrast to Gateshead and the Reeds, who excluded her, both Thornfield and Rochester have taken in the "bonny wanderer" (*JE*, 168). In both, Jane believes that she has found an abiding place that will uphold and cherish the full integrity of her person. Rochester confirms Jane's belief in his moonlit proposal, taking Jane as his wife—his equal and likeness—and assuring her that Thornfield is her true home, that her wanderings are over.

But Jane is wrong: there is no place in Rochester's home for a(nother) wife and, crucially, no place for herself in Rochester's vision of "Mrs. Rochester." Rochester wins Jane's hand by reiterating and reinforcing her own assertion that they are spiritual equals, but as morning comes, he reneges on his vow: he transforms his equal and likeness into his object and possession. His boastful conquest and insistence upon adorning Jane with jewels and silks rekindle the Gateshead feelings of entrapment and her need for rebellion: "the more he bought me, the more my cheek burned with a sense of annoyance and degradation" (*JE*, 338). Like John Reed, Rochester lords his economic virility over her—even though it is a "loving tyranny" by comparison, it is a force that Jane cannot keep in check as she can his sexual power with vexing and teasing.[16] Like John Reed, Rochester transforms her: the "bad animal" is now taken to be a "doll," a "second Danaë," (*JE*, 338) "a very angel as my comforter" (*JE*, 327). But Jane resists these objectifications as a denial of self, asserting, "I am not an angel . . . and I will not be one till I die: I will be myself" (*JE*, 327). It is the "master," who converts women into dolls and angels, that Jane rejects, the prospect of a union that does not accommodate herself that Jane dreads.

"Mrs. Rochester" thus becomes a figure of fear to Jane, a menacing potentiality, an abyss of selfhood. Jane's decision to write to her uncle in Madeira and make herself known to him *before* her marriage—before she becomes this "Mrs. Rochester"—signals her unconscious wish to forestall what she senses will be a self-sacrificing union. Her resolution also suggests that her search for kinship will not be fulfilled by marriage to Rochester at this point in the novel. While Jane assures Rochester she has "no kindred to interfere" with their union (*JE*, 321), she calls upon her kindred to prompt an interference. As her letter to her uncle is the "signifier of her desire," so Mason and the solicitor Briggs are the living representatives of her letter, who arrive to halt the wedding ceremony by revealing the existence of Rochester's first wife.[17]

Richard Mason also acts as a representative of the Mason and Rochester families: he is the brother defending his sister's "honor," and he is an agent for Rochester's departed father and brother, still able to exert their influence from beyond the grave and keep up the consequence of the family name by preventing Rochester from marrying a lowly governess, a familial interloper who has overstepped the boundaries of caste and the limits of her "place." The announcement of an "insuperable impediment" (*JE*, 365) to the marriage marks the climax of the family's power over the novel's protagonists: family secrets are forced out, bringing the course of action to an abrupt halt. The impediment is literally Bertha but also, implicitly, Jane, who is again deemed unworthy of membership in a "gentleman's" family because of her monetary want. At the same time, although the family surfaces ultimately as an obstacle to Rochester and Jane's union, the secrets revealed deliver Jane from the degradation of a bigamous marriage and the fate of being a kept woman like Bertha (even more of a kept woman, one could say, since Bertha is the legitimate wife)—a fate that would simply reinstate her Gateshead position.

In many ways, Bertha is the adult personification of the child Jane at Gateshead: she is the passionate dependent who must be restrained; the "bad animal" who must be locked away; the "heterogenous thing" Jane sees in the mirror before her wedding, which recalls Jane's own distorted image in the red room's mirror. These parallels have led Gilbert and Gubar to interpret Bertha as "Jane's truest and darkest double," "the angry aspect of the orphan child" that Jane still carries with her and that is projected outward onto a woman who acts out the orphan's anger.[18] Yet, what Gilbert and Gubar imply, but do not make explicit, is that the adult Bertha's likeness to the child Jane in her passion and rage arises from their analogous positions within the family. They are both, in a sense, family secrets, sources of family shame that must be locked away from view, threats to family security. While Bertha is victimized by the Rochesters and Masons for her money and imprisoned in the third story of Thornfield, Jane is comparably victimized by the Reed family because she has no money, imprisoned in the red room of Gateshead.

Both Jane and Bertha rebel against their containment within family-enforced prisons—Bertha replays Jane's childhood rebellion. Jane rebukes Mrs. Reed "like something mad, or like a fiend" (*JE*, 290), while the mad Bertha burns Rochester's bed and house in defiance of his control. Jane and Bertha each draw blood from their blood relations, Jane in her retaliation against the bullying of John Reed, Bertha in her attack on her brother Richard. Bessie and Abbot threaten to tie Jane to a chair in the red room, and Bertha is tied to a chair after she springs at Rochester. Yet, while Jane gains freedom from Gateshead and self-possession at Lowood, Bertha remains the "rebel slave." Bertha achieves her ultimate rebellion—administering her own poetic justice—in her suicidal destruction of the patriarchal house, the symbol of the family practices of primogeniture and marital transaction, in which she has been imprisoned.

Before her aborted wedding, Jane has two foreboding dreams in which she is burdened with a piteous wailing child who fetters her movement and prevents her from reaching Rochester. The dream-child is both a dependent and an impediment, and, thus, the child symbolizes both Jane and Bertha, each a dependent and each acting as an impediment (however subconsciously on Jane's part) to Jane's union with Rochester. The dream-child, however, can also be viewed in light of the Christian pilgrim's burden in Bunyan's *Pilgrim's Progress*. What Jane says of the burdensome child resounds with Christian's complaint over his own burden: "I might not lay it down anywhere, however tired were my arms—however much its weight impeded my progress, I must retain it" (*JE*, 357).

The child, then, is not simply an emblem of Jane's past, or even her present dependence, as numerous critics have held, but of her present *self-dependence*—a self-dependence that seeks to make progress in the world without acknowledgment of, or assistance from, God.[19] At Lowood, Helen had insisted to Jane that "the sovereign hand that created you and put life into it, has provided you with other resources than your feeble self, or than creatures feeble as you" (JE, 81). Symbolically, it is Jane's refusal to look beyond her "feeble self" that impedes her progress; it is her striving wholly for Rochester, whom she has made "her hope of heaven" (JE, 346) that leaves her quest unfulfilled.

Christian's burden falls when he comes to the cross, and so too, according to the Christian topography of the novel, will Jane's. Having been crowned with thorns at Thornfield, Jane is next bound for Whitcross Moor, the scene of her symbolic dying, where she will lay down the burden of self-reliance and turn to God. And after three days of wandering, she will be resurrected into the arms of a family, brought into her earthly and spiritual inheritance.

Jane Eyre at Moor-House: Answering the Call of Mother Nature and Father God

With her wedding interrupted and the hope of a life with Rochester made impossible by the presence of his "other/already" wife, the "ardent, expectant woman," Jane sees herself as a "cold, solitary girl again" (JE, 373). The reactivation of Jane's childhood position and feelings closes volume two and signals a return to the beginning of the novel: Jane's dissatisfaction with her position at Thornfield and her desire to depart from this "home" mark the recapitulation of her discontentment at Gateshead, where she was originally a "cold, solitary girl." Before leaving Rochester and Thornfield, Jane dreams she is once again in the Reeds' red room. She is confronted with a vision of kinship, not the ghostly Uncle Reed but a mother-figure, who urges Jane to "flee temptation" and embark on a new journey (JE, 407). This figure operates similarly to the Evangelist at the opening of *Pilgrim's Progress*, who urges Christian to leave the City of Destruction with the message "*Fly from the wrath to come.*"[20] In fleeing Thornfield, Jane thus escapes both the temptation of an immoral union with Rochester (becoming yet another of his mistresses) and the destructive wrath-to-come of Bertha Mason, who burns her prison-house to the ground.

Thornfield and marriage to Rochester, which was to be the culmination of Jane's wanderings, incorporate both the unsuccessful ending to Jane's first search for kinship and wholeness, and the beginning of a new search, which will, in the end, right the first. In volume three, the bildungsroman pattern is repeated anew, but with a difference. As Jane is alone in her room after her aborted wedding, "self-abandoned . . . longing to be dead," she asserts, "One idea only still throbbed life-like within me—a remembrance of God" (*JE*, 374). A prayer in the words of Psalm 22:11 rises to her mind, unbidden and unuttered: "Be not far from me, for trouble is near: there is none to help" (*JE*, 374). As a child at Gateshead, Jane had communicated her dislike of Psalms to Mr. Brocklehurst. Her invocation of this verse at the close of volume two suggests that Jane is reinterpreting her relationship to God. This reinterpretation is the thematic thrust of volume three, in which Jane comes to recognize the hand of God working in her life and learns to call on God as her help in the midst of trouble.

Volume three opens with Jane's question "What am I to do?" (*JE*, 379), echoing the words of Bunyan's Christian pilgrim at the outset of his trials of faith. This question signals that Jane is embarking on a journey of a new kind, one of spiritual progress. Michael Mason has noted that the section that details Jane's sufferings and wanderings following her departure from Thornfield is the most critically neglected portion of the novel.[21] Jane's three nights on Whitcross Moor are, however, crucial to her spiritual epiphany. Before her arrival at Moor-House, where she is taken in by a family who prove at last to be her true kin, Jane seeks out and claims kinship with two important figures who play a defining role in her future: Mother Nature and Father God.

The vision of maternal guidance in the red room dream that spurred Jane to flee Thornfield becomes a figure of maternal comfort and repose in "the universal mother, Nature," whom Jane claims as her only relative (*JE*, 412). Unlike Mrs. Reed, who withheld from Jane a mother's love, Nature is "benign and good: I thought she loved me, outcast as I was," and Jane clings to this mother with "filial fondness" (*JE*, 413). But Nature is ultimately seen to be part of "His works" (*JE*, 414), and in the arms of the universal mother, Jane at last feels the presence of God. God, according to Mr. Brocklehurst, followed the example of Mrs. Reed in not claiming the young Jane Eyre as his own. But now as Jane feels the protection and acceptance of Mother Nature, her attention is drawn to God's paternal love for her, and she is able finally to reject Brocklehurst's vision of the divine and see herself rightly as a "child of God."

Tortured by the fear of Rochester's self-abandonment (he, in their parting, accused Jane of flinging him back on "lust for a passion—vice for an occupation" [*JE*, 404]), Jane raises her hands in prayer:

> Looking up, I, with tear-dimmed eyes, saw the mighty-milky way. Remembering what it was—what countless systems there swept space like a soft trance of light—I felt the might and strength of God. Sure was I of His efficiency to save what He had made: convinced I grew that neither earth should perish, nor one of the souls it treasured. I turned my prayer to thanksgiving: the Source of Life was also the Saviour of Spirits. Mr. Rochester was safe: he was God's, and by God would he be guarded. (JE, 414)

As Beaty has rightly perceived, "This is not the voice of the first, the rebellious and skeptical Jane, but a second, more knowledgeable Jane"— one who is tempered and who has come to be sure of God's powers, whereas before she had simply expressed assurance in her own.[22] In this scene, God proves that He is not far from Jane; He fulfills his role in Bessie's song:

> Yet distant and soft the night-breeze is blowing,
> Clouds there are none, and clear stars beam mild;
> God, in His mercy, protection is showing,
> Comfort and hope to the poor orphan child.
>
> Ev'n should I fall, o'er the broken bridge passing,
> Or stray in the marshes, by false lights beguiled,
> Still will my Father, with promise and blessing,
> Take to His bosom the poor orphan child. (JE, 21)

There are numerous parallels between these two verses and Jane's experience on the moors: Jane prays under a cloudless night with the "clear stars" beaming down; she falls twice crossing the marsh; and, most important, she displays the spiritual conviction of the "poor orphan child." The child Jane who hounded Helen with her questions, "Where is God? What is God?" now has the faith of a "child of God." Her confidence in God's power and promise of salvation for all echoes Helen's belief that God is "My Maker and yours; who will never destroy what he created. I rely implicitly on his power, and confide wholly in his goodness. . . . God is my father; God is my friend" (JE, 96). Jane is comforted in the belief that God will watch over Rochester as He does her, taking both homeless wanderers to His bosom.

Jane's journey of spiritual education in volume three leads her to recognize that God is not simply watching but actively guiding, an arbitration that she first senses at the outset of her journey from Thornfield. Driven away by the dictates of conscience and the indomitable need to care for herself, Jane is, nevertheless, soon tempted to return, but she realizes, "I could not turn, nor retrace one step. God must have led me on" (*JE*, 410). Later, when Jane is a schoolteacher at Morton, she recalls her escape from Thornfield, remarking, "Yes; I feel now that I was right when I adhered to principle and law. . . . God directed me to the correct choice: I thank His providence for the guidance!" (*JE*, 459). Jerome Beaty has identified a providential ontology that is central to *Jane Eyre*, though it only becomes clear to Jane and her readers in volume three: "Men and women in Brontë's moral universe must earn salvation. They must acknowledge their reliance on God, seek and choose to submit to providential guidance, read signs, and choose to heed warnings so as to find the path." The providentialism of *Jane Eyre* does not, however, undermine the novel's valuation of female self-help or independent will. As Beaty asserts, "God shows signs, but we may choose to notice and follow or not." Like the Christian pilgrim, Jane finds the path through a combination of active intervention and active response; she is an agent in her own salvation.[23]

Wandering and lost on the moors, on the point of death from hunger and fatigue, Jane makes her first direct supplication to Father God: "Oh, Providence! sustain me a little longer! Aid—direct me!" (*JE*, 421). Beaty has noted that here Jane is addressing not a general providence but a "specifically interventionist" or "extraordinary Providence," who intervenes almost immediately (less than four paragraphs later).[24] Jane's prayer is answered, her faith rewarded: having endured the torturous "banishment from my kind" (*JE*, 428), she is brought to a place of deliverance which houses her "kind." Mother Nature and Father God ultimately lead Jane to the marsh's end—not by "false light beguiled" but by the steady light of Moor-House, also known as Marsh End. And Moor-House is home to the Rivers siblings, who are eventually revealed to be Jane's cousins. At first Jane is shunned by the servant Hannah, to which exclusion Jane responds, "I can but die . . . and I believe in God. Let me try to wait his will in silence" (*JE*, 429). Overhearing this profession of faith, the clergyman St. John Rivers takes her in, suggesting that such is God's will for Jane.

From the outset, it is clear that the kind of "fellow-feeling" for which Jane has been searching abides in Moor-House. Hannah's description of the sibling community of St. John, Diana, and Mary Rivers can be read as an idealized portrait of the Brontë siblings: "There was nothing like them in these parts, nor ever had been: they had liked learning, all three, almost from the time they could speak; and they had always been 'of a mak' of their own' . . . they always said there was no place like home: and then they were so agreeable with each other—never fell out nor 'threaped.' She did not know where there was such a family for being united" (*JE*, 438). Upon recovering from exposure and exhaustion, Jane soon finds herself drawn to the sisters Diana and Mary Rivers, who bear a close resemblance to Emily and Anne Brontë. Emily is clearly reflected in the strong-minded "leader" Diana, who instructs Jane in German (which both Charlotte and Emily studied in Brussels), while Anne is represented by the quiet, docile Mary.

Not only are the Rivers sisters alike (when Jane first peers in the window of Moor-House she cannot tell the difference between them, recalling Ellen Nussey's description of Emily and Anne as "like twins"), but Jane immediately recognizes her affinity to them: "I liked to read what they liked to read: what they enjoyed, delighted me; what they approved, I reverenced. They loved their sequestered home. I, too . . . found a charm, both potent and permanent. . . . Thought fitted thought; opinion met opinion: we coincided, in short, perfectly" (*JE*, 446–47). This idealized picture of sisterly solidarity can be seen in the context of the Brontë family relations in the 1840s, as Charlotte compensated for her increasing estrangement from Branwell, her former confidante and creative spur, by turning to her sisters for both emotional and creative support. Despite Hannah's presentation of the Riverses' sibling unity, St. John is significantly peripheral to the female community in Moor-House. He is unable to share in their domestic harmony, as Branwell was, by 1846, distanced from his sisters.

Jane's fellowship with Diana and Mary Rivers marks the domestic fulfillment of Lowood, where Jane was "treated as an equal" in the company of women. At Moor-House, she experiences a "reviving pleasure" in the sisters' companionship (*JE*, 446), regaining a sense of contentment and composure following her Thornfield traumas, which recalls the "more harmonious thoughts" and "better regulated feelings" Jane gains in the company of Helen and Miss Temple following her embittered childhood at Gateshead (*JE*, 99).

Aware of Jane's longing for the company of her "kind" throughout the novel, it is not surprising to us (though it is to St. John) that Jane's joy in learning that the Rivers siblings are her cousins far outweighs her pleasure in learning that she is an heiress. When St. John informs Jane of her inheritance from her uncle, John Eyre, her happiness is clouded by the belief that she has lost her last remaining kinsman: "My uncle I had heard was dead—my only relative; ever since being made aware of his existence,

I had cherished the hope of one day seeing him: now, I never should. And then this money came only to me: not to me and a rejoicing family, but to my isolated self" (*JE*, 488). Money alone cannot fulfill Jane's isolated self, and, in the search for kinship that dominates the novel, economic independence must be just a prelude to the discovery of her family (her blood kin) and, later, reunion with Rochester (her spiritual kin). Kinship is "wealth indeed!—wealth for the heart!" (*JE*, 491). The money simply signifies her rightful (i.e., blood) claim to the Rivers family and provides Jane with the "independency" to ensure a domestic comfort in which they all can live. When St. John protests her dividing her inheritance among them, Jane quickly silences him: "you . . . cannot at all imagine the craving I have for fraternal and sisterly love. I never had a home, I never had brothers or sisters; I must and will have them now" (*JE*, 494).

Not only does the Rivers family fulfill Jane's desire for an earthly home and human kin, the Moor-House section is essential to the structural unity of the novel. Its picture of family harmony and solidarity, of which Jane is an essential part, wipes out the Reed portrait. Both Reed and Rivers sections are ten chapters long, and the Rivers siblings, St. John, Diana, and Mary, are generally regarded as benevolent versions of John, Eliza, and Georgiana Reed. Thus, the family injustices Jane has suffered are righted within identical chapter and sibling structures. Jane progresses from dependent of the Reed family to provider for the Rivers family; from an inferior outcast, excluded from "the cordiality of fellow-feeling" at Gateshead (*JE*, 14), to a full member in a family of equals at Moor-House, where Jane at last shares "*full* fellow-feeling" with her kindred (*JE*, 495, my italics).

The "calm of domestic life" (*JE*, 502) that Jane's inheritance and newly found family bring to bear is, however, disturbed by St. John's resolve to become Jane's husband. Yet, even before he informs Jane of his intentions, it is obvious that St. John and Jane lack the affinity Jane shares with his sisters. He is certain Jane will take his offer to teach at Morton: "for in your nature is an alloy as detrimental to repose as that in mine; though of a different kind" (*JE*, 452). But, as Terry Eagleton has deftly put it, "The difference . . . is finally what counts."[25] Jane values the repose of "domestic endearments and household joys" as "the best things the world has!" (*JE*, 499). St. John's ambition is always looking higher—beyond the domestic and the secular—and Jane realizes that the peaceful society of family holds no attraction for him: "he would never rest; nor approve of others resting round him. . . . I comprehended all at once that he would hardly make a good husband: that it would be a trying thing to be his wife" (*JE*, 501). As St. John rejects the lull of "domestic endearments," Jane rejects the idea of a marital union without these endearments—a union "formed for labour, not for love" (*JE*, 514). In St. John's eyes, marriage to Jane is an indispensable part of his missionary work in India: it is the *only* means of answering both his and Jane's call to God's service. Yet, while Jane agrees to her role as a missionary at St. John's side, she regards the idea of becoming his wife as an unnecessary and unbearable self-sacrifice: "Alas! If I join St. John I abandon half myself. . . . As his sister, I might accompany him—not as his wife: I will tell him so" (*JE*, 516–17). St. John's definition of a "wife"—"a soul helpmeet I can influence efficiently in life and retain absolutely till death" (*JE*, 518)—appears as a form of sacred slavery, another enforced dependence of which, it seems clear, Jane will again be reproachful.

To persuade her, St. John projects himself as God's own messenger, with an exacting conviction that his plan for Jane is also God's and a warning that a rejection of his plan is a rejection of God. Margaret Smith has recognized the weight of Jane's dilemma: "Previously false religion had taken forms which Jane found it natural and easy to reject—the pompous, harsh dogmatism of Brocklehurst, or the narrow formalism of Eliza Reed. But in St. John's faith she sees a religion which is neither absurd nor selfish; she recognizes in him a self-control similar to that which she herself has achieved."[26] But Jane also recognizes in St. John her own annihilation, and God has faithfully directed her on the path of self-preservation. She reasons with her cousin, "God did not give me my life to throw away; and to do as you wish me, would, I begin to think, be almost equivalent to committing suicide" (*JE*, 528).

Worse, however, than the physical and emotional death that Jane fears will be her fate in India is the "second death" of damnation which St. John foretells as Jane's punishment for choosing the "track of selfish ease and barren obscurity" (*JE*, 532, 522). He reads aloud from Revelation with his eye fixed on her: "He that overcometh shall inherit all things; and I will be his God, and he shall be my son. But . . . the fearful, the unbelieving, &c., shall have their part in the lake which burneth with fire and brimstone, which is the second death" (*JE*, 532).[27] St. John's biblical shaming recalls the spiritual bullying of Mr. Brocklehurst, who likewise deemed Jane's acceptance into the heavenly community conditional on her submission to his will. Still Jane hesitates, unconvinced that St. John's will is also God's. "I sincerely, deeply, fervently longed to do what was right," she confesses, "and only that" (*JE*, 535).

At this moment of crisis, Jane anticipates Caroline Helstone's questioning in *Shirley*, "Does virtue lie in abnegation of self?" (S, 194). Does kinship with God and service to God require self-renunciation and a life without earthly love? Unable to answer with the firm conviction of Caroline's "I don't believe it" (S, 194), Jane appeals to God, imploring, "Shew me—shew me the path!" (*JE*, 535). And again, at this intercession, God shows Himself to be an active mediator in Jane's life journey, fulfilling His role as her guide and protector. In response to her petition, she hears Rochester's call, which she interprets as "the work of nature" (*JE*, 536) and, ultimately, "the will of Heaven" (*JE*, 538): it is an assurance from both Mother Nature and Father God that her path lies apart from St. John's, that it lies with a spiritually reformed (though physically deformed) Rochester in marriage.

Rochester's call has been criticized by many readers of *Jane Eyre* as a silly, melodramatic device, which Penny Boumelha, among others, has accounted for in both secular and feminist terms by arguing that the "call" is of Jane's own making—Jane "decides" to return to Rochester.[28] But according to the providential ontology of the novel as a whole, and volume three in particular, I would argue that the call is meant to be a kind of deus ex machina: a direct intervention by God. The call thus serves both the religious and romantic themes of the novel, underlying the fact that Jane's reunion with Rochester is, in the words of *Shirley*'s Caroline Helstone, "romantic, but it is also right" (S, 690).

We are further assured of the sanctity of the call by Rochester's revelation to Jane that he has come to recognize his blindness, his crippled body, and his desolation as an apportionment of "Divine justice" and has asked God's pardon for his past sins: "Of late, Jane—only of late—I began to see and acknowledge the hand of God in my doom. I began to experience remorse, repentance; the wish for reconcilement to my Maker. I began sometimes to pray: very brief prayers they were, but very sincere" (*JE*, 571). Beaty has thus remarked that Rochester's path "has been in its way similar to that which Jane has trod, from rebellion to humility, from self-reliance to acknowledgment of Providence."[29] Rochester's call is made in a prayer for mercy in the midst of God's judgment, and it is accordingly answered in renewed and restored kinship with Jane. Like Rochester, Jane views their reunion as the answer to her prayers and sees her marriage as her earthly reward, sanctioned by God: "Mr. Rochester, if ever I did a good deed in my life—if ever I thought a good thought—if ever I prayed a sincere and blameless prayer—if ever I wished a righteous wish,—I am rewarded now. To be your wife is, for me, to be as happy as I can be on earth"

(*JE*, 569). Through their faith, Jane and Rochester gain both the "peace of God" (*JE*, 449) and the "calm of domestic life" (*JE*, 502) that St. John ever lacks in his zeal.

At the novel's conclusion, Ferndean seems finally to house both self and kin: Jane is confident that her self is not lost in her union with Rochester, maintaining that "in his presence, I thoroughly lived; and he lived in mine" (*JE*, 559) and professing "I am my husband's life as fully as he is mine" (*JE*, 576). We are reassured that Jane will not be subsumed in this marriage, or degraded by economic dependency; that fate is prevented not only by her new identity as an "independent woman" (*JE*, 556), but also by Rochester's enlightenment: "Never mind fine clothes and jewels, now," Rochester tells Jane, "all that is not worth a fillip" (*JE*, 570). Rochester may be physically blind, but he sees clearly now, beyond the limits of earthly wealth. Many critics have argued that Charlotte Brontë must, in the end, "wound" Rochester so that her heroine does not utterly succumb to the romantic, virile hero as Charlotte's female characters in the juvenilia tended to do.[30] Even Elizabeth Hastings, though she is able to resist Sir William's compromising overtures, can only rise to a position of freedom through the downfall of another male, her brother Henry. It cannot be overlooked, however, that Charlotte Brontë conceals the feminist emasculation of Rochester behind the Christian motif of divine justice: the patriarchal God ultimately renders Rochester fit to marry Jane.

Jane, too, is rendered fit to marry Rochester by renouncing her self-reliance and affirming the paternal God as her pillar and guide. Jane is indeed a materially "independent woman," but she secures her spiritual kinship with God, the father who was at first neglected in favor of her policy of self-help and then eclipsed by her romantic desire for Rochester. In following the providential terrain of the novel, what underlies Jane's equality and communion with Rochester in marriage at Ferndean is the pair's mutual ability to throw off the "state of proud independence" (*JE*, 570) and to recognize their relationship at Thornfield as essentially idolatrous. Having set each other up as idols—Jane to adorn with gold and jewels and Rochester to worship above the Creator—they both now see clearly the right relationship with each other and with God. Rochester's wounding is thus the counterpart to Jane's wandering; both characters come to acknowledge their dependence on God, which is the necessary preface to embracing their mutual dependence on each other. The result is a return to Eden and the prelapsarian bond between man and woman, ever more absolutely bone of each other's bone and flesh of each other's flesh.

The novel ends with the penultimate verse of Revelation and the anticipation of St. John's "sure reward" in God's heavenly home (*JE*, 578). He writes to Jane, trusting that she is "not of those who live without God in the world, and only mind earthly things" (*JE*, 575). The spiritual pilgrimage of volume three confirms that the Jane Rochester who writes her life story is a woman who serves God "in my way—a different way to St. John's, but effective in its own fashion" (*JE*, 537), suggesting that, although St. John's way to the Celestial City is not Jane's, she, along with Rochester, is assured of her heavenly reward, accepted and loved as God's own children. The poor orphan child becomes an independent woman who chooses companionship and service in marriage as both her earthly fulfillment and spiritual calling.

Jane Eyre specifically promotes the female as an individual valued by God. Through her journey of providential self-help, Jane rejects the conventional view that female morality and salvation lie in self-denial and self-renunciation. *Jane Eyre* suggests that a woman can be a pilgrim in her own right, not merely a saving angel, as Rochester first envisions Jane, or a self-denying helpmate, as St. John seeks to make her. The autobiography of Jane Eyre records a woman's journey to a faith and family of her own making, and, in conclusion, asserts that these are the sites of Jane's self-fulfillment.

CHAPTER FOUR

Wuthering Heights
The Boundless Passion of Catherine Earnshaw

"I'm tired, tired of being enclosed here."

FEMALE IDENTITY, both in the late-eighteenth-century Yorkshire setting of *Wuthering Heights* and in the mid-nineteenth-century culture in which Emily Brontë wrote, was bound to a family. Women were socially recognized in their roles as daughters, sisters, wives, and mothers, leading to the now-popular designation of Victorian women as "relative creatures," a term derived from Sarah Ellis's 1839 conduct book *The Women of England*. Female agency, like female identity, was also bound by family ties. In 1844, Ann Richelieu Lamb observed, "Woman not being permitted by our present social arrangements and conventional rules, to procure a livelihood through her own exertions, *is compelled* to unite herself with some one who can provide for her."[1] Chief of the family man's responsibilities was to provide for daughters, sisters, and wives, thus securing a woman's dependency on, and containment within, a family—her father's or her husband's—throughout her life.

The world of *Wuthering Heights* is one of dominant patriarchs who control domestic space and govern kinship structures, seeking to enforce female relativity and limit female activity. All female movement in the novel is regulated between the two families of Wuthering Heights and Thrushcross Grange and is entirely dependent upon marital exchange. Even Nelly Dean's relocation from the Heights to the Grange and back again is dependent upon the marriages of the two Catherines. For Catherine Earnshaw, the journey is a one-way transfer from her brother's house to her husband's—a restriction that she fails in enduring. Like Emily Brontë, Catherine never successfully moves beyond her childhood home.

Following Helene Moglen's view that *Wuthering Heights* is fundamentally "Catherine's story," this chapter examines Catherine's story as a historically specific struggle and protest against her relativity and the terms of female exchange from one family to another.[2] Catherine's protest is carried out through her relationship with Heathcliff, which challenges not only the conventional notion of male and female relations, but also the relative nature of female identity. The tragedy of Catherine's story arises from her failure to negotiate the marital exchange: her physical and positional relocation from daughter and sister at Wuthering Heights to "the lady of Thrushcross Grange" (WH, 153) is ultimately foiled by her "unmovable" identification with Heathcliff and her unsatisfied longing in adulthood to return to her childhood home.

"Home" in the novel is figured as a psychological and emotional state, a condition of self-fulfillment that is associated with domestic structures and kinship relations, but never actually realized in them. In seeking to attain this home, Catherine Earnshaw tests various sites and relationships, but the sense of being "at home" is continually deferred, and any domestic enclosure remains imprisoning. Catherine's sense of confinement within domestic spaces is indicative of her position within family structures, first as a daughter/sister at the Heights and later as a wife/expectant mother at the Grange. Her pubescent dissatisfaction with Wuthering Heights compels her relocation to the only available alternative, Thrushcross Grange, which itself becomes dissatisfying, and she longs for a return to the Heights and, finally, for death.

Yet even the vision of an angelic family in heaven cannot sustain or fulfill Catherine's search. In the dream she relates to Nelly, Catherine maintains that "heaven did not seem to be my home" (WH, 99), and she rejects its attempts to contain her as well. Emily Brontë's feminism, unlike Charlotte's, does not foresee a traditional heaven as the ultimate home for her heroine, and *Wuthering Heights* significantly lacks an active providential intervener. Rather, Emily stresses female agency in the struggle for a selfhood independent of familial and social constraints, though she acknowledges the limitations of that agency. Catherine is ultimately unable to "go home"—literally unable to return to her childhood home once she is installed at the Grange and figuratively unable to find fulfillment during her lifetime. Insofar as she remains a "relative creature" until her death, Catherine reflects certain nineteenth-century female realities. Her story, therefore, can be considered as Emily Brontë's commentary on the familial positioning of female selfhood, which, for Catherine, proves to be ultimately destructive.

Before we focus on Catherine's move to the Grange, the family environment at the Heights requires a close look as an original defining community. In this environment, individual sense of self is shown to be dependent upon family status not simply for Catherine but for the entire group of "siblings," of which I consider Nelly Dean a significant member. The arrival of Heathcliff forces a hostile shuffling of family positions and, consequently, a reevaluation of self-perceptions.

Sibling Rivalry at the Heights and the Role of Nelly Dean

Like many family histories, Nelly Dean's narrative opens with the arrival of a child. The introduction of Heathcliff into the Earnshaw family is, however, a perverse birth: he is delivered by a father, as opposed to a mother, who insists that the foreign child be accepted as a natural addition to the family. The advent of Heathcliff sets the Earnshaws in uproar against the patriarch and his unexpected "gift": Hindley cries when he learns that the fiddle he was promised has been crushed by the cumbersome child; Catherine spits at the strange being when she learns that her longed-for riding whip was purchased but lost; and Mrs. Earnshaw lashes out at her husband for burdening her with another mouth to feed. As Nelly testifies, from the first Heathcliff "bred bad feeling in the house" (WH, 47). He is regarded as a violation of the sanctity of the established family by Mrs. Earnshaw and her children, and "bad feeling" manifests itself in terms of familial competition, both among the siblings and between the Earnshaw patriarch and his dependents.

This transgression by the Earnshaw father—overstepping the limits of his natural family function by "giving birth" to a child—initiates the novel's pattern of patriarchal assertions of power through the manipulation of family structures. Old Earnshaw inserts an unnatural member into the family, but his son Hindley, when he becomes head of the household, revokes Heathcliff's family membership and expels him from the house. Heathcliff's calculated revenge on the Earnshaw and Linton families in the second half of the novel succeeds through his ability to manipulate family structures through marriage, which brings both family properties under his control. This patriarchal maneuvering is, however, met with corollary acts of defiance by women and children, who also manipulate family structures to their advantage: Catherine's sibling alliance with the alien Heathcliff, for example, enables her to challenge the authority of both her father and his "detestable substitute," Hindley (WH, 24).

The blood siblings, Catherine and Hindley, join in the initial act of defiance against the father, when they vehemently refuse to have Heathcliff in bed with them. Nelly responds by leaving the child on the staircase landing for the night, hoping that by morning "it" will be gone and domestic peace will be restored. Like Jane Eyre, Heathcliff is an alien intruded upon the family; like Jane, he is regarded as a heterogeneous thing, hardly human. Nelly's use of the impersonal pronoun "it" to originally "name" Heathcliff emphasizes his apparent difference and inferiority compared to the members of the "natural" family, of which, significantly, Nelly considers herself one. Heathcliff even lacks the family language, speaking only "some gibberish that nobody could understand" (*WH*, 45). His liminal position is ultimately manifested by his placement on the threshold of the interior family bedrooms: he is neither completely in nor out.

Unlike Jane Eyre, this poor orphan child has a patriarch who acts as his protector and champion, and the patriarch's authority prevails. The "gypsy brat" (*WH*, 45) succeeds in gaining a place within the family—and his position is reinforced when he is christened "Heathcliff," the name of an Earnshaw son who died in childhood; however, Heathcliff is not christened with the surname of Earnshaw: "Heathcliff," Nelly tells us, serves "both for Christian and surname" (*WH*, 46). The name thus signifies his acceptance but also his difference and implied inferiority: in lacking the family name, he lacks *full* membership in the family. Heathcliff's introduction in the guise of a sibling nevertheless unsettles the existing dynamics and alliances at the Heights. Leo Bersani has pertinently observed that *Wuthering Heights* contains "all the signs of a drama of sibling recognition": Catherine and Hindley's initial protest against Heathcliff resembles a child's ambivalent feelings about the birth of a rival sibling. Emily Brontë, Bersani argues, splits the ambivalent emotions generated by sibling recognition between Hindley, who comes to embody all the passionate hostility against the new sibling, and Catherine, who comes to embody all the passionate attachment.[3]

Nelly Dean's role in the childhood drama at the Heights is often overlooked for her primary function as a framing narrator with Lockwood, and as a foster mother to the children of the second generation. But the fourteen-year-old Nelly is a vital participant in the sibling rivalry that arises with the coming of Heathcliff—an occurrence that threatens to disrupt her position in the family, as well as Hindley's and Catherine's. Recalling her early years to Lockwood, Nelly evidently takes pride in the fact that her mother nursed Hindley, and that, aside from being sent on a few errands, she was the constant companion of the Earnshaw siblings. When

Mr. Earnshaw embarks on his journey to Liverpool, he offers to bring her a gift of apples and pears, in addition to the fiddle and whip promised Hindley and Catherine. Nelly is Heathcliff's predecessor, a child not related by blood who is nevertheless "adopted" and treated as a member of the Earnshaw family.[4] Despite her claim that she "had no more sense" (*WH*, 46), Nelly's decision to put Heathcliff on the staircase landing, in defiance of Mr. Earnshaw's charge that the boy sleep with Hindley and Catherine, is clearly a self-protective measure, an attempt to avoid being replaced by the new child.

But this rebellious act, when discovered by the master, prompts Nelly's temporary banishment from the family and, consequently, a gap in her narrative during the crucial period of sibling realignments. When Nelly returns to the Heights, she finds that Catherine and Heathcliff have already become "very thick" (*WH*, 46): Catherine has forsaken her blood ties to Hindley and accepted the alien outsider as a brother. Nelly's narrative is dependent upon her direct access to first the Earnshaw and later the Linton family, and it is inevitably colored by her personal involvement, as her early representation of the intruding "it" attests.[5] Heathcliff's arrival temporarily displaces both Nelly and her narrative. With Nelly's banishment, Emily Brontë specifically disables her ability to relate the origins of Catherine and Heathcliff's bond. As the bond exists beyond the boundaries of the natural family, it also arises outside the limits of Nelly's narrative; thus, it carries an aura of unaccountability throughout her tale.

Yet even before Heathcliff's insertion at the Heights, Nelly's position indicates that the boundary between family and nonfamily is not fixed. Gilbert and Gubar maintain that Nelly is an outsider, by her own self-definition as a "poor man's daughter" (*WH*, 78) and by her role as the family's servant. Heathcliff, they argue, becomes a "desirable third" for Catherine in the early sibling drama, a counterbalance to the pressures of her brother's domination.[6] Yet Nelly is not removed to the kitchen until Hindley returns as the new patriarch following old Earnshaw's death. While Catherine aligns herself with the newcomer, Nelly and Hindley unite in their opposition to him. The siblings are four, not three—paired in opposing alliances, not unlike the Brontë siblings in their juvenile writing. Nelly and Hindley cooperate in affording Heathcliff "blows" and "pinches" (*WH*, 46), which serve as their only means of retaliation against his usurpation of Nelly's position as adopted child and of Hindley's position as Catherine's bed partner.

Beyond describing her early alliance with Hindley, Nelly gives little detail of their childhood relationship. It is clear, however, that they shared a kind of brother-sister bond. Nelly calls herself Hindley's "foster sister" (*WH*, 81), and Stevie Davies refers to Nelly as Hindley's "twin," a relation that parallels, and perhaps stood as a model for, Catherine and Heathcliff's sibling identification.[7] Although Nelly does not react to the adolescent separation from Hindley with the mental anguish that plagues Heathcliff and Catherine, she nonetheless recalls her childhood bond with a half-disguised longing throughout her narrative. When Nelly approaches the sand pillar at the crossroads in volume one, chapter eleven, she remembers that "Hindley and I held it a favourite spot twenty years before" (*WH*,133). Overcome by "a gush of child's sensations," she envisions her "early playmate" in the figure of his son, Hareton, seated near the guidepost (*WH*, 133)—the son whom Nelly has nursed since infancy and whom she regards as "Hareton, *my* Hareton" (*WH*, 134). Nelly suffers more at Hindley's death, she admits, than at Catherine's: "ancient associations lingered round my heart; I sat down on the porch and wept as for a blood relation" (*WH*, 228). Although romantic attachment or unrequited love on Nelly's part is strictly conjecture, her allegiance to Hindley, despite his dissipated and destructive behavior as an adult, reinforces Emily Brontë's thematic emphasis on the enduring power of the childhood bond, to which Catherine and Heathcliff violently bear witness.

When the children fall ill with measles following the death of Mrs. Earnshaw, Nelly is called to tend them, forced to "take on me the cares of a woman at once" (*WH*, 47) and assume the matronly role with which she is usually associated. Softened by Heathcliff's silent suffering, as opposed to the Earnshaw children's terrible harassment, Nelly relaxes her allegiance to Hindley, and "thus Hindley lost his last ally" in tormenting his foe (*WH*, 47). Bitter over his isolation, Hindley blames Heathcliff for stealing his previously unrivaled position in the affections of his "sisters" and of Mr. Earnshaw, who becomes furious with Hindley when he sees him persecuting the "poor, fatherless child" (*WH*, 46). Through Earnshaw's unnatural favoritism toward Heathcliff, Hindley comes to "regard his father as an oppressor rather than a friend, and Heathcliff as a usurper of his parent's affections and his privileges" (*WH*, 47). Heathcliff is not only a sibling rival for the family's love and esteem but also a challenger to Hindley's "privileges" as the only son and sole heir of Wuthering Heights and its adjacent lands.

Attuned to this threat, Hindley denounces Heathcliff as a "beggarly interloper" and accuses him of trying to "wheedle my father out of all he has" (*WH*, 49). Yet, upon Mr. Earnshaw's death, it is apparent that Heathcliff is not provided for in Earnshaw's will (if he had one), despite his role as the father's "favourite" (*WH*, 50), and that Hindley is the sole inheritor of both property and position. Hindley's first act as patriarch is to assert his legitimacy over the pretender-son, expelling the "vagabond" from the family circle, depriving him of the instructions of the curate, and reducing him to his "right place" on the farm (*WH*, 27), laboring outdoors "as any other lad" (*WH*, 56). To secure the legitimacy of his descendants, Hindley christens his firstborn son Hareton, the name of the first patriarch and founder of the house.

Hindley lords his inherited position and power over Heathcliff specifically to reverse the favored treatment the interloper received from old Earnshaw, thereby earning the scorn of Catherine, who denounces him in the pages of her diary as a "detestable substitute" (*WH*, 24). But journal writing is not Catherine's primary means of expressing discontent under her brother's rule. The separation that Hindley enforces between Catherine and Heathcliff is the origin of her discontent; her willful union with Heathcliff becomes the outlet for her rebellion.

Catherine and Heathcliff: A Doubled Likeness

The mutinous acts recorded in Catherine's diary—Catherine and Heathcliff's deliberate destruction of Joseph's devotional tracts and their clandestine scamper on the moors—serve as testimony to the "rebellious identification" that Catherine forms with Heathcliff shortly after his arrival at the Heights.[8] The "poor, fatherless child" (*WH*, 46) is clearly everything that Catherine is not. He lacks origins, relations, even a name; he belongs to no one; he exists in the mysterious realm that lies outside the patriarchal family. As daughter and sister, Catherine's identity is wholly contained within and determined by the patriarchal family to which she belongs. For Catherine to claim an identification with Heathcliff is inconceivable according to the socially sanctioned boundaries that segregate genders and classes, as well as the familial and the nonfamilial (except through the unifying force of marriage, and even this was to operate within the bounds of class endogamy).

And yet Catherine asserts her belief that she *is* Heathcliff. This assertion is all the more unsettling because it is not "conditioned by ties of blood"; their symbolically incestuous merging does not involve bodies so much as beings.[9] Catherine tells Nelly, "he's always, always in my mind—not as a pleasure, any more than I am always a pleasure to myself—but, as my own being" (*WH*, 102). Catherine's identification with Heathcliff is not a passive recognition of affinity, but rather a conscious act of rebellion against a state of containment imposed by her patriarchal family. Heathcliff becomes "the project" of Catherine's desire: he is a crucial player in her longing to break boundaries of selfhood imposed by a family and society that construct female identity in terms of prohibitions and limitations. Reacting to Hindley's prohibition against her association with Heathcliff, Catherine vows in her diary, "H. and I are going to rebel" (WH, 24). Catherine knows herself to be limited and confined at the Heights, and she knows that only by appropriating Heathcliff to herself—by acting as "H. and I"—can she attain and experience an expanded selfhood beyond that provided by her femaleness and familial position. In Hegelian terms, Catherine enacts a transgressive appropriation of the Other, and that Other is ultimately understood to be constitutive of her own being, so that "H. *and* I" is ultimately expressed as "I *am* H."[10]

Catherine's insistence on complete identification with Heathcliff subverts the conventional female self-in-relation that denotes her identity in connection with her father, brother, and, eventually, her husband. "I am Heathcliff" offers a symmetry and autonomy that the significations "I am Earnshaw's daughter and Hindley's sister and Edgar Linton's wife" deny. Catherine and Heathcliff's kinship is based on the equality and likeness of twins, but Catherine is not unaware of the gender difference between them: she forms their relationship with a keen sense of her disadvantages as the female half. Even at six years old, she asks her father for a whip, an appendage of self-empowerment. Mr. Earnshaw, significantly, does not grant her desire, bringing instead another male to add to the family, another instrument of patriarchy to which she will potentially "relate."

Catherine, however, shapes her father's gift into her own desire, and Heathcliff, a veritable tabula rasa, allows her this agency of creation. Heathcliff serves as her metaphorical whip, her appendage of self-empowerment, and Catherine wields her "whip" to disrupt the family order and challenge the patriarchal authority that governs life at Wuthering Heights.[11] She delights in her ability to taunt her father with her superior command over Heathcliff, claiming that the boy "would do *her* bidding in anything, and *his* only when it suited his own inclination" (WH, 52). When old Earnshaw asks, "Why canst thou not always be a good lass, Cathy?" she, with Heathcliff's head in her lap, is able to equalize the charge, responding, "Why cannot you always be a good man, father?" (WH, 53). Catherine and Heathcliff likewise challenge Hindley, the father's substitute, scorning his edict of forced separation and laughing at his punishments. Joseph, too, with his oppressive patriarchal Calvinism, meets with defiance as Heathcliff mirrors Catherine's act of hurling her prayerbook into the dog kennel, attesting to her shaping influence over him.

Patsy Stoneman and other literary critics have suggested that Catherine and Heathcliff's relationship is based on an early stage of psychological development in which a child seeks to affirm his or her identity in a mirror image, often found metaphorically in another child, usually a brother or sister.[12] Yet if Catherine is the agent behind this identification—creating Heathcliff as her mirror image—then she understands him as not simply reflecting her but "doubling" her. Catherine claims Heathcliff as both a likeness *and* a double, fulfilling her own narcissistic desire to have an identity that is both herself and beyond herself. She tells Nelly, "surely you and every body have a notion that there is, or should be, an existence of yours beyond you. What were the use of my creation if I were entirely contained here?" (WH, 101). Heathcliff is an existence of Catherine's beyond her, providing a vision of escape from her multiple levels of containment: her femaleness, her status within the patriarchal family, even her corporeality. She concludes, "if all else perished, and *he* remained, I should still continue to be" (WH, 101).

Catherine's quest for transcendent selfhood, however, is finally contained by the social construct of her gender. Her confession to Nelly that Heathcliff "is more myself than I am" (WH, 100) is an acknowledgment of the societal limitations of her femaleness by which Heathcliff, her other self, is not fettered. It is a crucial statement of difference in a speech generally examined for Catherine's assertion of identification with Heathcliff. While Catherine moves in marriage from one house to another, one relational identity to another, Heathcliff embarks on "a mysterious adventure of self-creation" without her. When he returns a "self-made" man, Heathcliff can do things that Catherine, as a woman, cannot, such as manipulate the social structures to his own advantage.[13] This difference is made obvious in his ability to become master of both Wuthering Heights and Thrushcross Grange, consuming everything in his path, while Catherine, consumed by her inability to have control over her selfhood, longs in vain to be a girl again, "half savage and hardy, and free" (WH, 153).

Catherine even seems to lose control over her other self, and in her final meeting with Heathcliff, she rebukes his aloofness to her: "That is not *my* Heathcliff. I shall love mine yet; and take him with me—he's in my soul" (WH, 197). At this moment, Catherine imagines two Heathcliffs: the one that stands before her with his threatening autonomy, and the Heathcliff that she will take with her in her death-wish fantasy of eternal union in an expansive, undifferentiated state of being. For Catherine, death proves to be the longed-for escape from containment of self. But she first seeks a worldly escape from her patriarchal family in marriage and womanhood at Thrushcross Grange.

Wuthering Heights to Thrushcross Grange: Female Escape and Exchange

In *Wuthering Heights*, the ability to move freely in and out of the family is a male prerogative: Mr. Earnshaw makes an unexplained journey to Liverpool; Hindley is allowed to go to college. The child Catherine learns to view the world beyond the Heights as a place of adventure and acquisition. Her brother and father return "altered considerably" (WH, 56) and bring tokens of the outside world with them, Mr. Earnshaw carrying Heathcliff and Hindley escorting his wife, Frances. Catherine is attracted to both "tokens" in turn; she responds to Heathcliff's savagery and Frances's ladyhood as wholly alien to her own experience as a daughter and sister. The outsiders are, however, quickly assimilated into the world of Wuthering Heights. Heathcliff becomes, in one critic's view, "more an Earnshaw than the Earnshaws themselves," while Frances is literally overcome by life at the Heights and, after producing an heir, dies.[14]

Despite her connection with Heathcliff, Catherine is still attracted to the world outside the family home. She and Heathcliff delight in temporary escapes to the moors, away from the tyrannical domesticity Hindley and his new bride impose indoors. Catherine's curiosity leads the pair to Thrushcross Grange to obtain a glimpse of its alternative world. Peeping in the drawing-room window, they declare the view to be heavenly, not only for the sumptuous interior of the room but also for the freedom Edgar and his sister Isabella possess in having the room entirely to themselves. When Catherine is caught by the Lintons' bulldog, she is carried inside and recognized as "Miss Earnshaw"; Heathcliff, by contrast, is pronounced a "wicked boy . . . quite unfit for a decent house" (WH, 62) and dismissed, the door secured against him. The Lintons of Thrushcross Grange thus administer the crucial moment of separation for Catherine and Heathcliff. Heathcliff stands faithful near the window, ready to shatter "their great glass panes to a million fragments, unless they let her out" (WH, 62). But Catherine makes no protest at their division; she is seduced by the world of Thrushcross Grange with its lavish surroundings and lavish attentions. Heathcliff returns to the Heights alone, leaving Catherine "as merry as she could be" (WH, 63).

Although Catherine's stay at the Grange and her separation from

Heathcliff are only temporary, the alternative to life outside her own family, released from her brother's rule, makes a lasting impression. Hindley's recourse to drink and "reckless dissipation" (*WH*, 81) following the death of his wife transforms the Heights into an "infernal house": as Nelly recalls, "The curate dropped calling, and nobody decent came near us, at last; unless Edgar Linton's visits to Miss Cathy might be an exception" (*WH*, 81–82). For a female, unable to move freely in and out of the family, marriage is the only escape, and, in the prospect of marriage, Catherine reasserts her longing for the expansive, uncontained selfhood that she originally sought in her sibling relationship with Heathcliff. Marriage to the wealthy Edgar Linton, however, offers Catherine an escape that marriage to Heathcliff cannot, namely, a comfortable one. So she encourages Edgar's timid and uninspired courtship, gaining the "admiration of Isabella, and the heart and soul of her brother—acquisitions that flattered her [Catherine] from the first, for she was full of ambition" (*WH*, 82–83). Like her brother and father, Catherine "acquires" a token of the world beyond, but unlike Earnshaw and Hindley, who bring their acquisitions into the family, Catherine's acquisition fulfills her ambition by taking her *out*.

When Catherine informs Nelly that she has accepted Edgar's proposal of marriage, Nelly congratulates her on managing her liberation: "Your brother will be pleased. . . . The old lady and gentleman will not object, I think—you will escape from a disorderly, comfortless home into a wealthy respectable one; and you love Edgar, and Edgar loves you. All seems smooth and easy—where is the obstacle?" (*WH*, 98). The obstacle is, of course, Catherine's love for Heathcliff, who, Nelly affirms, "kept his hold on her affections unalterably" (*WH*, 82). In marrying Edgar, Catherine leaves Wuthering Heights and her family of origin behind, exchanging one house and one family for another, the natural course for the transition from daughter/sister to wife. Yet Catherine tries to exempt Heathcliff from this exchange. She denies any intention of ever separating from him, refusing to let the act of marriage alter her or her relationship to him: "I shouldn't be Mrs. Linton were such a price demanded! He'll be as much to me as he has been all his lifetime" (*WH*, 101). Nelly is astounded by Catherine's "folly," convinced that she is either "ignorant of the duties you undertake in marrying; or else, that you are a wicked, unprincipled girl" (*WH*, 102).[15]

But Catherine's principles simply do not acknowledge the exclusive love symbolized by the wedding band. She clearly envisions marriage as a means to satisfy three participants, not two: in marrying Edgar, she will appease his desire and be his wife, and she will provide an escape from familial containment for both herself *and* Heathcliff. Catherine ultimately blames Hindley for the step she is forced to take: "I've no more business to marry Edgar Linton than I have to be in heaven; and if the wicked man in there had not brought Heathcliff so low, I shouldn't have thought of it" (*WH*, 100). Marriage to Edgar, Catherine believes, will finally place both Heathcliff and herself out of her brother's "infernal house": she is again acting as "H. and I," rebelling against Hindley's patriarchal power. Ironically, by marrying Edgar, Catherine is also fulfilling her brother's desire, for Hindley "wished earnestly to see her bring honour to the family by an alliance with the Lintons" (*WH*, 110).

Although Catherine's speech to Nelly makes clear that she has chosen a marriage of wealth and comfort over a marriage of poverty and degradation, and Thrushcross Grange over Wuthering Heights, it does not suggest that she has chosen Edgar Linton over Heathcliff. Catherine is determined to maintain relationships with both men, to hold her two loves and two identities together, despite their differences. She wants Edgar's "frost" and Heathcliff's "fire," and she takes no warning from their obvious incompatibility (*WH*, 100). She intends to be "Mrs. Linton," a social, relational, "outside" identity, with the money and position that Heathcliff cannot give her, *and* Heathcliff, her true "inside" identity, the eternal rocks beneath Edgar's ever-changing trees. This resolution accounts for the "double character" she adopts upon her return from Thrushcross Grange, assuming a ladylike politeness in Edgar's presence and her usual "unruly nature" in Heathcliff's (*WH*, 83).

Catherine's decision to "choose both" (and, thereby, to "be both") is ultimately an attempt to dodge the operations of marital exchange. Yet in trying to have both worlds, refusing, as Catherine has always done, to be limited or contained, she irreparably splits herself between the two men and the two houses. Just as she weeps to return to earth from heaven in the dream she relates to Nelly, so will she long to return to Wuthering Heights from the imagined "heaven" of Thrushcross Grange. The storm that follows Heathcliff's self-exile from the Heights splits a tree at the corner of the house, a foreboding sign that Catherine will likewise be rent apart, and this sundering will be her prison.

"This Shattered Prison": Catherine's Thwarted Return to the Heights of Girlhood

The imagery of dungeon walls and prison bars abounds in *Wuthering Heights*. Upon his arrival at the Heights, Lockwood criticizes the inhospitality of its "wretched inmates" and vicious guard dogs (WH, 11). The house serves as a literal prison for Isabella, Linton, Hareton, Nelly, and the younger Cathy, with Heathcliff as its terrible warden. Both Catherine and her daughter experience the family of origin as imprisoning, whether at Wuthering Heights or Thrushcross Grange. The younger Cathy's longing to move outside of her childhood home at the Grange for the tantalizing vista of Penistone Craggs and Wuthering Heights parallels her mother's desire to exchange the Heights for the Grange.

For mother and daughter, movement beyond the original family is associated with the transition from girlhood to womanhood, a seemingly enlarged identity that promises freedom and agency. Leonore Davidoff and Catherine Hall have noted that women in the eighteenth and nineteenth centuries assumed their full adult status in marriage. When Catherine accepts Edgar's proposal, Nelly remarks, "she esteemed herself a woman, and our mistress" (WH, 110). The younger Cathy anticipates journeying beyond the closed gates of her girlhood home "when I am a woman" (WH, 234).[16] When Nelly discovers Cathy's clandestine meetings with Linton at the Heights, she scolds her charge for exceeding both physical boundaries and the bounds of acceptable behavior. Cathy defends her actions on the grounds that "The Grange is not a prison, Ellen, and you are not my jailer. And besides, I'm almost seventeen. I'm a woman" (WH, 295). But the vision of freedom offered by the alternative house and the elevated status of womanhood is illusory. Heathcliff turns Wuthering Heights into a prison for the younger Cathy, forcing marriage and its attendant womanhood upon her.

For Catherine, the heaven-haven of Thrushcross Grange soon ends. The concessions Edgar affords her, fearful of "ruffling her humour" (WH, 113), prove fleeting, as does her contentment in being the lady of the house. "Well," Nelly concludes, "we *must* be ourselves in the long run . . . it ended when circumstances caused each to feel that the one's interest was not the chief consideration in the other's thoughts" (WH, 114). The latitude Catherine envisioned for herself at the Grange is not fulfilled, a disappointment aggravated by the return of Heathcliff. Family bonds are even more constricting at the Grange than they were at the Heights: only blood ties and class associations are recognized. The Grange does not accommodate the kinship shared by Catherine and Heathcliff. Edgar implies as much when he designates the kitchen as the most suitable place to receive "the gypsy—the plough boy" (WH, 117) and admonishes his wife for "welcoming a runaway servant as a brother" (WH, 118).

Heathcliff's return tests the viability of Catherine's intention to maintain a double character in her relationships with Edgar and Heathcliff. Despite her confidence that, for her sake, Edgar will befriend Heathcliff, and that Heathcliff "comprehends in his person" (*WH*, 101) the nature of her feelings for him and Edgar, neither man accepts the Edgar-Catherine-Heathcliff bond that Catherine desires. They regard each other as rivals for her and battle for exclusive right of possession.[17] Their mutual animosity culminates in a confrontation in the Grange kitchen. Catherine locks Edgar and Heathcliff in, hoping to force some kind of resolution between them. But when the scene ends in violence—Edgar striking Heathcliff on the throat and Heathcliff smashing the bolted door to make his hasty exit—Catherine literally cannot comprehend their inability to share her affections and tolerate one another: "I'm delightfully rewarded for my kindness to each! After constant indulgence of one's weak nature, and the other's bad one, I earn, for thanks, two samples of blind ingratitude, stupid to absurdity!" (*WH*, 141).

With Heathcliff momentarily banished from the Grange, Edgar finally forces the choice that Catherine has never intended to make: "Will you give up Heathcliff hereafter, or will you give up me? It is impossible for you to be *my* friend and *his* at the same time; and I absolutely *require* to know which you choose" (*WH*, 144). This impossibility makes the world of Thrushcross Grange, with its wifehood and womanhood, a prison. To be forced to choose is to be forced to accept a limited selfhood—to be denied access to Heathcliff is to be denied that part of herself that is beyond herself.

When Nelly informs Heathcliff of Catherine's subsequent illness, he expresses contempt for her "frightful isolation" (*WH*, 187) at the Grange with images of constriction: Edgar "might as well plant an oak in a flower pot, and expect it to thrive" (*WH*, 187); "Catherine has a heart as deep as I have; the sea could be as readily contained in that horse-trough, as her whole affection be monopolized by him" (*WH*, 182). But Catherine blames the two men equally, telling Heathcliff that he *and* Edgar have broken her heart. Part of Catherine's refusal to see herself as a "relative creature"—exclusively determined by her relationship to one man and one family—is her attempt to redefine both Edgar and Heathcliff *in relation to her*. When Heathcliff appears at the Grange, Catherine tells Edgar, "for my sake, you must be friends now" (*WH*, 117). But the men cannot be friends, even for Catherine's sake, for each understands her solely in terms of her relationship to *himself*. Catherine rejects the exclusive rights of her husband and resists his demand that she choose to be either his friend or Heathcliff's. Instead, she plans a self-destructive revenge that she hopes will devastate both men: "I'll try to break their hearts by breaking my own. That will be a prompt way of finishing all" (WH, 143). If she cannot have an identity that encompasses Heathcliff *and* Mrs. Linton, she looks forward

> for the time when I shall sleep
> Without identity—
> And never care how rain may steep
> Or snow may cover me![18]

Catherine's final protest against her relativity is made on her deathbed, when she refuses to be buried with the departed Earnshaws or with the Lintons under the chapel roof. Her final resting place is out on a green slope, free from both family enclosures, where, in the end, both Edgar and Heathcliff come to her.

Isabella Linton Heathcliff accomplishes the most dramatic, if tentative, victory over her relative identity. In many ways, she is the most relational character in the novel: she is introduced first as Edgar's sister, and she is known subsequently as Catherine's sister-in-law, as her "brother's heir" (WH, 131), as Heathcliff's wife, and, finally, as Linton's mother. Isabella's marriage and movement from Thrushcross Grange to Wuthering Heights parallels Catherine's: the two families exchange their daughters/sisters, though Isabella's marriage is not approved by her brother as Catherine's is approved by Hindley. Upon hearing of her marriage to Heathcliff, Edgar emphasizes the finality of the exchange from sister to wife, proclaiming her thereafter "only my sister in name" (WH, 162). In marriage, Isabella is quickly disillusioned; her premarital vision of Heathcliff as "a hero of romance" destroyed, she asks Nelly if he is really a madman or a devil (WH, 183). She regrets that she has exchanged her identity as Isabella Linton for that of Isabella Heathcliff, lamenting to Hindley upon her arrival at the Heights that her name "*was* Isabella Linton" (WH, 168). Isabella's heart, like Catherine's, longs for the home of her childhood and her past self. "*I can't follow it, though*" (WH, 166), she writes to Nelly, emphasizing the physical and legal bonds that prevent her return. But while Catherine simply allows her imprisonment and unfulfilled longing to overcome her, Isabella actively contrives an escape.

Following Catherine's death, Isabella finds an opportunity to flee the prison of her marriage and the physical prison of the Heights for the Grange. There, with "childish spite" (WH, 209), she vows to smash and burn her wedding band, the symbol of her marital bond and bondage. The

Grange, she tells Nelly, "is my right home" (*WH*, 210), but she knows she cannot stay there unmolested and unclaimed by her husband. In one of the most radical escapes allowed a woman in a Victorian novel, Isabella flees, pregnant and alone, to live and raise her child by herself, anticipating the escape Anne's Helen Huntingdon makes in *The Tenant of Wildfell Hall*. Like Helen, Isabella must live with the constant threat of her husband's legal right to force her return and to claim their child. Unlike Helen, Isabella, having fled, is extinguished as a character; although she gains a kind of victory over her relative identity as Heathcliff's wife, her identity is erased from the novel, and we only hear of her death.

Catherine's delirious return to childhood and Wuthering Heights prefaces her ultimate escape to her home among the dead, a place "without identity." In a moment of "feverish bewilderment" (*WH*, 149), she believes herself to be back at Wuthering Heights, the mirror in her chamber transformed into the black press in the room that she and Heathcliff shared as children. Terrified of the face she sees in the press/mirror, she does not recognize it as her own, despite Nelly's insistence that "It was *yourself*, Mrs. Linton; you knew it a while since" (*WH*, 151). But, in her delirium, she dissociates her idea of herself from the image she sees in the glass; her fear arises from seeing "Mrs. Linton," the figure of a woman (and, dreadfully, a pregnant woman), as opposed to Catherine Earnshaw, the child she thinks she is, lying in her chamber at Wuthering Heights. Catherine relinquishes her womanhood, her marriage, and her ties to Thrushcross Grange, telling Nelly that in her vision, "the whole last seven years of my life grew a blank! I did not recall that they had been at all. I was a child; my father was just buried, and my misery arose from the separation that Hindley had ordered between me and Heathcliff—I was laid alone, for the first time" (*WH*, 153).

Catherine's current state of "frightful isolation," self-exiled to her bedchamber in protest of the separation her husband seeks to impose between her and Heathcliff, recalls the original separation imposed by Hindley—and the separation she herself imposed in exchanging Wuthering Heights for the Grange. Yet, significantly, Catherine reinvents her removal from the Heights to conform with her present feelings of powerlessness: "But supposing at twelve years old I had been wrenched from the Heights, and every early association, and my all in all, as Heathcliff was at that time, and been converted at a stroke into Mrs. Linton, the lady of Thrushcross Grange, and the wife of a stranger; an exile, and outcast, thenceforth, from what had been my world—You may fancy a glimpse of the abyss where I grovelled!" (WH, 153). In this version, Catherine—a twelve-year-old child instead of the eighteen-year-old woman she was when she left the Heights—is "wrenched" from Heathcliff and her home, as opposed to actively desiring and pursuing her escape. Her desired haven, Thrushcross Grange, is converted to a place of exile, and she becomes an outcast from her true home. Catherine is trapped in the exchanges she has made—Earnshaw for Linton, Wuthering Heights for Thrushcross Grange—and she longs to undo the original exchange. "I wish I were a girl again, half savage and hardy, and free. . . . Why am I so changed?" she asks herself (WH, 153). The changes Catherine recognizes—her womanhood and wifehood, of which her pregnancy is the most obvious sign—preclude the longed-for return to childhood.

This return is an attempt to recapture a time when Catherine felt herself to be whole, a feeling inextricably bound to a time when Heathcliff was "my all in all." With Heathcliff, Catherine envisions the "ideal of a nontransforming union,"[19] a vision also advanced in Emily Brontë's poem "The Death of A. G. A.," in which Angelica identifies A. G. A. as

> my all-sufficing light—
> My childhood's mate, my girlhood's guide,
> My only blessing, only pride.[20]

But, similarly, as A. G. A. is transformed from an "all-sufficing light" to Angelica's "mortal foe" in the Gondal saga, a time comes in *Wuthering Heights* when Catherine no longer recognizes Heathcliff as her "all in all." She appropriates Edgar in marriage, hoping to regain a lost sense of "all in all." But, while Catherine maintains that Heathcliff will be as much to her as he has always been, her marriage to Edgar transforms and relocates her from a daughter and sister at Wuthering Heights to "the lady of Thrushcross Grange" (WH, 153).

Catherine never fully negotiates the exchange. Stevie Davies has argued that "Catherine Linton never leaves off being Catherine Earnshaw" and that "Emily Brontë authorises an opposite journey: the way home is always potentially open." But the return home is realized only in Catherine's feverish delusions. She never returns to Wuthering Heights once she is installed at the Grange. Her visions of the Heights and Heathcliff as the original lost sites of her self-fulfillment are also feverish delusions. Writing on George Eliot's *The Mill on the Floss* (1860), Mary Jacobus argues that, at the conclusion of the novel, Tom and Maggie Tulliver long for an idyllic childhood past that never truly existed.[21] This assertion is equally applicable to Catherine. The childhood world of Wuthering Heights was one of family conflict, patriarchal oppression, sibling rivalries and jealousies, beatings, punishments, and enforced separation. Catherine formed her bond with Heathcliff in the pursuit of escape from the family, and the two children are never so happy as when they are tucked away together in the oak-paneled bed or out on the moors by themselves. Catherine longs not to return to the reality of her childhood home, but to the dream-place of self-fulfillment where she enjoys undisturbed union with Heathcliff. Imagination provides a temporary return; death promises a permanent one.

Emily Brontë ultimately authorizes Catherine's longed-for return to her childhood home by proxy. The novel concludes with the promise of the younger Cathy's return to the Grange, where she will live out her married life with her cousin, Hareton, whom many critics identify as a brother figure occupying a position in his relationship with Cathy at the Heights similar to that which Heathcliff occupied with Catherine.[22] Cathy is allowed an "opposite journey," reversing the one-way course her mother took from her childhood home to her marital home. For the younger Cathy, fraternal love and married love can cohabit; she is not forced to choose between them. By marrying the brother figure and by returning to her beloved childhood home, Cathy fulfills the domestic desires of her mother. The symbolic incest between Catherine and Heathcliff is actualized by Cathy and Hareton but also licensed, since Hareton is Cathy's cousin. The two are bound by blood ties but spared the taboo of an incestuous bond. Cousins in Brontë fiction occupy a position halfway between siblings and lovers; thus, romance and marriage between cousins is always a viable possibility (e.g., Jane Eyre and St. John Rivers in *Jane Eyre,* and Caroline Helstone and Robert Moore in *Shirley*). In addition to securing a union with the sibling-lover, Cathy also manages the domestic subversions that her mother and her aunt Isabella were not able to negotiate: she successfully returns to inhabit her original home, thereby escaping the irreversible relocation that marriage typically required of a wife.

The names that Lockwood discovers carved into the windowsill at Wuthering Heights can now be interpreted in light of Catherine's protest against female identity exclusively determined by family relationships and irreversibly transferred from father to husband upon marriage. The writing, "a name repeated in all kinds of characters, large and small—*Catherine Earnshaw,* here and there varied to *Catherine Heathcliff,* and then again to *Catherine Linton*" (WH, 23), is not necessarily a young woman's attempt to weigh her choices in marriage against dependent daughterhood or sisterhood, or to question her true identity. Rather, the writing expresses her desire to be all Catherines at once. Catherine tells Nelly that she never means to forsake Heathcliff for Edgar, intending to sustain a relationship with both, and so too Catherine never means to substitute one name for another, as is the usual course for a woman upon marriage. Catherine Earnshaw-Heathcliff-Linton can be read as a single identity encompassing all of its guises, just as a man has one name for all his guises as son, brother, husband, father. This inclusive identity is capable of incorporating all of the names, so expansive that to Lockwood "the air swarmed with Catherines" (WH, 24).

The tragedy of Catherine's story rests on her inability, in the end, to fulfill her desire to be Catherine Earnshaw-Heathcliff-Linton. She cannot escape the exclusive and linear progression from her family name to her married name—a transference that passes over her bond with Heathcliff, never recognizing it. Once she has exchanged the Earnshaw name for Linton, she can never return to it, despite her desperate longing to be a girl again. Even the ghost child that Lockwood encounters announces herself as "Catherine Linton," though she is cast in the form of Catherine Earnshaw and is begging to reenter the home of her youth.

"Earnshaw" and "Linton" are the signifiers of Catherine's dependency on and subordination to her father and her husband and their respective families. The identity of Catherine Heathcliff is expressed in the novel only in its terms of equality and complete identification, "I am Heathcliff." Catherine's bond with Heathcliff is not relational or hierarchical; it does not designate her membership in a family. Rather, "Catherine Heathcliff" is a signifier of her desire to break free of family systems of determination and her relational identity as a female. But the name of Catherine Heathcliff and union with Heathcliff are not realized in Catherine's lifetime, and neither is her desire.

Heathcliff's Revenge: Appropriating Women's Property and Women as Property

While Catherine Earnshaw feels her social reality as a "relative creature" to be psychologically and emotionally imprisoning, Isabella and the younger Cathy Linton experience their relativity in terms of physical bondage. The Linton women play pivotal roles in Heathcliff's successful appropriation of Wuthering Heights and Thrushcross Grange, through which he secures his revenge against the families who worked to separate him from "his heart's darling" (WH, 35). Emily Brontë has been praised for her remarkable knowledge of family succession and property laws, which Heathcliff shrewdly manipulates. But Heathcliff's revenge ultimately succeeds by his ability to exploit the female's role in the inheritance of property—more specifically, by his ability to exploit woman's position *as* property.

Randolph Trumbach has written: "Patriarchy presumed that there was property not only in things but in persons and that ownership lay with the heads of households. It meant that some men were owned by others, and all women and children by their husbands or fathers."[23] Heathcliff moves from being at the mercy of this patriarchal system to assuming the role of the patriarch himself. *Wuthering Heights* traces Heathcliff's evolving relationship to property, from penniless orphan to ardent protocapitalist and master of both the Heights and the Grange. As a boy, he first witnesses the battle for possession in the Linton children's struggle over the exclusive right to hold their dog, in which they nearly tear it in two. Heathcliff scorns them and rejects their world, remarking to Nelly, "When would you catch me wishing to have what Catherine wanted?" (WH, 59).

Part of Heathcliff's introduction to the world at the Heights, and undoubtedly part of his socialization process during his three-year absence, is his realization that possession, whether of houses and lands or women and children, is power.[24] Hindley's power over Heathcliff and Catherine derives from his claim to Wuthering Heights. When Hindley mortgages the land to fund his "mania for gaming" (WH, 231), Heathcliff takes possession of the Heights, thus reversing the dynamics of power and securing his domination over both Hindley's person and property. Likening Catherine to a piece of property, Heathcliff strives to take possession of her, believing that only by treating her as a possession, as Hindley did and Edgar does, can he hope to secure her entirely for himself. Catherine thus becomes the object over which he and Edgar struggle for exclusive possession, a tug-of-war that does eventually split her in two.

Heathcliff's desire to possess Catherine becomes, after her death, a relentless quest to possess all things connected with her. Steven Vine has argued that Heathcliff substitutes property gain for Catherine's loss in a desperate attempt to retain his hold on her.[25] His first act as master of Thrushcross Grange is to appropriate Catherine's portrait and instruct that it be transported to Wuthering Heights—an attempt to substitute the portrait for the departed reality. Catherine thus becomes part of the property he possesses and controls, like his wife, Isabella, and daughter-in-law, Cathy.

Relationships in *Wuthering Heights* are repeatedly expressed in the language of ownership. Upon his arrival at the Heights, Lockwood is uncertain whether Heathcliff or Hareton is the "favoured possessor" of the younger Cathy (*WH*, 16). When he finds Heathcliff without an "owner" in Liverpool, Mr. Earnshaw assumes possession of him and carries him home along with his children's other gifts (*WH*, 45). Heathcliff ominously refers to Linton as "my property" (*WH*, 253) and assumes his ownership of Hindley's son, Hareton, upon Hindley's death, despite Nelly's insistence that "There is nothing in the world less yours than he is!" (*WH*, 230). The head of the household assumed legal custody of children and wives: being in "custody" at Wuthering Heights is tantamount to physical imprisonment and domestic violence with no recourse to the law for protection.

Through ownership of people, specifically women, Heathcliff secures the ownership of property. It is not entirely clear whether Mr. Linton made a will or whether Thrushcross Grange was entailed, though the logical order of inheritance in either case would be first Edgar, then his sons, then Isabella, then her sons. Cathy would inherit the Grange only in the last instance, being passed over in favor of first Isabella and then her son, Linton. Both women are potential property owners, but they maintain a precarious hold. Theorists of property ownership, such as Thomas Hobbes and John Locke, failed to clarify "how women's control of property and their expected subordination within the family could be reconciled."[26]

A woman's property, like her identity, fell under the rule of coverture. Under common law, all of a woman's liquid property (i.e., money, stocks, jewels, clothes, etc.) became her husband's at marriage, and the husband was entitled to the possession and usufruct of his wife's freehold property. Unless a father or male guardian made a particular stipulation in his will or created a trust, "a woman's inheritance passed to the legal control and use of her husband."[27] Marriage, then, as Heathcliff seems fully aware, is the quickest way to usurp a woman's position in the line of inheritance and thereby claim her inherited property. This is his all-but-stated purpose in marrying Isabella, and it is his clear design in arranging the marriage of his and Isabella's son, Linton, to Catherine and Edgar's daughter, Cathy. And Heathcliff clearly informs Linton of his prerogative as Cathy's husband over her body and her property, both of which are legally the objects of male ownership. Linton delights in the prospect of owning Thrushcross Grange upon his marriage and Edgar's death: "I'm glad, for I shall be master of the Grange after him—and Catherine always spoke of it as *her* house. It isn't hers! It's mine—papa says everything she has is mine" (*WH*, 340).

The Linton order of succession implies, however, that it would not be necessary for Linton to marry the younger Cathy in order to inherit the estate when Edgar dies. Yet Linton's failing health and the possibility of his death preceding Edgar's make the marriage with Cathy urgent to Heathcliff's plan to secure the estate for himself. Nelly argues with him that when Linton dies, Cathy will become the sole heir. But Heathcliff denies this: "There is no clause in the will to secure it so; his property would go to me; but, to prevent disputes, I desire their union, and am resolved to bring it about" (WH, 263). The marriage of the younger Cathy to Linton would necessarily prevent any disputes over rightful ownership of Thrushcross Grange. James H. Kavanagh has argued that "it hardly matters what the inheritance laws say, since Cathy's marriage transfers all the personal wealth she has just inherited to her new husband, who immediately leaves it to Heathcliff."[28]

Edgar likewise desires his daughter's union with his heir, but he envisions their marriage as a means of protecting her from Heathcliff and allowing her to remain in "the house of her ancestors" (WH, 315–16). He resolves to alter his will so that her fortune (i.e., her personal property) is guarded by trustees for use by her and any children she may bear, and thus, is protected against Heathcliff's claim should Linton die. The trust, as Davidoff and Hall explain, recognized the vulnerability of female property and served to protect it after marriage. Heathcliff, however, is able to prevent Edgar from taking this precaution, delaying the lawyer Edgar has summoned. Edgar dies before his will can be changed, leaving his daughter at the mercy of his greatest enemy, who takes control of the Grange. Nelly questions the legality of Heathcliff's claim to ownership: since Linton was a minor when he died, he cannot by law devise real property, but Heathcliff claims the lands "in his wife's right, and his also" (WH, 356), implying his double claim under coverture and the terms of Linton's will.[29] At any rate, there is little that Nelly or Cathy, both penniless, property-less women, can do to disturb his possession. Cathy nonetheless remains indignantly sensible of the injustice done to her. When Heathcliff berates her for planting flowers at the Heights, she retorts, "You shouldn't grudge a few yards of earth for me to ornament, when you have taken all my land!" (WH, 388).

The appropriation of property marks Heathcliff's quest for fulfillment in Catherine's absence. But, like Catherine's search, it is unsuccessful. The houses and lands that he has worked methodically to acquire give him no pleasure and provide no compensation for his loss. He comes to regard his property only as a burden he must relinquish before he can join Catherine in death: "I have not written my will yet, and how to leave my property, I cannot determine! I wish I could annihilate it from the face of the earth" (WH, 407). Catherine, for whom his earthly possessions are inadequate substitutes, eludes him still. She remains, until Heathcliff's death, "incomparably beyond and above" him (WH, 197), and yet he sees everything in relation to her: "The entire world is a dreadful collection of memoranda that she did exist, and that I have lost her!" (WH, 394). Even Hareton and the younger Cathy, the remaining victims of his revenge, whose persons and properties are his possessions, look at him with the elusive eyes of Catherine Earnshaw, reminding Heathcliff that she remains beyond possession. By depriving the cousins of their rightful land and money, Heathcliff unwittingly makes possible the bond of love that defeats him: there is no threat of degradation to keep them apart, and, in their love, they appear as beyond his power to control as the ghostly Catherine.

Following Heathcliff's death, the novel concludes with the restoration of the "the lawful master and the ancient stock" (WH, 411) in Hareton Earnshaw who, in marriage to Cathy, will assume control of both the Heights and the Grange. Joseph's unbridled joy over Hareton's accession seems to indicate a reassertion of a world of dominant patriarchy, this time with a less-rebellious relative female in the younger Cathy. But the final journeys for the lovers of both generations are ultimately female-directed: Cathy, after leading Hareton through a course in literacy, leads him to the "house of *her* ancestors" (WH, 315–16, my italics), and Catherine calls Heathcliff to her in death with the promise of a shared heaven. Catherine Earnshaw's struggle against female containment within kinship structures is finally realized not in unlimited female agency, but in a male and female relationship that promises to be "enabling and operative, rather than repressive and restrictive."[30] Cathy and Hareton represent a compromise between ultimate possession and unbounded freedom, shaping the excesses of Catherine and Heathcliff into a viable domestic relationship.

CHAPTER FIVE

Agnes Grey and *The Tenant of Wildfell Hall*
Lessons of the Family

> And this I say, not, of course, in commendation of myself, but to show the unfortunate state of the family. . . .
>
> *Agnes Grey*

THROUGHOUT THE NINETEENTH CENTURY and well into the twentieth, Anne Brontë was known primarily by her relation to the authors of *Jane Eyre* and *Wuthering Heights*. In 1897, Angus M. MacKay maintained that Anne's immortality would forever be "due to her sisters." In the same year, Margaret Oliphant insisted, "The youngest of all, the gentle Anne, would have no right to be considered at all as a writer but for her association with these imperative spirits." Anne has suffered most in a comparison of the Brontës' writing, partly owing to Charlotte's setting of the tone for evaluations of her literary merit and personal character. In Charlotte Brontë's "Biographical Notice," which first revealed Anne to be Acton Bell, Charlotte described Anne only as she compared with Emily, presenting her as "milder and more subdued" and concluding that "she wanted the power, the fire, the originality of her sister." Literary criticism to the present day has repeated this pronouncement of Anne's want and extended it in comparison not only with Emily but also with Charlotte.[1]

Recent studies, however, including Elizabeth Langland's *Anne Brontë: The Other One* (1989) and Maria H. Frawley's *Anne Brontë* (1996), have undertaken to carve out a place of Anne's own, reevaluating her literary corpus and rejecting past tendencies to read her works as unsuccessful mimicry of those by Charlotte and Emily. Anne's moral energy and didactic aims distinguish her novels from her sisters', aligning her more with eighteenth-century neoclassicism than with the romantic and gothic traditions drawn upon by Charlotte and Emily. Like the neoclassical writers of the eighteenth century, Anne Brontë followed the Horatian edict, which insisted that art should both inform and delight, thereby imparting both pleasure and applicability to life. She approached this end with evangelical fervor. Anne was adamant that her art should serve a moral purpose and refused to limit her authorial ambition to simple amusement: "time and talents so spent, I should consider wasted and misapplied. Such humble talents as God has given me I will endeavour to put to their greatest use; if I am able to amuse I will try to benefit too."[2]

Within the Brontë corpus, the moral didacticism of Anne's fiction links it most closely with the writings of her father, Patrick Brontë, who also professed to write "In the attempt to profit, whilst he pleased." Patrick's religious fiction illustrates the moral education and enlightenment of characters as means to educate and enlighten his readers; thus, the subject of writing serves his purpose in writing. In the preface to *The Maid of Killarney* (1818), Patrick Brontë informed his readers that "his main object throughout has been, he trusts, to do some good and no harm; to correct certain errors, and establish certain truths, which to him appeared to be of no small consequence." In the preface to the second edition of *The Tenant of Wildfell Hall*, Anne seems to echo him, "My object in writing the following pages, was not simply to amuse the Reader, neither was it to gratify my own taste, nor yet to ingratiate myself with the Press and Public: I wished to tell the truth, for truth always conveys its own moral to those who are able to receive it" (*TWH*, xxxvii). Anne's commitment to representing truth for moral and didactic ends—particularly those "unpalatable" truths of domestic life—defines her works (*TWH*, xxxviii). It also distinguishes them. Patrick Brontë certainly never exposed his readers to scenes and characters like those in *Wildfell Hall*. As Langland has recognized, "in wedding explicit representation of Huntingdon's debauchery with moral emphasis, Anne Brontë was charting her own course."[3]

Like her father, Anne sees that the purpose in writing is served by the subject of her writing. Both *Agnes Grey* and *The Tenant of Wildfell Hall* take moral education as their subject, particularly the moral development of the young as directed by a family. Both novels reinforce the Victorian view of the family as the institutional locus of morality and underscore the formative power of the family over its members. Anne's didactic presentation of fictional families is meant to expose and reform "the errors and abuses of society"—errors and abuses that Anne judged to be originally engendered in the family (*TWH*, xxxvii). Anne's female protagonists, Agnes Grey and Helen Huntingdon, serve her didactic aims: they are voices of moral judgment in materialistic and morally repugnant families, criticizing the misuse of the family's formative power and stressing the lasting damage of misguided lessons passed from parents to children. In the course of their narratives, Agnes and Helen, in turn, are educated by their family experiences—Agnes as a governess employed in the households of self-indulgent, imprudent, and unprincipled persons, and Helen as a wife and mother living with a degenerate, alcoholic, and abusive husband. In her writing, Anne sought to reveal the truth about lessons given and learned in the domestic sphere, hoping that what she revealed would itself be a lesson to benefit the Victorian family.

Agnes Grey: The Governess and Family Lessons

Agnes Grey begins, "All true histories contain instruction" (AG, 3). Following this claim that the novel is "true history," Anne immediately sets forth the didactic overtones of Agnes's story, both, as Frawley has suggested, "in her evocation of Agnes Grey's work as a governess and in the style Agnes adopts as a narrator." Apart from recognizing the exemplary Christian fortitude displayed by its central governess figure, the earliest reviews of *Agnes Grey* largely dismissed its instructive purpose. *Douglas Jerrold's Weekly Newspaper* briefly remarked that "neither [the Bloomfield nor Murray families] is a favourable specimen of the advantages of home education," but did not elaborate. The general impression of *Agnes Grey* was "no impression at all," as the *Atlas* maintained. The *Britannia* likewise found "nothing to call for special notice."[4]

The publishing history of *Agnes Grey* accounts for much of its early critical neglect. Reviewers focused on its companion, *Wuthering Heights*, which seemed to baffle "all regular criticism," and, because *Agnes Grey* appeared after the popular reception of *Jane Eyre*, though it had been written before, Agnes was recurrently viewed as "a sort of younger sister to Jane Eyre; but inferior to her in every way." The novel itself was considered to be one of a rising corpus of governess novels, which portrayed the governess as a victim of class discrimination and economic and emotional hardship. Patricia Thomson has recognized that the fictional governess of the period had certain conventional attributes, which Agnes Grey clearly possesses: she "was bound to be a lady—preferably the daughter of a clergyman; she was always impoverished, unprotected, and, by virtue of her circumstances, reasonably intelligent and submissive."[5] Furthermore, *Agnes Grey* is typical of the genre in presenting its governess-heroine as an uncomplaining, dutiful Christian, who endures social humiliation with quiet dignity. In this, it followed the example set by Barbara Hofland's Ellen Delville in *Ellen, the Teacher* (1814), Mrs. Sherwood's Caroline Mordaunt in *Caroline Mordaunt; or, The Governess* (1835), Harriet Martineau's Maria Young in *Deerbrook* (1839), and Elizabeth Missing Sewell's Emily Morton in *Amy Herbert* (1844).

As numerous studies have pointed out, discrimination against the governess (be she real or fictional) was a reaction against her "status incongruence," or ambiguity of position in the family and society. Mary Poovey has argued that, because the governess was like a mother in the work she performed but like a working-class woman in the wages she earned, she threatened to collapse class boundaries and blur categories of womanhood. The presence of a governess in the home also disturbed the boundaries between family life and the public world of work and between family relations and nonkinship relations. The resident governess was an unnatural addition to the nuclear family, and her physical and emotional isolation within the home was often the result of awkwardness felt by both employee and employers, as well as a need to mark social distance between the governess and the "ladies" of the house, even though the governess herself was often middle class, and, therefore, a "lady."[6] This demarcation was especially evident when the family went out in public. Agnes recognizes her predicament in accompanying the Murray girls on their outings, finding it awkward to walk beside them, ignored by both themselves and their companions, and disagreeable to walk behind "and thus appear to acknowledge my own inferiority" (AG, 111).

Many Victorian conduct-book writers recognized and sympathized with the governess's precarious position in the private family. In 1847, the same year *Agnes Grey* was published, Mrs. Elizabeth Whately wrote that the "loneliness of position,—the being *in* a family, and not yet of it" was one of the "inevitable evils" of the governess's situation: she is "transplanted into a foreign soil, and not even intended to take root there." Charlotte Brontë praised Whately's *English Life, Social and Domestic in the Middle of the Nineteenth Century* for its accurate and compassionate presentation of governesses. Also in 1847, Mary Maurice offered advice to mothers and governesses designed to ease the tension generated by a governess's presence in the home. Maurice encouraged mothers to include governesses in family gatherings and to insist that their children treat them with respect, and she cautioned governesses not to succumb to a false pride that would keep them aloof.[7]

In her posts as a private governess, Charlotte Brontë was painfully aware of her status incongruence—being in and not yet of the family—and she largely kept to herself rather than risk an uncertain reception in the family rooms. Her aversion to this prospect is obvious in a letter she sent to Ellen Nussey from her first position with the Sidgwick family, explaining that she had to write with a pencil because "I cannot just now procure ink without going into the drawing room—where I do not wish to go." Charlotte concluded that the "chief requisite" for being a governess was the power "of making oneself comfortable and at home wherever we may chance to be—qualities in which all our family are singularly deficient." Anne's discomfort, particularly her feelings of isolation and homesickness, are reflected in her poems and in *Agnes Grey*. She was the first of the sisters to go out as a governess, serving the longest time away from home with the Inghams of Blake Hall from April to December 1839 and with the Robinsons of Thorp Green from May 1840 through June 1845. *Agnes Grey* and *Wildfell Hall* are thus both "true histories" in the sense that they are informed by her experiences and impressions.[8]

Although Anne details Agnes's sufferings at the hands of unruly children and condescending parents, *Agnes Grey* is not primarily a critique of the unhappy condition of the Victorian governess in the private home. Rather, it is a commentary on the upper- and rising middle-class Victorian family—the context in which the governess was becoming a "standard furnishing." Anne considers the mistreatment of the governess to be a critical reflection of the "unfortunate state" of the families that Agnes serves (AG, 66). Kathryn Hughes asserts that "[b]y 1850 the question of the governess' domestic comfort had become a litmus test which measured the gentility and morality both of the family that employed her and that of society at large."[9] The governess's duality as both insider and outsider, confidante and "hireling," allows Agnes, as narrator, to regard the family with both an intimate and a critical eye, which serves the didactic purposes of the novel even as Agnes reveals the emotional taxation of her status ambiguity. Agnes, however, is the medium, not the focus, of Anne Brontë's criticism: through her, Anne exposes family relations and values as morally flawed.

This criticism of family life is not primarily class based. Terry Eagleton has argued that *Agnes Grey* is ultimately "ambivalent about how far morality is *class*-morality." Eagleton points out that while Agnes's mother blandly reminds her daughter and the reader that "there are good and bad in all classes" (AG, 56), implying thereby that virtue is "classless," it is also implicit in the novel's structure that the virtues of compassion, generosity, and honesty are exhibited by members of the working and modest middle classes like the Greys and Mr. Weston and are pointedly absent from the "purse-proud" nouveau riche Bloomfields (AG, 56) and the aristocratic Murrays.[10] As a novel dealing foremost with education, however, *Agnes Grey* seeks to reveal the educative source of those faults that we read as class oriented—vanity, materialism, egoism, selfishness, disrespect for the lower classes. Agnes, for example, expresses her conviction that the Murray girls are rude to their father's tenants—laughing at their manner of eating and speaking and deriding them to their faces—not because of inherent class differences but "chiefly owing to their defective education" (AG, 89). Rosalie's belittling of Agnes as "a hireling, and a poor curate's daughter" is judged to be "rather the effect of her education than her disposition" since "she had never been properly taught the distinction between right and wrong; she had, like her brothers and sisters, been suffered from infancy to tyrannize over nurses, governesses, and servants" (AG, 66). Children, Anne suggests, are not initially products of class but of families; her object is to show the family as the defining community that engenders individual values and social attitudes.

This aim is underpinned by an Evangelical emphasis on the importance of early home lessons in determining an individual's character. The belief that habits of the family become habits of the self forms the basis of educational thought in such guidebooks as Maria Edgeworth's *Parent's Assistant* (1796) and Harriet Martineau's *Household Education* (1849), both of which stressed the formative influence of parental example. In his popular conduct guide *Self-Help* (1859), Samuel Smiles maintained, "The education of character is very much a question of models; we mould ourselves so unconsciously after the characters, manners, habits, and opinions of those who are about us." Writing *Agnes Grey* more than a decade earlier, Anne Brontë had also testified to this belief: "Habitual associates are known to exercise a great influence over each other's minds and manners. Those whose actions are for ever before our eyes, whose words are ever in our ears, will naturally lead us . . . to act and speak as they do" (AG, 102). This is not only Agnes's fear for herself as she is placed in families of selfish, vulgar, and vain individuals, it also forms her chief anxiety for her pupils. Smiles insisted, "Example in conduct . . . even in apparently trivial matters, is of no light moment, inasmuch as it is constantly becoming inwoven with the lives of others, and contributing to form their characters for better or for worse. The characters of parents are thus constantly repeated in their children."[11]

Agnes Grey serves to illustrate this educational maxim, depicting parents who contribute to form the characters of their children *for worse* through their examples in conduct, which are invariably characterized, according to Agnes, by a "sad want of principle" (AG, 66). Agnes alone is genuinely concerned with instilling principles of right and wrong in her charges; in her initial enthusiasm to be a governess, she hopes "to make Virtue practicable, Instruction desirable, and Religion lovely and comprehensible" (AG, 12). Yet, in contrast to the parents, who impart all-too-effective lessons through their actions, the governess is presented as an ineffectual instructor, unable to realize her educational goals. At first it seems that Agnes's progress is impeded by her employers' refusal to let her exert any discipline over her charges beyond the gentle reminder. Soon, however, it becomes evident that her primary obstacle is not a parentally imposed restraint on her manner of instruction, but a parental presence that undermines the moral content of the lessons themselves.

The episodic nature of Agnes's experiences in her two posts operates to underline repeatedly the power of parental example in counteracting the lessons of the governess. Even when parents are not consciously constructing themselves as examples to be followed, Agnes's accounts show that they invariably succeed in "undoing, in a few minutes, the little good it had taken me months of labour to achieve" (AG, 46). Agnes's "lessons in the art of instruction" (AG, 16)—what she herself learns and what she hopes to teach through her history—is that the family, not the governess, makes a lasting impression.

Thus she demonstrates that mistreatment of the governess is taught through parental example. In her first post with the Bloomfield family, the monstrous Bloomfield children, Tom and Mary Ann, follow their parents' example of disregard for the governess: Mrs. Bloomfield speaks to Agnes with a "cool, immutable gravity" (AG, 18), and Mr. Bloomfield scarcely speaks to her at all, and when he does, he is brusque and uncivil. The children mimic their parents' dismissal of Agnes as an underling who can be treated with derision. As Agnes is insignificant, her instructions and entreaties lack authority. She must acknowledge that the "name of governess . . . was a mere mockery as applied to me" (AG, 27), as she watches helplessly while the children throw her desk out the window and burn her workbag.

Anne's primary concern in *Agnes Grey* is to show the grievous effects of these family lessons not on the governess, but on the children themselves. The focus of her concern in the Bloomfield family is the only son, Tom. Tom believes his father and Uncle Robson epitomize manliness. They demonstrate a rough physicality and verbal authority before which he and his sister cower and to which his mother submits, clearly delineating both men as masters of their domain. Tom strives to mirror their behavior, and they encourage him, glad to see that he is beyond the "petticoat government" of mother and governess (AG, 49). During his visits, Uncle Robson introduces Tom to alcohol, instructing the boy to "imitate him in [drinking] to the utmost of his ability, and to believe that the more wine and spirits he could take, and the better he liked them, the more he manifested his bold and manly spirit, and rose superior to his sisters. Mr. Bloomfield had not much to say against it, for his favourite beverage was gin and water; of which he took a considerable portion every day" (AG, 47). In this observation, Agnes suggests that the association of masculinity with heavy drinking is introduced in the family to reinforce gender-based hierarchies: through his drinking, Tom learns, he both affirms his masculinity and rises superior to the female population around him. Tom Bloomfield can be seen as a prototype for the young Arthur Huntingdon, whose father likewise teaches him to "be a man" through drink and to scorn the petticoat government of his mother. A corollary theme of Anne's criticism of family lessons in *Agnes Grey* is devoted to denouncing the association of drink, particularly overindulgence in drink, with masculine virility. The destructive nature of such overindulgence is made explicit in *Wildfell Hall:* it costs Huntingdon his life and forces Helen to flee with her son in order to prevent him from following his father's example. The drunken antics of Huntingdon and his friends illustrate the repulsive and morally corrupt consequences of those "bold and manly spirits" encouraged in youth.

Watching his father, Tom has learned to assert a "manly" domination in the feminized home not only through drinking, but also through physical brutishness. He considers it his masculine prerogative to physically abuse his sister, Mary Ann (not unlike John Reed, who bullies the young Jane Eyre), and he sees nothing wrong with extending this control over his governess by what Agnes describes as "violent manual and pedal applications" (AG, 28). It is his role to keep his sister and governess "in order" (AG, 28) just as his father keeps Mrs. Bloomfield "in order" during his harrowing tirade at the dinner table. Tom goes farther, committing atrocities against animals in yet another attempt to follow in his father's footsteps. When Agnes admonishes Tom for the "extremely wicked" act of catching birds in traps and then dismembering them with his penknife, he easily defends himself:

> "Papa knows how I treat them, and he never blames me for it; he says it's just what *he* used to do when *he* was a boy...."
> "But what would your mama say?"
> "Oh, she doesn't care—she says it's a pity to kill the pretty singing birds, but the naughty sparrows, and mice and rats, I may do what I like with. So now, Miss Grey, you see it is *not* wicked." (AG, 22)

Because his parents approve of his actions, Tom cannot conceive of them as cruel or morally wrong, despite Agnes's counseling. Even her warnings of divine retribution are brushed aside because "Papa" never offers any censure. With no sense of religious principle, Tom's notion of morality is entirely dependent upon familial example and approbation.

There is a disturbing parallel between Tom's torturing birds and his persecuting Mary Ann and Agnes—all the more disconcerting because the matriarch endorses her son's behavior, reminding Agnes that such lower creatures "were created for our convenience" (AG, 49). By implicitly linking women with the lower creatures created for "convenience," Mrs. Bloomfield reinforces the gender-determined superiority that her husband and brother teach by word and example. Because Mrs. Bloomfield makes no effort to subdue Tom's tyrannies and disrespectful behavior to the women around him, even to herself, Anne Brontë leaves little doubt that the character of the father will be repeated in the son.

In the Murray household, the moral threat derives not from the male but from the female example and standards of behavior. Despite her insistence on Agnes's "unimpeachable morality" as her children's governess (AG, 57), Mrs. Murray makes no effort to ensure a moral grounding in the education of her daughters.[12] As Mrs. Murray enlightens Agnes concerning her duties, Agnes perceives that she simply wishes her daughters, Rosalie and Matilda, to be "as superficially attractive, and showily accomplished, as they could possibly be made without present trouble or discomfort to themselves"—or indeed to herself (AG, 64). In both the Bloomfield and Murray families, the mothers regard mothering as burdensome "trouble," rather than, as Evangelical writers on the family held, a supreme duty or "delightful task" assigned to them by Providence. Sarah Lewis is typical in her exaltation of mothers' role "as the guardian angels of man's infancy" to whom "is committed the implanting that heavenly germ to which God must indeed give the increase; but for the early culture of which they are answerable."[13]

By the early nineteenth century, many domestic advice writers acknowledged the practical need for a private governess, since a mother's duties as household manager, in addition to her social and philanthropic commitments, often precluded the uninterrupted time necessary to educate her children. But, with the increasing numbers of governesses taking on responsibilities previously charged to mothers, writers such as Lewis and Mary Maurice saw mothers relinquishing their educative role to the governesses.[14] Because of the governess's likeness to the mother in her educational charge (and her lack of other potentially distracting social or domestic responsibilities), she threatened to displace the figure around which the ideology of the family revolved. Kathryn Hughes argues,

> The challenge that the governess represented to this ideal of motherhood was profound. Her presence in the household signalled that some women chose not to dedicate themselves to full-time child-rearing but preferred to hire other women to carry out these duties on their behalf. Moreover, the fact that the childless governess could perform many of the functions of a mother suggested that, far from being instinctual, maternal affection was something that might be bought.[15]

To suppress these ideological challenges, Lewis and others emphasized the centrality of motherhood to "woman's mission." In an 1849 tract titled *Governess Life*, Mary Maurice issued a stern warning to mothers, stressing their irreplaceable responsibility for directing the education of their children: "the duties and cares of a mother are of that kind that no one else can estimate, and she has no right wholly to cast off the care of her children. She has a helper, but she cannot have a substitute. What God has given her to do, she can never devolve on any other. Such conduct, would, indeed, be sinful, and instances are but too frequent in which children have been thus wholly left to instructors to form their minds and characters."[16] In *Agnes Grey*, Anne Brontë follows the aims of domestic advice literature in criticizing mothers for relinquishing the responsibility to educate their children's minds as well as mold their characters, offering examples from the fictional Bloomfield and Murray families. The unruly behavior of the young Bloomfields, for example, is a censorious reflection on their upbringing by a mother who claims to have had "so little time" (AG, 18) to tend to their instruction, leaving them to be supervised by nurses.

In each of her posts, Agnes serves as the means by which the mothers neglect their duties as primary educators. Mrs. Murray advises Agnes on her role, demanding, "Who is to form a young lady's tastes, I wonder, if the governess doesn't do it!" (AG, 159). The irony of this remark is obvious: the reader is clearly intended to think, as Agnes does, that the mother is the right person to form a young lady's tastes. Agnes desires "to give the lady some idea of the fallacy of her expectations," but Mrs. Murray sails out of the room, casually exonerating herself from any character-forming responsibility (AG, 160).

Mrs. Murray's hypocrisy is also obvious in her scolding of Agnes for her carelessness in chaperoning the eldest daughter, Rosalie, who has gone past the boundaries of her father's grounds in the hopes of meeting one of her suitors, the rector Mr. Hatfield. "Oh!" Mrs. Murray declares, "if you—if *any* governess had but half a mother's watchfulness—half a mother's anxious care—I should be saved this trouble" (AG, 120). Her spouting about "a mother's watchfulness" is laughable, since she has only happened to spy Mr. Hatfield's approach from the window of her dressing room, where, we are meant to realize, she spends most of her time. She charges Agnes to impress upon her daughter what is "proper" conduct, again relinquishing her own part in this responsibility. The repeated inference that the governess should be "half a mother" underscores Agnes's predicament in relation to the family matriarch: she is expected to alleviate the trouble of mothering—to be, in other words, the mother's "double." But, in practice and authority, compared with the mother, she is "but half," and therefore can never replace her. Again, Anne Brontë's point is that, even when the governess has the best intentions, parental example prevails, and family proves to be the most effective teacher and model.

Through her own influence, Mrs. Murray succeeds in making Rosalie superficially attractive and wholly self-concerned. As Agnes observes, Rosalie's "ruling passion" is the "all absorbing ambition, to attract and dazzle the other sex" (AG, 67), a passion that is encouraged by her mother. At her coming-out ball, Rosalie assures Agnes that "[t]he ladies, of course, were of no consequence to me. . . . the best, mama told me,—the most transcendent beauties among them, were nothing to me" (AG, 79). Mrs. Murray pits her daughter against the other "beauties," hoping to obtain for her a profitable union with Sir Thomas Ashby—a man of wealth and status but also a bad-tempered, drunken philanderer. When Agnes asks Rosalie if her mother is aware of Sir Thomas's indiscretions and yet still wishes her to marry him, Rosalie replies nonchalantly, "To be sure she does! She knows more against him than I do, I believe: she keeps it from me lest I should be discouraged. . . . he'll be all right when he's married, as mama says; and reformed rakes make the best husbands, *every* body knows" (AG, 123). Agnes judges this to be a purely mercenary tactic and is "amazed and horrified at Mrs. Murray's heartlessness, or want of thought for the real good of her child" (AG, 147). Mrs. Murray's understanding of Rosalie's "real good," however, is measured exclusively in terms of class status and financial prosperity, for which she is willing to trade her daughter's moral well-being. The fact that Rosalie voices no objection to Mrs. Murray's scheming testifies that she has adopted her mother's materialistic ambitions. "I *must* have Ashby Park," Rosalie declares, "whoever shares it with me" (AG, 123). She is accordingly incredulous when she hears that Agnes's elder sister, Mary, is to be married to a country vicar and reside in "[a] quiet little vicarage." "O stop!" she responds, "you'll make me sick. How *can* she bear it?" (AG, 77). Rosalie is more concerned about the nature of the house than the nature of the husband, whom Agnes assures her is good, wise, and amiable. Anne presents this skewed value system, which privileges wealth and social prestige over mutual love, as Rosalie's ultimate undoing.

Rosalie's justification of her impending union with Sir Thomas also invokes a characteristic belief of female nature: her redemptive potential. Rosalie takes for granted her salvational powers, believing, as both Mrs. Murray and feminine ideology encourage, that as a wife she will naturally make Sir Thomas "all right." Rosalie's assumptions anticipate the naïveté of Helen Huntingdon in *The Tenant of Wildfell Hall*. In both cases, Anne Brontë "explodes the myth of domestic heaven and exposes the domestic hell" that results when a marriage is formed assuming the saving power of an angelic wife over a reprobate husband.[17] Unlike Helen Huntingdon, Agnes recognizes the inevitable harm that will come from habitual association with such a man. She tries to counteract Mrs. Murray's influence, but her warnings and exhortations go unheeded as usual: "Miss Murray only laughed at what I said" (AG, 147).

Agnes Grey and Rosalie Murray: Foils of Female Education

The chapters relating to Rosalie's life as Lady Ashby demonstrate the tragic consequences of the lessons and values imparted by her family. Like Emily Brontë's Catherine Earnshaw, Rosalie envisions the transfer from her father's house to her husband's as liberation. Her experience of marriage, however, illustrates that the metaphorical movement from dependent daughterhood to a state of womanhood signified by marriage may simply mark imprisonment in an even more constricting domestic structure. The bridal mansion, which Rosalie declared she *must* have, proves to be her prison-house, where, married to a man she "detests," she maintains that she "must be a prisoner and a slave" (AG, 193). She has simply exchanged the boundaries of her father's park at Horton Lodge for even narrower parameters, with a husband who will do as he pleases—namely, drink, gamble, and philander—and who insists that his wife take her only enjoyment in him. Sir Thomas thus shows himself to be an early version of Arthur Huntingdon, whose wife, Helen, like Rosalie, suffers in an imprudent marriage also misguided by the belief that she could make him "all right." Unlike Helen, Rosalie is not concerned to lead her husband's reformation, insisting, "It's the husband's part to please the wife, not hers to please him. . . . And as for persuasion, I assure you I shan't trouble myself with that: I've enough to do to bear with him as he is, without attempting to work a reform" (AG, 190).

During her visit to Ashby Park, Agnes suggests that Rosalie take comfort in raising her infant daughter, but Rosalie's ideas of maternal responsibility are as empty as her own mother's, and again she cannot take the trouble. She praises her infant daughter as "the most charming child in the world, no doubt . . . and all the more so, that I am not troubled with nursing it—I was determined I wouldn't be bothered with that" (AG, 181). Having witnessed the lessons Mrs. Murray imparted, Agnes is not surprised to see that Rosalie regards her child "with no remarkable degree of interest or affection" but shows off the furniture and paintings in her grand house with animation and pleasure (AG, 184). And yet, Agnes observes, Rosalie's gratification "was followed by a melancholy sigh; as if in consideration of the insufficiency of all such baubles to the happiness of the human heart"(AG, 186). But this reflection, like her character-forming education, is merely superficial, and Rosalie goes on to ring for tea. She briefly offers hope that her daughter will grow up differently, wanting Agnes to "bring it up in the way it should go, and make a better woman of it than its mama" (AG, 181). Despite her apparent recognition of the good principles Agnes regularly preached and practiced, Rosalie is not willing to accept her own role in the process of making her daughter "a better woman": she protests, "I can't centre all my hopes in a child; that is only one degree better than devoting one's self to a dog" (AG, 194).

Rosalie's self-centeredness is a lesson of the family deeply ingrained—deeper than any "natural" maternal instinct ascribed to the female sex generally—and it recalls Agnes's earlier assessment of Rosalie's upbringing: "she had not been taught to moderate her desires, to control her temper or bridle her will, or to sacrifice her own pleasure for the good of others" (AG, 66). Rosalie will no doubt neglect and misdirect her daughter just as her mother did her. The child will be handed over to a governess, but she will have already learned her lessons.

As a wife and mother, Rosalie is clearly intended to be a foil to Agnes, whose marriage to the curate Mr. Weston is characterized by mutual affection and modest means, and whose children, Agnes promises, "shall want no good thing that a mother's care can give" (AG, 208). Weston himself is the antitype of Bloomfield manliness. Following instead a model advocated by Anne's beloved Cowper, whose writings "validated a manliness centred on a quiet domestic rural life," Weston is kind to animals, generous to the poor, devoted to God.[18] Even in Agnes's brief description of her life as Mrs. Weston, we are convinced that she is fulfilled, just as we are certain that Lady Ashby is miserable. Anne succeeds in showing that Lady Ashby of Ashby Park is "poor" in contrast to Agnes, who enjoys the riches of the good life in the quiet vicarage that Rosalie once scorned.

Anne Brontë also suggests that Rosalie's and Agnes's fates are, at least in part, the result of their different upbringing. Unlike Rosalie, Agnes has a mother who takes her children's education wholly on herself. Mrs. Grey raises Agnes and her elder sister, Mary, in the Evangelical "way it should go," instilling moral principle, piety, compassion for the poor, appreciation of employment, as well as the accomplishments of music, singing, drawing, French, Latin, and German—attainments that fit Agnes to be a governess in the first place, despite her family's objections to the idea. To Agnes's regret, however, she is also raised "in the strictest seclusion," so that her "only intercourse with the world" (AG, 4) until her nineteenth year is an occasional tea party and visit to paternal relations.

Agnes recognizes her particular disadvantages as the "pet" of the family, who spoil her "by ceaseless kindness to make me too helpless and dependent, too unfit for buffeting with the cares and turmoils of life" (AG, 4). She records her sense of an unrealized potential that her family situation imposes, acknowledging a discrepancy between her own and her family's sense of her selfhood: "though a woman in my own estimation, I was still a child in theirs" (AG, 9). Both mother and sister repeatedly tell Agnes that it is far easier for them to do the household chores and sewing themselves than to teach her how to do them. Their conception of her abilities is so limited that Mary even wonders how Agnes will manage as a governess "without me or mama to speak and act for you" (AG, 11).

In her critique of education in and by the family, Agnes does not spare her own. Despite being an accomplished and conscientious instructor, Mrs. Grey is faulted for her overprotection even as Mrs. Bloomfield and Mrs. Murray are faulted for their neglect. Agnes protests her restricted upbringing, saying to her mother, "You do not know half the wisdom and prudence I possess, because I have never been tried" (AG, 11). When the Greys are threatened with economic ruin, Agnes views the family's misfortune primarily as a chance for personal growth: "To go out into the world; to enter upon a new life; to act for myself; to exercise my unused faculties; to try my unknown powers" (AG, 12). She therefore embraces the chance to be a governess as a means to secure a broader field of experience and education for herself.

It is true, as Cates Baldridge has argued, that Agnes's experiences outside her family essentially serve to lead her back to where she started, to recognize what a good upbringing she has had, despite her complaints about its limitations.[19] Following her trials with the Bloomfields, Agnes acknowledges how greatly she has come to "love and value [her] home" (AG, 52). This concession bolsters the ideological agenda of the novel, which endorses the kind of education Agnes received in her parsonage home. Agnes's steady perseverance in the face of vice, selfishness, conceit, and other moral failings works to confirm that child-rearing by the mother in a bourgeois Evangelical home is indeed the "way it should go" in producing spiritually rich and principled adults. But in its focus on Agnes's experiences *outside* her family, the novel also suggests Anne's ideological commitment to the importance of trying the home values beyond the family *as part of* the formative experience.

The lessons Agnes acquires in her intercourse with the world cannot be taught but must be tried: perseverance through adversity and humiliations, self-possession in dealing with untamed children and unreasonable mothers, and the self-reliance that she is specifically denied by her mother, under whose authority Agnes is not "many degrees more useful than the kitten" (AG, 10). Agnes testifies to her out-of-family education: "I had been seasoned by adversity and tutored by experience" (AG, 52). These sentiments are faithful to Anne's own: after a year with the Robinson family, she wrote in her diary paper, "I have the same faults that I had . . . only I have more wisdom and experience, and a little more self-possession."[20]

The story of Agnes's maturation as a governess thus widens Anne Brontë's critique of family-conducted education in *Agnes Grey* to consider not only the quality of moral education in the family but also the educational benefits of practical acquaintance with the world. Anne implicitly challenges the story of courtship as female education—a course that is shown to be tragic for Rosalie—as well as the notion that female education must be limited to the domestic sphere to protect an inherent female morality. The harm of restricting girls' moral education, as well as of neglecting boys', lies at the heart of her educational philosophy in *The Tenant of Wildfell Hall*.

By the end of *Agnes Grey*, Agnes is no longer the suppressed parsonage pet: she has proven her intelligence, usefulness, moral courage, and perseverance to her mother as well as to herself, and, following the death of Agnes's father, they run a boarding school as equal partners. Only after Agnes has reaped the benefits of experience as a self-determining individual does the novel resume a traditional marriage plot with the reappearance of Mr. Weston. For her own children, Agnes declares that she will be their primary educator "for the time being" (AG, 208). From her experiences, Agnes recognizes the importance of passing beyond the family boundary as part of the development of selfhood, and her concluding remarks suggest that she will not be an overprotective mother—that she will encourage both her son and daughters to go out into the world and act for themselves. Thus, the end of the novel balances moral education in the family with the chance for self-determination beyond it: Agnes's children will have both.

The Tenant of Wildfell Hall: A Call for Equality in Moral Education

Anne Brontë clearly intended *Agnes Grey* as instructive fiction, exposing the self-perpetuating harm of misguided family lessons and irresponsible parental examples. After her opening statement, which suggests a didactic purpose in relating her story, Agnes reiterates that her design in enumerating "the vexatious propensities of my pupils" and "the troubles resulting from my heavy responsibilities" is not to recommend herself but "to benefit those whom it might concern . . . if a parent has, therefrom, gathered any useful hint, or an unfortunate governess received thereby the slightest benefit, I am well rewarded for my pains" (AG, 36–37). Whether any parent or governess benefited from Agnes's tale is unknown, but the novel itself impressed the reviewers as little as Agnes Grey impressed her pupils. This was not the case with *The Tenant of Wildfell Hall*.

Anne Brontë's second novel was repeatedly condemned for its graphic depictions of licentiousness displayed by Huntingdon and his associates;

Acton Bell was criticized for having "a morbid love of the coarse, if not of the brutal." As different as the two novels are in tone, *Agnes Grey* suggested the domestic situation that *Wildfell Hall* develops as its critical focus. *Wildfell Hall* gives an extended portrait of an imprudently made marriage similar to that between Rosalie and Sir Thomas, except that Helen Huntingdon is a wife anxious to direct her husband's spiritual reformation—who has, in fact, married for this specific purpose. Her efforts to this end are relayed through her diary, which occupies the central position in the novel's structure and its thematic consideration.[21] Compared with *Agnes Grey*, *Wildfell Hall* is structurally more complicated, its narrative more layered, its characters and themes more emotionally and philosophically complex, and its style more intense, but it takes up and advances Anne's concerns with the family's role in directing individual morality.

As *Agnes Grey* addressed the engendering of morality in the domestic sphere, *Wildfell Hall* turned its attention to the *gendering* of morality—the notion that boys and girls required different kinds of education to safeguard their virtue. Girls were generally thought to need more sheltering from, and less knowledge of, worldly vice than boys, who were given fewer constraints and often little moral direction for their entrance into the larger world. In chapter 3 of *Wildfell Hall*, Anne Brontë gives her heroine a forum to argue the disadvantages of gender-determined education; the harm of such education for both sexes is illustrated repeatedly in the characters that populate the novel and above all in the story of Arthur and Helen Huntingdon.

In the early reviews of *Wildfell Hall*, however, the novel was discredited by the very notion of gendered morality that it sought to overthrow. Writing for *Fraser's Magazine*, Charles Kingsley declared *Wildfell Hall* to be "utterly unfit to be put into the hands of girls." *Sharpe's London Magazine* regretted that the novel was "rendered unfit for the perusal of the very class of persons to whom it would be most useful, (namely, imaginative girls likely to risk their happiness on the forlorn hope of marrying and reforming a captivating rake,) owing to the profane expressions, inconceivably coarse language, and revolting scenes and descriptions by which its pages are disfigured." Such injunctions did not curb the popularity of *Wildfell Hall*, and when a second edition of it was released, Anne wrote a preface defending her presentation of profanity and scenes of drunken debauchery for a didactic purpose: "when we have to do with vice and vicious characters, I maintain it is better to depict them as they really are than as they would wish to appear. To represent a bad thing in its least offensive light is doubtless the most agreeable course for a writer of fiction to pursue; but is it the most honest, or the safest?" (*TWH*, xxxvii–xxxviii). Anne specifically objected to the notion of gendered censorship, insisting, "All novels are or should be written for both men and women to read" (*TWH*, xxxix). Leonore Davidoff and Catherine Hall explain that bowdlerized reading matter issued from "a concept of respectability which began to close off knowledge of the world outside family, friends, and co-religionists"—particularly female knowledge.[22]

Anne judged this restriction to be a clear threat to moral well-being, rather than a protective measure. She wrote in the preface, "O Reader! if there were less of this delicate concealment of facts—this whispering "Peace, peace," when there is no peace, there would be less of sin and misery to the young of both sexes who are left to wring their bitter knowledge from experience" (*TWH*, xxxvii). To Anne's mind, moral education was best served by an absolute commitment to truth, by revelation and acknowledgment of the "facts." Truth, she argued, however "unpalatable," should not be differentiated according to gender, and she clearly hoped that *Wildfell Hall* would benefit the young of both sexes, insisting that characters like Huntingdon and his profligate companions "do exist, and if I have warned one rash youth from following in their steps, or prevented one thoughtless girl from falling into the very natural error of my heroine, the book has not been written in vain" (*TWH*, xxxviii). Anne felt it was her authorial duty and Christian responsibility to reveal the facts, recognizing, as she had in *Agnes Grey*, "plain discrepancies between the Victorian mythos of the family and family realities."[23] She depicts drunken brawls in the drawing room, the slamming of bedroom doors, and a husband who hurls curses at his wife and engages in moonlight liaisons with the wife of one of his guests. And Anne does not spare us Milicent Hattersley's quiet but telling plea to the husband who manhandles her in front of the others: "Do let me alone, Ralph! remember we are not at home" (*TWH*, 278). Such a supplication leaves the reader to imagine what commonly goes on between husband and wife in the Hattersley household. These depictions provide some of the most harrowing moments in Victorian literature, which explode the idea of home as the place of peace.

There was little domestic peace in the parsonage when Anne was writing *Wildfell Hall*. Charlotte attributed the disturbance to Branwell, describing his behavior as increasingly "intolerable—to papa he allows rest neither day nor night—and he is continually screwing money out of him sometimes threatening that he will kill himself if it is withheld from him . . . he will do nothing—except drink, and make us all wretched."

Anne was clearly aware of Branwell's affair with Mrs. Robinson, which prompted Anne's resignation from her position at Thorp Green in June 1845 and Branwell's dismissal upon discovery in July. In her July 1845 diary paper, Anne recalled her time with the Robinsons, commenting, "during my stay I have had some very unpleasant and undreamt of experience of human nature." This remark can be seen in relation to both Branwell and the Robinsons' worldly social circle, of which Anne disapproved, seeing its effects on her brother. In her "Biographical Notice," Charlotte intimated that Branwell's downfall—his tragic lack of moral fortitude in the midst of temptation—was the driving force behind her sister's second novel: "She had, in the course of her life, been called on to contemplate, near at hand and for a long time, the terrible effects of talents misused and faculties abused. . . . She brooded over it till she believed it to be a duty to reproduce every detail (of course with fictitious characters, incidents, and situations) as a warning to others." While Charlotte appeared to recognize Anne's didactic purpose in writing *Wildfell Hall*, she publicly condemned the choice of subject as "an entire mistake." Charlotte's disparagement of the novel was largely prompted by her belief that the writing had exhausted Anne, both physically and mentally, aggravating her delicate health and her tendency to religious melancholy. It was also no doubt disturbing to see the faults of a once-admired brother displayed so candidly before the public.[24]

Charlotte did not comment or perhaps even perceive that the novel essentially advanced her own objections to the socially endorsed difference in the education given girls and boys. In January 1846, she shared her thoughts on the folly of boys' education with Margaret Wooler: "You ask me if I do not think that men are strange beings—I do indeed, I have often thought so—and I think that the mode of bringing them up i[s] strange, they are not half sufficiently guarded from temptation—Girls are protected as if they were something very frail and silly indeed while boys are turned loose on the world as if they—of all beings in existence, were the wisest and the least liable to be led astray." The sisters no doubt discussed their views on educational and experiential equality for boys and girls in the light of Branwell's moral collapse. Winifred Gérin maintains that "Branwell's sisters blamed the eventual failure of his life on the overindulgence of his upbringing and the mistaken confidence placed in his moral judgment by his doting elders."[25]

The gendered distinction in modes of upbringing and its implications for the formation of individual morality were also being discussed in the public sphere. Ann Richelieu Lamb considered the assignation of a gender to virtue "one of the deepest rooted errors of education." "Were virtue to be regarded as an indivisible whole," Lamb argued, "not frittered into shreds and patches, with male and female names tacked to them, how much better would it be for both parties."[26] This is precisely Helen's view, which she defends against the criticisms of Mrs. Markham and her son, Gilbert, upon her first visit to Linden-Car.

Helen rejects Gilbert's belief that a boy's virtue is bolstered "by temptation" (*TWH*, 29). Boys, she argues, are "not taught to avoid the snares of life, but boldly to rush into them," while girls are "taught to cling to others for direction and support, and [are] guarded, as much as possible, from the very knowledge of evil" (*TWH*, 29–30). Instead of eliciting "noble resistance," a boy's experiential "trials of virtue" too often prove overpowering (*TWH*, 27–28). Instead of serving to protect an inherent female virtue, education limited to the dictates of propriety leaves girls unprepared to encounter "vice and vicious characters" (*TWH*, xxxvii) and therefore easily victimized.

Helen essentially repudiates the notion of inherent virtue in either gender and insists that virtue must be taught before it can be tried. The young of both sexes are made victims to "the snares and pitfalls of life" (*TWH*, xxxviii)—the one because experience is their only teacher, the other because they are denied the lessons of experience. Helen informs Gilbert of her educational philosophy, which is also no doubt Anne Brontë's: "You would have us encourage our sons to prove all things by their own experience, while our daughters must not even profit by the experience of others. Now *I* would have both so to benefit by the experience of others, and the precepts of a higher authority, that they should know beforehand to refuse the evil and choose the good, and require no experimental proofs to teach them the evil of transgression" (*TWH*, 30–31).

Helen is adamant that "experience" will not be her son's only teacher. Unlike the Bloomfield and Murray matriarchs in *Agnes Grey*, she takes seriously her role as young Arthur's moral educator, upholding the divine nature of her charge. At his birth, she rejoices that "God has sent me a soul to educate for Heaven" (*TWH*, 240). Helen's view of motherhood is typical of nineteenth-century Evangelicalism. Sarah Lewis, for example, asserted, "What is a child in relation to a mother? An immortal being, whose soul it is her business to train for immortality."[27] Helen understands her motherly as well as her wifely role in terms of training a soul; her notion of education is underpinned by religion and ultimately seen in the context of ensuring salvation.

Yet Helen's insistence on educating young Arthur herself meets with objections from Gilbert's mother, who warns Helen that her son "will be the veriest milksop that ever was sopped!" (*TWH*, 27). In Charlotte Brontë's *The Professor*, Hunsden Yorke similarly criticizes Frances Henri for making a milksop of her son, Victor, implying, as Mrs. Markham does, that too much maternal attention is "foolish fondness" (*TWH* 25) and will produce an effeminate, spiritless youth. Helen and Frances insist, however, on their responsibility to guide and protect their sons until they have the moral fortitude to go forth into the world. The mothers respond to their critics in very similar language. Frances declares, "Better a thousand times [Victor] should be a milk-sop than what he—Hunsden, calls 'a fine lad'" (*P*, 262–63). Helen tells Gilbert, "if I thought [Arthur] would grow up to be what you call a man of the world . . . I would rather that he died to-morrow!—rather a thousand times!" (*TWH*, 31).

At this point in the novel, neither the Markhams nor the reader is aware that the "widow" Mrs. Graham has come to this conclusion through her own painful experience, delivering Arthur from a father who teaches him to be "a man of the world" through drink and contempt of maternal affection. In a less sinister though not dissimilar way, Mrs. Markham advances a notion of male development dependent on cultivating a taste for alcohol and a sense of shame in loving one's mother. She argues that Helen's home-schooling, particularly her severe tactics intended to eradicate Arthur's taste for alcohol, hinder the development of his manly spirit. "Only think what a man you will make of him," she protests (*TWH*, 27), implying a direct correlation between imbibing alcoholic "spirits" and exuding manly spirit or vigor. As with the young Tom Bloomfield in *Agnes Grey*, Anne Brontë challenges the indoctrination of manliness through exposure to alcohol. The excessive consumption of alcohol stands as the most obvious manifestation of male overindulgence throughout *Wildfell Hall*. In showing this self-indulgence and its appalling results to be a consequence of Mrs. Markham's philosophy of raising boys, Anne Brontë means to redirect the critique of motherhood against *her*.

Anne's condemnation of male indulgence and her insistence on the need for moral instruction in boys' upbringing advances a concern of many domestic writers in the 1830s and 1840s. In *The Wives of England* (1843), Sarah Ellis blamed men's selfishness on "a want of that moral training which ought ever to be made the prominent part of education." Earlier in 1839, Sarah Lewis had argued that "men are said to be more selfish than women. How can they help it? no pains are taken in their education to make them otherwise. . . . Is it astonishing that these boys should hereafter be selfish husbands and tyrannical fathers?"[28] In *Wildfell*

Hall, as in Agnes Grey, Anne Brontë also suggests that male self-indulgence is instilled as habit by the family, resulting from the prominence and license granted boys and the self-sacrifice expected from the female members for their comfort and promotion. The Markham household aptly illustrates this gender differentiation. As Gilbert's sister Rose complains, "I'm told I ought not to think of myself" but only to consider "what's most agreeable to the gentlemen of the house"—"a very good doctrine," according to Mrs. Markham (*TWH*, 53). It is one she stringently followed with her late husband, candidly admitting she would "as soon have expected him to fly, as to put himself out of his way to pleasure me" (*TWH*, 54).

Spoiled by his mother's pampering, Gilbert admits the ease with which he "might sink into the grossest condition of self-indulgence and carelessness about the wants of others, from the mere habit of being constantly cared for myself, and having all my wants anticipated or immediately supplied" (*TWH*, 54). Also spoiled by an indulgent mother, Walter Hargrave becomes "too selfish" to consider the financial comfort of his mother and sisters; he is concerned only with maintaining his reputation as a "man of fashion in the world" (*TWH*, 232). To this end, Hargrave and his mother push his sister, Milicent, into a lucrative but imprudent marriage with Hattersley. Ironically, Helen is able to convince Hattersley, Milicent's husband, to mend his profligate ways, while she makes no headway with her own husband, Arthur. Arthur Huntingdon stands as the supreme example of a son ruined by an indulgent mother. Helen blames (and, in a sense, justifies) Huntingdon's lack of self-restraint on the influence of a "foolish mother," who "indulged him to the top of his bent" and encouraged in him "those germs of folly and vice it was her duty to suppress" (*TWH*, 177). Anne Brontë's ruthless portrait of Huntingdon's adult behavior goes furthest in criticizing Mrs. Markham's ideas of boys' education, showing the injury that early indulgence and neglect of moral guidance brings on both men and their families.

"His Wife Shall Undo What His Mother Did!": Moral Education of the Husband

Helen understands her wifely mission to be reeducating her husband, instilling in him a new moral code of conduct that will replace the delinquent impressions made by his family of origin. Helen's guardian, Aunt Maxwell, firmly objects to her marriage, accusing Helen of falling victim to Huntingdon's charms and ignoring his moral deficiencies and history of indiscretions: "How you can love such a man I cannot tell, or what pleasure you can find in his company: for 'What fellowship hath light with darkness; or he that believeth with an infidel?'" (*TWH*, 177). Aunt Maxwell likens the differences between Helen and her suitor to those between a saint and a sinner, between light and darkness. Although Helen rejects this opposition, she nonetheless envisions herself as a kind of heavenly light breaking through Huntingdon's debased darkness. The fact that Huntingdon is an "infidel" appeals to Helen's religiosity and makes marriage and the prospect of reforming him all the more desirable. She tells her aunt, "I shall consider my life well spent in saving him from the consequences of his early errors, and striving to recall him to the path of virtue" (*TWH*, 147). Helen's self-appointed mission evokes the redemptive power of the domestic Angel (a figure to be immortalized in Coventry Patmore's sequence of poems "The Angel in the House," 1854–1863), which is rooted in the belief that women can recall men to the humanity their worldly experiences continually undermined. This belief has biblical foundations, for as St. Paul says, "the unbelieving husband is made holy through his wife. . . ." Helen believes that Heaven has designed her to recall Huntingdon, and he plays into this rhetoric, promising to be a receptive convert, forever striving to remember and perform the injunctions of his "angel monitress" (*TWH*, 200).[29]

A scene from Patrick Brontë's *The Cottage in the Wood* (1815) perhaps provided the inspiration for the exchanges recounted above. In Patrick's story, the heroine, Mary, refuses a proposal of marriage from William Bower, who is described as "an agreeably accomplished rake," by reciting the same scripture verses Aunt Maxwell uses in Anne's novel. Like Huntingdon, Bower appeals to Mary's religiosity and presents himself as a willing disciple. "As I love you," Bower tells Mary, "you may in time bring me over to your way of thinking, and then all will be well. I even now feel, as if I could be every thing your heart could wish." Unlike Helen, however, Mary rejects this prospect as a threat to her well-being, telling Bower that "[s]ome rash women . . . have made the experiment, which you allude to; but, for one that has had reason to rejoice it, a thousand have had cause for sorrow." In detailing Helen's sufferings as the wife of an "agreeably accomplished rake," *Wildfell Hall* testifies to the folly of attempting such an experiment.[30]

Helen is, however, initially confident of her ability to be her husband's moral guide, and she sees Huntingdon's reeducation as a means to his earthly fulfillment and ultimate salvation. The Christian figure of the saving wife dominated ideas of femininity within marriage: implicitly likened to Christ, a wife could influence and "save" through gentle persuasion and self-sacrifice. As Anne demonstrates in the character of Lord Lowborough, this figure was seductive not only to women, who envisioned their influence over men as a divinely ordained form of power (though, again, like Christ's, a passive power), but also to "world-weary men," who longed for restorative peace.[31] Having gambled away his fortune and turned to drink for solace, Lowborough meets the beautiful and lively Annabella Wilmot, and he is convinced that she will enable his salvation: "She is the most generous, high-minded being that can be conceived of. She will save me, body and soul, from destruction. Already, she has ennobled me in my own estimation, and made me three times better, wiser, greater than I was" (*TWH*, 198). Lowborough's faith in Annabella, however, is wholly misplaced, and Huntingdon laughingly reveals that "the artful minx loves nothing about him, but his title and pedigree, and 'that delightful old family seat'" (*TWH*, 198). Both Lowborough and Helen are seduced by the idea of saving wifehood; both are eventually forced to confront the infidelity of their partners and the impossibility of their visions.

It soon becomes clear that Helen cannot effect any kind of moral regeneration in her husband. After assuring her that she could lead him onto the path of virtue, he blocks her efforts by claiming that she is "too austere in [her] divinity," making his excuses as a "poor, fallible mortal" (*TWH*, 237). He claims sexual difference as justification for his flirtations with Lady Lowborough, telling Helen, "It is a woman's nature to be constant—to love one and one only, blindly, tenderly, and for ever . . . you must give us a little more licence" (*TWH*, 237). Finally, he accuses Helen of driving him to drink by her "unnatural, unwomanly conduct" (*TWH*, 323). Failing to raise Huntingdon to her level of moral responsibility, Helen instead finds herself brought down by his indiscretions, and she struggles to reconcile his behavior with her own self-conception and moral convictions, repeatedly judging herself in terms of her husband's character.

The sexual difference that lay at the heart of ideological assumptions of male/female relations—and that asserted moral superiority as a function of female difference—was converted into an idyllic oneness in marriage through the wife's "perfect identity of self" with her husband. This identification was necessarily key to the notion of a wife's redemptive potential: woman's character became linked to her husband in marriage, thus facilitating his moral edification. Oneness in marriage was also a legal reality. In 1854 Barbara Leigh Smith Bodichon explained that "a man and wife are one person in law; the wife loses all her rights as a single

woman, and her existence is entirely absorbed in that of her husband."³²
Within marriage, then, female selfhood was both ideologically sacrificed
and legally denied. The Brontës clearly knew the legal bonds of married
women, forced by law to forfeit property, money, and children to their
husbands—as we have seen in *Wuthering Heights*. In Charlotte Brontë's
Shirley, Mrs. Pryor attests to her sufferings with an abusive husband and
without the protection of the law: "This world's laws never came near
us—never! They were powerless as a rotten bulrush to protect me!—impotent as idiot babblings to restrain him!" (S, 490).

In *Wildfell Hall*, Anne Brontë exposes the legal and ideological "oneness" of husband and wife in marriage to be a threat to Helen's physical, psychological, and, crucially, moral autonomy. When Huntingdon returns from one of his London escapades, sick from overindulgence in drink and reckless living, Helen pleads for him to make amends, desperate that her own selfhood is at stake: "Don't you know that you are a part of myself? And do you think you can injure and degrade yourself, and I not feel it?" (*TWH*, 257). In the pages of her diary, Helen takes Huntingdon's sins as her own: "since he and I are one, I so identify myself with him, that I feel his degradation, his failings, and transgressions as my own; I blush for him, I fear for him; I repent for him, weep, pray, and feel for him as for myself; but I cannot act for him; and hence, I must be and I am debased, contaminated by the union, both in my own eyes, and in the actual truth" (*TWH*, 263).

Helen's diary chronicles her disillusionment with the idea of her "perfect identity of self" with Huntingdon. Although George Moore and Winifred Gérin have criticized the device of the diary as a structural weakness, placing the drama of Helen's married life "at one remove," the diary format allows the reader to follow Helen's process of disillusionment.³³ Her feelings and impressions are recorded at the time when they are fresh and not, as they would be if Helen had told her story to Gilbert, hardened or exaggerated by the passage of time. Thus, we feel Helen's fervor when she assures her aunt that she has such confidence in Huntingdon "that I would willingly risk my happiness for the chance of securing his" (*TWH*, 147). We perceive her reluctance when she is forced to admit, "His very heart, that I trusted so, is, I fear, less warm and generous than I thought it" (*TWH*, 187). We sense her dread when she confesses, "There are times when, with a momentary pang—a flash of wild dismay, I ask myself, 'Helen, what have you done?' But I rebuke the inward questioner" (*TWH*, 209–10). On the contrary, the diary allows the inward questioner space and voice. It serves as the site of Helen's struggle with ideology and reality—the conflict between her religious convictions, her notions of wifely duty, and her desire to "save" Huntingdon, on the one hand, and the preservation of herself and, most important, her son, on the other.

At the end of her forbearance, Helen rebels against her husband and the notion of the domestic Angel: "I am tired out with his injustice, his selfishness and hopeless *depravity*—I wish a milder word would do—I am no angel and my corruption rises against it" (*TWH*, 268). "I am no angel" marks Anne Brontë's most direct challenge to Victorian categories of female identity and the promotion of woman's divinely inspired influence. With this declaration, Helen delivers herself from the burdensome ideological responsibility to "save." While she cannot claim legal separation from Huntingdon, she asserts her moral separation, protesting, "he may drink himself dead, but it is NOT my fault!" (*TWH*, 324).

Through Helen's inability to convert Huntingdon, Anne Brontë stresses the difficulty of reforming habits established in youth, thereby reinforcing the vital responsibility of parents to direct their children's moral upbringing that is emphasized in *Agnes Grey*. In 1839, Sarah Lewis had likewise argued, "The importance of early impressions—of *home* impressions—is proved by the extreme difficulty of eradicating or counteracting them, if bad."[34] The wife in *Wildfell Hall*, like the governess in *Agnes Grey*, proves unable to undo the early lessons of the family. Instead, the wife falls victim to the self-indulgence cultivated by the mother.

Educating Arthur: Saving Son and Self

With the birth of her son, Arthur, Helen transfers her salvational mission from husband to child, the tabula rasa on which she can impress her Christian principles at the outset, not following thirty-six years of self-indulgence. "Mother" becomes Helen's primary identity, and, in contrast to Rosalie, she comes to center all her hopes in her child. Learning of Huntingdon's affair with Annabella and receiving his refusal to grant her a divorce or custody of their child, Helen can only inform him that "henceforth, we are husband and wife only in the name . . . I am your child's mother, and *your* housekeeper—nothing more" (*TWH*, 307). The limitations of Helen's agency as a wife are emphasized when she compares her situation with that of Lowborough, who is free to leave Annabella and claim their children. Still, for most midcentury readers, Helen's injunction would be taken as a radical redefinition of a wife's "relative duties" (as Sarah Ellis specified them) to exclude her sexual obligations. Writing in the early twentieth century, May Sinclair remarked on its audacity: "Thackeray, with the fear of Mrs. Grundy before his eyes, would have shrunk from recording Mrs. Huntingdon's ultimatum to her husband. The slamming of that bedroom door fairly resounds through the long emptiness of Anne's novel."[35] Through Helen's prioritizing of her motherly role over her wifely one, *Wildfell Hall* essentially challenges the fusing of wife and mother into a single, unified state of domestic womanhood.

That these two roles could be in conflict—that the well-being of children could be threatened by a wife's legal submission to her husband—was only beginning to be recognized by Parliament. Debate over the 1838 Infant Custody Bill, for example, centered on the primacy of motherhood versus wifehood. As Laura C. Berry has explained, throughout the second half of the nineteenth century, "women's role in the family shifted from an all-important emphasis on wifedom and its financial implications to a crucial consideration for the sentimental tentacles of motherhood."[36] Caroline Norton famously campaigned for the passage of the custody bill, which became law in 1839, granting a separated wife access to her children and enabling her to gain temporary custody of children under seven, provided she was deemed by the court to be of good character. This law, of course, would not have applied to Helen, who makes her escape in October 1827. With no legal recourse, she must make a moral choice between loyalty to her marriage vows and her maternal responsibilities.

Upon her son's birth, Helen initially hopes that the child will function as an agent of reform and that fatherly affection will "elevate and purify [Huntingdon's] mind" where Helen's efforts have not (*TWH*, 241). Instead, it becomes increasingly clear to Helen that Huntingdon's parental example threatens to ruin the child. Helen abandons her struggle to "save" her husband; she must now save her son *from* Huntingdon. Mother and father engage in a custody battle over young Arthur's impressionable mind and morals. In this battle, Helen sees Huntingdon as her "greatest enemy" (*TWH*, 310), and she is forced to contend against family likeness—"the father's spirit in the son" (*TWH*, 326)—and Huntingdon's efforts to "make a man" of his progeny, counteracting the lessons of self-control and moral responsibility Helen imparts. Under his father's tutelage, Arthur learns "to tipple wine like papa, to swear like Mr. Hattersley, and to have his own way like a man, and [to send] mamma to the devil when she tried to prevent him" (*TWH*, 354). Encouraging Arthur in this behavior and in his "manly" rejection of his mother becomes one of Huntingdon's "staple amusements" (*TWH*, 354) and his primary means of tormenting Helen. His tactics culminate in his declaration that Helen is unfit to teach Arthur herself and his decision to secure a private governess for Arthur's tuition, who is, in fact, another of Huntingdon's mistresses.

As the chapter title denotes, this maneuver is the "boundary past" (*TWH*, 387)—the final violation of Helen's "higher and better self," which remains "unmarried" (*TWH*, 244), committed only to rearing her son to avoid the example of his father. Her bonds as a wife are broken when her claims as a mother are threatened: "I am a slave, a prisoner," she declares in language reminiscent of Lady Ashby, "but that is nothing; if it were myself alone, I would not complain, but I am forbidden to rescue my son from ruin" (*TWH*, 373). In Helen's mind, the moral rescue of her son supersedes all legal and ideological ties by which she is bound, and she flees with young Arthur to her family home of Wildfell Hall in defiance of marriage and child custody laws. The Reverend Millward's insistence that "nothing short of bodily ill-usage" could justify the violation of a woman's "sacred duties as a wife" (*TWH*, 467) is implicitly refuted by the novel's commitment to the higher responsibilities of the mother.

In Charlotte Brontë's first novel, *The Professor*, Frances and William Crimsworth discuss what Frances "would have been had she married . . . a profligate, a prodigal, a drunkard or a tyrant" (*P*, 255). Such a scenario, as well as Frances's response that she would endure the evil until she found it "intolerable and incurable" and then leave her torturer "suddenly and silently," could have likely inspired the similar course Helen Huntingdon takes (*P*, 255).[37] Anne, however, takes pains to present Helen's escape from Huntingdon as the moral choice of a mother to rescue her son, not a rebellion carried out by a discontented and abused wife.

Although not devised to save herself, this escape allows Helen a form of self-determination otherwise unavailable to her under the laws of marriage. At Wildfell Hall, she takes her mother's maiden name and pretends to be a widow. These acts of "reselfing," while necessary protection against Huntingdon's legal right to claim her son, signify Helen's determination to embrace a selfhood unconnected to, and undetermined by, her husband and centered in motherhood rather than wifehood. Even when Helen returns to minister to her dying husband, thereby fulfilling her wifely duty and satisfying her own conscience, Helen is thinking primarily of the "higher duty" she owes to her son (*TWH*, 439): her first act, therefore, is to compel Huntingdon to sign a contract giving her custody of the boy, which is finally ensured by Huntingdon's death.

As Helen's diary records her failure in saving her husband, it also records a mother's success in reclaiming her son from Huntingdon's "contaminating influence" (*TWH*, 307). Langland has noted that the diary additionally serves to educate Gilbert Markham, who, through his reading, comes to appreciate and endorse Helen's domestic "violations" and her insistence on directing the moral education of her son: "I see that she was actuated by the best and noblest motives in what she has done" (*TWH*, 438).[38]

Like Helen Huntingdon, Anne Brontë was actuated by noble motives. She considered it her authorial role and responsibility to be a moral educator, and *Agnes Grey* and *Wildfell Hall* can be read in a tradition of instructive fiction and domestic "improving" literature. Anne was aligned with contemporary Evangelical writers on the family in stressing the importance of the family's, and particularly the mother's, educative charge, but she was also committed to an unconventional idea of gender equality in moral education as the best means to serve the young of both sexes. Furthermore, her insistence on laying bare the unpalatable facts of domestic life in her fiction was a radical approach to moral didacticism, one which earned her critical scorn. Nevertheless, Anne's purpose in writing, as she herself insisted, was not simply to amuse but to benefit her readers, and to this end she sought to reveal the truth about family lessons.

CHAPTER SIX

The Professor and *Shirley*
Industrial Pollution of Family Relations and Values

> Nothing refines like affection. Family jarring vulgarizes—
> family union elevates.
>
> *Shirley*

ALTHOUGH THE PROFESSOR (1846; published posthumously 1857) and *Shirley* (1849) are rarely examined together, their similarities locate them within a mid-Victorian debate over the effects of industrialization in the public and private spheres. Both novels present portraits of the Yorkshire countryside eclipsed by an industrial Moloch, the mill. Both feature millowners who own "no God but Mammon" (*P*, 23) and whose unrelenting desire to generate personal wealth pollutes the environment surrounding their mills. Edward Crimsworth's mill emits soot from "its iron bowels" (*P*, 17), covering the locality with a "dense, permanent vapour" (*P*, 15). Robert Moore's "gaunt mill-chimney" releases "an occasional sulphur-puff from the soot-thick column of smoke" (*S*, 141). Charlotte Brontë knew firsthand the topography of the industrial north, which she described to W. S. Williams as "our northern congregations of smoke-dark houses clustered round their soot-vomiting Mills."[1] As John Ruskin would recognize in *The Storm-Cloud of the Nineteenth Century* (1884), she saw a direct relation between industrial pollution and the kind of society that produced it: "There is analogy between the moral and physical atmosphere," she writes in *Shirley* (*S*, 326). The "dark Satanic Mills" of *The Professor* and *Shirley* foul the atmosphere not simply with smoke and soot but with competition, materialism, and self-interest. Charlotte Brontë presents these as values of a contemporary industrial society that threaten the virtues of cooperation, benevolence, and selflessness associated with the family.

This chapter considers *The Professor* and *Shirley* as novels of social criticism, which take as their theme the corruption of family values and affections by a spirit of industrialism. In a sense, these novels complement Anne Brontë's critique in *Agnes Grey* and *The Tenant of Wildfell Hall*: while Anne charges individual families with prioritizing material values over the "real good" of its members, Charlotte extends this criticism to society at large. She depicts societies wholly lacking in fraternity, composed of individuals who disown any personal responsibility for the welfare of their fellow men. The value of personal relations in both novels is measured strictly in economic, utilitarian terms. Hunsden Yorke exemplifies this view in *The Professor* when he questions Frances Henri, "Mademoiselle, what is an association? I never saw one; what is its length, breadth, weight, value—aye *value*—What price will it bring in the market?" (P, 236). Charlotte Brontë is concerned to portray the damage inflicted upon private and public associations that are conceived solely according to market values, as shown by Edward Crimsworth's and Robert Moore's valuation of mill over family and self-interest over community.

The opening "industrial" chapters of *The Professor*, which portray the sibling antagonism between Edward and William Crimsworth, gesture to the socially critical theme of brotherhood forsaken, which is explicitly formulated in *Shirley*. *The Professor* keeps the theme of sibling rivalry between master and worker at a literal level, while *Shirley* expands it figuratively; in both, friction is generated by the pursuit of material advantage. Both *Shirley* and *The Professor* can be located in a framework of midcentury industrial novels and nonfictional prose that present social division in terms of brotherhood disowned and make a case for reconciliation by advocating the alteration of social relations to resemble family ones.

The family itself, however, is not safeguarded against the intrusion of marketplace values, and Charlotte Brontë represents "family jarring" (S, 99) as both a result of this intrusion and a reflection of larger social strife. In *The Professor* and *Shirley*, market values are mediated to the individual millowners specifically through the family of origin: Charlotte points out that both Edward Crimsworth and Robert Moore are nurtured to regard the making of money as self-validation. Materialistic self-interest engendered in the family and encouraged in the public world of trade is shown to make men unfeelingly mechanistic—an attitude that disrupts both domestic and social harmony and becomes the focal point of Charlotte Brontë's criticism. The primary victims of this attitude are the millowners' relations: Edward Crimsworth's brother, William, and Robert Moore's cousin, Caroline Helstone. These individual victims represent those classes exploited by an increasingly capitalistic and self-interested society, namely, working-class men and middle-class women.

The Industrial and Ideological Context of *The Professor* and *Shirley*

The Professor and *Shirley* are informed by competing ideologies of the family and the marketplace as models for personal relations. Relationships within the private world of the family and the public world of commerce were taken to be motivated by different rationales. Whereas the family was united and sustained by the principles of cooperation, mutual consideration, and personal sacrifice for the collective good, relations in the marketplace were driven by the "master principle of self-interest." In his seminal economic text *An Inquiry into the Nature and Causes of the Wealth of Nations* (1776), Adam Smith argues that the benevolence that holds a family together does not sustain the marketplace, despite the interdependence of individuals for goods and services: "But man has almost constant occasion for the help of his brethren, and it is in vain for him to expect it from their benevolence only. He will be more likely to prevail if he can interest their self-love in his favour, and shew them that it is for their own advantage to do for him what he requires of them. . . . It is not from the benevolence of the butcher, the brewer, or the baker, that we expect our dinner, but from their regard to their own interest."[2]

On the principle of self-interest, Smith and his nineteenth-century followers, including Thomas Robert Malthus, David Ricardo, and John Ramsay McCulloch, advocated the laissez-faire policies of free trade and free labor. Self-interested behavior, they insisted, would naturally promote collective prosperity. As Gary F. Langer has noted, their "vision of the good society was ordered by the competitive market in which individual effort and sacrifice were rewarded and guided by the market in the best interests of society. The duty of the individual was to look after his own interests and abstain from interfering in the interests of others." This ideology of a self-regulating market, in which individual effort (as opposed to social charity) was rewarded, encouraged the middle-class Protestant ethic of self-help. Under the precepts of self-help, industriousness and frugality were promoted as moral virtues, and monetary success was seen as a sign of God's favor. Instructive self-help tracts, which extolled the virtues of self-reliance and perseverance, flourished in the 1840s and 1850s. The most popular of these was Samuel Smiles's *Self-Help* (1859), which features a collection of biographical sketches intended to serve as models of the successful practice and rewards of self-help. Heather Glen has noted that *The Professor* is offered to the reader as a fictional "exemplary biography of the self-made man." William Crimsworth's goal throughout the novel is to be in a position to help himself. Through his diligence, he scales a worldly "hill of Difficulty" (P, 3–4) and achieves economic and social success.

Yet the social realities of the 1840s were such that not all men could help themselves. The economy in Haworth and the surrounding areas was dependent on woolen manufacture and trade. J. Horsfall Turner has estimated that in 1838 there were approximately twelve hundred hand-loom weavers in Haworth, who constituted almost half the village population. The advent of power looms in the 1830s and 1840s, which produced cloth more efficiently and cheaply, forced hand weavers and wool combers to take employment in the mills. According to Benjamin Hershel Babbage, by 1850 there were three factories in Haworth, employing over one thousand workers. Sally Shuttleworth has noted that those who continued to work out of their homes, as well as those who took to the factories, "would have been working for a small fraction of the wages they could previously have commanded."[3]

In addition to the shift from home-based to factory-based labor, West Yorkshire in the 1820s, 1830s, and 1840s suffered through cycles of depression in the textile trade, which brought low wages and high unemployment. The Poor Law Amendment Act (1834) eliminated the outdoor relief that had previously been administered by the parish so that the only public support for the indigent was to be found in the dreaded workhouses. Patrick Brontë encouraged the people of Haworth to petition Parliament to repeal the act, pleading "the cause of the poor" and expressing his fear that "starvation, deprived of relief, would break into open rebellion." Patrick had firsthand experience of machine-wrecking rebellion and violence carried out by Luddites in his curacy at Hartshead-cum-Clifton. In her "Reminiscences," Ellen Nussey maintained that Charlotte's father "materially helped to fix her impressions" of the Luddite discontent that drives the plot of *Shirley*.[4] We can hear Patrick's sentiments echoed in William Farren's assessment that "starving folk cannot be satisfied or settled folk" (S, 366).

The new law was predicated upon an attitude to poverty influenced by the ethics of self-help and laissez-faire economics. It was the responsibility of every man to look after his own interests; privation was viewed as the result of idleness and waste, the sinful neglect of one's duty. In the late 1830s and 1840s, the essayist Thomas Carlyle turned his attention to the present and future condition of the working classes and became one of the most dynamic voices challenging an "immoral" marketplace ideology devoid of philanthropic considerations. Carlyle followed the advocates of self-help in condemning idleness, maintaining that work was "of a religious nature," but in *Chartism* (1839), he asked a crucial question: "Can the poor man that is willing to work, always find work, and live by his work?" Carlyle suggested that a man's poverty did not necessarily arise from a heathen lack of desire to work but from the lack of opportunity to work. He argued that the social philosophy of laissez-faire and "Every man for himself" led to an unjust abdication of responsibility on the part of government and, more crucial, of those who "preside over work" to provide assistance for those who could not help themselves.[5]

In *Past and Present* (1843), Carlyle attributed the dissolution of social brotherhood to England's worship of the "Gospel of Mammonism":

> about one thing we are entirely in earnest: The making of money.... We have profoundly forgotten everywhere that *Cash-payment* is not the sole relation of human beings; we think, nothing doubting, that *it* absolves and liquidates all engagements of man.... Verily Mammon-worship is a melancholy creed. When Cain, for his own behoof, had killed Abel, and was questioned, "Where is thy brother?" he too made answer, "Am I my brother's keeper?" *Did I not pay my brother his wages, the thing he had merited from me?*[6]

As the obligation between master and worker was reduced to cash payment, laborers were reduced to "mercantile commodities" or "working machines," useful when they generated profit but dispensable when they constituted an expense.[7]

By midcentury, novelists such as Charles Dickens and Elizabeth Gaskell were voicing Carlyle's sentiments against a dehumanizing, morally defunct religion of trade. *Hard Times* (1854), *Mary Barton* (1848), and *North and South* (1854–1855) are literary responses to the changes in social relations brought about by industrialization; each condemns a factory owner for regarding his workers simply as cogs in an economic machine. Dickens and Gaskell were admirers of Carlyle—Dickens inscribed *Hard Times* to him, and Gaskell used an extract from one of his essays as the title-page epigraph in *Mary Barton*. Furthermore, the reformation of the millowner Mr. Thornton in *North and South* is based on his becoming a Carlylean

"Captain of Industry." Carlyle called upon England to embrace "a noble Chivalry of Work" beyond "mere Supply-and-demand." He specifically charged industrial leaders to be "Noble Master[s], among noble Workers," guided in their relations by "God's justice" rather than "gold purses." Gaskell's Thornton essentially answers Carlyle's charge, even using a Carlylean term to express his awakening desire to cultivate "some intercourse with the hands beyond the mere 'cash nexus.'"[8]

Charlotte Brontë predates Gaskell in centering a novel on the moral reformation of an individual millowner after the manner of Carlyle's captain of industry. It is clear from Charlotte's letters that she knew Carlyle's works, though it is not explicitly clear that she had read *Chartism* or *Past and Present*. Nevertheless, Barry V. Qualls argues that in *Shirley*, "Brontë so draws her characters and their contexts that any 1840s reader would almost certainly have seen Carlyle's analysis behind her ideas and *dramatis personae*, no matter what the author's sources."[9] *Shirley* critically illustrates the selfishness of an individual millowner who, like Dickens's Bounderby and Gaskell's Thornton, embodies a class of masters that neglect their personal responsibility to men in pursuit of profit. As Charlotte insists in *Shirley*, the difference between an individual and a society is a difference only in degree, not in kind:

> All men, taken singly, are more or less selfish; and taken in bodies they are intensely so. The British merchant is no exception to this rule: the mercantile classes illustrate it strikingly. These classes certainly think too exclusively of making money: they are too oblivious of every national consideration but that of extending England's (*i.e.* their own) commerce. Chivalrous feeling, disinterestedness, pride in honour, is too dead in their hearts. A land ruled by them alone would too often make ignominious submission—not at all from the motives Christ teaches, but rather from those Mammon instils. (S, 185–86)

Charlotte's social analysis is infused with Carlylean language and tone. The setting and protest of *Shirley* is placed against this vision of a Mammon-worshiping, profit-seeking, chivalry-lacking, mercenary world of trade.

In a land ruled by man's materialistic self-interest, the Victorian family was recurrently seen as an unsullied haven of morality. The cooperative relations associated with the family were promoted as a natural social order, which the rise of capitalism had interrupted and corrupted. Catherine Gallagher has argued that industrial novelists, as well as domestic ideologues and social reformers, made "the connection between family and society one of their main themes and primary organizing devices," advocating the need for society to be infused with a "harmonious spirit of family life" which would counteract the discordant spirit of trade.[10] The family contributed to social reformation by standing as an example on which relations in the public sphere should be modeled.

As, ideally, social relations would resemble familial ones, the present flawed society was recurrently likened to a dysfunctional antifamily in order to emphasize the "unnaturalness" of man's treatment of his fellow man. In the same year that Carlyle was blasting the policies of laissez-faire for social injustice and disorder in *Chartism* (1839), Sarah Ellis was extolling the family as a virtuous refuge amidst social injustice and disorder in *The Women of England*. Although works by Carlyle and Ellis would not seem to lend themselves to comparison, both writers draw on family-society analogies, employing the trope of sibling rivalry to describe social relations. Carlyle presents a society devoid of all fraternal feeling and accuses men of "killing" their brothers in "Cain's rude way" and then disavowing responsibility for their actions.[11] Sarah Ellis blames society for its worship of "the mammon of unrighteousness—the moloch of this world," which transforms brothers into foes:

> Alas! there is no union in the great field of action in which [man] is engaged; but envy, and hatred, and opposition, to the close of the day—every man's hand against his brother, and each struggling to exalt himself, not merely by trampling upon his fallen foe, but by usurping the place of his weaker brother, who faints by his side, from not having brought an equal portion of strength into the conflict, and who is consequently borne down by numbers, hurried over, and forgotten.[12]

There are obvious echoes of this image in Dickens's depiction of the Coketown population as "an unnatural family, shouldering, and trampling, and pressing one another to death."[13]

Although Carlyle and Ellis similarly present class conflict as brotherhood disowned, they take different views on the means by which strife could be repaired and brotherhood restored in the industrial world. Both hold that a personal code of ethics would have to prevail against a system that encouraged, even demanded, the ruthless and unceasing pursuit of "pecuniary success." Carlyle's *Chartism* and *Past and Present* are addressed to a "nation of men," specifically the "Working Aristocracy," whom Carlyle designated as "Mill-owners, Manufacturers, Commanders of Working

Men," insisting that "[t]he Working Aristocracy must strike into a new path; must understand that money alone is *not* the representative either of man's success in the world, or of man's duties to man; and reform their own selves from top to bottom, if they wish England reformed." Carlyle's is a world of working men. Although he employs the family trope of brotherhood as a model for social relations, he makes no mention of actual families or women playing a part in social reformation. Individual men must be the agents of their own reform.[14]

Ellis, by contrast, addresses the wives, mothers, daughters, and sisters of the "Working Aristocracy," insisting that "the society of woman in her highest moral capacity" is best calculated to win individual men away from industrial competition. Man's spiritual regeneration is not simply in woman's power to effect, it is her "especial duty." Ellis argues that man has need of woman's "sisterly services": "under the pressure of the present times, he needs them more than ever, to foster in his nature, and establish in his character, that higher tone of feeling, without which he can enjoy nothing beyond a kind of animal existence—but with which, he may faithfully pursue the necessary avocations of the day, and keep as it were a separate soul for his family, his social duty, and his God." Ellis envisioned the domestic environment as a recuperative oasis in which the principles of order, justice, and benevolence were exemplified and instilled not only in children but also in husbands whose engagements in the public sphere threatened to impart a value system that would undermine ideas of Christian manhood. Thus, in her vision of social reformation, the family held a dual role as a model and a school. Gallagher maintains that "Sarah Ellis wanted to reduce the dissimilarity between the ethics of public and private life, but she did not indicate that the differences could or should be completely erased."[15] For Ellis, the family's reformative power was located in its difference and protected detachment from larger society. Similarly, a woman's moral capacity was dependent upon her isolation from the male world of strife, thereby justifying her containment in the domestic sphere, where she could best perform her "sisterly services."

The Professor and *Shirley* operate in this industrial and ideological context. Whether or not Charlotte read *Chartism, Past and Present*, or *The Women of England*, she would have known Carlyle's and Ellis's visions of man's interactions in the public sphere as "part of the conscience of the age and part of what was happening about her in the industrial north." Like Carlyle and Ellis, Charlotte Brontë employs sibling rivalry as a metaphor for industrial strife between men who should serve one another as brothers but instead act as oppressor and victim. While Charlotte subscribed to the vision of a conflict-driven public sphere, she specifically challenged Ellis's vision of the private sphere as protected and isolated from marketplace strife by woman's redeeming influence. The reformative power is expressly denied Mrs. Crimsworth in *The Professor* and only ambiguously granted to Caroline Helstone in *Shirley*. Charlotte instead aligns women with Ellis's "weaker brother" in order to probe the affinities she recognized between the positions of middle-class women and working-class men that made them similarly disadvantaged in a "mercenary male world."[16]

Sibling Rivalry in the Mill: The Relevance of the Opening Chapters of *The Professor*

The Professor is concerned with the male dismissal of brotherhood brought about by a spirit of competition and self-promotion. In her opening portrayal of the millowner Edward Crimsworth and his younger brother and clerk, William, Charlotte Brontë proposes an analogy between family conflict and social conflict. Family is not a refuge from the world of strife but a reflection of it. In her discussion of the Gradgrind family in *Hard Times*, Gallagher argues, "Instead of presenting us with an ideal family on which society should model itself, he [Dickens] depicts a family that is itself no more than a mirror of an exploitative society. At the onset, the Gradgrind family does not represent potential relations of social harmony, but actual relations of domination, denial, and oppression." Dickens himself proposes an "analogy between the case of the Coketown population and the case of the little Gradgrinds," who are equally oppressed by the materialist philosophy of their "fathers": "the relations between master and man"—like that between Gradgrind and his children—"were all fact." Benevolence is as foreign to Bounderby as fancy is to Gradgrind.[17]

The portrait of sibling antagonism between the brutish Yorkshire millowner Edward Crimsworth and his subservient younger brother, William, has been cited as a chief flaw in Charlotte's first novel. Kathleen Tillotson, for example, considers the Crimsworth story a false start, raising interest but leading nowhere. While she staunchly defended the Brussels section of *The Professor*, Charlotte herself considered the opening chapters "very feeble," and they are frequently dismissed as cardboard melodrama reminiscent of the juvenilia. Yet the Crimsworth sibling rivalry is thematically significant as a metaphor for industrial strife, which is implicit in *The Professor* and made explicit in *Shirley*. The brothers' opposition also serves as an archetype for the dynamics of relationships in the rest of the novel. Heather Glen has asserted that the pervasive image of human relations in *The Professor* "is of conflict, or, at best, friction between self-defensive and self-seeking individuals." In both its Yorkshire and Brussels settings, the world of *The Professor* recalls Carlyle's assessment of his own society: "Our life is not a mutual helpfulness; but rather . . . it is a mutual hostility."[18]

The rivalrous nature of William's relationships is prefigured in the opening letter to a former Eton schoolfellow, Charles, to whom he proposes to tell his story. When he recalls their boyhood bond, William claims to have "never experienced anything of the Pylades and Orestes sentiment for you" (P, 5) and assures Charles that "your sardonic coldness did not move me—I felt myself superior to that check *then* as I do *now*" (P, 6). William's underlying purpose in sending the letter is to assert his continued superiority over Charles by relating his successful journey of self-help, which, upon receiving no reply from Charles, he offers to the general public. William Crimsworth's journey of self-help wholly lacks the Pylades and Orestes sentiment. It is presented as a series of antagonistic associations through which William "progresses" according to Ellis's portrait of man's struggle with his fellow man—by defeating a combatant and exalting the self. In each struggle he proves himself superior, renouncing his dependency on a series of individuals who each attempt to "master" him, ultimately gaining the position of mastery for himself.[19]

The opening portrait of sibling antagonism specifically links the novel's atmosphere of mutual hostility to a rising industrial society. Edward Crimsworth is, in Helene Moglen's words, "a representative of a developing class which is antithetical to personal humane values: a product and prophet of industrialization." He stands for the Carlylean Mammon-worshiping society that has "profoundly forgotten everywhere that *Cash-payment* is not the sole relation of human beings."[20] Taking William as his clerk, Edward perceives their association strictly in terms of the hierarchical bond that joins employer and employee: "hear once for all what I have to say about our relationship, and all that sort of humbug! . . . I shall excuse you nothing on the plea of being my brother; if I find you stupid, negligent, dissipated, idle, or possessed of any faults detrimental to the interests of the House—I shall dismiss you as I would any other clerk. . . . I expect to have the full value of my money out of you" (P, 19). To Edward, the "interests of the House" and the "full value" of his relationship with William have "a one-dimensionally economic meaning."[21] Edward recognizes no "higher" familial bond between the inmates of his house. His speech demonstrates the power granted by his money and his role as "master" of the house and serves to put William in his "proper" place. This gesture is not unlike Hindley's assertion of power over Heathcliff, when he returns as master of Wuthering Heights, or John Reed's over Jane, exemplified in his boast that "all the house belongs to me" (*JE*, 8).

William, suffering Edward's abuses like "any other clerk," in turn disowns their fraternity: "I had long ceased to regard Mr. Crimsworth as my brother—he was a hard, grinding Master, he wished to be an inexorable tyrant—that was all" (*P*, 31). When William resolves to suffer his dependency no longer, he, like Edward, uses the language of the counting-house to terminate their public and private association. William tells Edward, "It is time you and I wound up accounts," to which Edward responds by offering William a horsewhipping as his "wages" (*P*, 42–43). Not only is their relationship reduced to an economic transaction, but the term *wages* is perverted to mean an allocation of physical violence. Translated into the public sphere, Edward and William have become foes like Ellis's brothers, "each struggling to exalt himself" with hands raised against one another. Edward's attitude toward his "weaker" sibling serves Charlotte Brontë's criticism as both a result and a reflection of the unforgiving atmosphere of the public world of trade and business, where men have exchanged fraternity for competition.

Charlotte underlines her criticism of the "unnaturalness" of Edward's treatment of his brother (both his literal brother, William, and his figurative "brothers," his other dependent laborers) when he is publicly denounced in the town hall as being in the class of "family despots," of "monsters without natural affection" (*P*, 44). The millowner Hunsden Yorke, at whose instigation Edward is condemned, suggests that there is no difference between Edward's public and private behavior. Hunsden rightly predicts that as Edward is a "tyrant to his workpeople, a tyrant to his clerks," so, too, will he "some day be a tyrant to his wife" (*P*, 50). Even though Crimsworth Hall is located four miles from Edward's mill, so that the inhabitants may evade its noxious smells and smoke, they cannot escape the intrusion of his workplace attitude. His relationship with his girlish wife moves from "playful contention" (*P*, 13) to the suggestion of physical and emotional abuse when Edward is driven to bankruptcy.

Regarded by her husband simply as a prized commodity, Mrs. Crimsworth apparently has no "secret influence" over Edward, able to preserve his humanity from the savage workings of the market. Beneath Edward's "hard surface" there is no "heart as true to the kindly affections of [woman's] nature" that Ellis and others maintained was in a wife's power to elicit.[22] Rather, Mrs. Crimsworth is, like William, a victim of Edward's ruthless materialism, another recipient of his physical violence when his position is threatened. An undeveloped character, Mrs. Crimsworth appears in the narrative to prove that her husband is indeed a tyrant at work and at home. Thus, in its presentation of her relationship with Edward, *The Professor* establishes a damaging link between the public and private spheres. Charlotte Brontë's first novel also suggests that she had recognized a correlation between the persecution of workers in the public sphere and women in the private sphere by the unchecked Mammonism of men in power over them. In *Shirley*, she would develop this parallelism of oppression more fully in presenting the related sufferings of Robert Moore's dispossessed mill workers and his cousin Caroline Helstone.

"Reproach of my Dependence": *The Professor*'s Parallels with *Jane Eyre*

While the conflict between millowner and disgruntled worker anticipates the subject of *Shirley*, William's bildungsroman course in *The Professor* looks forward to much in *Jane Eyre*. Like Jane, William begins his life journey from a position of familial dependence and subservience, and, like Jane, he is full of reproach. Edward treats William as John Reed does Jane, lording his economic advantages and possessions over his younger dependent relation. Edward even owns the portrait of their mother, the only family member with whom William feels any sympathy. Like John with the books that Jane treasures, Edward demonstrates his advantage and power through his possessions, which are signs of his legitimacy and the legitimacy of the profession by which he comes to own them.

The brothers' rivalry, therefore, is representative not only of social conflict between masters and men, but, on another level, of that between a rising manufacturing class and a fading aristocracy, each scornful of the means by which the other comes by its wealth. Class conflict is translated into a family conflict between the manufacturing Crimsworths and the aristocratic Tyndales/Seacombes over the transgressive marriage of Edward and William's parents. As in *Jane Eyre*, family serves as protectors of class status. The Seacombes in *The Professor* and the Reeds in *Jane Eyre* disown women for marrying "beneath" them, Jane's mother to a poor clergyman, William's to a tradesman. Brought up by the Crimsworths, Edward learns to bear "determined enmity" against William as a representative of the aristocratic "house of Seacombe" on whose "bounty" he is raised (*P*, 8). Edward's goal in treating William as a clerk and not as a brother is to emphasize William's position as a member of the working class, despite his aristocratic demeanor and Eton education. During a party at Crimsworth Hall, William is left isolated and unacknowledged, "weary, solitary, kept down—like some desolate tutor or governess—"; his brother, William notes, is therefore "satisfied" (*P*, 23). This snub marks the triumph of Crimsworth over Seacombe, trade over aristocracy. Furthermore, in associating William's degradation with the "feminized" position of a governess, Charlotte Brontë was not only recalling and expressing her own feelings as a governess through her narrator (which accounts for his gender confusion), but also suggesting a more general connection between gendered and class oppression. It is not without a sense of poetic justice that Charlotte has William rise above his familial dependence and make his way in the world as a tutor, just as Jane makes her way as a governess.

William's journey is launched by his sense of "self-dissatisfaction" (*P*, 40) as a ward of the Seacombes and then as Edward's clerk, and so he orphans himself, claiming neither aristocrat nor manufacturer as his kin, as Jane claims neither wealthy Reeds nor poor Eyres. His decision to become a tutor signifies his determination to "make" himself outside of the defining community of family. William's story is one of successful self-help that fuses his natural "mental wealth" (*P*, 31), his brother's material wealth, and what Jane calls "wealth for the heart" (*JE*, 491) in a family of his own making. Yet, in William's quest, there is "no sense of a supportive context" or "mutual helpfulness" for his achievements.[23] Unlike Jane, who finds sympathetic and nurturing communities at Lowood, Thornfield, and Moor-House, William encounters only discord, opposition, debasement. He moves from an "atmosphere of brutality and insolence" in Edward's Yorkshire mill (*P*, 69) to a Brussels schoolroom environment hardly more compassionate or civil. William describes the "tone" of Mademoiselle Reuter's establishment as "rough, boisterous, marked by a point-blank disregard of all forbearance toward each other or their teachers; an eager pursuit by each individual of her own interest and convenience, and a coarse indifference to the interest and convenience of every one else" (*P*, 97–98). The schoolroom is a microcosm of a society composed entirely of self-interested individuals, whose idea of "relationship" is trampling another to elevate the self. William observes, "Human beings . . . seldom deny themselves the pleasure of exercising a power which they are conscious of possessing, even though that power consist only in a capacity to make others wretched" (*P*, 132). William's employer, Monsieur Pelet, thus treats his

Flamand ushers "with perpetual severity and contempt" (P, 69). The directrice, Mademoiselle Reuter, maintains that Frances Henri "needs keeping down" (P, 150) and actively works to do so, dismissing Frances as a teacher when she judges her to be a rival for William's attention. Even Hunsden's rescue of William from his countinghouse bondage is not done so much to help the young man—"for whom I personally care nothing" (P, 49)—as to overthrow the tyrant Edward and to put William in his debt.

William also discovers the pleasure of exercising power over others, and, unlike Jane Eyre, he seeks to establish himself as "master," not "kin," in his relationships. Pursued by Mademoiselle Reuter, he responds to her "slavish homage" with "despotism" (P, 129). He enjoys the feeling of being "half [Pelet's] master" when he discovers the secret liaison between Pelet and Reuter (P, 113). He relishes his own courtship of Frances Henri from the position of schoolmaster, taking pleasure in dictating faster than she can comprehend and forcing her to speak English. After their marriage, William seems to derive a kind of sexual satisfaction from making her read Wordsworth: "she had to ask questions; to sue for explanations; to be like a child and a novice and to acknowledge me as her senior and director" (P, 253). Frances, too, seems to appreciate the master-pupil dynamic of their interactions, insisting on calling William "Monsieur" after their marriage and maintaining, "I should never have suited any man but Professor Crimsworth" (P, 256). The portrait of Frances is, however, both framed and interpreted by her "master's" narrative, leading many feminist critics to question how accurately William understands and presents her. Rebecca Rodolff persuasively argues that, as Frances comes to occupy more of the reader's attention in the last third of the novel, we can detect Charlotte Brontë's growing desire to write an autobiographical journey of self-help from a female perspective, exploring obstacles and emotions symptomatic of "femaleness" in a patriarchal society.[24] Charlotte thus turned to Jane Eyre and, finally, in a revisioning of *The Professor*, Lucy Snowe.

A Family Haven or the Return of Edward Crimsworth?

William Crimsworth's progress in the novel is marked by his rise from familial dependent to patriarch, from dissatisfaction in an original family to supreme self-satisfaction in a family of his own making, from victim to master. *The Professor* is the only one of Charlotte Brontë's novels to have an extended portrait of life after marriage. William returns with his wife, Frances, and son, Victor, whose name symbolizes William's personal "victory" in the world, to the vicinity of his brother's mill in Hunsden Wood, where they settle in "a region whose verdure the smoke of mills has not yet sullied, whose waters still run pure, whose swells of moorland preserve in some ferny glens, that lie between them, the very primal wildness of nature" (P, 257). This natural sanctuary is another indication of William's success: he has at last fulfilled his heart's "panting desire for freer and fresher scenes," which he felt under "the closeness, smoke, monotony and joyless tumult" surrounding Edward's mill (P, 30). The domestic sphere serves both as a symbol of personal success and a pastoral antithesis to the opening industrial environment. But does this peaceful, untainted physical atmosphere correspond to a harmonious family atmosphere? With his "smug portrait of blissful domesticity," William would like his reader to think so.[25] His sense that he has achieved a haven of peace where reason and love prevail is the reason he decides to send Victor to Eton: his son must be prepared for a very different world of conflict beyond the home.

But *The Professor* circles back to the theme of family as a site of contention and violence. Charlotte again suggests an analogy between social conflict and family conflict; again the Crimsworth family "does not represent potential relations of social harmony, but actual relations of domination, denial, and oppression."[26] There is a disturbing sense that William, now in the position of master, exercises his power to make his son wretched, as Edward lorded over him. His resemblance to Edward is most clear in his threatening to "whip" out Victor's unruly temper, or what William calls his "violence" (P, 266). It is ironic that William recognizes violence in his son's conduct but not, apparently, in his actions as a father, which consist of shooting Victor's beloved mastiff and resolving to force the "fearful operation" in sending Victor to Eton (P, 266). William seems to take a kind of perverse pleasure in cataloging the future misery of his son: "to leave home will give his heart an agonized wrench" (P, 266), and his time at Eton will be "utter wretchedness" (P, 265); nevertheless, Victor will be "cheap of any amount of either bodily or mental suffering which will ground him radically in the art of self-control" (P, 266), without which he will "someday get blows instead of blandishments—kicks instead of kisses" (P, 267). It is certainly difficult to find an atmosphere of domestic harmony in the vignettes William gives us: Victor wailing on the grave of his dead dog and swearing that he can love his father no more;

Frances and Hunsden arguing over Victor's education; and Frances roving with an "unexpressed anxiety" (P, 267) around her child while Hunsden preaches "mutinous maxims and dogmas" to him (P, 263).

William's shooting of Victor's dog, Yorke, named after Hunsden, is done to protect the family against the threat of rabies, which William suspects the dog carries. But the gesture is clearly symbolic of his attempt to "put down" Hunsden himself, who is a force of disruption and contamination in the Crimsworths' walled garden, both as Victor's mentor in mutiny and as a figure of industry. Despite his retirement from trade, Hunsden is still a voice of radical liberalism, promoting a future of ever-expanding capitalism. He intrudes upon the domestic environment with his "talk of free trade" (P, 259) and his news of Edward's recovered wealth in railway speculations. Whereas, in *Jane Eyre*, there is a sense of grim poetic justice in the demise of the economic bully John Reed as a debtor, there is no such permanent justice for Edward. Concluding her novel of self-help with an account of Edward's financial recovery, Charlotte Brontë suggests that, while the William Crimsworths of the world can rise through steady self-improvement, materialistic, ruthless self-interest still reaps its reward in an increasingly capitalistic and competitive society.

Shirley: Brothers Divided and the Call to Fathers

The materialistic self-interest that corrupts the Crimsworths' fraternal bond divides an entire society in *Shirley*. Set in the West Riding in 1811–1812, *Shirley* portrays an industrializing society "in the throes of a sort of moral earthquake" (S, 37), which has created a "great gulf" between masters and workingmen, rich and poor (S, 502). The world of *Shirley* is racked by divisions and confrontations on all fronts: England is at war with France; Whigs clash with Tories over the government's handling of the war effort; the Church collides with Dissenters (enacted in the Whitsuntide procession); Luddites challenge the masters, who are determined to replace man with machine.

In preparing to write *Shirley*, Charlotte Brontë sent for copies of the *Leeds Mercury* from 1812 to 1814 in order, according to Gaskell, "to understand the spirit of those eventful times." Although the novel is set in the early nineteenth century, the mood of discontent is analogous and the social criticism applicable to her own times. Terry Eagleton has argued that contemporary Chartism is the "unspoken subject of *Shirley*." Chartist discontent was an explicit subject of many of Shirley's contemporaries, such as Benjamin Disraeli's Sybil (1845), Gaskell's Mary Barton, and Charles Kingsley's Alton Locke (1850), another novel heavily influenced by the writings of Carlyle. Gaskell's John Barton, like the narrator of Shirley, describes a world divided, where masters and workers exist "as separate as Dives and Lazarus, with a great gulf betwixt us." Disraeli's Sybil, or Two Nations insisted, as the full title suggests, that the gulf had destroyed national unity, creating instead "Two Nations of England, the Rich and The Poor." Chartism—its aims, its obstacles, and its dangers— was clearly on Charlotte's mind during the writing of Shirley, for she exchanged a series of letters with W. S. Williams on the subject in the spring of 1848. "Your remarks respecting the Chartists seem to me truly sensible," she wrote; "their grievances should not indeed 'be neglected, nor the existence of their sufferings ignored.'" Although Charlotte judged the Chartists as heading an "ill-advised movement," she called on the government "to examine carefully into their causes of complaint and make such concessions as justice and humanity dictate." With echoes of Carlyle, Charlotte expressed the need for reconciliation between the classes through the "substitution of mutual kindliness" for mutual hostility.[27]

The reformist agenda of Shirley seeks to bridge the gulf of social division. The disregard of common brotherhood lies at the heart of Charlotte Brontë's social criticism; her hope for reform is centered on the awakening of conscience in the self-interested individual, illustrated in the mill-owner Robert Moore. Robert initially views "Progress" as personal profit, and he is willfully blind to the larger repercussions of his goal. The narrator of Shirley explains that "he did not sufficiently care when the new inventions threw the old work-people out of employ: he never asked himself where those to whom he no longer paid weekly wages found daily bread; in this negligence he only resembled thousands besides" (S, 36).

Robert's domestic relationships, like his industrial ones, are reduced to a question of personal economic advantage. Caroline Helstone stands as Charlotte's representative victim when cash payment is the sole relation between men and women, as well as between master and men. Cast aside when Robert realizes that she desires a marriage he deems "unprofitable," Caroline is left to scrounge for emotional sustenance as Robert's unemployed workers are left to scavenge for their "daily bread" unassisted and unheeded. Throughout Shirley, Charlotte draws parallels between the oppression of women and workers, of whose physical and emotional sufferings "nobody took much notice" (P, 37). Caroline's confinement in the parsonage with an uncle unresponsive to her needs is the domestic equivalent of the workers' imprisonment in industrial structures by masters unconcerned for their well-being. As Robert refuses to grant his men any employment concessions, Helstone likewise refuses to grant Caroline's plea for employment as a governess, declaring it to be incomprehensible nonsense.

As numerous critics have argued, the parallels between the suffering of dispossessed women in the private sphere and dispossessed workers in the public sphere bring thematic unity to a novel that, from its first appearance, was criticized as "a portfolio of random sketches," rather than an organic whole. Gilbert and Gubar maintain that *Shirley* "deliberately seeks to illustrate the inextricable link between sexual discrimination and mercantile capitalism" as forces of marginalization. Charlotte Brontë makes this link explicit when she articulates the opinion of society that "old maids, like the houseless and unemployed poor, should not ask for a place and occupation in the world: the demand disturbs the happy and rich: it disturbs parents" (S, 441). As the husbandless are united with the houseless in their needs, the happy and rich in the public sphere are united with parents in the domestic sphere in their neglect.

Throughout the novel, Charlotte Brontë employs the rhetoric of brotherhood in advocating an end to social division, but she proposes a working solution of paternalism. As Rosemarie Bodenheimer explains, paternalist ideology recalled feudal arrangements, espousing that "relations between employers and workers should be constituted in moral as well as economic terms and that society was properly seen as a hierarchical order in which the wealthy and powerful would protect the poor in return for their deference and duty." Relations in the workplace ultimately should be modeled on relations in the home, a home ideally governed and protected by a benevolent father who, through his benevolent provision, earns the respect of his children. Bodenheimer has recognized that "paternalism is an assumption central to Brontë's imagination of human relations" in both public and private spheres.[28]

Contrary to the opinion of a laissez-faire society, *Shirley* argues that the husbandless and houseless are right to demand places and occupations because it is the responsibility of "parents" in both spheres to provide them. The novel is propelled by these demands. It is not Charlotte's intention to overturn the hierarchical social order that puts the fate of workers in the hands of masters and the fate of women in the hands of men: *Shirley* insists on responsive and responsible masters and men. Through the characters of Caroline Helstone and Robert's workers, Charlotte Brontë calls for a reassertion of domestic and social paternalism—for fathers to see the sufferings of their dependents, to hear their complaints, and to "alter these things" (S, 443).

The Paternalistic Failings of Robert Moore and Their Effects in the Domestic Sphere

Robert Moore inherits his father's position as millowner, but, as we learn from Hiram Yorke (another millowner named Yorke), he is a poor substitute, literally and figuratively, because of his inherited debts and his lack of paternalist inclinations. Charlotte Brontë cannot, however, vilify Robert as she does Edward Crimsworth, for the young millowner is the hero of her novel even as he is the focus of her social criticism. She takes care, for example, to assure her reader that Robert does not beat the children in his mill, but this is the only paternal feeling he displays toward his "family" of workers. Charlotte attempts to mitigate Robert's lack of benevolence toward his workers by repeatedly alluding to the fact that he is not a full-blooded Yorkshireman. When Yorke (whose name signifies his full Yorkshire blood) warns that Robert has made enemies of his former workers, Robert retorts, "What do I care for that? What difference does it make to me whether your Yorkshire louts hate me or like me?" Yorke responds, "Ay, there it is. The lad is a mak' of an alien amang us; his father would never have talked i' that way. Go back to Antwerp, where you were born and bred, mauvaise tête!" (S, 52). As Eagleton has argued, Robert Moore is "critically measured against the robust traditions of Yorkshire paternalism" evinced in the millowner Yorke.[29] It is Yorke who dismisses Shirley's defense of Robert on the basis of his foreignness: "If Moore had behaved to his men from the beginning as a master ought to behave, they never would have entertained their present feelings towards him" (S, 413). Robert's paternalistic failings, Yorke maintains, cannot be ascribed to his foreignness but to his selfishness.

In a conversation with Caroline, Robert rationalizes his drive for capital by claiming to have been "brought up only to make money" so that now he "lives to make it, and for nothing else, and scarcely breathes any other air than that of mills and markets" (S, 138). This attempt by Robert to justify his actions is also part of Charlotte's critique of the mistaken conflation of family and material values in his upbringing. Like Hunsden Yorke in *The Professor*, who engages in trade "to pay off some incumbrances by which the family heritage was burdened" (P, 258), Robert runs his mill determined "to rebuild the fallen house of Gérard and Moore," (S, 34–35) the two manufacturing firms joined by his parents' marriage, now encumbered with debt. Robert views his own constrained circumstances as an excuse for his "narrow" sympathies (S, 82). But Caroline, expressing Charlotte's view, rejects this social outlook. In his concern for the *concepts* of family name and family honor (which, in Robert's mind, are wholly dependent on his economic status), he neglects the living, breathing workmen who constitute a broader "family" for whom he should take responsibility.

Charlotte Brontë takes pains to show that Robert Moore does not rightly value family. He is more at home in his countinghouse, where he regularly sleeps and takes his meals, than in the house he shares with his sister, which holds "no particular attraction" for him, being "one within which the wings of action and ambition could not long lie folded" (S, 72). While Hollow's Cottage offers a temporary respite from the cares of mill and market, it does not prove to be the site of Robert's spiritual regeneration that Ellis maintained. As they enjoy their evening reading together, Caroline performs her "sisterly services" in seeking to impress upon Robert his likeness to Caius Marcius in Shakespeare's *Coriolanus*, the "proud patrician who does not sympathize with his famished fellow-men, and insults them" (S, 103). "I know," she insists, "it would be better for you to be loved by your workpeople than to be hated by them, and I am sure that kindness is more likely to win their regard than pride. If you were proud and cold to me and Hortense, should we love you? When you are cold to me, as you *are* sometimes, can I venture to be affectionate in return?" (S, 105). Caroline clearly sees herself in a position similar to that of Robert's workers, all of them dependent on Robert's will and oppressed by his cold and proud manner. Like Margaret Hale in Gaskell's *North and South*, Caroline "applies a single standard of behavior to both private relations and the relations between the classes."[30] She judges Robert's manner to his workpeople as an example of "brotherhood in error" (S, 104) and attempts to persuade him that his attitude in the workplace should resemble his attitude in the home, where is he generally kinder and gentler.

Robert sees himself divided into two incompatible natures: "one for the world and business, and one for home and leisure" (S, 287). In practice, however, he, too, applies a single standard of behavior to both his private and public relations—the callous, profit-seeking, self-interest of the marketplace, which he displays to both heroines of *Shirley* in casting off Caroline and in proposing a loveless but advantageous marriage to Shirley.

Instead of prompting Robert's moral improvement, Caroline becomes another victim of his "mechanistic-materialist philosophy": like the Yorkshire workmen, she is "let go" when deemed an unprofitable investment.[31] Caroline's inability to convince Robert of his personal injustice, like Helen Huntingdon's inability to save her husband, shows the limits of woman's reformative power and underscores the power of the original family environment in shaping personal values.

Despite Caroline's insistence to Robert that it is "unjust to include all poor working people under the general and insulting name of 'the mob'" (S, 105), Charlotte Brontë is not wholly successful in presenting the out-of-work Yorkshiremen as something other than a mob. Apart from William Farren, the workers are not fleshed out; they are most memorable as the threatening, disembodied collective that attacks Robert's mill in the middle of the night. But it seems that Charlotte initially intended to elicit sympathy for the group by reminding Robert Moore and her readers that they are "family men" whose distress arises from their inability to support their dependent families. The attack on Robert's frames is announced as "a warning from men that are starving, and have starving wives and children to go home to when they have done this deed" (S, 40).

William Farren is Charlotte's representative of the "worker as family man." Farren appeals for a slower integration of the new machines on behalf of the workers' "poor and pined" families (S, 153). While Charlotte makes clear that Farren is not of the same order as the Luddite rabble—separating him from the angry mob that threatens Robert under the leadership of the radical Moses Barraclough—she nonetheless suggests his potential for violence. Farren admits, "I'm getting different to mysel': I feel I am changing. I wad n't heed, if t' bairns and t' wife had enough to live on; but they're pinched—they're pined—" (S, 157). Farren promises to be another John Barton, the unemployed father in Gaskell's *Mary Barton*, who is driven to violence against the masters as a last resort in turning their attention to the plight of the Manchester workers. Both men are helpless witnesses to the suffering of their families, and their impotence makes them "changed." Unlike Gaskell, however, Charlotte does not challenge our (or her own) sympathy for Farren by bringing him to violence: he is significantly absent from the attack on Robert's mill, and we see him again as a caring father tending his children at church and Caroline in her illness.

Like Caroline, Farren seeks to impress upon Robert the social consequences of his actions. But Robert can only respond to Farren's pleas with harsh economic pragmatism, arguing, "If I did as you wish me to do, I should be bankrupt in a month: and would my bankruptcy put bread into your hungry children's mouths?" (S, 154). Robert's unfeeling words, however, are followed by an uncharacteristic act of paternalist intervention. He secures Farren a position tending the fruit gardens at Yorke Mills, which signals the reader that the hero of *Shirley* is not without conscience and which rescues the Farrens from the fate of the Bartons. Yet this isolated, secret gesture seems somewhat empty; Robert appears to regard it as a sentimental lapse in his laissez-faire philosophy. His single paternalistic act stands in contrast to the open philanthropy of Yorke, who agrees to take on Farren. Yorke is "much beloved by the poor, because he was thoroughly kind and very fatherly to them. To his workmen he was considerate and cordial: when he dismissed them from an occupation, he would try to set them on to something else; or, if that was impossible, help them to remove with their families to a district where work might possibly be had" (S, 57–58). Charlotte does not sentimentalize Yorke's benevolence, emphasizing his intolerance to those above him and his readiness to crush those below him at the first sign of rebellion. But Yorke is meant to stand as an example of the active paternalism that conciliates class differences and preserves social harmony.

As Yorke is a good father to his "family" of workers, he is also a good father to his family at Briarmains, a replica of the Taylor family home, the Red House in Gomersal. The Yorkes are the only intact family in the novel, the "first and oldest in the district" (S, 58). As Moglen argues, "On the face of it, the Yorkes are a good, 'successful' family": Mr. Yorke is "an advocate for family unity" (S, 165), proud of, and attentive to, his children, and Mrs. Yorke is described as "a very good wife, a very careful mother" (S, 165). In an 1850 letter, Mary Taylor congratulated Charlotte for assembling in the Yorkes a faithful portrait of her own Dissenting family—"peculiar, racy, vigourous; of good blood and strong brain; turbulent somewhat in the pride of their strength, and intractable in the force of their native powers; wanting polish, wanting consideration, wanting docility, but sound, spirited, and true-bred as the eagle on the cliff or the steed in the steppe" (S, 170).[32]

The Yorkes appear to represent an ideal family on which society should model itself. But, like the family exchanges among the Gradgrinds and between the Crimsworth brothers, domestic relations in *Shirley* do not offer an exemplary vision of harmonious social relations; instead, they mirror existing social conflict. The Yorkes are a family divided by "Cain and Abel strife" (S, 655); at Briarmains, brother's hand is literally turned against brother in fistfights as the younger boys rebel against the tyranny of the eldest son, Matthew. The narrator alludes to the fate of the House of Thebes in describing the boys' interactions: "The dragon's teeth are already sown amongst Mr. Yorke's young olive-branches: discord will one day be the harvest" (S, 168). Charlotte Brontë colors her portrait of the upstanding Yorkes with disturbing biblical and classical allusions of sibling treachery that leads to death and destruction. The strife among the Yorke brothers epitomizes those interactions in the world beyond the family, where men lack fraternal feeling for one another and where the discord predicted within the Yorke family is presently being reaped.

The Yorke family is also seething with female discontent and barely suppressed rebellion, embodied in the eldest daughter, Rose (modeled on Mary Taylor), whose mind is filled with "the germs of ideas her mother never knew" and whose ideas are often "trampled on and repressed" (S, 166). Rose's demand to "do more" than society concedes reinforces the link between daughters and workers who ask for places and occupations in the world and whose demands are trampled on and repressed. The Yorke family portrait has been criticized as an extraneous picture in *Shirley*'s "portfolio," but it serves the purposes of Charlotte's domestic and social commentary, supporting her presentation of family relations in the private sphere as adversely affected by the public world of mutual hostility and competition. The Yorke family represents in microcosm *Shirley*'s larger social concerns with male conflict and with female containment, which is also the focus of Caroline's story.

Cash Payment between Man and Woman: The Corruption of Marriage in *Shirley*

When we first meet Robert Moore, he is discussing marriage with the curate Mr. Malone in the countinghouse of his mill. Malone puts forward a notion of marriage guided by self-interest and materialism: "If there is one notion I hate more than another, it is that of marriage; I mean marriage in the vulgar weak sense, as a mere matter of sentiment; two beggarly fools agreeing to unite their indigence by some fantastic tie of feeling—humbug! But an advantageous connection, such as can be formed in consonance with dignity of views, and permanency of solid interests, is not so bad—eh?" (S, 29). Through his actions, Robert clearly subscribes to this view. He decides to spurn Caroline's affection and suppress his own feelings of love for her in exchange for the financial benefits he would enjoy by marrying the wealthy Shirley Keeldar. In his one-dimensional economic outlook, Robert regards marriage as a personal investment of the same type as the purchase of new machinery: "speculations most important to his interests depended on the results to be wrought by them" (S, 39). Women, like Robert's workers, are seen as physical capital, and marriage is simply a means to a profitable end.

As Robert's unemployed workers are the victims of his self-interested designs in the public sphere, Caroline Helstone is the corollary victim in the private sphere. We see the workers' sufferings only in the brief portrait of the Farren household, but Caroline Helstone's physical and emotional devastation is painfully vivid. Through her portrayal of Caroline's suffering, Charlotte Brontë is concerned to reveal the struggle for female livelihood and self-development endured by those women who have lost their marriageable "worth" and are yet prevented, by the opinion of society and their own limited education, from aspiring to anything else. Caroline is faced with the agony of securing a valued sense of self not dependent on the roles of wife and mother.

Despite her uncle Helstone's view that all marriages are more or less unhappy, an opinion that is later corroborated by Mrs. Pryor, Caroline's raison d'être is to become Robert Moore's wife. Love for Robert is the "predominant emotion of [Caroline's] heart ... always there, always awake, always astir" (S, 192). But Caroline's domestic ambitions ultimately lose out to Robert's industrial ones. The dilemma that Caroline faces when she loses the chance to become Robert's wife underscores the difference in man's and woman's position: for Robert, who is brought up to make money and who has the opportunity to earn a living, marriage and love are merely "superfluities"; for Caroline, who is brought up specifically *not* to make money and who has no means of supporting herself, marriage constitutes the essence of her future hopes.

When she is disappointed by Robert's cold, aloof manner to her, Caroline realizes how completely her sense of self has been defined by the prospect of their marriage: "Caroline was feeling at her heart's core what a dreaming fool she was; what an unpractical life she led; how little fitness there was in her for ordinary intercourse with the ordinary world. She was feeling how exclusively she had attached herself to the white cottage in the Hollow; how in the existence of one inmate of that cottage she had pent all her universe: she was sensible that this would not do, and that some day she would be forced to make an alteration" (S, 124). Unlike Caroline Vernon or Mina Laury in Charlotte's juvenilia, Caroline Helstone awakens to the fact that she cannot exist solely for her "Zamorna." With this painful revelation, Caroline suffers a crisis of identity, forced to wrestle with the overwhelming question that remains: if not for Robert, then for whom or what does she exist? "Till lately," she reflects, "I had reckoned securely on the duties and affections of wife and mother to occupy my existence.... What was I created for, I wonder? Where is my place in the world?" (S, 194).

Robert's rejection leads Caroline to look for answers in the examples of other unmarried women. She visits the "old maids" Miss Mann and Miss Ainley with the intention of modeling herself on these sisters of charity, and thereby channeling her aimless grief into benevolent activity. But these women only offer Caroline depressing portraits of potentiality in their narrow and loveless existence. The stern and sober Miss Mann bears a "starved, ghostly longing for appreciation and affection" (S, 201) that mirrors and projects indefinitely Caroline's own starved and haunting longing—her "funereal inward cry" (S, 206)—suggesting that a loveless existence cannot be compensated and must simply be endured. Caroline ultimately comes to the same conclusion that Frances Henri voices in *The Professor*: "an old maid's life must doubtless be void and vapid, her heart strained and empty" (P, 256).

Caroline's overwhelming need for reciprocated love following Robert's dismissal prompts her to envision another relationship that will give her life meaning. Caroline transfers her idea of herself from a wife to a daughter, seeking to replace the lost husband with a long-lost mother: "She longed for something else: the deep, secret, anxious yearning to discover and know her mother strengthened daily" (S, 208). But the absent mother cannot offer Caroline an identity that sustains her any more than the distant Moore can. Her last resort is to propose a plan to become a governess, but Caroline does not embrace this project with the enthusiasm of Agnes Grey. She resolves to be a governess simply because "she could do nothing else" (S, 208). Employment is her last "hope of relief" (S, 208), but it is a poor substitute for marriage.

Caroline's attitude earned the condemnation of Mary Taylor, who recognized employment as woman's "first duty" and denounced Charlotte as "a coward & a traitor" for treating "this great necessity" merely as an outlet "that *some* women may indulge in—if they give up marriage & don't make themselves too disagreeable to the other sex." But Charlotte's feminism was different from Mary's: it was "less clear, less radical, more troubled."[33] Charlotte regularly presented dilemmas without providing straightforward solutions. She does not condemn Caroline for having domestic ambitions—for thinking of employment as a dreary alternative rather than as a "first duty." But Charlotte Brontë does signal the need for socially accepted alternatives to marriage, which she shows in Caroline's illness to prey on the mind, body, and spirits.

Caroline is temporarily rescued from her confinement in the parsonage not by employment—nor the longed-for satisfaction of wifehood or daughterhood—but by a sisterhood with the wealthy heiress Shirley Keeldar. Able to support herself, Shirley is a figure of female freedom, unburdened by the need, either financial or emotional, to be a wife or mother. Despite differences in station and personality, Caroline and Shirley enjoy a companionship founded on freedom of expression. Shirley offers Caroline an outlet for her opinions on the condition of unmarried women, and Shirley replies with her own feminist visions and condemnations of misogyny (Milton is soundly denounced for creating Eve in the image of his cook). Caroline indulges her visionary friend but ultimately feels herself disconnected from the mermaids and Titan-women that inspire Shirley. Caroline admits to Mrs. Pryor that, as much as she likes Shirley, their friendship "does not make me strong or happy" (S, 271)—nor does it provide answers to her life questions.

As with Jane and the Rivers sisters, female community does not long remain undisturbed by the prospect of marriage. Nor does Caroline and Shirley's friendship remain untouched by the prevailing atmosphere of contention. The rivalry that develops between the two women over Robert's attention is understated and repeatedly suppressed by Caroline's protestations of sisterly affection—"affection that no passion can ultimately outrival" (S, 296). But the motif of sibling rivalry persists, as Caroline watches her "sister" take her place by Robert's side at the school feast and in their moonlit walk. As Jane Eyre falls far short of the beautiful and wealthy Blanche Ingram in Jane's self-portrait, Caroline too appears, "compared with the heiress, as a graceful pencil-sketch compared with a vivid painting" (S, 280). Like Jane, Caroline resigns herself to the upcoming marriage of her kinsman.

In wanting to be counted a "man of business" and in taking a personal interest in Robert's business, Shirley seeks to associate herself with the handsome millowner and unwittingly robs Caroline of her hope of reunion with her cousin. Judging Shirley initially as a flirt, Robert soon comes to see her as a profitable opportunity. Knowing how greatly Robert desires to be rich, Caroline generously concludes that marriage to Shirley would be in his best interest, since Shirley promises to be a far more effective helpmate in fulfilling his desire than Caroline could: "I am poverty and incapacity," she concludes. "Shirley is wealth and power: and she is beauty too, and love—I cannot deny it" (S, 292). Shirley seems to offer everything.

Caroline thus feels herself divided from both Robert and Shirley, destined to become nothing to them after their marriage. As Robert's cousin, Caroline has, throughout the novel, occupied a delicate position halfway between his sister and his lover. Denied the opportunity to become his wife, she refuses to play the role of sister: "As for being his sister and all that stuff, I despise it. I will either be all or nothing to a man like Robert: no feeble shuffling or false cant is endurable" (S, 292). At the height of Caroline's isolation, Charlotte Brontë's voice comes through clearly in protest against her heroine's orphaned condition: "I believe single women should have more to do—better chances of interesting and profitable occupation than they possess now" (S, 441). Women without husbands "have no earthly employment, but household work and sewing; no earthly pleasure, but an unprofitable visiting; and no hope, in all their life to come, of anything better. This stagnant state of things makes them decline in health: they are never well; and their minds and views shrink to wondrous narrowness. The great wish—the sole aim of every one of them is to be married, but the majority will never marry: they will die as they now live" (S, 442). Charlotte places Caroline's dilemma in its larger social context: like so many girls, Caroline's sole aim and opportunity is marriage. She is not given any life-alternatives to marriage; she is not encouraged to think of herself as anything but a "relative creature," dependent upon her uncle until her dependency is transferred onto a husband. Caroline, Charlotte Brontë suggests, is ultimately victimized by her upbringing. Her uncle, whose notion of a "clever woman" is a female accomplished in "shirt-making and gown making, and pie-crust making" (S, 111), does not trouble to offer her an education that would prepare her for any occupation other than wifehood and motherhood. Her cousin Hortense does little to expand her sphere beyond the accomplishments of French and fine needlework.

In objecting to this narrow middle-class female existence, Charlotte Brontë echoes the protest of other women prose writers of the 1840s, including Harriet Martineau and Anna Jameson. Jameson maintained that there was a fundamental discrepancy between the ideal "feminine" education and a social reality that required more and more middle-class women to support themselves:

> She is educated for one destiny, and another is inevitably before her. Her education instructs her to love and adorn her home—"the wom-

an's *proper* sphere,"—cultivates her affections, refines her sensibilities, gives her no higher aim but to please man, "her protector";—and allows her no other ambition than to become a good wife and mother. Thus prepared, or rather unprepared, her destiny sends her forth into the world to toil and endure as though she had nerves of iron.[34]

As she does in the industrial world, Charlotte places the responsibility for the present situation and for future change on the father figures: "Men of England! look at your poor girls.... Fathers! cannot you alter these things? Perhaps not all at once; but consider the matter well when it is brought before you.... You would wish to be proud of your daughters and not to blush for them—then seek for them an interest and an occupation" (S, 443–44). *Shirley* thus couples the call for social paternalism with a call for domestic paternalism. Both daughters and workers acknowledge their dependency within the patriarchal structures of family and society; Caroline's plea to the men of England, like Farren's plea to Robert Moore, is for fathers to help their dependents help themselves.

In *Household Education*, published the same year as *Shirley*, Harriet Martineau stresses that female self-sufficiency is vital in the face of female redundancy, when, as in *Shirley*, the matrimonial market is overstocked like the cloth market. Crucial to Charlotte Brontë's plea is that interest and occupation are necessary for both economic maintenance and emotional well-being. As evidence of the harm caused by the "stagnant state" of single women's lives, Caroline suffers a psychosomatic illness that brings her to death's door: it is an appropriate fulfillment of Rose Yorke's assertion that life confined in Briarfield Rectory must be nothing but "a long, slow death" (S, 451)—as indeed it was for Helstone's wife, Mary Cave.

Paradoxically, however, following Charlotte's/Caroline's call for occupation as a means to rescue female existence from "that useless, blank, pale, slow-trailing thing it too often becomes to many" (S, 441), Charlotte "cures" Caroline's physical and mental crisis of identity *not* by granting her earthly employment through which she can achieve self-determination, but by giving her a new "relational" identity as a daughter. The restoration of Caroline's mother in Mrs. Pryor seems to give all the interest and occupation that Caroline needs—so much so "that she forgot to wish for any other stay" (S, 496–97). Caroline's sense of self-worth is revitalized with her health, and she concludes, "I am a rich girl now: I have something I can love well, and not be afraid of loving" (S, 505). At this point in the novel, Caroline simply makes the transition from daughter to wife. The feminist "call to fathers" seems to be drowned out by wedding bells.

Shirley's journey to wifehood symbolically overturns the view of marriage presented by Malone at the opening of novel: Shirley privileges mutual sentiment over personal interest. She recognizes that Robert's offer of marriage is defiled by the language of economic necessity and repulses him, saying, "You spoke like a brigand who demanded my purse, rather than like a lover who asked my heart" (S, 607). She is also aware that Robert's mill is the only "queen of his heart" (S, 384) and he has proposed simply to procure Shirley's money for the true object of his affection. She scorns his attempt "to make a speculation" of her: "You would immolate me to that mill," she accuses, "your Moloch!" (S, 608).

Shirley's own family, the Sympsons, seek to immolate her to a marriage made for their convenience and attempt to rein in her autonomous "audacity" with the decorous and deferential examples of her Sympson cousins Gertrude and Isabella. Defending her personal freedom, Shirley defies her Uncle Sympson's attempt to "make a speculation" of her, refusing to marry the wealthy Sam Wynne and the painfully poetic Sir Philip Nunnely. She denounces her uncle's participation in the worldly business of "making marriages" for economic gain:

> Your god, sir, is the World. . . . Behold how hideously he governs! See him busied at the work he likes best—making marriages. He binds the young to the old, the strong to the imbecile. He stretches out the arm of Mezentius, and fetters the dead to the living. In his realm, there is hatred—secret hatred: there is disgust—unspoken disgust: there is treachery—family treachery: there is vice—deep, deadly, domestic vice. In his dominions, children grow unloving between parents who have never loved: infants are nursed on deception from their very birth; they are reared in an atmosphere corrupt with lies. Your god rules at the bridal of kings—look at your royal dynasties! Your deity is the deity of foreign aristocracies—analyze the blue blood of Spain! Your god is the Hymen of France—what is French domestic life? All that surrounds him hastens to decay: all declines and degenerates under his sceptre. *Your* god is a masked Death. (S, 633–34)

Marriages, Shirley insists, not rooted in mutual respect, love, and trust but formed out of worldly interests are the sources of domestic strife, the corrupting agents of family life. Shirley's tirade also bears a nationalistic tone, warning of the threat to England's families—its symbols of civility and

Christian morals—if England "really becomes a nation of shopkeepers" (S, 186). A society ruled by greed, Shirley implies, breeds a kind of European immorality.

In defiance of Robert Moore, Sympson, and the god who manufactures marriages like any other goods, Shirley declares that her heart and her conscience—and "*they only*" (S, 634, original emphasis)—will guide her choice in marriage. To this, Sympson demands, "Will your principles permit you to marry a man without money—a man below you?" "Never a man below me," Shirley retorts (S, 631). In agreeing to marry her former tutor, Louis Moore, below her in "station and estate" (S, 709) but master of her heart, Shirley redefines the value of human relationships from a singularly monetary standard. She rescues marriage from the marketplace.

Shirley's "Winding Up": The Restoration of Family Values?

The concluding chapters of *Shirley* seek systematically to replace the marketplace values that have governed human interactions in the novel with Christian "family" values. Robert Moore learns to view his industrial and domestic relations as something more than mere cash payments. His reformation is brought about by his experience of "Cain-like desolation" (S, 610) following Shirley's rejection of his proposal. On his journey to Birmingham and London, he witnesses the social parallel to Caroline's domestic confinement in an "ill" society, "where there was no occupation and no hope" (S, 616). Wandering the slums, he is finally awakened to the causal relationship between his individual acts of selfishness and the general sufferings of the poor and unemployed, realizing that his own attitude and actions have been "Cain-like," bringing death and despair to those whom he should look upon as his brothers. To Yorke, he acknowledges his personal responsibility to be his "brother's keeper": "Something there is to look at, Yorke, beyond a man's personal interest. . . . Unless I am more considerate to the ignorant, more forbearing to suffering, than I have hitherto been, I shall scorn myself as grossly unjust" (S, 616).

Robert's forbearance is tested in his own suffering when he is shot down by the half-crazed weaver Mike Hartley. In his enforced convalescence at Briarmains, under the supervision of the formidable Mrs. Yorke and the dragon-nurse Mrs. Horsfalls, Robert learns what it means to be at the mercy of caretakers who mistreat and neglect—the equivalent experience of Caroline and his own workers. From his conversation with Caroline, he is also alerted to the causal relationship between his selfish dismissal of her affections and her subsequent illness, and in this, too, he prays to be "spared to make some atonement" (S, 664).

As part of that atonement, Robert comes to value Hollow's Cottage as something more than an adjunct to his mill. "I am pleased to come home," he tells Hortense upon his return, having "never before called the cottage his home" (S, 679). Robert also comes to value marriage as more than a vehicle of "Credit and Commerce" (S, 611). In at last proposing marriage to Caroline, he acknowledges his need for a "helpmate," not a wealthy business asset but a supportive and edifying companion who, he professes (in language highly reminiscent of Sarah Ellis's), elicits "pure affection, love of home, thirst for sweet discourse, unselfish longing to protect and cherish" that replace "the sordid, cankering calculations of [his] trade" (S, 614). In taking Caroline as this helpmate, Robert assures her that the "proud patrician" in him is rightfully humbled and that her lessons will no longer go unheeded: "I *will* do good," he vows, "you shall tell me how: indeed, I have some schemes of my own, which you and I will talk about on our own hearth one day" (S, 736). These schemes, in which Robert proposes to line the Hollow with cottages and cottage gardens surrounding his mill, promise to balance industrial progress with humanitarian responsibility. Even the conflict-ridden Yorke family promises to be reformed by the sprightly Martin Yorke, who feels "as if it were my vocation to turn out a new variety of the Yorke species" (S, 673). *Shirley*, then, "winds up" with the assurance of reform in both family and community.

But *Shirley* ultimately ends ambiguously, throwing doubt on the permanence of Caroline's domesticating influence and Robert's reformation. In a kind of epilogue, the narrator passes through the Hollow and recounts its appearance some years after the marriages of Caroline and Shirley to the Moore brothers: "there I saw the manufacturer's day-dreams embodied in substantial stone and brick and ashes—the cinder-black highway, the cottages, and the cottage-gardens; there I saw a mighty mill, and a chimney, ambitious as the tower of Babel" (S, 739). This portrait of a transformed countryside raises numerous questions about the quality of life in the Hollow. How does the physical atmosphere reflect the moral atmosphere? Have Robert's schemes polluted the "blue hill-country air" as Caroline feared (S, 737)? Does paternalist responsibility persist underneath the chimney of the mighty mill, the symbol of Robert's personal ambitions realized? Does Robert live and work as a Carlylean captain of industry, "a noble Master, among noble Workers," or is the allusion to Babel an ominous sign that dissonance and division are the results of man's industrial ambition?[35] Charlotte Brontë concludes *Shirley* with a description of the physical atmosphere but leaves the reader to look for the moral.

Charlotte also leaves the "woman question" that *Shirley* proposes unanswered. From a feminist perspective, it is perhaps the most frustrating aspect of *Shirley* that only the working-class petitioners are granted "a place and occupation." Of Charlotte's novels, *Shirley* most directly poses a demand for middle-class female occupation outside the domestic sphere, but *Shirley* is also the only one of Charlotte's novels in which the heroine who seeks employment never achieves it. Outside of family and marriage, the novel offers no solution to the dilemma of the young, unmarried Caroline as she wonders, "What am I to do to fill the interval of time which spreads between me and the grave?" (S, 193). The "interest and occupation" given to Caroline and Shirley is marriage and those philanthropic activities that they carry out as wives. Self-sufficiency is vanquished as a priority in the novel, as Caroline gives herself over to Robert's daydreams and Shirley is reduced to total dependency on Louis.

Shirley does propose alternatives to marriage in independent female employment and female community but ultimately fails to realize them. Both alternatives are promised in the Yorke sisters who rebel against their mother's designs to limit their development to "womanly and domestic employment" (S, 453). But, as Moglen has argued, there seems to be no place in England for their feminism, and they ultimately must immigrate to a foreign land to achieve their desired "living."[36] That "living," however, ends in death for the younger sister, Jessy, and loneliness for Rose beyond the pages of the novel. For the females in *Shirley*, death, marriage, and the alienation of "old maidism" are the fearful alternatives, all of which must be faced by the heroine of Charlotte's final novel.

CHAPTER SEVEN

Villette
Authorial Regeneration and the Death of the Family

> Death takes from him what he loves, roots up and tears violently away the stem round which his affections were twined—a dark, dismal time, a frightful wrench—but some morning—Religion looks into his desolate house with sunrise, and says that in another world, another life, he shall meet his kindred again.
>
> *The Professor*

IN JUNE 1849, CHARLOTTE BRONTË sat in the empty dining room of the parsonage, "stripped and bereaved" of the siblings with whom she had lived, written, and published. In the aftermath of family death, Charlotte was forced into a process of self-regeneration, both as an author and a woman deprived of those "who understood me, and whom I understood."[1] This process can be traced in the letters she wrote during and after a series of deaths that rocked the Brontë family and in *Villette*, Charlotte's literary response to death.

Villette marks Charlotte Brontë's creative attempt to deal with loss and memory amidst the realities of a solitary existence—a journey that is also ventured by her most compelling and autobiographical heroine, Lucy Snowe. Lucy adopts a strategy of displacement in articulating the impact of death on her life story. Her use of the metaphorical family shipwreck and the open-ended fate of M. Paul place death beyond the narrative parameters of her tale, making death intangible and elusive. Many readers and critics of *Villette* view this tactic as cowardly or delusional avoidance on Lucy's part and a sign of her essentially weak nature. But these forms of narrative displacement ultimately allow both Lucy and her creator to achieve consolation and control over their memories of death.

Recording the Death of the Family, 1848–1852

In an 1850 letter, Charlotte Brontë characterized death as "that dread visitant before whose coming every house[hold] trembles." Late 1848 through 1852 was an intense period of letter writing for Charlotte. In these letters she documented the series of deaths that destroyed a lifelong writing partnership, and they served as Charlotte's primary outlet for her grief—grief that remained largely hidden from her shared sufferer, Patrick Brontë, for fear of aggravating her father's own precarious health and spirits.[2] Written often daily, even when her literary efforts had stalled, the letters stand as a chronicle of grief and memory, of Charlotte's quest for religious consolation and justification in the face of death, and of her search for emotional and imaginative mainstays as she continued to write—the last sounding Bell.

In her correspondence, Charlotte sought kindred spirits who might provide the emotional and artistic support she could no longer receive from Emily and Anne, finding sustenance in her dialogues with W. S. Williams, Ellen Nussey, George Smith, Elizabeth Gaskell, and (before their quarrel over *Villette*) Harriet Martineau. But writing itself became her "best companion." As the juvenile writing she had shared with her siblings had served to relieve the loss of their mother and maternal elder sisters, Charlotte again found in writing "a curative and comforting power." She assured Ellen Nussey, "crushed I am not—yet: nor robbed of elasticity nor of hope nor quite of endeavor—Still I have some strength to fight the battle of life . . . still I can *get on*."[3]

A review of her letters shows that Charlotte did not hesitate to write in passionate detail about her siblings' deaths and her emotional devastation at their loss—even to the man of business W. S. Williams. This may seem surprising in light of our notions of Victorian propriety and our modern, more subdued interactions in response to death. Such verbosity, however, was not uncommon in what Patsy Stoneman has called a "death-orientated society." High mortality rates, particularly in Haworth, as Benjamin Hershel Babbage's 1850 report confirmed, ensured that death was a pervasive topic of discourse. Pat Jalland has noted, "Death evoked the most intense emotions in family life, and Evangelicalism and Romanticism encouraged early and mid-Victorians to give full scope to their expression." Death was viewed as a family event, with members called on to provide physical and spiritual comfort and to gather around the deathbed in the final moments. While the moment of death was intensely private, surviving family members could discuss the event and aftermath with persons outside the family circle as an acceptable form of mourning.[4]

On October 2, 1848, one week after the death of Branwell, Charlotte began a letter to Williams, "We have buried our dead out of our sight." Out of sight but not out of mind, the death scenes of Charlotte's siblings would haunt her. Many of her letters reflect on the ending of life and on life beyond the end for both the deceased and the survivors. The mid-nineteenth century was rife with questions relating to Christian eschatology, or the nature of the "four last things": death, judgment, heaven, and hell. Death was generally regarded as God's will to be met with submission by both the afflicted and his loved ones. What seemed a random and cruel deprivation was justified as either a test of Christian fortitude or a punishment for past sins.[5]

Charlotte chose to view Branwell's death as a deliverance for both him and the family: "The removal of our only brother must necessarily be regarded by us rather in the light of a mercy than a chastisement. Branwell was his father's and his sisters' pride and hope in boyhood, but since manhood the case has been otherwise." Charlotte's sentiment seems to be one of relieved finality, as death put an end to Branwell's bouts of insomnia, depression, and self-destructive behavior, and to her father's anxiety over Branwell's financial debts and moral abandonment. Biographers have noted Charlotte's loss of sympathy for her brother and her bitter disappointment in what she considered his wasted genius. At his death, she admitted to Williams, "I do not weep from a sense of bereavement—there is no prop withdrawn, no consolation torn away, no dear companion lost—but for the wreck of talent, the ruin of promise, the untimely dreary extinction of what might have been a burning and a shining light." In Charlotte's mind, Branwell's self-propelled decline had already destroyed her confidante, literary rival, and creative spur. Death did not deprive her further.[6]

If Branwell's life had troubled Charlotte, his death finally brought peace of mind: it was an appropriate end to his Byronic excesses and, at the same time, a textbook Evangelical conversion. Charlotte described to Williams the "strange change" that came over Branwell in his final hours when he seemed to open his heart to the worth of religion and principle. Charlotte's confidence that there was at last "peace and forgiveness for him in Heaven" reiterated Anne's belief in her brother's ultimate salvation, expressed by *Wildfell Hall*'s Helen Huntingdon at the death of her reprobate husband, Arthur: "God, who hateth nothing that He hath made, *will* bless it in the end!" (*TWH*, 456).[7]

Emily's illness followed on the heels of Branwell's funeral, and Charlotte described the course of Emily's consumptive decline as a "relentless conflict" between "the strangely strong spirit and the fragile frame." It was also a struggle for Charlotte, forced by Emily's stubborn refusal of medical assistance, to "sit still, look on, and do nothing." Emily did not allow her family to call for a doctor until the morning of her death on December 19, 1848, and by then she was beyond any help that the village doctor could give. As with Branwell, the distress of the death scene subsided to an atmosphere of calm, and Charlotte affirmed her faith that her departed sibling was at peace: "Yes—there is no Emily in Time or on Earth now—yesterday, we put her poor, wasted mortal frame quietly under the Church pavement. We are very calm [a]t present, why should we be otherwise?—the anguish of seeing [he]r suffer is over. . . . We feel she is at peace."[8]

In her turn, Anne succumbed to consumption at the end of May 1849. Unlike Emily—perhaps even to counteract the pain Emily had caused her family by her intractability—Anne submitted to the numerous doctor calls and attempted remedies. Her last thoughts were of the sister she would leave behind, charging Ellen to "be a sister in my stead" and Charlotte to "take courage" in her solitude. Ellen Nussey's account of Anne's death at Scarborough reads like an Evangelical norm, what Pat Jalland has called the "good death," which required piety and fortitude in the face of suffering. In her correspondence, Charlotte repeatedly contrasted Anne's gentle passing and Christian acceptance of a divinely willed death with Emily's last struggles, "torn conscious, panting, reluctant though resolute out of a happy life." She admitted to Williams that "[Anne's] quiet Christian death did not rend my heart as Emily's stern, simple, undemonstrative end did—I let Anne go to God and felt He had a right to her. I could hardly let Emily go—I wanted to hold her back then—and I want her back hourly now." As Emily never seemed able to resign herself to death, Charlotte clearly found it most difficult to endure the loss of the sibling to whom she had felt the closest, and whose literary talents had promised the greatness that Charlotte had previously looked for in Branwell. But, whereas Branwell had actively and steadily ruined himself, Charlotte maintained that Emily had been "rooted up in the prime of her own days, in the promise of her powers."[9]

Unable to hold any of her siblings back, Charlotte reflected on the devastation her family had suffered: "It is over. Branwell—Emily—Anne are gone like dreams—gone as Maria and Elizabeth went twenty years ago. One by one I have watched them fall asleep on my arm—and closed their glazed eyes—I have seen them buried one by one—and—thus far—God has upheld me. [F]rom my heart I thank Him."[10]

The loneliness that Charlotte endured after her sisters' deaths forced her to reaffirm her faith in an afterlife where she might hope to see Emily and Anne again. The idea of heaven as a final home where family and friends would ultimately be reunited in happiness was the most characteristic of the Victorian age. The nineteenth-century Christian Socialist F. D. Maurice (1805–1872) wrote that "among those things in heaven and earth that are so to be restored, the sympathies and affections of the family are some of the chief." Charlotte wrote to Williams shortly after Anne's death, "Had I never believed in a future life before, my Sisters' fate would assure me of it. There must be a Heaven or we must despair—for life seems bitter, brief—blank."[11] This sentiment is echoed by Tennyson in mourning for his departed friend Arthur Hallam in *In Memoriam* (1850). Tennyson writes:

> My own dim life should teach me this,
> That life shall live for evermore,
> Else earth is darkness at the core,
> And dust and ashes all that is. . . .[12]

Charlotte was reading Tennyson's celebrated elegy during the composition of *Villette*, but she found the poem rather forced: "if Arthur Hallam had been somewhat nearer Alfred Tennyson—his brother instead of his friend—I should have distrusted this rhymed and measured and printed monument of grief. What change the lapse of years may work—I do not know—but it seems to me that bitter sorrow, while recent, does not flow out in verse."[13]

Charlotte was clearly interpreting *In Memoriam* in the context of her own recent family loss and the fact that she had attempted to write verses following the deaths of Emily and Anne but found the task too arduous. She also seems to forget that *In Memoriam* was written and revised over a period of seventeen years. In the poem itself, Tennyson admits that verse gives grief only "in outline and no more," but he finds "the sad mechanic exercise" of measured language to be consoling, granting him artistic control over the pain of loss and memory.[14] In writing *Villette*, Charlotte Brontë would finally achieve artistic control over her memories of death.

The emptiness of Charlotte's life in the aftermath of her siblings' deaths was elicited by the conspicuous emptiness of the parsonage. She confessed to Ellen, "To sit in a lonely room—the clock ticking loud through a still house—and to have open before the mind's eye the record of the last year with its shocks, sufferings losses—is a trial."[15] The parsonage was now a constant reminder of death and loss, and although her home was her sanctuary and, more important to the duty-conscious daughter, her rightful place as her father's only remaining child, she could not completely subdue her desire to escape. In the years following her siblings' deaths, Charlotte Brontë, now revealed to be the author Currer Bell, found that escape in travel. She accepted an unprecedented number of excursions beyond Haworth, journeying to London where she met her literary idol, William Makepeace Thackeray, and Harriet Martineau, and to Edinburgh and the Lakes where she met and later visited Elizabeth Gaskell.

Although these journeys to the wider world were welcome distractions, Charlotte was determined not to avoid home and its memories. She told Gaskell, "It will not do to get into the habit of running away from home, and thus temporarily evading an oppression instead of facing, wrestling with and conquering it, or being conquered by it." Charlotte repeatedly reproached herself for making visits or inviting visitors to Haworth and thus delaying the inevitable solitary wrestling in the empty, silent house. Like the biblical Jacob who wrestles with the angel until the break of dawn, Charlotte was nightly accosted by memory: "Late in the evenings and all through the nights," she wrote to Williams, "I fall into a condition of mind which turns entirely to the Past—to Memory, and Memory is both sad and relentless."[16]

In her letters, Charlotte contemplated the painful nature of memory as "presence-in-absence." Memory assumed Death's place as "a sad—dreary guest" in the parsonage, taking on a haunting life of its own. "Many seem to recall their departed relatives with a sort of melancholy complacency," Charlotte wrote, "but I think these have not watched them through lingering sickness nor witnessed their last moments—it is these reminiscences that stand by your bedside at night, and rise at your pillow in the morning." Memory is personified as a cohabitant in the house, as death had been personified, usurping the place of the once living. To Ellen, Charlotte expressed her despair, knowing that "Solitude, Remembrance and Longing are to be almost my sole companions all day through—that at night I shall go to bed with them, that they will long keep me sleepless—that next morning I shall wake to them again—Sometimes—Nell—I have a heavy heart of it." Charlotte's recourse to personifying abstractions emphasizes her loneliness and sense of disconnection with the living, and it is clearly recognizable as a feature of Lucy Snowe's narration, in which abstractions such as Reason and Imagination serve as "companions" with whom Lucy converses, lacking the outlet of family and friends.[17]

Writing in the Face of Death

Charlotte's correspondence in the years following her siblings' deaths documents her ongoing attempt to wrestle with the effects of memory and loss on the solitary self. An isolated woman's struggle for self-mastery in the face of death becomes her dominant theme of exploration in *Villette*. With the death of her sisters and coauthors, Charlotte suffered a crisis of identity—or what Sally Shuttleworth has called a "destabilization of selfhood"—both as Charlotte Brontë and as Currer Bell. Charlotte wrote to Williams: "The two human beings who understood me, and whom I understood, are gone...." The loss of this sisterly understanding—the loss of identity *as a sister*—felt to Charlotte like a loss of self. As Cassandra Austen wrote at the death of her beloved sister Jane, "it is as if I had lost a part of myself."[18]

Confessing to recurring periods of "nervousness," Charlotte recognized the effects of bereavement on her sense of self, remarking to Williams, "The loss of what we possess nearest and dearest to us in this world, produces an effect upon the character...." Her difficulties in embarking on a new novel without the consultation of Ellis and Acton Bell testify to the interrelatedness of identity, sibling relationship, and writing, which had characterized the Brontës' creative partnership and which was now dissolved. Her psychological and imaginative dysfunction can be viewed as symptomatic of the loss of an internal security provided by the sibling bond. Throughout her life, Charlotte had been a writer dependent upon "the gentle spur of family discussion," and she now had to reconstitute herself as a solitary author. "The great trial is when evening closes and night approaches," she wrote to Ellen. "At that hour, we used to assemble in the dining-room—we used to talk—Now I sit by myself—necessarily I am silent." Charlotte concluded, "If I could write I daresay I should be better but I cannot write a line."[19]

It is well known that the family trials of 1848 and 1849 interrupted the writing of *Shirley*, which was begun shortly after the publication of *Jane Eyre*. Throughout this period, Charlotte's thoughts were "caught away from imagination, enlisted and absorbed in realities the most cruel." During Emily's illness, Charlotte wrote to Williams, "My book, alas! is laid aside for the present; both head and hand seem to have lost their cunning; imagination is pale, stagnant, mute." During Anne's decline, she declared, "My literary character is effaced for the time. . . . Should Anne get better, I think I could rally and become Currer Bell once more—but if otherwise—I look no farther." Again and again, Charlotte stressed that her authorship was dependent upon a "healthy" sibling relationship; without it, Currer Bell's abilities seemed to fail her.[20]

Despite Gaskell's suggestion that Charlotte did not resume work on *Shirley* until after Anne's death—with the appropriately titled chapter "The Valley of the Shadow of Death"—Charlotte's letters indicate that she was writing occasionally during Anne's illness. In April 1849 she confided to Williams: "I try to write now and then. The effort was a hard one at first. It renewed the terrible loss of last December strangely—Worse than useless did it seem to attempt to write what there no longer lived an 'Ellis Bell' to read: the whole book with every hope founded on it, faded to vanity and vexation of spirit." Along with her Christian faith, Charlotte's hope for survival became increasingly founded and focused on her writing. She worked feverishly to complete *Shirley* in the three months following Anne's death, confessing to James Taylor of Smith, Elder that the last volume of *Shirley* was "composed in the eager, restless endeavour to combat mental sufferings that were scarcely tolerable."[21]

Yet, I would argue that the portrait of Caroline Helstone's illness, which opens the last volume of *Shirley*, was not composed simply in an effort to suppress painful memories and felt absences, but to construct them in an imaginative space where they could be rendered more emotionally manageable. In Caroline's illness, Charlotte Brontë projects her memories of Emily's and Anne's illnesses, as well as her own questioning of God's justice and mercy in the face of affliction. Her description of Caroline's religious doubts and petitions for faith emanate from her own: Caroline, like Charlotte, "believed, sometimes, that God had turned his face from her" (S, 394). Through her portrayal of Caroline's emotional and physical wasting away, Charlotte imaginatively wrestles with the inevitability of death, but, in the end, she cannot face the consequences. Death is averted, family is restored, and the two heroines, who resemble Charlotte's sisters in both appearance and character, marry in health and prosperity.

Although she could not let Caroline die, or Mrs. Pryor's petitions for her daughter's life go unheeded, Charlotte felt compelled to narrate a scene in which the dying and the watcher of death are not spared—an alternative that mirrored her own reality: "Not always do those who dare such divine conflict prevail. Night after night the sweat of agony may burst dark on the forehead; the supplicant may cry for mercy with that soundless voice the soul utters when its appeal is to the Invisible. 'Spare my beloved,' it may implore. 'Heal my life's life. Rend not from me what long affection entwines with my whole nature. God of heaven—bend—hear—be clement!'" (S, 498). Yet, Charlotte writes, the supplicant "knows that it is God's will his idol shall be broken, and bends his head, and subdues his soul to the sentence he cannot avert, and scarce can bear" (S, 498). This scene of death is undoubtedly a description of Charlotte's own desperation and struggle for resignation at the bedsides of her siblings, with whom long affection entwined her whole nature. Although the realization of this scene is carefully avoided in the plot of *Shirley*, it is significant as a foray into the imaginative wrestling with death that Charlotte will fully undertake in *Villette*. The scene also conveys Charlotte's sense that death and suffering are preordained by God, a belief she again turns to in her final novel. In *Shirley*, Charlotte exchanges her "dark and desolate reality" for "an unreal but happier region" of imaginative wish-fulfillment.[22] She does not allow herself this luxury in *Villette*: death is not contained in a narrative aside but pervasive, and Lucy Snowe must continuously grapple with "the King of Terrors" (V, 633).

When she had completed the manuscript of *Shirley*, Charlotte Brontë wrote to Williams, acknowledging that the work had done her good: "The faculty of imagination lifted me when I was sinking three months ago, its active exercise has kept my head above water since—its results cheer me now." She assured him that, without her writing, she would be like Noah's raven, "weary of surveying the deluge and without an ark to return to."[23] These sea and storm images carry over to *Villette*, taking the place of any literal explanation for the family disaster that leaves Lucy adrift and isolated in the world. Lucy's "homeless, anchorless, unsupported mind" (V, 69) is like the raven without an ark, the half-drowned survivor searching for a buoy. Lucy, like Charlotte Brontë, turns to writing in her need.

Charlotte, however, found it difficult to press forward with a new novel after *Shirley*. She wrote to Ellen, "I thought to find occupation and interest in writing when alone at home—but hitherto my efforts have been very vain—the deficiency of every stimulus is so complete." She again tried to persuade Cornhill to publish *The Professor*, perhaps finding comfort and confidence in a text written in collaboration, rather than attempting to write without her sisters to consult. Once again her publisher declined, and Charlotte finally consigned her novel to the cupboard, where it remained until after her death. Whereas *Jane Eyre* was written with poetic fury, the writing of *Villette* progressed slowly, in fits and starts. When the novel was finally near completion at the end of October 1852, Charlotte wrote to George Smith, testifying to the difficulties she had encountered in her efforts to write without her family: "You must notify honestly what you think of 'Villette' when you have read it. I can hardly tell you how I hunger to hear some opinion besides my own, and how I have sometimes desponded and almost despaired because there was no one to whom to read a line, or of whom to ask a counsel. 'Jane Eyre' was not written under such circumstances, nor were two-thirds of 'Shirley.'" She concluded the letter, "Remember to be an honest critic of 'Villette,' and tell Mr Williams to be unsparing: not that I am likely to alter anything, but I want to know his impressions and yours."[24] These statements surely grant insight into the nature of the Brontë sisters' collaboration and consultation: Emily and Anne could probably be as hardheaded as Charlotte when defending their work, and as unsparing in their criticisms. Yet each sister to some degree "hungered for" and valued the opinions of her sibling critics.

On January 28, 1853, *Villette* was published. The novel returned to the master-pupil love theme and Brussels setting of *The Professor* but employed the female autobiographical perspective that earlier had earned Charlotte critical acclaim and popular regard in *Jane Eyre*. Unlike Jane, who recalls her life story ten years after her marriage to Rochester, Lucy Snowe narrates with the distance of many decades, reconstructing her past life and departed loves, her hair lying "white under a white cap, like snow beneath snow" (V, 61). Gilbert and Gubar have read *Villette* as Charlotte's last fictional attempt to "come to terms with her own loveless existence," specifically recalling the loss of M. Heger's friendship.[25] For Charlotte, *Villette* is a reconstruction of the past but not a past strictly limited to her Brussels experience. The painful reality of Charlotte's "loveless existence" was no doubt made sharper by the absence of familial love, which had been her constant support. In coming to terms with her solitary existence through writing, Charlotte connects the earlier loss of Heger with the more recent loss of her family. Thus, Lucy Snowe writes from the perspective of a double bereavement: the loss of M. Paul and the death of *her* family. As the two "authors" of *Villette*, both Charlotte and

Lucy write of, and *out of*, bereavement. Mourning is channeled into creative art; *Villette* is born out of death.

For Lucy, as for Charlotte, bereavement leads to a crisis of identity. Helene Moglen has described *Villette* as "the confrontation of the self by the self."[26] The "self" that both Lucy and Charlotte must confront is specifically one dispossessed by death and forced to reestablish an identity out of loss and memory, and through the act of writing. Both Charlotte, whose sense of self as a sister and an author is destabilized by death, and Lucy, who is twice stripped and bereaved, write as a means to understand and recreate the self in solitary existence. In answering the overwhelming question of the novel, "Who *are* you, Miss Snowe?" (V, 440), Lucy pointedly declares, "I am a rising character" (V, 442). Lucy's journey within the novel, as well as her writing of that journey, seeks to create a self out of destruction and death—a kind of phoenix rising from the ashes.

Villette is also a confrontation of, and artistic victory over, death; it is a tangible symbol of Charlotte's "getting on" as a solitary author. But the representation of death in the novel is largely evasive: the death of Lucy's family is only presented as a metaphorical shipwreck, and the death of M. Paul is left to the reader's imagination to construct. Charlotte includes none of the social and literary conventions to depict the final passage— there are no detailed deathbed scenes, no coffins, no funerals or graves, none of the trappings of death with which Charlotte was all too familiar. Lucy's reticence on the subject of death draws attention to her narrative as a collection of painful memories, which Gilbert and Gubar maintain Lucy "conveniently 'forgets,'" and which Moglen suggests Lucy represses in the face of "a past too threatening to be confronted." Mary Ann Kelly also asserts that Lucy fails to "articulate and therefore grieve her original loss."[27]

Within a novel dominated by happenings and feelings of loss that are beyond literalization for Lucy's experiencing self, Lucy as autobiographer/ narrator employs the metaphorical shipwreck as a means of articulating death and her role as the lone survivor. Rather than arguing that the use of metaphor is simply a self-protective mechanism, or a testimony to Lucy's continuing repression and powerlessness in the face of death, this chapter explores the figurative representation of death and the displacement of death outside the novel as forms of deliberate artistic control, through which both Charlotte and her heroine govern the nature of loss and the operations of memory. *Villette* reconstructs not only the past, but also the memory of that past. The ability to manipulate these reconstructions serves as a source of strength and consolation for both Charlotte Brontë and Lucy Snowe.

The Shipwrecked Family: Memory and Metaphor

Villette is a story of life after death. Virtually every character lives with death: Mrs. Bretton, Mr. Home, and Madame Beck are widowed; Paulina and Graham have each lost a parent; Miss Marchmont has been deprived of her beloved Frank; M. Paul and the "family-junta" (V, 670) that surrounds him mourn the death of Justine Marie; and even the king of Labassecour shows "the effects of early bereavement" (V, 304). Lucy also takes pains to reveal that Death does not spare Graham and Paulina in their blissful marital union. They too "had to pay their tribute to the King of Terrors" (V, 633), as their parents are taken in "the fulness of years" (V, 633) and a beloved child is snatched away.

Unlike Charlotte's other protagonists, who appear in the novels already orphaned, Lucy Snowe attempts to narrate the death of her family. Yet she does not give literal expression to the circumstances surrounding this death. Instead, she employs the image of a violent storm and shipwreck as the tragedy that deprived her of her loved ones. Within the metaphor, Lucy is victim, survivor, and captain of the ill-fated voyage, imaginatively transforming the "dry bones of the real" (V, 581) and resurrecting the past on her own terms.

Lucy opens her life story with a family history, but, in the first of her many acts of narrative displacement, the family history is not her own. The title of chapter 1, "Bretton," is the name of both a family and a place. Lucy says of her godmother, Louisa Bretton: "Her husband's family had been residents there for generations, and bore, indeed, the name of their birthplace—Bretton of Bretton" (V, 5). This name doubling suggests the family's rootedness, durability, and, ultimately, its strength as an institution. In the course of the novel, however, the long family prosperity is interrupted: the Brettons face financial difficulties and are uprooted. Despite their seemingly successful attempt to reestablish themselves in a virtual replica of their English home in Villette, the precarious state of the family is underlined. Even with the Bretton family, the domestic paragon of comfort and affection, "all had not gone smoothly" (V, 252). Lucy's family will not recover from its adversities.

Even before the metaphorical shipwreck wipes out Lucy's kinsfolk, they already appear to be a "wreck" of a family. Lucy feels more at home in the "large peaceful rooms" (V, 5) at Bretton than she does in the company of her own family, who, though we know nothing specific about them, impart to Lucy "an unsettled sadness" and a perpetual sense of impending doom (V, 6). By contrast, Lucy comments, "Time always flowed smoothly for me at my godmother's side; not with tumultuous swiftness, but blandly, like the gliding of a full river through a plain. My visits to her resembled the sojourn of Christian and Hopeful beside a certain pleasant stream, with 'green trees on each bank, and meadows beautified with lilies all the year round'" (V, 6–7). Bretton functions as a temporary lull in the tumultuous storm of Lucy's family life and, later, as a haven from the storm of her life without a family. The allusion to *Pilgrim's Progress* at the outset of Lucy's story signals the arduous journey that lies ahead, but it also suggests, as in *Jane Eyre*, that the pilgrim will not be without God. In *Villette*, this promise is fulfilled by Lucy's Greatheart, M. Paul Emanuel, whose name is derived from "Emmanuel," meaning "God with us."[28]

At the opening of the novel, Mrs. Bretton has claimed Lucy for a time from some unspecified "kinsfolk" for reasons unclear even to Lucy. Lucy reflects, "I believe she then plainly saw events coming, whose very shadow I scarce guessed" (V, 6). Lucy's godmother seems to have an insight into her family life that is denied to the child Lucy, nor does the adult Lucy reveal it to the reader when she narrates after the mysterious "events" have passed. Our sense of Lucy's family as unsettled, even dangerous, is affirmed when a letter arrives at Bretton and Lucy fears that it is a "disastrous communication" (V, 7) from her own home. The letter is instead a communication from "Home"—Mr. Home—announcing the arrival of his daughter Polly, who becomes the new focus of both the Brettons' and the reader's attention, prompting Lucy's self-marginalization in her own autobiography. Only when Lucy is called to rejoin her family after six months absence does she return the focus to herself.

Describing her family reunion, Lucy remarks, "It will be conjectured that I was of course glad to return to the bosom of my kindred. Well! the amiable conjecture does no harm, and may therefore be safely left uncontradicted" (V, 46). But Lucy allows her readers their amiable conjectures and conventional expectations only to subject them to a crushing contradiction in the harsh realities of her experience. In a mid-Victorian culture that deified the family as a place of fulfillment and serenity, Lucy's family, by contrast, appears to threaten her personal well-being. Using the images of placid seas and smooth sailing, Lucy invites her reader on a pleasant voyage of family life, but then she disorients, tossing the reader around in an unexpected storm. She begins: "I will permit the reader to picture me, for the next eight years, as a bark slumbering through halcyon weather, in a harbour still as glass—the steersman stretched on the little deck, his face up to heaven, his eyes closed: buried, if you will, in a long prayer. A great many women and girls are supposed to pass their lives something in that fashion; why not I with the rest?"(V, 46). With this image, Lucy invokes the domestic ideal of childhood and womanhood within the family: like a boat sheltered within a placid harbour, kept on course by a steersman who enjoys the blessings of heaven, so women and children are guided and protected within the family. "Why not I with the rest?" Lucy asks, but she has already led us to believe that neither she nor her family are like the imagined "rest."

"Picture me then," she repeats, "idle, basking, plump, and happy, stretched on a cushioned deck, warmed with constant sunshine, rocked by breezes indolently soft" (V, 46). Lucy has shifted her position in the metaphor: she is no longer "a bark" but now a passenger on a seafaring vessel, still, however, enjoying the tranquil waters. The next section breaks the spell of this figurative language—clouds gather quickly, and the tone darkens. Lucy proposes to reveal the truth of her family situation, but it is a truth still veiled in images of shipwreck and perishing in the sea:

> However, it cannot be concealed that, in that case, I must somehow have fallen over-board, or that there must have been a wreck at last. I too well remember a time—a long time, of cold, of danger, of contention. To this hour, when I have the nightmare, it repeats the rush and saltiness of briny waves in my throat, and their icy pressure on my lungs. I even know there was a storm, and that not of one hour nor one day. For many days and nights neither sun nor stars appeared; we cast with our own hands the tackling out of the ship; a heavy tempest lay on us; all hope that we should be saved was taken away. In fine, the ship was lost, the crew perished. (V, 46–47)

In one of the most complex passages of the novel, Lucy presents "a picture of death" that seems to be an intricate interplay of memory and metaphor, created out of skewed recollections and nightmare images.[29] She asserts, "I too well remember," but what she remembers is not specific, only "a long time, of cold, of danger, of contention," which could be a description of her life within the family, or her account of a prolonged family decline and death. "I even know there was a storm," she maintains, as if grasping for some basis in reality for her storm-driven metaphor. Yet when Ginevra Fanshawe asks Lucy on the deck of the *Vivid* if she is fond of a sea voyage, Lucy maintains that she has never been on one.

It is tempting to search Lucy's allusions to her domestic tragedy for what *really* happened to her family. While we should not attempt to undermine Lucy's shipwreck metaphor with conjecture, it seems fairly obvious that the family suffered disgrace, financial and/or marital, as well as death. Lucy, for example, says that her aunt "plainly saw events coming, whose very shadow I scarce guessed." It seems unlikely that the vigilant Lucy, even though a child, would not be aware of a grave illness in the family that would inevitably lead to the "event" of death, but it is quite possible that the child was shielded from knowledge of impending financial ruin or embarrassing marital collapse. Her description of the family atmosphere "of cold, of *danger*, of *contention*" (my italics) also suggests an internal domestic struggle more characteristic of a family suffering severe financial or marital troubles than a prolonged illness. The visual image of the sinking ship in which all hands are casting out the tackling reinforces the idea that Lucy's family had to jettison all superfluous material possessions in a futile attempt to "save" themselves. And, most tellingly, Lucy's family, like Jane Eyre's, has left her no money, and it seems clear that they had none to leave her.

Perhaps Lucy never fully knew the reality of her childhood trauma, or perhaps as an old woman she has repressed the memory of it. She later comments, "Certain junctures of our lives must always be difficult to recall to memory. Certain points, crises, certain feelings—joys, griefs, and amazements—when reviewed, must strike us as things wildered and whirling, dim as a wheel fast spun" (V, 702). In attempting to articulate her family's death in narrative form, Lucy must exercise control over her memory of that death, "wildered and whirling, dim as a wheel fast spun." She does this by calling on a more recent memory: the final loss of M. Paul in a shipwreck while on a voyage from the West Indies. This more recent loss governs Lucy's narration of her previous loss of family: her childhood memories are interpreted through and shaped by her adult reality.

M. Paul's final voyage also provides the thematic structuring of Lucy's life story. Her narrative is a voyage through the recurring storms of death and its memories. Death in *Villette* (Lucy's family's, Miss Marchmont's, M. Paul's) is always heralded by storm, and Lucy's ship metaphor, following the Latin translation of "metaphor," is the "figure of transport" on which she weathers the storm. Grief can be expressed, loss endured, and blanks of memory filled in only through the metaphor of shipwreck: it is a means of "narrating the unnarratable." The metaphor creates a new reality out of which Lucy shapes her entire narrative, portraying herself as both victim and survivor of storm and shipwrecks. The metaphor becomes, in Terence Hawkes's words, "a way of thinking and of living; an imaginative projection of the truth." The metaphor *becomes* the memory.[30]

Lucy's Voyage from Death to Life (and Death Again)

The absence of family is a determining factor in Lucy's attempts at self-discovery and self-mastery. The significance of this absence for Lucy is emphasized by the lack of any clearly defined family history or background in the text, which heightens our sense of Lucy's social and psychological isolation. Charlotte Brontë's publishers at Cornhill criticized Lucy's lack of personal history as one of the novel's flaws, but Charlotte preferred to leave her heroine's past elusive and staunchly defended her creation: "You say that she may be thought morbid and weak, unless the history of her life may be more fully given. I consider that she *is* both morbid and weak at times; her character sets up no pretensions to unmixed strength, and anybody living her life would necessarily become morbid." Charlotte attributed Lucy's weakness and morbidity to her life-after-death circumstances, which Lucy laments as "a terrible oppression" (V, 62). Stripped and bereaved, Lucy is virtually without emotional or financial support. She is, as Ginevra avows, "nobody's daughter" (V, 203), and Ginevra, by contrast the daughter of a "gentleman of family," swears, "I would not be you for a kingdom" (V, 202). Lucy admits that her position as the sole survivor of her family is "anomalous, desolate, almost blank of hope" (V, 62). In Tony Tanner's terms, Lucy is an "unlocated individual."[31] Her journey out of deprivation is a quest to constitute herself though lacking a family, which traditionally granted social and economic identity for young women. "I know not that I was of a self-reliant or active nature," she maintains, "but self-reliance and exertion were forced upon me by circumstances" (V, 47). The only brief exception to this enforced self-reliance occurs at the beginning of chapter 6, when Lucy mentions her two uncles, Charles and Wilmot, who were frequent visitors at the inn where Lucy takes temporary lodgings in London. This family connection, however, does little for her, only earning her the added courtesy of the previously arrogant maid and waiter.

The actual event of death repeatedly goads Lucy to exertion, however much she wishes simply to remain the "anesthetized survivor" of her family tragedy.[32] Still in her mourning dress, she becomes a companion and nurse to an old spinster, Miss Marchmont, who stands as an "irascible mother" to Lucy (V, 49) and with whom Lucy contentedly narrows her lot, hoping to "escape occasional great agonies by submitting to a whole life of privation and small pains" (V, 50). "Fate," she concludes, "would not be so pacified; nor would Providence sanction this shrinking sloth and cowardly indolence" (V, 50). Upon Miss Marchmont's death, Lucy is again bereaved of a "family" connection and forced out into the world "to live." Wandering around the city of London before her departure to Villette, Lucy enjoys a "prodigious" amount of life (V, 65). But, as Charlotte herself testified, "The crisis of bereavement has an acute pang which goads to exertion—the desolate after feeling sometimes paralyzes."[33] This "desolate after feeling" or paralysis, which characterized Charlotte's life after her ardent efforts to complete *Shirley*, also characterizes Lucy's existence as a teacher at the Pensionnat de Madame Beck. Following her momentary "ecstasy of freedom and enjoyment" in London (V, 66), she describes her escort to the *Vivid*, the ship that will take her to Villette, as a return to the world of the dead: "I thought of the Styx, and of Charon rowing some solitary soul to the Land of the Shades" (V, 68). Upon arriving in Villette, Lucy resolves to be a shade, to hold the "quick" of her nature "in catalepsy and a dead trance" (V, 152).

Lucy's resolution manifests itself in her fierce efforts at self-regulation, which are, in turn, reinforced by, and externalized in, the regulatory atmosphere of surveillance throughout the Pensionnat, headed by Madame Beck, who glides "ghost-like through the house, watching and spying everywhere" (V, 100). But Lucy's self-imposed damper on the stirrings of life is never secure: as Lucy admits before entombing herself with Miss Marchmont, "I still felt life at life's sources" (V, 48). Lucy's penchant for life is first elicited by M. Paul, who propels her onto the stage as part of the fête-day celebrations. She discovers that "a keen relish for dramatic expression had revealed itself as part of my nature," but self-control ultimately wins out: "the strength and longing must be put by; and I put them by, and fastened them in with the lock of resolution which neither Time nor Temptation has since picked" (V, 197).

The only "joys of fancy" Lucy allows herself to indulge in are "strange" and, significantly, "necromantic" (V, 105), suggesting a form of communication with the dead. Lucy indeed attempts to communicate with the ghostly nun who haunts the Pensionnat, believing the spirit to have a message for her from beyond the grave. But with Dr. John's diagnosis of the nun as only one of Lucy's "joys of fancy," she is "left secretly and sadly to wonder, in my own mind, whether that strange thing was of this world, or of a realm beyond the grave; or whether indeed it was only the child of malady, and I of that malady the prey" (V, 361). With "secret horror" (V, 358), Lucy realizes that her mind is populated with visions of the dead. The spectral nun functions as a visible projection of the dead that continue to live in Lucy's mind and resurface in dreams and memory.

The Long Vacation: Dreaming of the Well-Loved Dead

The long vacation marks Lucy's most harrowing communion with death and the dead in the recesses of her mind. Lucy's feeling of isolation at the Pensionnat becomes a physical reality during the vacation; the act of abandonment, which she suffered at her family's death, is replayed. Lucy even lacks the props of employment and routine that have thus far sustained her. Her solitude is shared with a deformed crétin student, but the presence of this "hapless creature" only intensifies Lucy's sense of confinement and dislocation: "it was more like being prisoned with some strange tameless animal, than associating with a human being" (V, 220). She is relieved when the crétin is finally claimed by an aunt, but the student's removal ultimately mocks Lucy's circumstances: Lucy has no one to claim her and no claim to anyone. Even the deformed and senseless crétin enjoys a familial bond.

In the absence of family and friends, memory intervenes. Violent storms bring the dead to life in Lucy's mind, stirring her half-buried grief. The storms Lucy endures at the Pensionnat revive the memory of a past stormy time, forcing her to confront her past and present condition of deprivation and undermining her precarious sense of anesthetized emotions and self-control: "Oh, my childhood! I had feelings: passive as I lived, little as I spoke, cold as I looked, when I thought of past days, I *could* feel" (V, 151). Lucy's delirium during the long vacation testifies to feelings out of control. The turbulence of her "homeless, anchorless, unsupported mind" (V, 69) is projected onto the outside world—everything becomes associated with death. The roof of the Pensionnat becomes "crushing as the slab of a tomb" (V, 225). In the empty dormitory, "the ghostly white beds were turning into spectres—the coronal of each became a death's head, huge and snow-bleached" (V, 224). The equinoctial storms rage outside, as well as in Lucy's mind: "At last a day and night of peculiarly agonizing depression were succeeded by physical illness; I took perforce to my bed. About this time the Indian summer closed and the equinoctial storms began; and for nine dark and wet days, of which the Hours rushed on all turbulent, deaf, dishevelled—bewildered with sounding hurricane—I lay in a strange fever of the nerves and blood" (V, 222). Charlotte Brontë admitted to Elizabeth Gaskell that the autumnal equinox was a strangely trying time for her, leaving her depressed in both mind and body. She attributed the cause to it being "the anniversary of my poor brother's death, and of my Sister's failing health. I need say no more."[34] Clearly for Charlotte, her physical and mental maladies emanated from disturbing memories of the "well-loved dead," and, as Lucy falls ill amidst the sounding hurricane, memories of the departed rise before her in a vengeful dream.

Maintaining that her dream experience is "nameless," Lucy can only describe it as having "the hue, the mien, the terror, the very tone of a visitation from eternity" (V, 223). This visitation forms the narrative crux of her dream: "Amidst the horrors of that dream," Lucy writes, "I think the worst lay here. Methought the well-loved dead, who had loved *me* well in life, met me elsewhere, alienated: galled was my inmost spirit with an unutterable sense of despair about the future" (V, 223). The feeling of estrangement, the "want of companionship" (V, 221), that is so oppressive during the long vacation invades Lucy's dream, tearing her away from a vision of past family unity. But Lucy has given the reader no indication that there was ever family unity. Like *Wuthering Heights*'s Catherine Earnshaw, Lucy longs for the *idea* of home, a place of self-fulfillment within community or companionship. But this home has no basis in Lucy's childhood reality, and the attainment of "home," for both Catherine and Lucy, is repeatedly deferred in their lifetimes.

Following the deaths of Charlotte's siblings, the oppression of memory upon sleep was a frequent topic of her letters. She wrote to Williams: "waking—I think—sleeping—I dream of them—and I cannot recall them as they were in health—still they appear to me in sickness and suffering—Still my nights were worse after the first shock of Branwell's death—they were terrible then—and the impressions experienced on waking were at that time such as we do not put into language." Here were Charlotte's own "nameless" dream experiences, which provoked an "unutterable sense of despair." It was not the first time she had been confronted with such a dream. Charlotte's friend Mary Taylor recalled that while they were schoolmates at Roe Head, Charlotte alluded to a disturbing dream involving her deceased sisters, Maria and Elizabeth. Despite Mary's insistence that she *"Make it out!"* Charlotte refused: "She said she would not; she wished she had not dreamed, for it did not go on nicely; they were changed; they had forgotten what they used to care for."[35]

Charlotte Brontë's dreams of departed and altered siblings form the basis of Lucy's dream experience. Charlotte's reticence in recalling these occasions clearly granted her a degree of control over the dreamworld and its unbidden memories, where she seemed deprived of control. Lucy also cannot control the oncoming of memory and dreams—they also leave her grappling with the "unutterable," the "unknown," the "nameless"—but, with authorial retrospect, she can govern their representation. The very act of writing *Villette* (by both Charlotte and Lucy) is a means to control, to shape, to understand those feelings and impressions evoked by disturbing memories of the departed which in their first instance "we do not put into language." Writing allows both authors of Lucy's story to narrate the unnarratable. Considerable narrative distance allows Lucy a controlled catharsis.

Waking from her dream, Lucy determines that there is no motive "why I should try to recover or wish to live; and yet quite unendurable was the pitiless and haughty voice in which Death challenged me to engage his unknown terrors. When I tried to pray I could only utter these words:— 'From my youth up Thy terrors have I suffered with a troubled mind.' Most true it was" (V, 223–24). Turning at last to religion for consolation, Lucy's memory triggers the words of Psalm 88. In this prayer, she hints at a preoccupation with death that arises from the experiences of her childhood.[36] Earlier in the narrative, when Lucy contemplates the possibility of her death away from her English homeland, she claims to be "inured to suffering: death itself had not, I thought, those terrors for me which it has for the softly reared. I had, ere this, looked on the thought of death with a quiet eye" (V, 67). In the most disturbing allusion to Lucy's family life, which suggests an intolerable atmosphere of internal strife or even abuse, or a series of external misfortunes, Charlotte Brontë obliterates the idea of home as a place of personal security and well-being. Lucy has not been "softly reared"; death is depicted as a welcome escape from the tortures of family.

Lucy's dream of her departed family evokes her longing for death's release but also elicits a resistance to its "unknown terrors." Her alienation from human companionship and confinement in the Pensionnat parallels the position of the supplicant in Psalm 88, who offers his lament to God: "my soul is full of troubles: and my life draweth nigh unto the grave.... Thou hast put away mine acquaintance far from me; thou hast made me an abomination unto them: I am shut up, and I cannot come forth."[37] But Lucy rebels against the lure of death; she comes forth from her crushing tomblike solitude, seeking comfort from God and man in the Catholic confessional. Yet, upon leaving the church, Lucy is still lost: her physical disorientation in unknown environs reflects her continuing emotional and spiritual dislocation. Volume one of *Villette* ends with Lucy's fainting fit in the storm, a literalization of Psalm 69, which concludes volume two of *Jane Eyre:* "the waters came into my soul; I sank in deep mire: I felt no standing; I came into deep waters; the floods overflowed me" (*JE*, 375). Like Jane, however, Lucy is rescued by Providence: from the arms of the well-loved dead, she is delivered into the arms of the well-loved living.

Graham Bretton's Correspondence: Entombing Memory

As with Jane Eyre, Lucy is providentially provided with a domestic shelter and family at the height of her solitary crisis; yet, unlike Jane, who is rescued from the threat of physical starvation, Lucy is delivered from an emotional hunger—"a want of companionship" (*V*, 221). Perhaps Charlotte was contrasting the plights of her two heroines when she wrote: "The world can understand well enough the process of perishing for want of food: perhaps few persons can enter into or follow out that of going mad from solitary confinement" (*V*, 392). From the perils of madness and death, Lucy is reborn into a family; she wakes in the bosom of "auld lang syne." Memory, which was so threatening in the Pensionnat, now comforts Lucy, transforming "an unknown room in an unknown house" (*V*, 237) into a familiar haven. A physical replica of her childhood abode in Bretton, La Terrasse recalls for Lucy the tranquility of her godmother's company. Here, in her "calm little room" which "seemed somehow like a cave in the sea," the turbulence in her mind subsides at last (*V*, 258).

As Lucy is reacquainted with Louisa and Graham Bretton (whom Lucy has previously recognized as the Pensionnat's visiting doctor, Dr. John), she attempts, at the request of her godmother, to narrate the death of her family: "for her satisfaction I had to recur to gone-by troubles, to explain causes of seeming estrangement, to touch on single-handed conflict with Life, with Death, with Grief, with Fate" (*V*, 252). As a narrator, Lucy continues to regulate her life-and-death story through metaphor—this time, a metaphor of battle. Charlotte employed a similar metaphor in an 1852 letter to Ellen Nussey: "Submission—courage—exertion when practicable—these seem to be the weapons with which we must fight life's long battle."[38] Even as Lucy's sole "familial" connection, the Brettons cannot serve as outlets for her grief. Lucy remains the solitary survivor of death, and she replays her metaphor of sea voyage and storm to justify her narrative reticence and her resolution that Louisa Bretton cannot be a confidante:

> The difference between her and me might be figured by that between the stately ship, cruising safe on smooth seas, with its full complement of crew, a captain gay and brave, and venturous and provident; and the life-boat, which most days of the year lies dry and solitary in an old, dark boat-house, only putting to sea when the billows run high in rough weather, when cloud encounters water, when danger and death divide between them the rule of the great deep. No, the "Louisa Bretton" never was out of harbour on such a night, and in such a scene: her crew could not conceive it; so the half-drowned life-boat man keeps his own counsel, and spins no yarns. (V, 258)

The danger and death that Lucy has endured as the "half-drowned life-boat man" determines her difference and isolation. Her silence is finally broken by M. Paul, with whom the sufferings of death and grief form a common bond, not a difference. To him, she can and will tell all.

Upon Lucy's return to the service of Madame Beck, Graham promises to write—"just any cheerful nonsense that comes into my head" (V, 326)—as a gesture of friendship and a token of remembrance. The letters remind Lucy, in her self-enforced seclusion, of her association with a family. They "reaffirm her connection to a pleasant childhood memory," recapturing the time at Bretton when she was "a good deal noticed" (V, 5) and providing a welcome reprieve from the haunting childhood memories that accosted her in the long vacation.[39] As she had likened her Bretton childhood to the peaceful sojourn of Christian and Hopeful by the stream called both the "River of God" and the "River of the Water of Life" in *Pilgrim's Progress*, Lucy again alludes to this scene of rest to describe her feelings of relief and renewal in the company of her "god-family." She associates Graham's letters with "that goodly river" (V, 420) that provides "vital comfort" (V, 362).

The family attentions that Lucy enjoys are interrupted by the return of the child Polly as Paulina Mary Home de Bassompierre. As she did at Bretton, Paulina intrudes on the family circle, usurping Lucy's place in Graham's regard and putting an end to his correspondence. With Paulina's return, Lucy acknowledges that the river "on whose banks I had sojourned, of whose wave a few reviving drops had trickled to my lips, was bending to another course: it was leaving my little hut and field forlorn and sand-dry, pouring its wealth of waters far away" (V, 420). Lucy describes her sense of loss when Graham's letters cease to arrive as suffering "weeks of inward winter" (V, 382). Longing to be remembered, she admits, "My hour of torment was the post-hour" (V, 383). These sentiments are faithful to those that Charlotte expressed to Ellen in 1850:

> I have had no letters from London for a long time—and am very much ashamed of myself to find—now when that stimulus is withdrawn—how dependent on it I had become—I cannot help feeling something of the excitement of expectation till post-hour comes and when day after day it brings nothing—I get low. This is a stupid, disgraceful, unmeaning state of things—I feel bitterly enraged at my own dependence and folly—It is so bad for the mind to be quite alone—and to have none with whom to talk over little crosses and disappointments and laugh them away.[40]

In the years before and during the writing of *Villette*, Charlotte cherished her correspondence with her publisher George Smith, who served as the model for Graham Bretton and who, like Graham, elicited feelings from his correspondent that perhaps extended beyond the boundaries of mere friendship. Both Charlotte and Lucy seek to resist a dependence on their correspondence, yet, at the same time, they hunger for the sense of connection that the letters provide, easing the solitude of the mind. What had become a treasured presence in Lucy's life now becomes another painfully felt absence, another abandonment, another deprivation that Lucy must face.

Lucy consigns the letters and her awakened feelings for Graham to memory, locking the packet of letters away as mementoes. But the seduction of memory proves irresistible: Lucy is drawn to reread the letters again and again, even though the reading "did not nourish me" (V, 384). Bitterly enraged at her own dependence and folly, Lucy imposes a control on her memory, for, she declares, "it is not supportable to be stabbed to the heart each moment by sharp revival of regret" (V, 421). Lucy decides to bury her dead out of her sight; she lays Graham's letters to rest underneath Methusaleh, the pear tree in "l'allée défendue," longing to bury her feelings and hopes for reciprocated love along with them.

The act of burial—the only burial scene in a novel preoccupied with death—plays out Lucy's narrative strategy for memory and loss: memory is both contained and controlled, whether physically, under the ground, or figuratively, under images of shipwreck and storm. These attempts at control aid Lucy's efforts to impose a form on her inexpressible grief. Embodied in the letters, grief and loss become tangible objects that can be manipulated and—ideally—managed. In burying the letters, Lucy also buries her sense of familial connection with the Brettons, concluding, "If life be a war, it seemed my destiny to conduct it single-handed" (V, 425). Resting beside her "newly-sodded grave" (V, 425), Lucy hopes for a sense of finality, but she later reflects on the unquiet tomb in which her emotions and memories lie buried: "Was this feeling dead? I do not know, but it was buried. Sometimes I thought the tomb unquiet, and dreamed strangely of disturbed earth, and of hair, still golden and living, obtruded through coffin-chinks" (V, 524). In a Poe-esque image of the dead beloved refusing to die, Lucy suggests a parallel between the legend of the nun buried alive for some passionate crime against her vow, and the burial of her own live feelings, both of which seem to rise unbidden from their graves. The well-loved "dead" (her family, her feelings, her letters, Graham) still haunt her dreams, threatening to overthrow her entombing control.

"Many Waters Cannot Quench Love, Neither Can the Floods Drown It . . . for Love Is Strong as Death."

Lucy's role as a shade among the living is one that she both invokes and rejects throughout the course of her narrative. Despite her acceptance of a life in "my own still, shadow-world" (V, 185) clothed in a "gown of shadow" (V, 183), she resists the imposition of shadow upon her, rebuking Graham's characterization of her as an "inoffensive shadow" (V, 454): "He wanted always to give me a rôle not mine" (V, 455). When Paulina's father offers to employ her as a companion to his daughter, Lucy again objects, "I was no bright lady's shadow. . . . Overcast enough it was my nature often to be; of a subdued habit I was: but the dimness and depression must both be voluntary" (V, 427). M. Paul elicits the light and life Lucy self-consciously keeps subdued. Lucy ponders, "You are well habituated to be passed by as a shadow in Life's sunshine: it is a new thing to see one testily lifting his hand to screen his eyes, because you tease him with an obtrusive ray" (V, 483).

Lucy's entire narrative has been a rejection of roles not her own, a refusal to follow the course of the other female narratives contained within hers—those of conventional femininity (represented by Paulina and the women of "La vie d'une femme"), empty coquetry (Ginevra), and sensual rebellion (Cleopatra, Vashti, and the nun). So long "unrelated" to anyone, she repeatedly insists on her difference and, therefore, her solitude.

Thus, whereas Jane Eyre recognizes and embraces her kinship with Rochester, Lucy Snowe must be convinced. It is Paul, not Lucy, who first proposes a friendship based on the closeness of siblings, "intimate and real—kindred in all but blood" (V, 588–89). In the chapter entitled "Fraternity," he asks Lucy to be his "sister" (V, 589), having previously told her:

> "I was conscious of rapport between you and myself. You are patient, and I am choleric; you are quiet and pale, and I am tanned and fiery; you are a strict Protestant, and I am a sort of lay Jesuit: but we are alike—there is affinity. Do you see it, mademoiselle, when you look in the glass? Do you observe that your forehead is shaped like mine—that your eyes are cut like mine? Do you hear that you have some of my tones of voice? Do you know that you have many of my looks? I perceive all this, and believe that you were born under my star." (V, 531–32)

Paul's insistence on their kinship is underlined by his noting their physical affinities, as if they really are related. This shared "rapport" overcomes their obvious differences in temper, nationality, and, especially, the differences in their Protestant and Catholic creeds, the last of which Paul's "family" uses to try to keep them apart.

But Paul is not misled; he avows to Lucy, "Donnez moi la main! I see we worship the same God, in the same spirit, though by different rites" (V, 553). Lucy, too, learns to recognize her affinity with the fiery little man. Despite his hardness and irritability, Lucy sees that Paul's heart is not "an ossified organ" (V, 489), just as, despite her own passive withdrawal, Lucy's heart burns with life. Like Lucy, he too *could* feel. Like her, "his nature was of an order rarely comprehended" (V, 290). But Lucy comes to comprehend.

Paul and Lucy's bond is finally sealed by death: death both affirms and ends their relationship. Paul is also committed to the memory of the departed, of whom Lucy learns on her errand to the residence of Madame Walvarens. The old woman's house, suitably located in the Basse-Ville, or lower city, seems to be one of living death. Madame Walvarens herself appears "to have outlived the common years of humanity" (V, 586); her ghoulish appearance reminds Lucy of Malevola, the evil fairy. A portrait of a young woman in nun's garb, dead twenty years, recalls the ghostly nun of the Pensionnat; the entire house is a shrine to the spirit of the departed girl. Detained by a storm in the "cell-like room," Lucy hears Père Silas's family romance of M. Paul and the woman in the portrait, Justine Marie—

the well-loved dead "still remembered, still wept" (V, 566). It is a tale of young love thwarted by family interest and pride: forbidden by her wealthy family to marry the pauper Paul, Justine Marie withdraws to a convent, burying herself and her grief, and finally dies. When her family is financially ruined, Paul sacrifices himself to care for them—an expression of the constancy of his love, unchanged even by death.

Père Silas's account of Paul's devotion to the dead affirms his connection with Lucy: he is also a perpetual mourner. Both Paul and Lucy are the "anesthetized survivors" of death, unable, on their own, to free themselves from their bonds with the dead. Conversing in "l'allée défendue," Paul reveals that he too has seen the mysterious nun who haunts the Pensionnat, remarking that "her business is as much with you as with me, probably" (V, 533). In her physical resemblance to the cloistered Justine Marie, the nun is a particularly haunting vision of the well-loved dead for Paul. When the nun comes upon Lucy and Paul together, she affirms their common affinity with her, an incarnation of living death, and with each other, two self-appointed shades leading their buried lives. Paul tells Lucy that his passion, like Lucy's well-beloved letters, "lies buried—its grave is deep-dug, well-heaped, and many winters old: in the future there will be a resurrection" (V, 499). The resurrection will be found in his growing love for Lucy, and hers for him, through which both Paul and Lucy forego their commitment to the dead and embrace a living bond with each other.

Despite his intention to discourage their union, Père Silas's account of Paul's undying love serves only to intensify Lucy's feelings. In revealing "the adytum of [Paul's] heart" (V, 575), the old priest testifies to the strength of Paul's love. It is a love strong as death, a love that "had laughed at Death himself, despised his mean rape of matter, clung to immortal spirit, and, in victory and faith, had watched beside a tomb twenty years" (V, 576). Whereas Père Silas and the "family-junta" (V, 670) conspire to raise another alienating vision of the dead in Lucy's mind—a ghost against whom Lucy must compete for Paul's love—Lucy draws confidence from her vision of M. Paul's life-giving love. "Was I, then," she asks, "to be frightened by Justine Marie? Was the picture of a pale dead nun to rise, an eternal barrier?" (V, 576).

Lucy's assurance of her place in Paul's heart is tested on her drugged excursion through the fête, where she sees M. Paul with a young girl and comes to believe that his love has been resurrected not in their shared bond, but in the nun's living namesake, his ward Justine Marie Sauveur, an orphan and an heiress whom the "family-junta" intend to be Paul's bride. Returning to the Pensionnat in the Rue Fossette and finding the "nun" lying on her bed, Lucy enacts a physical and psychological triumph over her visions of the dead: "I tore her up . . . I held her on high . . . I shook her loose . . . And down she fell . . . and I trode upon her" (V, 681). Lucy's vigorous destruction of the nun (who, with a dose of the "homely web of truth" [V, 672] is revealed to have been Ginevra's suitor, Count de Hamal, in disguise) resembles Vashti's attacking and ripping apart her grief and marks Lucy's final rejection of a suicidal passivity that characterized Justine Marie's life in the convent and her own life in the Pensionnat.

Whereas the loss of Graham elicited burial and suppression—acts that Lucy has ever maintained in dealing with death and bereavement—the imminent departure of M. Paul makes Lucy feel "what defied suppression" (V, 695). Although repulsed by Madame Beck, who attempts to impede Lucy's final meeting with Paul, she cannot withdraw; fearing to be forgotten, she must cry out, "My heart will break!" (V, 695). Lucy has thrown off the "language of passivity," and, encouraged by M. Paul, she can at last speak freely: "All leaped from my lips. I lacked not words now; fast I narrated; fluent I told my tale; it streamed on my tongue" (V, 708).[41] Paul's love and his loss stir Lucy to her most active role in confronting deprivation: he inspires her not only to tell her tale but, in the twilight of her life, *to write* her tale. In so doing, Lucy will not passively withdraw to a Carmelite convent to count her beads; or haunt l'allée défendue "revêche comme une religieuse" (V, 155); or hang in a museum "flat, dead, pale and formal" (V, 287), "cold and vapid as ghosts" (V, 288), like the women whose submission and silence Lucy ultimately rejects.

The "open" ending of *Villette*, which Garrett Stewart has called the Victorian period's "most notorious flouting of the conventional death scene," is Lucy's final act of authorial control over the telling of her life story. She ultimately leaves it to the reader to decide Paul's fate.[42] Like Rochester, Paul is compelled to go on a voyage to the West Indies to secure his "family's" interest. Before his departure, he sets Lucy to her tasks at Numéro 7, Faubourg Clotilde:

> "you shall live here and have a school; you shall employ yourself while I am away; you shall think of me sometimes; you shall mind your health and happiness for my sake, and when I come back—"
> There he left a blank. (V, 714)

Paul leaves Lucy with a "blank" to be filled in upon his return, and, in like manner, the time apportioned for his return is signaled by a hiatus or "blank" in the text. When Lucy takes up her pen again, she writes in the present tense and present day: three years have passed and "he is coming" (V, 714).

Lucy's anticipation of Paul's arrival is the last specific mention of him in the text; when she returns to a retrospective past tense to give an account of the Atlantic storm that has strewn the ocean floor with wrecks, Paul is significantly absent, though readers generally infer that Paul's ship was one of those wrecked. But Lucy will not tell us. Refusing any literal representation of Paul's death, she guarantees that, in her narrative at least, he is *ever* coming—even in absence, ever present. Roland Barthes suggests that to stage absence in language is "to remove the death of the other [. . .] to manipulate absence is to prolong the moment [. . .] where the other will move from absence to death." Lucy maintains that Paul's absence has been the "three happiest years of my life" (V, 711): she is the faithful steward of his property and a successful schoolmistress, sustained in the knowledge of his faithful love for her. In her narrative she prolongs this absence indefinitely. She stages what Steven Vine has called "preservative textual encryptment," thereby making Paul "more my own" (V, 714).[43]

Lucy's authorial control in staging an "open" ending (and, therefore, no ending at all) counters her powerlessness as a participant in that ending, a watcher of the storm: "wander as I may through the house this night," she attests, "I cannot lull the blast" (V, 715). The experiencing self cannot control the storm, but the narrating self can control the representation of it. As the teller of the tale, she can, like Christ at Galilee, command the sea to quiet, "Peace, be still!" and conclude that what she has imparted to us is "enough said" (V, 715).[44] Throughout her narrative, Lucy has acknowledged the providentiality of her storm-tossed life and of the "shipwrecks" that twice bereave her. At the commencement of the long vacation, Lucy remarks, "I concluded it to be part of his great plan that some must deeply suffer while they live, and I thrilled in the certainty that of this number, I was one" (V, 220). Elizabeth Gaskell concluded that Charlotte also "believed some were appointed beforehand to sorrow and much disappointment; that it did not fall to the lot of all—as Scripture told us—to have their lines fall in pleasant places; that it was well for those who had rougher paths to perceive that such was God's will concerning them, and try to moderate their expectations, leaving hope to those of a different doom, and seeking patience and resignation as the virtues they were to cultivate." The process of writing for both Lucy and Charlotte in the aftermath of deprivation is not simply to come to terms with loss, but to accept that loss as God's will and to be consoled by a Father who loveth, even as he chasteneth. Lucy's refusal to let Paul "die" in the text is not necessarily a refusal to accept God's will, nor a denial or deferral of the truth, but an assertion of a higher truth. "He is coming" is a statement of narrative consolation highly charged with religious overtones—in Tennyson's words, "Of comfort clasp'd in truth revealed."[45]

The ending of *Villette* anticipates the coming of "Emmanuel" with whom Lucy and all Christian pilgrims will make an everlasting home and enjoy an everlasting life: "for final home His bosom, who 'dwells in the height of Heaven;' for crowning prize a glory, exceeding and eternal. Let us so run that we may obtain; let us endure hardness as good soldiers; let us finish our course, and keep the faith, reliant in the issue to come off more than conquerors: 'Art thou not from everlasting mine Holy One? WE SHALL NOT DIE!'" (V, 634-35).[46] The conclusion of *Villette*, then, is a profession of faith in the constancy of "Emmanuel," who is both M. Paul and God the Father, and who is, for the "faithful steward" Lucy, "her Christian hero" (V, 577), her Greatheart leading her to the Celestial City—"with us" even in—and beyond—suffering and death.[47] This is also the belief that closes Charlotte Brontë's other female autobiography, *Jane Eyre*, exemplified by the Greatheart St. John Rivers, who responds to the coming of his own death with "faith steadfast," declaring, like his namesake at the conclusion of the Book of Revelation, "'Amen; even so come, Lord Jesus!'" (JE, 579).

Peter Allan Dale has argued that, as Protestants and descendants of Bunyan, both Charlotte and Lucy have always understood that "it is in the Word that salvation lies." Salvation also lies in the writing of their own words. Unlike Dale, I believe that the two are not incompatible: the latter gives testimony to the former, and both sustain.[48] With faith in the saving potential of the Word and their own words, Charlotte and Lucy can live—and, more important, write—with loss. Lucy will not be a "woe-struck and selfish woman" like Miss Marchmont, grieving away her life after the death of her lover (V, 55). With faith in and love for Emanuel, Lucy discovers a new self: she is no longer "desperate, nor yet desolate; not friendless, not hopeless, not sick of life, and seeking death" (V, 697).

Lyndall Gordon has suggested that, in Lucy Snowe's love for Paul Emanuel—a love that transcends absence and death and provides, as Christ does, "real food that nourished, living water that refreshed" (V, 594)—Charlotte Brontë projected her own dream of love: "She wanted a love which could sustain itself as a spur to action—or a spur to art."[49]

Charlotte had felt this kind of love: she had felt it for her "master" Monsieur Heger; she had felt it to some extent in her relationships with George Smith and James Taylor; and perhaps, had she lived, her marriage to Arthur Bell Nicholls would have continued to spur her writing. But, above all, Charlotte Brontë had known this kind of love in the intense family affection she shared with her siblings: it had underlain her Angrian partnership with Branwell and her publishing efforts with Emily and Anne. *Villette* testifies to the enduring power of these loves as spurs to art.

Conclusion
Life after *Villette*

LUCY SNOWE SPENDS THE "three happiest years of my life" (*V*, 711) in self-sufficient employment but always in anticipation of M. Paul's return and the reunion that will preface their marital union. The autonomy forced upon her by Paul's death is not what Lucy desires, but it is what she endures. Selfhood without Paul and the prospect of shared domestic tranquility is not the blank void that Mina Laury and Caroline Helstone fear—but neither is it complete. This is why Lucy constructs her narrative so that Paul is ever coming: as she sustains herself through writing, Lucy provides her own narrative consolation—the promise of earthly and spiritual communion with "Emanuel."

Following the publication and generally favorable reception of *Villette*, Charlotte Brontë continued to find sustenance in her writing. Still perhaps unsure of how to begin without her sisters to consult, she revisited a recurrent theme of the juvenilia, which she had featured in the opening chapters of the yet-unpublished *Professor*. The same violent sibling rivalry that occurred between the industrial tyrant Edward and his dependent younger brother, William, links the fragments that constitute "The Story of Willie Ellin," written between April and July 1853. In November, however, Charlotte began anew, turning from two contentious brothers to a solitary girl. In "Emma," William Ellin figures as an enigmatic gentleman observer in the drama that unfolds. A Mr. Fitzgibbon arrives at an English girls' school and presents a "new pupil in the shape of his daughter." To the mistress of the boarding school, Matilda is a show pupil, displayed for her finery and given preferential treatment for her fortune, which leaves the child isolated and despised by the other pupils. Her manner is detached, which the pupils take for airs, but she suffers from bouts of sleepwalking and nervous fits, which suggests that some mental anguish lies at the root of the girl's alienation. The crisis comes when the child's father is revealed to be a phoney, his name and address untraceable, and the girl is declared an "impostor." She is, in the eyes of the schoolmistress, "no longer acceptable" because no longer in possession of a stately name and grand fortune. With this verdict rendered against her, it is clear how completely family connections have defined Matilda Fitzgibbon. As Lyndall Gordon has remarked, "if her father does not exist, her own identity, her very existence is called into question."[1]

The manuscript of "Emma" ends with a climatic scene in which the schoolmistress demands of the child, "Who are you?" Overcome and unable to answer, the girl can only utter a cry and fall until Mr. Ellin gathers from the floor "what had fallen on it."[2] At this moment of interrogation, the child, in the manner of Lucy Snowe, endures a metaphorical death of the family, a shocking blow that leaves her adrift, both socially and mentally. Visibly traumatized, she cannot speak; she cannot say who she is without the referential family support. She has stood upon her family connection as the foundation of her identity, and, now stripped of her position, she falls, literally and metaphorically. In the narrative, the child is reduced from a "who" to a "what," a degradation that none of Charlotte Bronte's heroines have had to endure, not even Lucy Snowe, to whom is put the same question, "Who are you?" Gordon has observed that "who" is a social identity granted to the girl based on who her father is. Deprived of this identification, society, in the form of the schoolmistress, can only see her as a "what." Matilda Fitzgibbon stands in the most anomalous position of Charlotte's female characters. She is most fully orphaned, with no surrogate family like the Reeds or the Brettons, no given role, no defining community at all. Charlotte Brontë is setting new boundaries here, and, with her last novel fragment, she tantalizes the reader with how she would have sent this orphan out into the world. Still, in the child's journey of self-development, another mysterious family background promises to play a pivotal role.

This last period of writing was interrupted by a wedding. Although Charlotte Brontë referred to marriage as one of the "fearful alternatives" for her fictional heroine Lucy Snowe, it was one that she herself embraced. The years 1853 and 1854 saw the proposal, rejection, continuing courtship, and eventual acceptance of Arthur Bell Nicholls, Patrick Brontë's curate. In the end, Charlotte was not asked to make the transfer from her father's house to her husband's. She and Nicholls lived with Charlotte's father in the parsonage, her childhood home and the setting in which she had produced her art. But though the setting was the same, the family was significantly different, and the freedom to write was necessarily hindered as increased daughterly and now wifely duties were pressed upon her.

In April 1860, *Cornhill Magazine* published "Emma" as the last fragment of the dearly departed authoress Charlotte Brontë. Public sentiment for Charlotte was high following Elizabeth Gaskell's 1857 biography, which presented Charlotte as an icon of suffering familial devotion. In a preface to "Emma," William Thackeray drew on Gaskell's sentimental portrait of "that family of poets in their solitude yonder on the gloomy northern moors." He then recounted the following scene: "One evening, at the close of 1854, as Charlotte Nicholls sat with her husband by the fire, listening to the howling of the wind about the house, she suddenly said to her husband, 'If you had not been with me, I must have been writing now.' She then ran upstairs, and brought down, and read aloud, the beginning of a new tale."[3] It is difficult to read Charlotte's comment to her husband without inferring a tone of nostalgia, a longing for the past, even for the recent past when, alone and grieving over the loss of her siblings, she was at least fulfilling her vocation as a writer. But it is clear that she did not mean to give up her vocation. She did not mean to choose between being a wife and being a writer, and this scene records her attempt to be both. In it, Charlotte does not sit resigned by the fireside but jumps up to retrieve her work and present it for critical review. Charlotte turned to her husband as she had her sisters; she read to him aloud and asked his opinion of her work-in-progress, seeking from her new family the support and spur that she had always enjoyed in her original family environment. But with his mundane comments, the husband proved to be a poor substitute for the sibling critics on whom Charlotte had depended and with whom she had written some of the greatest works of literature in the English language.

Even after the deaths of her siblings, Charlotte Brontë still understood herself as an author animated by the domestic circle. But her new domestic circle did not seem to provide the incentive that her family of origin had provided, and thus Charlotte's decision to marry Nicholls is viewed by many as a tragic silencing or interment. Marriage was but one alternative in her life journey; Charlotte Brontë recognized this, and it was the alternative that she embraced until her death. In the few months of her marriage, she tried to realize herself fully as a wife, as she had, in the past, realized herself fully as an author. Whether or not her life with

Arthur Bell Nicholls would have eventually allowed for the kind of creativity that she shared with her siblings—whether her marital family would have come to assist her writing—will continue to be debated.

For the Brontë siblings, it could be said that without the family, there would have been no writing. The family enabled their art and underpinned their literary achievements. The very phrase "We are three sisters," by which the Brontës were first made known to the world (or, at least, to a publishing house in London) encapsulates the interdependence of identity, family relationship, and writing that was fundamental to their experiences as authors. In life and in fiction, the Brontës recognized that family was crucial in defining the self.

There is, in the end, no common Brontë "vision" of the family or verdict on contemporary family life. Rather, this study has shown that the Brontës recognized the multifaceted nature of the family—what it offered the individual, what it denied, what it suppressed, how it controlled and contained, how it excluded, how it fulfilled. In drawing out these distinctions, I have hoped to open the framework in which we read the Brontës and to emphasize the importance of the family as a formative community in the Brontës' fictional journeys of self-development and self-discovery. To approach the novels with a strict notion of the Brontës as revolutionary feminists and a preconception of female experience in the Victorian family as unilaterally imprisoning, repressive, and unfulfilling is to underestimate the complexity of Jane Eyre, the "rebel" who ultimately finds self-fulfillment as a wife and mother. It is to miss the paradox of Wuthering Heights, which is viewed by Catherine Earnshaw simultaneously as a haven and a prison. It is to overlook the doubleness of Helen Huntingdon, who is both the domestic violator and ideal mother. And it is to suppress the contradictions of Caroline Helstone, who is at once Charlotte Brontë's strongest voice advocating female employment beyond the domestic sphere and a character who overwhelmingly longs to be a "relative creature." Through these complexities, the Brontës continue to challenge our readings and our understanding of them as mid-Victorian women.

ABBREVIATIONS IN NOTES

Works and persons frequently cited have been identified by the following abbreviations:

AB	Anne Brontë
Alexander, *EEW*	*An Edition of the Early Writings of Charlotte Brontë*. Ed. Christine Alexander. Oxford: Basil Blackwell, Vol. 1, 1987; Vol. 2, parts 1 and 2, 1991.
Alexander, *EW*	Christine Alexander, *The Early Writings of Charlotte Brontë*. Oxford: Basil Blackwell, 1983.
BB	Branwell Brontë
BST	*Brontë Society Transactions*
CB	Charlotte Brontë
EB	Emily Brontë
EG	Elizabeth Gaskell
ELH	*English Literary History*
EN	Ellen Nussey
GS	George Smith
LCB	Elizabeth Gaskell, *The Life of Charlotte Brontë*. Ed. Elizabeth Jay. London: Penguin, 1997.
PB	Patrick Brontë
PMLA	*Publications of the Modern Language Association*
RES	*Review of English Studies*
SEL	*Studies in English Literature, 1500–1900*

Smith	*The Letters of Charlotte Brontë with a Selection of Letters by Family and Friends*, Vol. 1, 1829–1847, Vol. 2, 1848–1851. Ed. Margaret Smith. Oxford: Clarendon, 1995, 2000.
WS	*The Brontës: Their Lives, Friendships and Correspondence.* Ed. T. J. Wise and J. A. Symington. 4 vols. Oxford: Basil Blackwell, 1932.
WSW	William Smith Williams

Whenever possible when quoting from Brontë correspondence, I have used the more reliable *Letters of Charlotte Brontë*, edited by Margaret Smith. For correspondence not found in Smith or dated 1852 or later, I have consulted Juliet Barker's *The Brontës: A Life in Letters* and, only in the last instance, Wise and Symington's less accurate *The Brontës: Their Lives, Friendships and Correspondence*.

NOTES

Introduction: Family as Context and Content

1. [Ellen Nussey], "Reminiscences of Charlotte Brontë," 31; rpt. in Smith, 1:601; Juliet Barker's final sentence reads, "Without this intense family relationship, some of the greatest novels in the English language would never have been written" (*The Brontës*, 830).
2. See, for example, Maurianne Adams, "Family Disintegration and Creative Reintegration: The Case of Charlotte Brontë and *Jane Eyre*," in *The Victorian Family: Structure and Stresses*, ed. Anthony S. Wohl, 148–79; Robert Keefe, *Charlotte Brontë's World of Death*; Dianne F. Sadoff, *Monsters of Affection: Dickens, Eliot and Brontë on Fatherhood*; and Irene Tayler, *Holy Ghosts: The Male Muses of Emily and Charlotte Brontë*.
3. I have taken the term *defining community* from the philosopher Charles Taylor, *Sources of the Self: The Making of Modern Identity*, 36. Taylor asserts that identity formation and self-understanding require a referential context: "One is a self only among other selves. A self can never be described without reference to those who surround it" (35).
4. Preface, *JE*, xxxi; CB to EG, September 20, 1851, Smith, 2:695. CB criticizes an anonymous article on the enfranchisement of women in the *Westminster Review* 55 (July 1851): 289–311, saying, "I think the writer forgets that there is such a thing as self-sacrificing love and disinterested devotion." CB mistakenly believed that the article was written by John Stuart Mill, but it was, in fact, written by his collaborator, Harriet Taylor, whom he married in April 1851.
5. Paula Marantz Cohen, *The Daughter's Dilemma: Family Process and the Nineteenth-Century Domestic Novel*, 5.
6. Jenni Calder, *Women and Marriage in Victorian Fiction*, 9.
7. Catherine Waters, *Dickens and the Politics of the Family*, 20; Sarah Ellis, *The Women of England: Their Social Duties, and Domestic Habits*, 155.
8. Susan Fraiman, *Unbecoming Women: British Women Writers and the Novel of Development*, 144.
9. Caroline Helstone's inability to leave the domestic environment despite her desire for self-development in the larger world is the critical focus of her frustrated bildung.
10. I have recognized the protagonists as Jane Eyre, Catherine Earnshaw, Agnes Grey, Helen Huntingdon, William Crimsworth, Caroline Helstone, and Lucy Snowe.
11. Tom Winnifrith argues, for example, that "vague references to the Brontës working together and a natural tendency to regard the three sisters as one author should be balanced against the considerable differences between the three novelists and their novels" (*A New Life of Charlotte Brontë*, 75). Elizabeth Langland also maintains, "We shall do most justice to each sister if we acknowledge the differences rather than persist in a romantic myth of oneness" (*Anne Brontë: The Other One*, 41).

Notes

CHAPTER ONE
The Victorian Context: Self, Family, and Society

1. See Lawrence Stone, *The Family, Sex and Marriage in England 1500–1800*; Randolph Trumbach, *The Rise of the Egalitarian Family: Aristocratic Kinship and Domestic Relations in Eighteenth-Century England*; Peter Laslett and Richard Wall, *Household and Family in Past Time;* Alan MacFarlane, *Marriage and Love in England: Modes of Reproduction 1300–1840*.

2. Jean-Louis Flandrin, *Families in Former Times: Kinship, Household and Sexuality*, trans. Richard Southern, 4.

3. Ibid., 5.

4. James Mill, *Analysis of the Phenomena of the Human Mind*, 2:176; Stone, *Family, Sex and Marriage*, 147, 22.

5. When Tabby suffered a severe fracture in her leg, CB expressed to EN her distress at the occurrence, "for she was like one of our own family" (December 29, 1836, Smith, 1:159).

6. Penny Kane has noted that a high proportion of children in mid-Victorian England did not grow up in the presence of both their natural parents: "About a third of households in the 1851 Census did not contain a household head together with a spouse" (*Victorian Families in Fact and Fiction*, 2).

7. Steven Mintz, *A Prison of Expectations: The Family in Victorian Culture*, 3; Cohen, *Daughter's Dilemma*, 10; John Ruskin, "Of Queen's Gardens," in *The Works of John Ruskin*, ed. E. T. Cook and Alexander Wedderburn, 18:122.

8. Stone, *Family, Sex and Marriage*, 422–24.

9. Charles Dickens, *Great Expectations*, 208. Friedrich Engels, *The Origin of the Family, Private Property, and the State: In the Light of the Researches of Lewis H. Morgan*, examines changing family structures in relation to the rise of capitalism and private property and forms the basis for many Marxist studies of the family. Stone, *Family, Sex and Marriage*, 22.

10. See Jeffrey Weeks, *Sex, Politics and Society: the Regulation of Sexuality since 1800*.

11. PB delivered a speech against the New Poor Law to overflowing attendance at a meeting in the Haworth Sunday school room on February 22, 1837. The speech was printed in the *Times*, February 27, 1837: 6. For PB's disputes with Dissenters in the 1830s and 1840s, see Barker, *The Brontës*, 217–18, 240–41, 257–58.

12. Ruskin, "Of Queen's Gardens," 122; Catherine Gallagher, *The Industrial Reformation of English Fiction: Social Discourse and Narrative Form, 1832–1867*, 114–15. Gallagher explores the paradox specifically in industrial reform literature of the 1850s and 1860s, which encouraged society to be made similar to the family but maintained that it could be made similar only if the family remains isolated from, and uncorrupted by, the very society it sought to reform.

13. Louis Aimé-Martin, *The Education of Mothers of Families; or, The Civilisation of the Human Race by Women*, trans. Edwin Lee, 19; Mintz, *Prison of Expectations*, 28.

14. Philippe Ariès, *Centuries of Childhood*, trans. Robert Baldick, 10; George Potter, "The First Point of the New Charter: Improved Dwellings for the People," 555.

15. Jacques Donzelot, *The Policing of Families*, trans. Robert Hurley, 45.

16. In his study of the historical transformations of the word *family*, Raymond Williams notes that its use in the sense of aristocratic lineage extended into the nineteenth century: "Class distinction was expressed as late as the nineteenth century (and residually beyond it) in phrases like 'a person of no family,'" (*Keywords: A Vocabulary of Culture and Society*, 132). In *AG*, Rosalie Murray speaks of one of her suitors as being "rich enough, but of no family" (81). This comment is clearly intended to be a criticism of her class snobbery and an indication that she has not been raised in a good family.

17. Marianne Farningham, *Home Life*, 111; Alexander Scott, *Suggestions on Female Education: Two Introductory Lectures on English Literature and Moral Philosophy*, 52. See CB to WSW, March 19, 1850, Smith, 2:364–65.

18. Ariès traces an increasing attention to child development from the eighteenth centu-

ry. See *Centuries of Childhood*, part 1; Elisabeth Jay's discussion of Evangelical notions of childhood, *The Religion of the Heart: Anglican Evangelicalism and the Nineteenth-Century Novel*, 55–56, 139–42; Prov. 22:6; Legh Richmond, *Domestic Portraiture; or, The Successful Application of Religious Principle in the Education of a Family, Exemplified in the Memoirs of Three of the Deceased Children of the Rev. Legh Richmond, with a Few Introductory Remarks on Christian Education, by the Rev. E. Bickersteth*, 43; "My heart leaps up when I behold" (1807), *The Norton Anthology of Poetry*, 3d ed. (New York: Norton, 1983), 551.

19. Jay, *Religion of the Heart*, 139; Richmond, *Domestic Portraiture*, 15.

20. Richmond, *Domestic Portraiture*, 4; Benjamin Hershel Babbage, *Report to the General Board of Health on a Preliminary Inquiry into the Sewerage, Drainage, and Supply of Water, and Sanitary Condition of the Inhabitants of the Hamlet in Haworth, in the West Riding of the County of York*, 26. See Barker, *The Brontës*, 136–37.

21. For example, girls played with dolls and needlebooks; boys played with hoops and balls. Boys were taught to swim and dive, while vigorous outdoor activities were discouraged for girls as "unladylike." Leonore Davidoff and Catherine Hall, *Family Fortunes: Men and Women of the English Middle Class, 1780–1850*, 344–45.

22. George Eliot, *The Mill on the Floss*, 9, 12.

23. Hannah More, "Thoughts on the Cultivation of the Heart and Temper in the Education of Daughters," *Essays on Various Subjects, Principally Designed for Young Ladies*, 145; 1 Tim. 2:9–15.

24. Richmond, *Domestic Portraiture*, 137; Nancy Armstrong, *Desire and Domestic Fiction: A Political History of the Novel*, 17; Felicia Hemans, "The Homes of England," (ll. 33, 39–40), 392. The poem first appeared in *Blackwood's Edinburgh Magazine* in April 1827. The parsonage received *Blackwood's* from 1825 onward, so it is likely that the Brontës saw the poem in its first instance.

25. Aimé-Martin, *Education of Mothers*, 19.

26. A Woman, *Woman's Rights and Duties*, 397.

27. Harriet Martineau, *Household Education*, 269.

28. LCB, 42, 34, xxiii; Barker, *The Brontës*, 796; [John Skelton], "Charlotte Brontë," 570; review of LCB, 90.

29. See Barker, *The Brontës*, 107–10; Helene Moglen, *Charlotte Brontë: The Self Conceived*, 33–34; Barker, *The Brontës: A Life in Letters*, 266–71; LCB, 39.

30. Winifred Gérin, *Branwell Brontë*, 2.

31. Mintz, *Prison of Expectations*, 50.

32. In the advertisement to *The Rural Minstrel: A Miscellany of Descriptive Poems* (1813), for example, PB assures his readers that he "proceeded, according to the best of his conscience and judgment, endeavouring, as nearly as he could, to copy after the great Apostle, *who became all things to all men, that he might by all means save some*" (*Brontëana: The Rev. Patrick Brontë, A. B., His Collected Works and Life*, 71); 1 Tim. 2:11–15; Tayler, *Holy Ghosts*, 275–76.

33. LCB, 41. See also PB's and EG's reading of Day's *History of Sandford and Merton* (1783–1789), a best-selling children's tale promoting moral education and the appeal to reason, LCB, 461n17; Hannah More, *Moral Sketches of Prevailing Opinions and Manners, Foreign and Domestic: With Reflections on Prayer*, xvii. Barker, *The Brontës*, 145–46, notes that PB purchased this edition in Thornton and that the inscription on the flyleaf, though virtually erased, includes his signature and the dates 1819 and March 1820.

34. See Tom Winnifrith, *The Brontës and Their Background: Romance and Reality*, 31. Winnifrith notes that there were also impressive theological collections in the library at Ponden House and the Keighley Mechanics's Institute, from which the Brontës may have borrowed books, as well as in the library at Thorp Green, where AB and BB taught the Reverend Robinson's children. I am grateful to Ann Dinsdale, librarian at the Brontë Parsonage Museum, for providing a list of "Books belonging to or inscribed by Members of the Brontë Family and held in the Brontë Parsonage Museum." For a list of biblical allusions in CB's novels, see *P*, appendix 7, index A, 326–30.

35. CB to EN, June 1837, Smith, 1:171–72. According to Smith, CB may have known that her father had heard Richmond preach at a Church Missionary service in Bradford on November 7, 1817.
36. PB to EG, July 30, 1855, LCB, 46–47.
37. Ibid., 47. Lyndall Gordon maintains that Elizabeth was "designed for a future as a housekeeper by her father's decision to educate her at a lower standard than the others" (*Charlotte Brontë: A Passionate Life*, 14). In the Clergy Daughters' School's register, "governess" is written under the category "For what educated" next to the name of each girl, except for Elizabeth. See Barker, *Life in Letters*, 6–7.
38. *The Maid of Killarney*, *Brontëana*, 178.
39. Jean-Jacques Rousseau, *Émile*, trans. Barbara Foxley, 393.
40. Barker, *The Brontës*, 105. This was PB's salary at the time of his wife's death.
41. December 4, 1823, quoted in Barker, *The Brontës*, 118.
42. See Edward Chitham's chapter "Learning's Golden Mine," in *The Birth of Wuthering Heights: Emily Brontë at Work*, 17–32, for a detailed discussion of EB's knowledge of Latin. See Barker, *The Brontës*, 145–47, for a discussion of the books PB used in his home instruction.
43. William Makepeace Thackeray to WSW, October 23, 1847, Barker, *Life in Letters*, 171.
44. Chitham, *Birth of Wuthering Heights*, 18.
45. Gérin, *Branwell Brontë*, 24; More, *Moral Sketches*, 81; Jay, *Religion of the Heart*, 142.
46. Elaine Showalter, *A Literature of Their Own from Charlotte Brontë to Doris Lessing*, 21.
47. Robert Southey to CB, March 12, 1837, Smith, 1:166–67; CB to WSW, June 15, 1848, Smith, 2:73. See CB to EN, January 23, 1844, and March 24, 1845, in which she insists that it is her "duty" to restrain her feelings of discontentment at home, where she is needed to care for an ailing PB while BB and AB were employed at Thorp Green. Nevertheless, CB admits that she longs "to travel—to work to live a life of action" (Smith, 1:341, 385).
48. CB to Southey, March 16, 1837, Smith, 1:169.
49. CB to EG, August 27, 1850, Smith, 2:457.
50. Ann Richelieu Lamb, *Can Woman Regenerate Society?* 43; Mrs. Hugo Reid, *A Plea for Woman: Being a Vindication of the Importance and Extent of Her Natural Sphere of Action*, 27, 28.
51. CB to WSW, May 12, 1848, Smith, 2:66.
52. CB makes reference to salt water–stained copies of the *Lady's Magazine* in S (440). In a December 1840 draft of a letter to Hartley Coleridge, CB writes that her aunt "thinks the tales of the Lady's Magazine infinitely superior to any trash of Modern Literature. So do I for I read them in childhood and childhood has a very strong faculty of admiration but a very weak one of Criticism" (Smith, 1:237). *Lady's Magazine* was the only reading matter to be censored by PB, who burnt CB's copies "because they contained foolish love stories" (CB to Coleridge, December 10, 1843, Smith, 1:240).
See CB's letters to Hartley Coleridge for evidence of her familiarity with Richardson's novels, Smith, 1:236–42.
53. CB to WSW, January 10, 1850, Smith, 2:328; Sarah Ellis, "Review of *Shirley*, by the Author of *Jane Eyre*," 34–35.
54. CB to GS, March 16, 1850, Smith, 2:359. Making another connection between the Brontës and Sarah Ellis, Marianne Thormählen, "The Brontë Pseudonyms," suggests Ellis as the source for Emily's pseudonym, but there is no conclusive evidence that Emily read any of her works.
55. CB to WSW, February 1, 1849, Smith, 2:174, reports that AB is reading one of Bremer's tales. CB to EG, November 6, 1851, Smith, 2:711, discusses Bremer's works.
56. The list is transcribed in Barker, *The Brontës*, 948, and Smith, 2:361. See CB to WSW, April 12, 1850, Smith, 2:383.
57. Harriet Björk, *The Language of Truth: Charlotte Brontë, The Woman Question, and the Novel*, 17; CB to EG, August 27, 1850, Smith, 2:457.
58. Mary Taylor to CB, July 24, 1848, Smith, 2:87.
59. Mary Taylor, *Miss Miles, or A Tale of Yorkshire Life Sixty Years Ago*, 112.
60. Review of *Wuthering Heights* and *Agnes Grey*, 59; E. P. Whipple, "Novels of the Sea-

Notes 219

son," 368; [Elizabeth Rigby], review of *Vanity Fair, Jane Eyre* and the Governesses' Benevolent Institution, 173; [Margaret Oliphant], "Novels," 258, 259.

61. See the Clarendon editors' note to page 117, (S, 755–56). The excised passages are located in S, 117–18, 194–95, and appeared in *The Englishwoman's Domestic Magazine* 4 (1856), and the *Times Literary Supplement* 1 (July 1920): 423–24.

62. William Rathbone Greg, "Why Are Women Redundant?" 451.

63. Mary Wollstonecraft, *A Vindication of the Rights of Woman: With Strictures on Political and Moral Subjects*, 346–47; Martineau, *Household Education*, 215, 241–43.

64. According to Greg, "Why Are Women Redundant?" 441, in England and Wales in 1851 there were 1,248,000 unmarried women between the ages of 20 and 40 out of less than 3,000,000.

65. Martineau, *Household Education*, 243–44. In her autobiography, Martineau recorded, "'Currer Bell' told me . . . that she had read with astonishment those parts of 'Household Education' which relate my own experience," noting the affinity with her own ideas and feelings (Martineau, *Autobiography*, 2:324).

66. CB to WSW, July 3, 1849, Smith, 2:226; CB to Margaret Wooler, January 30, 1846, Smith, 1:448.

67. CB to WSW, July 3, 1849, Smith, 2:226; CB to WSW, June 15, 1848, Smith, 2:72.

68. CB to WSW, July 3, 1849, Smith, 2:226; CB to WSW, June 15, 1848, Smith, 2:73.

69. CB to WSW, July 3, 1849, Smith, 2:227; Armstrong, *Desire and Domestic Fiction*, 192.

CHAPTER TWO
The Family Context: Writing as Sibling Relationship

1. Andrew Elfenbein, *Byron and the Victorians*, 127. See Elfenbein's chapter on "Byron at the Margins: Emily Brontë and the Fate of Milo" for a thoughtful discussion of the Brontë family as a site of sibling and textual rivalries.

2. Shari Benstock quoted in Whitney Chadwick and Isabelle de Courtivron, *Significant Others: Creativity and Intimate Partnership*, 9; Sandra M. Gilbert and Susan Gubar, *The Madwoman in the Attic: The Woman Writer and the Nineteenth-Century Literary Imagination*, 251.

3. Elfenbein, *Byron and the Victorians*, 145. Elfenbein considers WH as a response to the "chilly realism" in *P*. For other criticism that considers the novels as commentaries on one another, see Margaret Mary Berg, "*The Tenant of Wildfell Hall*: Anne Brontë's *Jane Eyre*?" 10–15; and Langland, *Anne Brontë*, chapter 2—both of which consider TWH as a response to JE. Edward Chitham discusses TWH as AB's "corrective" to WH, "Diverging Twins: Some Clues to Wildfell Hall," in *Brontë Facts and Brontë Problems*, 91–109. Barbara Prentis, *The Brontë Sisters and George Eliot: A Unity of Difference*, 172.

4. Gilbert and Gubar, *Madwoman*, 83. Although EB did not spend prolonged periods away from home either as a student or a teacher, she was hardly a prisoner in the parsonage. Few daughters of clergymen could boast of being educated on the Continent, as EB was in Brussels. She was also allowed and greatly enjoyed an unchaperoned holiday to York with AB in June 1845.

EB's diary papers reveal her personal wishes for the maintenance of the family community. On June 26, 1837, she writes, "I guess this day 4 years we shall all be in this drawing room comfortable I hope it may be so" (*BST* 12 [1951]: 15). Four years later this is still her desire, as she happily muses on the sisters' plan to open a school together: "I guess that at the time appointed for the opening of this paper—we (i.e.) Charlotte, Anne and I—shall be all merrily seated in our own sitting-room in some pleasant and flourishing seminary, having just gathered in for the midsummer holyday" (July 30, 1841, Smith, 1:262). CB to EN, March 12, 1839, Smith, 1:187.

5. "Reminiscences of Charlotte Brontë," Smith, 1:589; Prefatory note to "Selections from

Poems by Ellis Bell," Smith, 2:753; Smith, 1:263; CB to EN, July 1, 1841, Smith, 1:258; CB to EN, August 7, 1841, and January 24, 1840, Smith, 1:266, 210.

6. There is extensive documentation of this phenomenon: Edward Chitham charts the occurrences of AB's Gondal and personal poems, noting the decline in turnout during her time as a governess. See "Table of Anne Brontë's Poems," in Chitham, *The Poems of Anne Brontë: A New Text and Commentary*, appendix 4 (a), 205–8. Derek Roper, *The Poems of Emily Brontë*, 2, notes that during the months EB spent in Brussels (February–November 1842), she completed only two poems and began only two. Alexander, *EW*, 139–45, has observed that CB mostly jotted down fragments in her spare moments while teaching at Margaret Wooler's school (July 1835–May 1838). For a time line of BB's juvenilia (though not a complete one), see Barbara Lloyd Evans and Gareth Lloyd Evans, *Everyman's Companion to the Brontës*.

7. January 1836, "Well here I am at Roe-Head," quoted in Barker, *The Brontës*, 249.

8. CB to Henry Nussey, May 9, 1841, Smith, 1:255.

9. PB to EG, July 30, 1855, *BST* 8 (1932): 94; Robert G. Collins, *The Hand of the Arch Sinner: Two Angrian Chronicles of Branwell Brontë*, xxi; PB to EG, July 24, 1855, *BST* (1932) 8: 92. See *The History of the Year*, "The Origin of the O'Deans," and "The Origin of the Islanders," all written on March 12, 1829, Alexander, *EEW*, 1:4–6.

10. See Alexander, general introduction to *EEW*, 1:xviii–xix.

11. "Biographical Notice of Ellis and Acton Bell," Smith, 2: 742.

12. In another of the early plays, known as the "Islanders' Play," the siblings appear as "Little King and Queens," a role comparable to the Genii in the Young Men's Play. The Young Men and Islanders developed concurrently for over a year until October 1830, when they emerge as the "single imaginary vision" of Glass Town (Alexander, *EW*, 53). *The History of the Young Men from Their First Settlement to the Present Time* (December 15, 1830–May 7, 1831), in *The Works of Patrick Branwell Brontë: An Edition*, vol. 1, *1827–1833*, ed. Victor A. Neufeldt, 153.

13. Alexander, *EEW*, 2.1:116. When CB learns that BB has killed her heroine, Mary Percy, she rewrites his account of Mary's demise in order that she can be "made alive" again. See BB's *History of Angria 8* (September 3–19, 1836), and CB's *The Return of Zamorna* (c. December 24, 1836), in *The Miscellaneous and Unpublished Writings of Charlotte Brontë and Patrick Branwell Brontë*, vol. 2, ed. T. J. Wise and J. A. Symington, 210–21, 281–314.

14. See *Corner Dishes* (May 28–June 16, 1834), Alexander, *EEW*, 2.2:108–9. See *My Angria and the Angrians* (October 14, 1834), Alexander, *EEW*, 2.2:246–49.

15. BB had nineteen poems published in local newspapers between 1841 and 1847, eighteen of them under his pseudonym. See Collins, *The Hand of the Arch Sinner*, xv–xliii; Barker, *The Brontës*, 523.

16. July 30, 1845, Smith, 1:405.

17. Imagined as a large island in the North Pacific, Gondal also has a different physical landscape compared to the West African Glass Town and Angria. The Brontë children constantly referred to the Rev. J. Goldsmith's *Grammar of General Geography for the Use of Schools and Young Persons* (1823) in laying out their imaginary kingdoms.

18. *BST* 12 (1951): 15. The expansion of Glass Town into Angria at the beginning of 1834, for example, is followed by EB's November 24, 1834, record of the Gondals' discovery and conquest of Gaaldine, a large island in the South Pacific. See WS, 1:124. From mid-summer 1835 and into 1836, CB and BB are chronicling the Republican revolution in Angria, while EB and AB are writing about the civil war between the Republicans and the Royalists in Gondal.

19. Several of CB's novel fragments are centered on the rivalry between two brothers, repeatedly named Edward and William. See Tom Winnifrith, introduction to *Charlotte Brontë: Unfinished Novels*, for a full discussion.

20. Margaret Oliphant, "The Sisters Brontë," in *Women Novelists of Queen Victoria's Reign: A Book of Appreciations*, 9; F. B. Pinion, *A Brontë Companion: Literary Assessment, Background and Reference*, 103.

21. *Captain Henry Hastings*, in *Five Novelettes*, ed. Winifred Gérin, 225; Alexander, *EW*,

66. CB retained the habit of including poems. She used some of her own composition in P and JE. AB included her own poems in AG and TWH.
22. "Biographical Notice," Smith, 2:743.
23. "*Branwells Blackwoods Magazine* July 1829," in Neufeldt, *Works 1*, 30; Alexander, textual introduction to *EEW*, 1:xxi.
24. Alexander, *EEW*, 1:94.
25. Ibid., 126; "Lines Spoken by a Lawyer" (l. 9), Alexander, *EEW*, 1:94.
26. Neufeldt, *Works 1*, 92.
27. Ibid., 94.
28. Alexander, *EEW*, 1:181, 191.
29. Alexander, *EW*, 72; *High Life in Verdopolis* (March 20, 1834), Alexander, *EEW*, 2.2:33.
30. Barker, *The Brontës*, 204. It is clear from CB to EN, July 4, 1834, in which CB recommends a selection of reading, that she is familiar with Byron's poetry and *The Letters and Journals of Lord Byron*, with a *Life* by Thomas Moore (1830), which PB purchased in 1832. See Smith, 1:129–32.
31. Alexander, *EEW*, 1:128; Barker, *The Brontës*, 188.
32. *Characters of the Celebrated Men of the Present Time*, Alexander, *EEW*, 1:124–25.
33. Alexander, *EEW*, 2.1:208, 209, 211.
34. *The Spell*, Alexander, *EEW*, 2.2:171–72. Subsequent references are cited parenthetically in the text.
35. Sally Shuttleworth, *Charlotte Brontë and Victorian Psychology*, 119.
36. See Alexander, *EW*, 161–64.
37. *Mina Laury* (January 17, 1838), Gérin, *Five Novelettes*, 165, 147.
38. *Captain Henry Hastings*, Gérin, *Five Novelettes*, 255. Subsequent references are located parenthetically in the text. The manuscript does contain several episodes in which Zamorna and Mary discuss his infidelity with Jane Moore, but these are unrelated to the plot concerning Elizabeth and Henry Hastings.
39. *Caroline Vernon* (c. late July/early August through late November/early December 1839), Gérin, *Five Novelettes*, 354. *Henry Hastings* and *Caroline Vernon* are neither signed nor dated, though dates appear in the stories themselves. Alexander uses these to date the manuscript, "since Charlotte made a habit of setting her stories at the time of composition" (Alexander, *EW*, 198). Keefe, *Charlotte Brontë's World of Death*, 81.
40. Barker, *The Brontës*, 302–3, provides convincing evidence that BB was home by the end of February.
41. Hatfield transcript 43 (13) copied at the Brontë Parsonage Museum (summer 1996); see Neufeldt, *The Works of Patrick Branwell Brontë: An Edition*, vol. 3, 1837–1848. Fannie Elizabeth Ratchford, *The Brontës' Web of Childhood*, 146.
42. Alexander, *EW*, 189. Alexander follows the views of Ratchford and Gérin, but Barker and Tom Winnifrith question the extent to which Elizabeth's dedication to Henry is "an accurate reflection of Charlotte's feelings toward her brother" (Winnifrith, *A New Life of Charlotte Brontë*, 43).
43. CB to EN, July 4, 1834, Smith, 1:130. The Clarendon editors note borrowed phrases from *The Heart of Midlothian* in JE and S. See P, appendix 7, 333.
44. Michael Cohen, *Sisters: Relation and Rescue in Nineteenth-Century British Novels and Paintings*, 118; Helena Michie, *Sororophobia: Differences among Women in Literature and Culture*, 17.
45. "Farewell to Angria," in *The Miscellaneous and Unpublished Writings of Charlotte Brontë and Patrick Branwell Brontë*, 2:404; CB to BB, May 1, 1843, Smith, 1:317.
46. On June 26, 1837, for example, EB records, "Anne and I writing in the drawing-room— Anne a poem beginning 'Fair was the evening and brightly the stars'—I Agustus-Almeda's life 1st v. 1–4th page from the last" (*BST* 12 [1951]: 15). Eight years later, on July 31, 1845, AB notes that EB has read "Emperor Julius's life" to her and adds that EB "is writing some poetry too I wonder what it is about" (Smith, 1:410).

47. Roper provides summaries of the various reconstructions of Gondal based on the extant poetry in *The Poems of Emily Brontë*, appendix 7, 305–7, 9. EB departed for Roe Head with CB in July 1835, to be replaced by AB in October. AB remained at Roe Head until December 1837. In October 1838, EB took up a teaching post at Law Hill, returning some time in March or April. AB became a governess to the Ingham family at Blake Hall in April 1839, but she was dismissed in December. She took her second post as a governess at Thorp Green, serving from May 1840 through June 1845.

Biographers and critics often cite AB's 1845 diary paper, in which she takes a far less cheerful view of the Gondal saga than EB does in her companion 1845 paper. AB maintains, "The Gondals in general are not yet in first rate playing condition—will they improve?" (Smith, 1:410). Roper, *The Poems of Emily Brontë*, 184–92. EB attempted to revise the poem on May 13, 1848. "Z——'s Dream," in *The Poems of Anne Brontë*, 136–39.

48. "Reminiscences of Charlotte Brontë," Smith, 1:598.

49. See Chitham, *The Poems of Anne Brontë*, 35–39, 194; and Langland, *Anne Brontë*, 76; November 1847–April 17, 1848, Chitham, *The Poems of Anne Brontë*, 156–57; Chitham, "Diverging Twins: Some Clues to *Wildfell Hall*," 91–109.

50. Roper, *The Poems of Emily Brontë*, 49–50; Chitham, *The Poems of Anne Brontë*, 63–64. EB designates her speaker as A. G. Almeda, AB as Alexandrina Zenobia, but it seems clear that the two names refer to the same character.

51. See CB to EN, January 4, 1838, Smith, 1:173–74.

52. Roper, *The Poems of Emily Brontë*, 128–29; Chitham, *The Poems of Anne Brontë*, 78–79.

53. The longing for companionship is a recurrent theme in Anne's poetry. See also "The Captive Dove" (October 31, 1843), in *The Poems of Anne Brontë*, 92–93.

54. Elfenbein, *Byron and the Victorians*, 144.

55. "Biographical Notice," Smith, 2:742. Barker, *The Brontës*, 480–81, notes that fifteen of the nineteen poems that CB included for publication had Angrian origins and about half of AB's twenty-one contributions were Gondal poems. Although it is more difficult to distinguish EB's personal poems from her Gondal ones, at least fifteen of her twenty-one contributions were clearly from Gondal.

56. Adams, "Family Disintegration," 148; "Biographical Notice," Smith, 2:743; *LCB*, 234–35.

57. CB to Aylott and Jones, April 6, 1846, Smith, 1:461. See Winnifrith, "*Wuthering Heights*: One Volume or Two?" in *Brontë Facts and Brontë Problems*, 84–90; Barker, *The Brontës*, 503; and Chitham, *Birth of Wuthering Heights*, esp. 85–96.

58. *Athenaeum* (December 25, 1847): 1324; Jerome Beaty, *Misreading Jane Eyre: A Postformalist Paradigm*, 2; *Examiner* (July 29, 1848): 483.

59. "Biographical Notice," Smith, 2:744; CB to WSW, June 22, 1848, CB to Mary Taylor, September 4, 1848, Smith, 2:79, 111–15.

60. July 22, 1848, see preface in *TWH*, xxxix.

61. CB to WSW, July 31, 1848, Smith, 2:94.

62. [Sydney Dobell], "Currer Bell," 164; "Biographical Notice," Smith, 2:747, 742.

63. Nicola Thompson, "The Many Faces of *Wuthering Heights*: 1847–1997," 31–45.

64. "Biographical Notice," Smith, 2:746.

CHAPTER THREE

Jane Eyre: The Pilgrimage of the "Poor Orphan Child"

1. Gilbert and Gubar, *Madwoman*, 339. For a good discussion of the female bildungsroman, see Susan Fraiman, *Unbecoming Women: British Women Writers and the Novel of Development*.

For one of the earliest discussions of the topography of JE, see Robert Martin, *The Accents of Persuasion: Charlotte Brontë's Novels*.

2. Gilbert and Gubar, *Madwoman*, 336; Margaret Soenser Breen, "Who Are You, Lucy Snowe?: Disoriented Bildung in *Villette*," 245; Barry V. Qualls, *The Secular Pilgrims of Victorian Fiction: The Novel as Book of Life*. See *P*, appendix 7, index B, 331, for specific references to *Pilgrim's Progress*. Margaret Smith, introduction to *Jane Eyre*, xv; Jerome Beaty, "Jane Eyre at Gateshead: Mixed Signals in Text and Context," 184.

3. Rosemary M. Colt, "Innocence Unleashed: The Power of the Single Child," 11, has observed that Jane Eyre disturbs the notion of the angelic Victorian child. Her passionate outbursts and her outrage at injustice and favoritism stand in stark contrast to the martyrlike resignation of other fictional Victorian orphans, such as Dickens's Little Dorrit and David Copperfield.

4. Gayatri Chakravorty Spivak, "Three Women's Texts and a Critique of Imperialism," 246.

5. Jenni Calder, *Women and Marriage in Victorian Fiction*, 17.

6. Gilbert and Gubar, *Madwoman*, 342.

7. Natalie J. McKnight, *Suffering Mothers in Mid-Victorian Novels*, 63; Sadoff, *Monsters of Affection*, 134.

8. Beaty, "Jane Eyre at Gateshead," 184.

9. Rod Edmond, *Affairs of the Hearth: Victorian Poetry and Domestic Narrative*, 51.

10. Beginning with EG, Brontë biographers and critics generally regard Helen as a fictionalized portrait of CB's eldest sister, Maria. Helen resembles Maria in her religious beliefs and early death from consumption brought about by the poor living conditions at the Clergy Daughters' School, Cowan Bridge, on which Lowood is based. See *LCB*, 56.

11. The threat of being deprived the hope of heaven (for the pits of hell) as punishment for naughty behavior or disobedience was a common disciplinary measure in children's religious education. For a detailed discussion, see Elisabeth Jay, *The Religion of the Heart: Anglican Evangelicalism and the Nineteenth-Century Novel*, 82–88. Jay notes Mr. Brocklehurst's resemblance to the Rev. William Carus Wilson, founder of the Cowan Bridge School and a "leading figure in the Calvinist wing of Anglican Evangelicalism" (*LCB*, 462, ch. 4, n. 2). Wilson was the editor of a monthly magazine, *The Children's Friend*, which regularly employed the threat of hell to encourage Christian behavior in the young. The "Child's Guide," which Brocklehurst gives to Jane, and which contains "an account of the awfully sudden death of Martha G—, a naughty child addicted to falsehood and deceit" (*JE*, 37), is characteristic of the tone and content of *The Children's Friend*.

12. AB is normally recognized for her belief in universal salvation (which her heroine Helen Huntingdon espouses in *TWH*), but it is one to which CB also subscribed. In CB to Margaret Wooler, February 14, 1850, CB regretted that the "Clergy" objected to her espousal and endorsement of the doctrine in *JE*: "I think it a great pity for their sakes, but surely they are not so unreasonable as to expect me to deny or suppress what I believe the truth!" (Smith, 2:343). In her preface to the second edition of *JE*, she insisted that "narrow human doctrines, that only tend to elate and magnify a few, should not be substituted for the world-redeeming creed of Christ" (*JE*, xxxi). See chapters 3 and 4 in Winnifrith, *Brontës and Background*, and Marianne Thormählen's *The Brontës and Religion* for comprehensive discussions of the Brontës' belief in universal salvation and the "equality of souls."

13. I have borrowed the phrase "controlling power of the family" from Kathryn Sutherland, "*Jane Eyre*'s Literary History: The Case for *Mansfield Park*," 420.

14. Stone, *Family, Sex and Marriage*, 72.

15. Adams, "Family Disintegration," 166.

16. Gilbert and Gubar, *Madwoman*, 357.

17. Sadoff, *Monsters of Affection*, 145.

18. Gilbert and Gubar, *Madwoman*, 360.

19. See, for example, Gilbert and Gubar, *Madwoman*, 358. Moglen, *Self Conceived*, 127; and McKnight, *Suffering Mothers*, 68.

20. John Bunyan, *The Pilgrim's Progress*, 9.
21. See Michael Mason, introduction to *Jane Eyre*, vii–xxxi.
22. Beaty, *Misreading Jane Eyre*, 160.
23. Ibid., 173, 174.
24. Ibid., 171.
25. Terry Eagleton, *Myths of Power: A Marxist Study of the Brontës*, 19.
26. Smith, introduction to *Jane Eyre*, xvi.
27. Rev. 21:7–8.
28. Penny Boumelha, *Charlotte Brontë*, 27.
29. Rochester's lost hand and eye evokes the biblical injunctions against adultery and temptation in Matt. 5:27–30. Beaty, *Misreading Jane Eyre*, 207.
30. For one of many instances of this argument, see Moglen, *Self Conceived*, 141–45.

CHAPTER FOUR
Wuthering Heights: The Boundless Passion of Catherine Earnshaw

1. Lamb, *Can Woman Regenerate Society?* 122.
2. Helene Moglen, "The Double Vision of *Wuthering Heights*: A Clarifying View of Female Development," 405. Many feminist studies displace Heathcliff as the novel's protagonist in favor of Catherine. Moglen, for example, discusses the entire novel as a linear progression of female maturation, which is only finally completed by the younger Cathy. See also Carol A. Senf, "Emily Brontë's Version of Feminist History: *Wuthering Heights*."
3. Leo Bersani, *A Future for Astyanax: Character and Desire in Literature*, 205.
4. Some critics have proposed that both Heathcliff and Nelly are related to the Earnshaws by blood, being Mr. Earnshaw's illegitimate children. Eric Solomon famously accounts for Earnshaw's strange devotion to Heathcliff on the basis that he is Earnshaw's bastard son, thus suggesting that the relationship between Catherine and Heathcliff is literally, rather than symbolically, incestuous. See Solomon, "The Incest Theme in *Wuthering Heights*." U. C. Knoepflmacher, *Emily Brontë: Wuthering Heights*, 46, has suggested that Nelly is also Earnshaw's illegitimate child.
5. This point is similarly noted by Paula Marantz Cohen, who argues that Nelly occupies "the position where family and fiction intersect" (*Daughter's Dilemma*, 107).
6. Gilbert and Gubar, *Madwoman*, 290, 264.
7. Stevie Davies, *Emily Brontë*, 103.
8. Steven Vine, "The Wuther of the Other in *Wuthering Heights*," 341.
9. Elfenbein, *Byron and the Victorians*, 154.
10. This argument is reflective of my readings of Georg Wilhelm Friedrich Hegel's ideas of subject formation and desire. Judith Butler's *Subjects of Desire: Hegelian Reflections in Twentieth-Century France* examines Hegel's *Phenomenology of Spirit* (1807), in which he asserts that the self desires "to find its own identity through the Other." The "project of desire" is therefore to achieve "the negation and assimilation of otherness and the concomitant expansion of the proper domain of the subject" (Butler, *Subjects of Desire*, 52, 46).
11. This point is noted by Gilbert and Gubar, *Madwoman*, 264.
12. See Patsy Stoneman, introduction to *Wuthering Heights*, xviii.
13. Patricia Yaeger, "Violence in the Sitting Room: *Wuthering Heights* and the Woman's Novel," 226. Heathcliff's ability to manipulate is noted by Elfenbein, *Byron and the Victorians*, 163.
14. Cecil W. Davies, "A Reading of *Wuthering Heights*," 259.
15. Arnold Kettle and others have concluded, following Nelly's notion of propriety and common sense, that Catherine is "kidding herself" in thinking she can openly express her love

for both men. Kettle, *An Introduction to the English Novel*, 1:145. Q. D. Leavis, "A Fresh Approach to *Wuthering Heights*," in *Lectures in America*, insists that "Catherine's innocent refusal to see that there is anything in her relation to [Heathcliff] incompatible with her position as a wife" is "preposterous" (90).

16. Davidoff and Hall, *Family Fortunes*, 322. Like Cathy, Jane Eyre, as a child, felt stifled in her family situation and laments that she "can never get away from Gateshead till I am a woman" (*JE*, 24).

17. See Stoneman's introduction for an extensive discussion of Catherine's intention to love both men. Stoneman proposes that "Catherine's 'naïve' assumption that people could love one another without conflict" is "a tragic commentary" on the free-love ideal of Shelley's "Epipsychidion" (xxxv).

18. "Enough of Thought, Philosopher," ll. 7–10 (February 3, 1845), *The Poems of Emily Brontë*. ed. Derek Roper, 165.

19. Bersani, *Future for Astyanax*, 221.

20. "The Death of A. G. A.," ll. 78–80 (January 1841–May 1844), Roper, *Poems*, 112.

21. Davies, *Emily Brontë*, 74; Mary Jacobus, "The Question of Language: Men of Maxims and *The Mill on the Floss*."

22. Stevie Davies, *Emily Brontë*, 106–7, for example, calls Hareton a "legitimized Heathcliff" and maintains that Hareton and the younger Cathy reassert the brother-sister bond, thereby fulfilling the yearning of the first generation.

23. Trumbach, *Egalitarian Family*, 119–20.

24. For a standard chronology of *WH*, see A. Stuart Daley, "A Revised Chronology of *Wuthering Heights*," 169–73.

25. Vine, "The Wuther of the Other," 354.

26. C. P. Sanger and James H. Kavanagh have written extensively on the order of inheritance of Thrushcross Grange. See Sanger, *The Structure of Wuthering Heights*, and Kavanagh, *Emily Brontë*. See also "Land Law and Inheritance in *Wuthering Heights*," in *WH*, appendix 6, 497–99. Davidoff and Hall, *Family Fortunes*, 275–76.

27. Joan Perkin, *Women and Marriage in Nineteenth-Century England*, 10–31, provides a useful outline of Barbara Leigh Smith Bodichon's *Brief Summary, in Plain Language, of the Most Important Laws of England Concerning Women; Together with a Few Observations Thereon*. Perkin notes that when the *Summary* was published, "very little had changed in Common Law since feudal times," so the laws therein are clearly applicable to both the late-eighteenth-century setting of *WH* and the mid-nineteenth century when EB was writing (11). There were no substantial changes in legislation until the Married Women's Property Act of 1870, which entitled a married women her separate earnings, as well as other specified inheritances. Davidoff and Hall, *Family Fortunes*, 276.

28. Kavanagh, *Emily Brontë*, 77.

29. Davidoff and Hall, *Family Fortunes*, 209–10; see "Land Law and Inheritance," *WH*, 499, for a dispute to Heathcliff's claims.

30. Lyn Pykett, *Emily Brontë*, 119.

CHAPTER FIVE
Agnes Grey and *The Tenant of Wildfell Hall*: Lessons of the Family

1. Angus M. MacKay, *The Brontës: Fact and Fiction*, 21; Oliphant, "The Sisters Brontë," in *Women Novelists of Queen Victoria's Reign: A Book of Appreciations*, 28–29; "Biographical Notice of Ellis and Acton Bell," Smith, 2:746.

2. Preface to the second edition, July 22, 1848, *TWH*, xxxix.

3. PB, advertisement to *The Rural Minstrel* (1813), *Brontëana: The Rev. Patrick Brontë, A.*

B., *His Collected Works and Life*, ed. J. Horsfall Turner, 71; PB, *Brontëana*, 132–33; Langland, *Anne Brontë*, 37.

4. Maria H. Frawley, *Anne Brontë*, 83; *Douglas Jerrold's Weekly Newspaper* (January 15, 1848): 77; *Atlas* (January 22, 1848): 59; *Britannia* (January 15, 1848): 43.

5. *Douglas Jerrold's Weekly Newspaper* (January 15, 1848): 77; Patricia Thomson, *The Victorian Heroine: A Changing Ideal, 1837–73*, 39. AG also fulfills readerly expectations of a governess novel by rewarding its heroine with marriage to a clergyman.

6. M. Jeanne Peterson, "The Victorian Governess: Status Incongruence in Family and Society," in *Suffer and Be Still: Women in the Victorian Age*, ed. Martha Vicinus, 3; Mary Poovey, *Uneven Developments: The Ideological Work of Gender in Mid-Victorian England*, 131. In her review of *JE*, *Vanity Fair*, and the Governesses' Benevolent Institution, Elizabeth Rigby maintained that "the real definition of a governess, in the English sense, is a being who is our equal in birth, manners, and education, but our inferior in worldly wealth" (176).

7. Elizabeth Whately, *English Life, Social and Domestic, in the Middle of the Nineteenth Century, Considered in Reference to Our Position as a Community of Professing Christians*, 141, 145; see CB to WSW, September 13, 1849, Smith, 2:251; and Mary Maurice, *Mothers and Governesses*.

8. CB to EN, June 30, 1839, Smith, 1:193; CB to EN, January 24, 1840, Smith, 1:210. See "Lines Written at Thorp Green" (August 28, 1840, and August 19, 1841) and "Home" (published 1846), *The Poems of Anne Brontë: A New Text and Commentary*, ed. Edward Chitham, 75, 79–80, 99–100. See Chitham, introduction to *Poems of Anne Brontë*, for a discussion of the discrepancies in dating AB's employment. See Barker, *The Brontës*, for a full discussion of Anne's experiences, and see CB to EN, April 15, 1839, Smith, 1:189, for similarities between Anne's troubles with the Ingham children and Agnes's trials with her Bloomfield charges.

9. Peterson, "The Victorian Governess," 3; Kathryn Hughes, *The Victorian Governess*, 89.

10. Eagleton, *Myths of Power*, 128, 127.

11. Samuel Smiles, *Self-Help with Illustrations of Character and Conduct*, 300, 294.

12. Insistence on the governess's morality stemmed not only from her role in reinforcing the home virtues by instruction and example, but also, implicitly, from the fact that the resident governess could easily be a sexual temptation to the men of the family, as Thackeray's Becky Sharp clearly is. See Poovey, *Uneven Developments*.

13. Sarah Lewis, *Woman's Mission*, 30–31.

14. The 1851 census recorded 21,000 governesses in England and Wales, increasing to about 25,000 in 1861. Pamela Horn, "The Victorian Governess," 333.

15. Hughes, *The Victorian Governess*, 56.

16. Mary Maurice, *Governess Life: Its Trials, Duties, and Encouragements*, 105.

17. Langland, *Anne Brontë*, 25.

18. Davidoff and Hall, *Family Fortunes*, 166.

19. See Cates Baldridge, "*Agnes Grey*—Brontë's Bildungsroman That Isn't," 31–45.

20. July 30, 1841, Smith, 1:264–65.

21. *Spectator* 21 (July 8, 1848): 663. As Lori A. Paige, "Helen's Diary Freshly Considered," 225–27, has noted, *Wildfell Hall* is divided into three parts, the first narrated by Gilbert Markham, the second narrated by Helen through her diary, and the third narrated by both Gilbert and Helen (through her letters to her brother Frederick).

22. [Charles Kingsley], "Recent Novels," 424; *Sharpe's London Magazine* 7 (August 1848): 184; Davidoff and Hall, *Family Fortunes*, 292.

23. Mintz, *Prison of Expectations*, 174.

24. CB to EN, June 17, 1846, Smith, 1:477–78; AB, diary paper, July 31, 1845, Smith, 1:410; "Biographical Notice," Smith, 2:745.

25. CB to Margaret Wooler, January 30, 1846, Smith, 1:448; Gérin, *Branwell Brontë*, 24.

26. Lamb, *Can Woman Regenerate Society?* 15.

27. Lewis, *Woman's Mission*, 23.

28. Sarah Ellis, *The Wives of England: Their Relative Duties, Domestic Influences, and Social Obligations*, 70; Lewis, *Woman's Mission*, 28–29.

29. Aunt Maxwell transposes 2 Cor. 6:14–15. 1 Cor. 7:14.
30. Patrick Brontë, *Brontëana*, 118, 112.
31. J. Baldwin Brown, *Young Men and Maidens: A Pastoral for the Times*, 38.
32. Ellis, *Wives of England*, 116; Bodichon, *A Brief Summary*, 6.
33. Winifred Gérin, introduction to *The Tenant of Wildfell Hall*, 14.
34. Lewis, *Woman's Mission*, 31.
35. May Sinclair, *The Three Brontës*, 54. For the Victorians, Mrs. Grundy became a symbol for excessive conformity to conventional morality. May Sinclair was the author of twenty-four novels and an enthusiast for female suffrage. For a good biography, see Suzanne Raitt, *May Sinclair: A Modern Victorian* (Oxford: Clarendon, 2000).
36. Laura C. Berry, "Acts of Custody and Incarceration in *Wuthering Heights* and *The Tenant of Wildfell Hall*," 33.
37. Helen's escape was also likely influenced by the account of a Mrs. Collins, who visited the parsonage and appealed to the Reverend Brontë for advice on fleeing from her debauched husband. For a full account of Mrs. Collins's story, see Barker, *The Brontës*, 341–42; and CB to EN, November 12, 1840, and April 4, 1847, Smith, 1:231, 521.
38. Langland, *Anne Brontë*, 134.

CHAPTER SIX

The Professor and *Shirley*: Industrial Pollution of Family Relationships and Values

1. CB to WSW, June 15, 1848, Smith, 2:72.
2. Gary F. Langer, *The Coming of Age of Political Economy, 1815–1825*, 14; *An Inquiry into the Nature and Causes of the Wealth of Nations*, in The Works and Correspondence of Adam Smith, ed. R. H. Campbell and A. S. Skinner, 26–27.
3. Langer, *Coming of Age*, 7; Heather Glen, introduction to *The Professor*, 10. According to the 1841 census, the village of Haworth had a population of 2,434. J. Horsfall Turner, *Haworth—Past and Present: A History of Haworth, Stanbury and Oxenhope*, 10, 128. Babbage, *Report to the General Board of Health*, 6; Shuttleworth, *Victorian Psychology*, 21.
4. See John Lock and Canon W. T. Dixon, *A Man of Sorrow: The Life, Letters and Times of the Rev. Patrick Brontë, 1777–1861*, for PB's speech, February 22, 1837, 332, and full account of PB's involvement with the Luddites, 100–15; [EN], "Reminiscences of Charlotte Brontë," Smith, 1:595.
5. Thomas Carlyle, *Past and Present*, book 3, chap. 11, 268; Thomas Carlyle, *Chartism*, 24; Carlyle, *Past and Present*, book 4, chap. 4, 361.
6. Carlyle, *Past and Present*, book 3, chap. 2, 198–99.
7. Carlyle, *Chartism*, 108.
8. Carlyle, *Past and Present*, book 4, chap. 4, 361, 365, 362, 367; EG, *North and South*, vol. 2, chap. 36, 431.
9. CB to WSW, June 15, 1848, comments on Carlyle's "peculiarities of style" (Smith, 2:74). Carlyle's *Critical and Miscellaneous Essays* (1838) were included in a parcel of books from Cornhill; in CB to WSW, April 5, 1849, she writes that "Carlyle's Miscellanies interest me greatly" (Smith, 2:197). In CB to WSW, April 16, 1849, she suggests that she has read Carlyle's *On Heroes, Hero-Worship, and the Heroic in History* (1841), for she admits that she does not "quite fall in with his hero-worship; but there is a manly love of truth, an honest recognition and fearless vindication of intrinsic greatness, of intellectual and moral worth—considered apart from birth, rank or wealth—which commands my sincere admiration" (Smith, 2:202). Smith, 2:204, also notes that CB would have known *Sartor Resartus* from *Fraser's Magazine* (1833–1834). Qualls, *Secular Pilgrims*, 47.
10. Gallagher, *Industrial Reformation of English Fiction*, 114, 115.

11. Carlyle, *Past and Present*, book 3, chap. 2, 199.
12. Ellis, *Women of England*, 52.
13. Charles Dickens, *Hard Times for These Times*, book 1, chap. 10, 63.
14. Ellis, *Women of England*, 53; Carlyle, *Past and Present*, book 3, chap. 2, 199; book 3, chap. 13, 239.
15. Ellis, *Women of England*, 53, 56, 58. Gallagher, *Industrial Reformation of English Fiction*, explores domestic ideology's representation of the family as "a model or a school of social reform" (115, 119).
16. Gordon, *Passionate Life*, 287; Igor Webb, *From Custom to Capital: The English Novel and the Industrial Revolution*, 146.
17. Gallagher, *Industrial Reformation of English Fiction*, 153; Dickens, *Hard Times*, book 1, chap. 5, 24, 23.
18. Kathleen Tillotson, *Novels of the 1840s*, 282; CB to WSW, December 14, 1847, Smith, 1:574. The opening section of *P* is essentially a reworking of BB's story, *The Wool Is Rising* (June 26, 1834), which describes the sibling antagonisms between Edward and William Percy, sons of Northangerland, and is partly set in the Yorkshire-based countinghouse of Edward's mill. Glen, introduction to *The Professor*, 16; Carlyle, *Past and Present*, book 3, chap. 2, 198.
19. In uncovering William's progress in these terms, Glen has argued that *P* shows a "chilling" side to the traditional self-help biography. See Glen, introduction to *The Professor*.
20. Moglen, *Self Conceived*, 89; Carlyle, *Past and Present*, book 3, chap. 2, 198.
21. Glen, introduction to *The Professor*, 27.
22. Ellis, *Women of England*, 53, 58.
23. Glen, introduction to *The Professor*, 27.
24. See, for example, Catherine Malone, "'We Have Learnt to Love Her More than Her Books': The Critical Reception of Brontë's *Professor*," 175–87; Rebecca Rodolff, "From the Ending of *The Professor* to the Conception of *Jane Eyre*," 71–89.
25. Annette Tromly, *The Cover of the Mask: The Autobiographers in Charlotte Brontë's Fiction*, 41.
26. Gallagher, *Industrial Reformation of English Fiction*, 153.
27. *LCB*, 298. The attacks on Hollow's Mill and on Robert Moore are based on accounts reported in the *Mercury* of William Cartwright and the raid on his Rawfolds Mill near Hartshead. See Herbert J. Rosengarten, "Charlotte Brontë's *Shirley* and the *Leeds Mercury*," 591–600; Lock and Dixon, *A Man of Sorrow*, 100–115; and Barker, *The Brontës*, 46–47. Eagleton, *Myths of Power*, 45, discusses Chartist agitation near Haworth in his chapter on *S*. Elizabeth Gaskell, *Mary Barton*, vol. 1, chap. 1, 45. With the publication of *Mary Barton* in 1848, CB wrote to WSW, February 1, 1849, that she was "dismayed to find myself in some measure anticipated both in subject and incident" (Smith, 2:174). CB to WSW, April 20, 1848, Smith, 2:51.
28. [G. H. Lewes], *Edinburgh Review* 91 (January 1850): 160. For discussions of these parallels and various views on the question of unity in *S*, see Asa Briggs, "Public and Private Themes in *Shirley*," 203–19; Janet H. Freeman, "Unity and Diversity in *Shirley*," 558–75; Jacob Korg, "The Problem of Unity in *Shirley*," 125–36; and Arnold Shapiro, "Public Themes and Private Lives: Social Criticism in *Shirley*," 74–84. Gilbert and Gubar, *Madwoman*, 375; Rosemarie Bodenheimer, *The Politics of Story in Victorian Social Fiction*, 21, 37.
29. Eagleton, *Myths of Power*, 50.
30. Gallagher, *Industrial Reformation of English Fiction*, 168.
31. Qualls, *Secular Pilgrims*, 45.
32. Moglen, *Self Conceived*, 166; Mary Taylor to CB, August 13, 1850, Barker, *The Brontës*, 290.
33. Mary Taylor to CB, c. April 29, 1850, Smith, 2:392; Moglen, *Self Conceived*, 168.
34. Anna Jameson, "'Woman's Mission' and Woman's Position," in *Memoirs and Essays Illustrative of Art, Literature, and Social Morals*, 230–31.
35. Carlyle, *Past and Present*, book 4, chap. 4, 362.
36. Moglen, *Self Conceived*, 168.

CHAPTER SEVEN
Villette: Authorial Regeneration and the Death of the Family

1. CB to WSW, June 13, 1849, Smith, 2:220; CB to WSW, September 21, 1849, Smith, 2:260.
2. CB to WSW, March 16, 1850, Smith, 2:354–55. Following EB's death, CB confided, "My Father says to me almost hourly 'Charlotte, you must bear up—I shall sink if you fail me.' [T]hese words—you can conceive are a stimulus to nature" (CB to WSW, December 25, 1848, Smith, 2:159).
3. CB to WSW, July 26, 1849, Smith, 2:232; CB to GS, March 31, 1851, Smith, 2:593; CB to EN, July 14, 1849, Smith, 2:230.
4. Patsy Stoneman, "The Brontës and Death: Alternatives to Revolution," in *The Sociology of Literature: 1848*, ed. Francis Barker et al., 79; Pat Jalland, *Death in the Victorian Family*, 4.
5. CB to WSW, October 2, 1848, Smith, 2:122. cf. Gen. 23:4, in which Abraham requests a burial place for his wife Sarah: "I am a stranger, and a sojourner with you: give me a possession of a burying place with you, that I may bury my dead out of my sight." See Michael Wheeler, *Death and the Future Life in Victorian Literature and Theology*, for a detailed discussion of views of death.
6. CB to WSW, October 2, 1848, Smith, 2:122. On Charlotte's view of Branwell, see, for example, Barker, *The Brontës*, 564–69; and Gordon, *Passionate Life*, 184–85. CB to WSW, October 2, 1848, Smith, 2:122. cf. John 5:35, in which Jesus praises John the Baptist as "a burning and a shining light."
7. CB to WSW, October 6, 1848, Smith, 2:124.
8. CB to WSW, December 25, 1848, Smith, 2:159; CB to WSW, December 7, 1848, Smith, 2:148; CB to EN, December 23, 1848, Smith, 2:157.
9. LCB, 295; Jalland, *Death in the Victorian Family*, 2–3; CB to EN, April 12, 1849, Smith, 2:200; CB to WSW, June 4, 1849, Smith, 2:220; CB to WSW, December 25, 1848, Smith, 2:159.
10. CB to WSW, June 13, 1849, Smith, 2:220.
11. Wheeler, *Death and the Future Life*, 6; Frederick Denison Maurice, *The Gospel of St. John: A Series of Discourses*, 318. See Marion J. Phillips, "Charlotte Brontë's Favourite Preacher: Frederick Denison John Maurice (1805–1872)," 77–87, for CB's acquaintance with Maurice. CB to WSW, June 13, 1849, Smith, 2:220.
12. Alfred Tennyson, *In Memoriam* (stanza 34, ll. 1–4), 64.
13. CB to EG, August 27, 1850, Smith, 2:457.
14. "My darling thou wilt never know" (December 24, 1848) and "There's little joy in life for me" (June 21, 1849), which appears unfinished. See *The Poems of Charlotte Brontë*, ed. Tom Winnifrith, 241–42. Tennyson, *In Memoriam* (stanza 5, ll. 12, 6), 41.
15. CB to EN, July 14, 1849, Smith, 2:230–31.
16. LCB, 355; CB to WSW, [November 19, 1850?], Smith, 2:513–14.
17. CB to EN, February 16, 1849, Smith, 2:184; CB to [WSW?], May 22, 1850, Smith, 2:403; CB to EN, July 14, 1849, Smith, 2:230.
18. Shuttleworth, *Victorian Psychology*, 247; CB to WSW, September 21, 1849, Smith, 2:260; Winchester Sunday, July 1817, "Letters from Cassandra Austen to Fanny Knight on Jane Austen's Death," in *Jane Austen: Selected Letters, 1796–1817*, ed. R. W. Chapman, appendix, 208.
19. CB to WSW, September 21, 1849, Smith, 2:260–61; CB to WSW, [November 19, 1850?], Smith, 2:513; CB to EN, June 23, 1849, Smith, 2:222; CB to EN, [February 16, 1850?], Smith, 2:347.
20. CB to WSW, February 1, 1849, Smith, 2:174; CB to WSW, [October 18, 1848?]; Smith, 2:128; CB to WSW, [January 13, 1849?], Smith, 2:168.
21. CB to WSW, April 16, 1849; Smith, 2:203; CB to James Taylor, September 5, 1850, Smith, 2:461.

22. CB to WSW, August 29, 1849, Smith, 2:241.
23. CB to WSW, September 21, 1849, Smith, 2:261; CB to WSW, July 3, 1849, Smith, 2:227. See Genesis 8:6–7.
24. CB to EN, October 23, 1850, Smith, 2:487; CB to GS, October 30, 1852, Barker, *The Brontës: A Life in Letters*, 353; CB to GS, October 30, 1852, WS, 4:14.
25. Gilbert and Gubar, *Madwoman*, 400.
26. Moglen, *Self Conceived*, 195.
27. Gilbert and Gubar, *Madwoman*, 59; Moglen, *Self Conceived*, 198; Mary Ann Kelly, "Paralysis and the Circular Nature of Memory in Villette," 343.
28. Greatheart guides Christiana on her journey to the Celestial City in part 2 of *Pilgrim's Progress*.
29. Hsiao-Hung Lee has also discussed how Lucy disorients the reader in her shipwreck metaphor in *"Possibilities of Hidden Things": Narrative Transgression in Victorian Fictional Autobiographies*, 68.
30. Wheeler, *Death and the Future Life*, xxi; Terence Hawkes, *Metaphor*, 39.
31. CB to WSW, November 6, 1852, WS, 4:18; Tony Tanner, introduction to *Villette*, 11.
32. Moglen, *Self Conceived*, 199.
33. CB to Margaret Wooler, March 24, 1849, Smith, 2:193.
34. CB to EG, November 6, 1851, Smith, 2:710.
35. CB to WSW, June 25, 1849, Smith, 2:224; Mary Taylor to EG, January 18, 1856, *LCB*, 81.
36. In *P*, William Crimsworth recognizes hypochondria as a malady arising from his boyhood experiences. His premarriage attack of hypochondria lasts nine days; similarly, Lucy's "strange fever of the nerves and blood" rages for "nine dark and wet days" (*V*, 222).
37. Ps. 88:3, 8.
38. CB to EN, August 13, 1852, WS, 4:4.
39. Kelly, "Paralysis and Circular Nature of Memory," 351.
40. CB to EN, [February 16, 1850?], Smith, 2:347.
41. Moglen, *Self Conceived*, 203.
42. Garrett Stewart, "A Valediction For Bidding Mourning: Death and the Narratee in Brontë's *Villette*," in *Death and Representation*, ed. Sarah Webster Goodwin and Elisabeth Bronfen, 52. CB maintained that the ending "was designed that every reader should settle the catastrophe for himself, according to the quality of his disposition.... Drowning and Matrimony are the fearful alternatives" (CB to GS, March 26, 1853, WS, 4:56). EG wrote that CB was not able to appease her father's expressed wish for a happy ending of marriage for the hero and heroine; instead, she could only "veil the fate in oracular words" (*LCB*, 392). Many feminist readings insist upon Paul's death as the only means by which Lucy can fully exercise her own powers, equating marriage to Paul with the death of Lucy's new-found independence, and therefore a "fearful alternative."
43. Roland Barthes, *Fragments d'un discours amoureux*, translated in Elizabeth Bronfen, "Dialogue with the Dead: The Deceased Beloved as Muse," in *Sex and Death in Victorian Literature*, ed. Regina Barreca, 246; Stephen Vine, "'When I am Not': Mourning and Identity in *Wuthering Heights*."
44. Nancy Sorkin Rabinowitz has similarly argued, "if [Lucy] cannot control her existence, she can at least control the telling of that existence" ("'Faithful Narrator' or 'Partial Eulogist': First-Person Narration in Brontë's *Villette*," 250). Mark 4:39.
45. *LCB*, 414. In *S*, CB had written, "Yet, let whoever grieves still cling fast to love and faith in God: God will never deceive, never finally desert him. "Whom he loveth, He chasteneth." These words are true, and should not be forgotten" (*S*, 394), adapted from Heb. 12:6. Tennyson, *In Memoriam* (stanza 37, l. 22) 67.
46. Adaptation of Rev. 19.
47. While I have focused on the Christian idea of "life everlasting" that M. Paul both represents and is given as a form of authorial consolation in Lucy's narrative, Irene Taylor pro-

vides a fascinating and broader reading of M. Paul as "the fictional embodiment of deity." See her chapters on V, in *Holy Ghosts*.

48. Peter Allen Dale, "Heretical Narration: Charlotte Brontë's Search for Endlessness," 16–17. Dale argues that Lucy's act of writing strives to "become a better Word than God himself has vouchsafed." Lucy, he maintains, is writing *against* the Word, since she can only find fulfillment in her human lover Paul (20).

49. Gordon, *Passionate Life*, 273.

Conclusion: Life after *Villette*

1. "Emma," in *Unfinished Novels*, 99, 112; Gordon, *Passionate Life*, 290; for an insightful reading of "Emma," see 289–92.

2. "Emma," 112, 113.

3. William Makepeace Thackeray, introduction to "Emma: The Last Sketch," in *Charlotte Brontë: Unfinished Novels*, 96. This fragment is from an October 11, 1859, letter from Arthur Nicholls to GS. Nicholls gave GS, founder of *Cornhill Magazine*, permission to print it as part of Thackeray's introduction.

BIBLIOGRAPHY

WORKS BY THE BRONTËS

Brontë, Anne. *Agnes Grey*. Edited by Hilda Marsden and Robert Inglesfield. Oxford: Clarendon Press, 1988.

———. *The Poems of Anne Brontë: A New Text and Commentary*. Edited by Edward Chitham. London: Macmillan, 1979.

———. *The Tenant of Wildfell Hall*. Edited by Herbert Rosengarten. Oxford: Clarendon Press, 1992.

Brontë, Charlotte. *An Edition of the Early Writings of Charlotte Brontë*. Vol. 1, *1826–1832*. Edited by Christine Alexander. Oxford: Basil Blackwell for Shakespeare Head, 1987.

———. *An Edition of the Early Writings of Charlotte Brontë*, Vol. 2, part 1, *1833–1834*. Edited by Christine Alexander. Oxford: Basil Blackwell for Shakespeare Head, 1991.

———. *An Edition of the Early Writings of Charlotte Brontë*, Vol. 2, part 2, *1834–1835*. Edited by Christine Alexander. Oxford: Basil Blackwell for Shakespeare Head, 1991.

———. *Five Novelettes*. Edited by Winifred Gérin. London: Folio, 1971.

———. *Jane Eyre*. Edited by Jane Jack and Margaret Smith. Oxford: Clarendon Press, 1969.

———. *The Poems of Charlotte Brontë*. Edited by Tom Winnifrith. Oxford: Basil Blackwell for Shakespeare Head, 1984.

———. *The Professor*. Edited by Margaret Smith and Herbert Rosengarten. Oxford: Clarendon Press, 1987.

———. *Shirley*. Edited by Herbert Rosengarten and Margaret Smith. Oxford: Clarendon Press, 1979.

———. *Unfinished Novels*. Stroud: Alan Sutton and the Brontë Society, 1993.

———. *Villette*. Edited by Herbert Rosengarten and Margaret Smith. Oxford: Clarendon Press, 1984.
Brontë, Emily. *The Poems of Emily Brontë*. Edited by Derek Roper with Edward Chitham. Oxford: Clarendon Press, 1995.
———. *Wuthering Heights*. Edited by Hilda Marsden and Ian Jack. Oxford: Clarendon Press, 1976.
Brontë, Patrick. *Brontëana: The Rev. Patrick Brontë, A. B., His Collected Works and Life*. Edited by J. Horsfall Turner. Bingley: T. Harrison & Sons, 1898.
Brontë, Patrick Branwell. *The Poems of Patrick Branwell Brontë*. Edited by Tom Winnifrith. Oxford: Basil Blackwell for Shakespeare Head, 1983.
———. *The Works of Patrick Branwell Brontë: An Edition*. Vol. 1, 1827–1836. Edited by Victor A. Neufeldt. New York: Garland Press, 1997.
———. *The Works of Patrick Branwell Brontë: An Edition*. Vol. 2, 1834–1836. Edited by Victor A. Neufeldt. New York: Garland Press, 1997.
———. *The Works of Patrick Branwell Brontë: An Edition*. Vol. 3, 1837–1848. Edited by Victor A. Neufeldt. New York: Garland Press, 1999.
Smith, Margaret, ed. *The Letters of Charlotte Brontë with a Selection of Letters by Family and Friends*. Vol. 1, 1829–1847. Oxford: Clarendon Press, 1995.
———. *The Letters of Charlotte Brontë with a Selection of Letters by Family and Friends*. Vol. 2, 1858–1851. Oxford: Clarendon Press, 2000.
Wise, T. J., and J. A. Symington, eds. *The Brontës: Their Lives, Friendships and Correspondence*. 4 vols. Oxford: Basil Blackwell for Shakespeare Head, 1932.
———. *The Miscellaneous and Unpublished Writings of Charlotte Brontë and Patrick Branwell Brontë*. 2 vols. Oxford: Basil Blackwell for Shakespeare Head, 1938.

CONTEMPORARY REVIEWS OF THE BRONTËS

[Dobell, Sydney]. "Currer Bell." *Palladium* 1 (September 1850): 161–75.
Ellis, Sarah. "Review of *Shirley*, by the Author of *Jane Eyre*." In *The Morning Call: A Table Book of Literature and Art*. Vol. 1:34–42. London: John Tallis, 1852.
[Kingsley, Charles]. "Recent Novels." *Fraser's Magazine* 39 (April 1849): 417–32.

[Lewes, G. H.]. Review of *Shirley*. *Edinburgh Review* 91 (January 1850): 153–73.
Review of *The Life of Charlotte Brontë*. *Christian Remembrancer* 34 (July 1857): 87–145.
"Mr Bell's New Novel." Review of *The Tenant of Wildfell Hall*. *Rambler* 3 (September 1848): 65–66.
[Oliphant, Margaret]. "Novels." *Blackwood's Edinburgh Magazine* 102 (September 1867): 257–80.
[Rigby, Elizabeth (Lady Eastlake)]. Review of *Vanity Fair, Jane Eyre* and the Governesses' Benevolent Institution. *Quarterly Review* 84 (December 1848): 153–85.
[Skelton, John]. "Charlotte Brontë." *Fraser's Magazine* 55 (May 1857): 569–82.
Review of *The Tenant of Wildfell Hall*. *Examiner*, July 29, 1848, 483–84.
Review of *The Tenant of Wildfell Hall*. *Sharpe's London Magazine* 7 (August 1848): 181–84.
Review of *The Tenant of Wildfell Hall*. *Spectator* 21 (July 8, 1848): 662–63.
Whipple, E. P. "Novels of the Season." Review of *The Tenant of Wildfell Hall*. *North American Review* 141 (October 1848): 354–69.
Review of *Wuthering Heights* and *Agnes Grey*. *Athenaeum*, December 25, 1847, 1324–25.
Review of *Wuthering Heights* and *Agnes Grey*. *Atlas*, January 22, 1848, 59.
Review of *Wuthering Heights* and *Agnes Grey*. *Britannia*, January 15, 1848, 42–43.
Review of *Wuthering Heights* and *Agnes Grey*. *Douglas Jerrold's Weekly Newspaper*, January 15, 1848, 77.

OTHER PRIMARY WORKS

Aguilar, Grace. *Woman's Friendship: A Story of Domestic Life*. London: Groomsbridge & Sons, 1850.
Aimé-Martin, Louis. *The Education of Mothers of Families; or, The Civilisation of the Human Race by Women*. Translated by Edwin Lee. London: Whittaker & Co., 1842.
Arnold, Arthur. *The Hon. Mrs. Norton and Married Women*. The Married Women's Property Committee. Manchester: A. Ireland, 1878.
Austen, Jane. *Jane Austen: Selected Letters, 1796–1817*. Edited by R. W. Chapman. Oxford: Oxford University Press, 1985.

Babbage, Benjamin Hershel. *Report to the General Board of Health on a Preliminary Inquiry into the Sewerage, Drainage, and Supply of Water, and Sanitary Condition of the Inhabitants of the Hamlet in Haworth, in the West Riding of the County of York*. London: Her Majesty's Staionery Office, 1850.

Beeton, Isabella. *Beeton's Book of Household Management*. London: Chancellor, 1982.

Bodichon, Barbara Leigh Smith. *A Brief Summary, in Plain Language, of the Most Important Laws Concerning Women; Together with a Few Observations Thereon*. London: John Chapman, 1854.

Brown, J. Baldwin. *Young Men and Maidens: A Pastoral for the Times*. London: Hodder & Stoughton, 1871.

Bunyan, John. *The Pilgrim's Progress*. Edited by N. H. Keeble. Oxford: Oxford University Press, 1984.

Carlyle, Thomas. *Chartism*. London: James Fraser, 1840.

———. *Past and Present*. London: Chapman & Hall, 1843.

Dickens, Charles. *Great Expectations*. Edited by Margaret Cardwell. Oxford: Clarendon Press, 1993.

———. *Hard Times for These Times*. London: Oxford University Press, 1955.

Eliot, George. *The Mill on the Floss*. Edited by Gordon S. Haight. Oxford: Oxford University Press, 1996.

Ellis, Sarah. *The Mothers of England: Their Influence and Responsibility*. London: Fisher, Son & Co., 1843.

———. *The Wives of England: Their Relative Duties, Domestic Influences, and Social Obligations*. London: Fisher, Son & Co., 1843.

———. *The Women of England: Their Social Duties, and Domestic Habits*. 3d ed. London: Fisher, Son & Co., 1839.

"Emily Brontë: A Diary Paper." *Brontë Society Transactions* 12 (1951): 15.

Engels, Friedrich. *The Origin of the Family, Private Property, and the State: In the Light of the Researches of Lewis H. Morgan*. Edited by Eleanor Burke Leacock. London: Lawrence & Wishart, 1972.

Farningham, Marianne. *Home Life*. London: James Clark & Co., 1869.

Gaskell, Elizabeth. *The Life of Charlotte Brontë*. Edited by Elisabeth Jay. London: Penguin, 1997.

———. *Mary Barton*. Edited by Stephen Gill. London: Penguin, 1985.

———. *North and South*. Edited by Angus Easson. Oxford: Oxford University Press, 1982.

Greg, William Rathbone. "Why Are Women Redundant?" *National Review* 14 (April 1862): 434–60.

Hemans, Felicia. "The Homes of England." *Blackwood's Edinburgh Magazine* 21 (April 1827): 392.

Jameson, Anna. "'Woman's Mission' and Woman's Position." In *Memoirs and Essays Illustrative of Art, Literature, and Social Morals*, 209–48. London: Richard Bentley, 1846.

Kavanagh, Julia. *Woman in France during the Eighteenth Century*. 2 vols. London: Smith, Elder & Co., 1850.

Lamb, Ann Richelieu. *Can Woman Regenerate Society?* London: John W. Parker, 1844.

Lewis, Sarah. *Woman's Mission*. New York: Wiley & Putnam, 1839.

Martineau, Harriet. *Autobiography*. 2 vols. London: Virago, 1983.

———. *Household Education*. London: Edward Moxon, 1849.

Maurice, Frederick Denison. *The Gospel of St. John: A Series of Discourses*. Cambridge: Macmillan, 1857.

Maurice, Mary. *Governess Life: Its Trials, Duties, and Encouragements*. London: John W. Parker, 1849.

———. *Mothers and Governesses*. London: John W. Parker, 1847.

Mill, James. *Analysis of the Phenomena of the Human Mind*. 2 vols. London: Baldwin & Craddock, 1829.

More, Hannah. *Moral Sketches of Prevailing Opinions and Manners, Foreign and Domestic: With Reflections on Prayer*. 2d ed. London: T. Cadell & W. Davies, 1819.

———. "Thoughts on the Cultivation of the Heart and Temper in the Education of Daughters." In *Essays on Various Subjects, Principally designed for Young Ladies*, 123–57. London: J. Wilkie & T. Cadell, 1777.

Morgan, Lady Sydney. *Woman and Her Master*. 2 vols. London: Henry Collburn, 1840.

Nightingale, Florence. "Cassandra." *Suggestions for Thought to the Searchers after Truth among the Artizans of England*. London: N.p., 1860.

[Nussey, Ellen.] "Reminiscences of Charlotte Brontë." *Scribner's Monthly* 2 (May 1871): 18–31. Reprinted in *The Letters of Charlotte Brontë*. Vol. 2, *1829–1847*, edited by Margaret Smith, 589–601. Oxford: Clarendon Press, 1995.

Potter, George. "The First Point of the New Charter: Improved Dwellings for the People." *Contemporary Review* 18 (November 1871): 547–58.

Reid, Mrs. Hugo. *A Plea for Woman: Being a Vindication of the Importance and Extent of Her Natural Sphere of Action*. Edinburgh: William Tait, 1843.

"The Reverend Patrick Brontë and Mrs. E. C. Gaskell." *Brontë Society Transactions* 8 (1933): 83–100.

Richmond, Legh. *Domestic Portraiture; or, The Successful Application of Religious Principle in the Education of a Family, Exemplified in the Memoirs of Three of the Deceased Children of the Rev. Legh Richmond, with a Few Introductory Remarks on Christian Education, by the Rev. E. Bickersteth.* Edited by E. Bickersteth. London: R. B. Seeley & W. Burnside, 1834.

Rousseau, Jean-Jacques. *Émile.* Translated by Barbara Foxley. London: J. M. Dent, 1993.

Ruskin, John. "Of Queen's Gardens." In *The Works of John Ruskin*, edited by E. T. Cook and Alexander Wedderburn, 18:109–44. London: George Allen, 1905.

Scott, Alexander. *Suggestions on Female Education: Two Introductory Lectures on English Literature and Moral Philosophy.* London: Taylor, Walton & Maberly, 1849.

Sewell, Elizabeth Missing. *Principles of Education, Drawn from Nature and Revelation, and Applied to Female Education in Upper Classes.* 2 vols. London: Longman, Green, 1865.

Smiles, Samuel. *Self-Help with Illustrations of Character and Conduct.* London: John Murray, 1859.

Smith, Adam. *An Inquiry into the Nature and Causes of the Wealth of Nations.* Glasgow Edition of The Works and Correspondence of Adam Smith, edited by R. H. Campbell and A. S. Skinner. Oxford: Clarendon Press, 1976.

Taylor, Mary. *The First Duty of Women: A Series of Articles Reprinted from the* Victoria Magazine, *1865–1870.* London: Emily Faithfull, 1870.

———. *Miss Miles, or A Tale of Yorkshire Life Sixty Years Ago.* New York: Oxford University Press, 1990.

Tennyson, Alfred. *In Memoriam.* Edited by Susan Shatto and Marion Shaw. Oxford: Clarendon Press, 1982.

Turner, J. Horsfall. *Haworth—Past and Present: A History of Haworth, Stanbury and Oxenhope.* Brighouse: J. S. Olicana Books, 1971.

Whately, Elizabeth. *English Life, Social and Domestic, in the Middle of the Nineteenth Century, Considered in Reference to Our Position as a Community of Professing Christians.* London: B. Fellowes, 1847.

Wollstonecraft, Mary. *Thoughts on the Education of Daughters with Reflections on Female Conduct, in the More Important Duties of Life.* New York: Garland, 1974.

———. *A Vindication of the Rights of Woman: With Strictures on Political and Moral Subjects.* London: J. Johnson, 1792.

A Woman. Review of *Woman's Rights and Duties*. *Blackwood's Edinburgh Magazine* 54 (September 1843): 373–97.
Wright, G. *Thoughts in Younger Life, on Interesting Subjects; or, Poems, Letters, and Essays, Moral, Elegiac, and Descriptive*. London: J. Buckland, 1778.

SECONDARY SOURCES

Aaron, Jane. *A Double Singleness: Gender and the Writings of Charles and Mary Lamb*. Oxford: Clarendon Press, 1991.
Abel, Elizabeth, ed. *Writing and Sexual Difference*. Brighton: Harvester Press, 1982.
Adams, Maurianne. "Family Disintegration and Creative Reintegration: The Case of Charlotte Brontë and *Jane Eyre*." In *The Victorian Family: Structure and Stresses*, edited by Anthony S. Wohl, 148–79. New York: St. Martin's Press, 1978.
———. "*Jane Eyre*: Woman's Estate." In *The Authority of Experience: Essays in Feminist Criticism*, edited by Arlyn Diamond and Lee R. Edwards, 137–59. Amherst: University of Massachusetts Press, 1977.
Alexander, Christine. *The Early Writings of Charlotte Brontë*. Oxford: Basil Blackwell, 1983.
Allott, Miriam, ed. *The Brontës: The Critical Heritage*. London: Routledge & Kegan Paul, 1974.
Argyle, Gisela. "Gender and Generic Mixing in Charlotte Brontë's *Shirley*." *Studies in English Literature, 1500–1900* 35 (1995): 741–56.
Ariès, Philippe. *Centuries of Childhood*. Translated by Robert Baldick. London: Pimlico, 1996.
———. *The Hour of Our Death*. Translated by Helen Weaver. London: Allen Lane, 1981.
Armstrong, Nancy. *Desire and Domestic Fiction: A Political History of the Novel*. New York: Oxford University Press, 1987.
Auerbach, Nina. *Communities of Women: An Idea in Fiction*. Cambridge: Harvard University Press, 1978.
———. *Romantic Imprisonment: Women and Other Glorified Outcasts*. New York: Columbia University Press, 1986.
Azim, Firdous. *The Colonial Rise of the Novel*. London: Routledge, 1993.
Bailin, Miriam. *The Sickroom in Victorian Fiction: The Art of Being Ill*. Cambridge: Cambridge University Press, 1994.

Baldridge, Cates. "*Agnes Grey*—Brontë's Bildungsroman That Isn't." *Journal of Narrative Technique* 23 (1993): 31–45.

Bank, Stephen P., and Michael D. Kahn. *The Sibling Bond*. New York: Basic, 1982.

Barker, Juliet. *The Brontës*. London: Phoenix, 1995.

———. *The Brontës: A Life in Letters*. Woodstock: Overlook Press, 1998.

Barnard, Robert. *Emily Brontë*. New York: Oxford University Press, 2000.

Barreca, Regina, ed. *Sex and Death in Victorian Literature*. Basingstoke: Macmillan, 1990.

Basch, Françoise. *Relative Creatures: Victorian Women in Society and the Novel, 1837–67*. Translated by Anthony Rudolf. London: Allen Lane, 1974.

Beaty, Jerome. "Jane Eyre at Gateshead: Mixed Signals in Text and Context." In *Victorian Literature and Society: Essays Presented to Richard D. Altick*, edited by James R. Kincaid and Albert J. Kuhn, 168–96. Columbus: Ohio State University Press, 1983.

———. *Misreading Jane Eyre: A Postformalist Paradigm*. Columbus: Ohio State University Press, 1996.

Beer, Patricia. *Reader, I Married Him: A Study of the Women Characters of Jane Austen, Charlotte Brontë, Elizabeth Gaskell, and George Eliot*. Basingstoke: Macmillan, 1974.

Bell, Arnold Craig. *The Novels of Anne Brontë: A Study and Reappraisal*. Braunton: Merlin, 1992.

Bentley, Phyllis. *The Young Brontës*. London: Max Parrish, 1960.

Berg, Margaret Mary. "*The Tenant of Wildfell Hall*: Anne Brontë's *Jane Eyre*?" *Victorian Newsletter* 71 (1987): 10–15.

Berry, Elizabeth Hollis. *Anne Brontë's Radical Vision: Structures of Consciousness*. English Literary Studies Monograph Series, no. 62. Victoria, B.C.: University of Victoria Press, 1994.

Berry, Laura C. "Acts of Custody and Incarceration in *Wuthering Heights* and *The Tenant of Wildfell Hall*." *Novel* 30 (1996): 32–55.

Bersani, Leo. *A Future for Astyanax: Character and Desire in Literature*. London: Marion Boyars, 1978.

Björk, Harriet. *The Language of Truth: Charlotte Brontë, The Woman Question, and the Novel*. Lund Studies in English, no. 47. Lund: CWK Gleerup, 1974.

Blake, Andrew. *Reading Victorian Fiction: The Cultural Context and Ideological Content of the Nineteenth-Century Novel*. Basingstoke: Macmillan, 1989.

Bloom, Harold, ed. *Modern Critical Views: The Brontës*. New York: Chelsea Press, 1987.
Bodenheimer, Rosemarie. *The Politics of Story in Victorian Social Fiction*. Ithaca: Cornell University Press, 1988.
Boumelha, Penny. *Charlotte Brontë*. Key Women Writers Series. Hemel Hempstead: Harvester Wheatsheaf, 1990.
Breen, Margaret Soenser. "Who Are You, Lucy Snowe?: Disoriented Bildung in *Villette*." *Dickens Studies Annual* 24 (1996): 241–57.
Briggs, Asa. "Public and Private Themes in *Shirley*." *Brontë Society Transactions* 13 (1958): 203–19.
Bronfen, Elizabeth. "Dialogue with the Dead: The Deceased Beloved as Muse." In *Sex and Death in Victorian Literature*, edited by Regina Barreca, 241–59. Basingstoke: Macmillan, 1990.
"The Brontës Then and Now: A Symposium of Articles Reprinted from Various Issues of the Brontë Society Transactions as a *Jane Eyre* and *Wuthering Heights* Centenary Tribute." Shipley: Brontë Society, 1949.
Buchen, Irving H. "Emily Brontë and the Metaphysics of Childhood and Love." *Nineteenth-Century Fiction* 22 (1967): 63–70.
Burgan, Mary. "'Some Fit Parentage': Identity and the Cycle of Generations in *Wuthering Heights*." *Philological Quarterly* 61 (1982): 395–413.
Burkhart, Charles. *Charlotte Brontë: A Psychosexual Study of Her Novels*. London: Victor Gollancz, 1973.
Butler, Judith. "Gender Trouble: Feminism and the Subversion of Identity." In *Feminist Literary Theory: A Reader*, edited by Mary Eagleton. 2d ed. Oxford: Blackwell, 1996.
———. *Subjects of Desire: Hegelian Reflections in Twentieth-Century France*. New York: Columbia University Press, 1987.
Butterfield, Mary, and R. J. Duckett. *Brother in the Shadow: Stories and Sketches by Patrick Branwell Brontë*. Bradford: Bradford Libraries and Information Service, 1988.
Calder, Jenni. *Women and Marriage in Victorian Fiction*. London: Thames & Hudson, 1976.
Carlisle, Janice. "The Face in the Mirror: *Villette* and the Conventions of Autobiography." *English Literary History* 46 (1979): 262–89.
Chadwick, Whitney, and Isabelle de Courtivron, eds. *Significant Others: Creativity and Intimate Partnership*. London: Thames & Hudson, 1996.

Chase, Karen. *Eros and Psyche: The Representation of Personality in Charlotte Brontë, Charles Dickens, and George Eliot*. New York: Methuen, 1984.
Chase, Karen, and Michael Levenson. *The Spectacle of Intimacy: A Public Life for the Victorian Family*. Princeton: Princeton University Press, 2000.
Chase, Richard. "The Brontës, or, Myth Domesticated." In *Forms of Modern Fiction: Essays Collected in Honor of Joseph Warren Beach*, edited by William Van O'Connor, 102–19. Minneapolis: University of Minnesota Press, 1948.
Chitham, Edward. *The Birth of Wuthering Heights: Emily Brontë at Work*. New York: St. Martin's Press, 1998.
———. "Diverging Twins: Some Clues to *Wildfell Hall*." In *Brontë Facts and Brontë Problems*, 91–103. Basingstoke: Macmillan, 1983.
———. "Gondal's Queen: Saga or Myth?" *Brontë Facts and Brontë Problems*, 49–57. Basingstoke: Macmillan, 1983.
———. *A Life of Anne Brontë*. Oxford: Basil Blackwell, 1992.
———. *A Life of Emily Brontë*. Oxford: Basil Blackwell, 1987.
Chitham, Edward, and Tom Winnifrith. *Brontë Facts and Brontë Problems*. Basingstoke: Macmillan, 1983.
Christ, Carol T. "Imaginative Constraint, Feminine Duty and the Form of Charlotte Brontë's Fiction." *Women's Studies* 6 (1979): 287–96.
———. "Victorian Masculinity and the Angel in the House." In *A Widening Sphere: Changing Roles of Victorian Women*, edited by Martha Vicinus, 146–62. London: Methuen, 1980.
Cohen, Michael. *Sisters: Relation and Rescue in Nineteenth-Century British Novels and Paintings*. Cranbury, N.J.: Associated University Presses, 1995.
Cohen, Paula Marantz. *The Daughter's Dilemma: Family Process and the Nineteenth-Century Domestic Novel*. Ann Arbor: University of Michigan Press, 1991.
Colby, Robert A. "*Villette* and the Life of the Mind." *Publications of the Modern Language Association* 75 (1960): 410–19.
Collins, Robert G., ed. *The Hand of the Arch Sinner: Two Angrian Chronicles of Branwell Brontë*. Oxford: Clarendon Press, 1993.
Colt, Rosemary M. "Innocence Unleashed: The Power of the Single Child." In *The Significance of Sibling Relationships in Literature*, edited by JoAnna Stephens Mink and Janet Doubler Ward, 11–22. Bowling Green, Ohio: Bowling Green State University Popular Press, 1993.

Costello, Priscilla H. "A New Reading of Anne Brontë's *Agnes Grey*." *Brontë Society Transactions* 19 (1987): 113–18.

———. "The Parson's Daughters: The Family Worlds of Charlotte, Emily, and Anne Brontë." Ph.D. diss., Union for Experimenting Colleges and Universities, 1983.

Craik, W. A. *The Brontë Novels*. London: Methuen, 1968.

Crosby, Christina. "Charlotte Brontë's Haunted Text." *Studies in English Literature, 1500–1900* 24 (1984): 701–16.

Crump, R. W. *Charlotte and Emily Brontë: A Reference Guide*. Boston: G. K. Hall, 1982.

Cunningham, Valentine. *Everywhere Spoken Against: Dissent in the Victorian Novel*. Oxford: Clarendon Press, 1975.

Dale, Peter Allen. "Heretical Narration: Charlotte Brontë's Search for Endlessness." *Religion and Literature* 16 (1984): 1–24.

Daley, A. Stuart. "A Revised Chronology of *Wuthering Heights*." *Brontë Society Transactions* 21 (1995): 168–73.

David, Deirdre. *Rule Britannia: Women, Empire, and Victorian Writing*. Ithaca: Cornell University Press, 1995.

Davidoff, Leonore, and Catherine Hall. *Family Fortunes: Men and Women of the English Middle Class, 1780–1850*. London: Hutchinson, 1987.

Davies, Cecil W. "A Reading of *Wuthering Heights*." *Essays in Criticism* 19 (1969): 254–72.

Davies, Stevie. *Emily Brontë*. Key Women Writers Series. Hemel Hempstead: Harvester Wheatsheaf, 1988.

Dawson, Terence. "The Struggle for Deliverance from the Father: The Structural Principle of *Wuthering Heights*." *Modern Language Review* 84 (1989): 289–304.

Dessner, Lawrence Jay. *The Homely Web of Truth: A Study of Charlotte Brontë's Novels*. The Hague: Mouton, 1975.

Dolin, Tim. "Fictional Territory and a Woman's Place: Regional and Sexual Difference in *Shirley*." *English Literary History* 62 (1995): 197–215.

Donzelot, Jacques. *The Policing of Families*. Translated by Robert Hurley. Baltimore: Johns Hopkins University Press, 1997.

Eagleton, Terry. *Heathcliff and the Great Hunger: Studies in Irish Culture*. London: Verso, 1995.

———. *Myths of Power: A Marxist Study of the Brontës*. 2d ed. Basingstoke: Macmillan, 1988.

Edmond, Rod. *Affairs of the Hearth: Victorian Poetry and Domestic Narrative*. London: Routledge, 1988.

Elfenbein, Andrew. *Byron and the Victorians*. Cambridge Studies in Nineteenth-Century Literature and Culture, no. 4. Cambridge: Cambridge University Press, 1995.

Ewbank, Inga-Stina. *Their Proper Sphere: A Study of the Brontë Sisters as Early-Victorian Female Novelists*. Cambridge: Harvard University Press, 1966.

Flandrin, Jean-Louis. *Families in Former Times: Kinship, Household and Sexuality*. Themes in the Social Sciences. Translated by Richard Southern. Cambridge: Cambridge University Press, 1979.

Foucault, Michel. *The History of Sexuality*. Vol. 1, *An Introduction*. Translated by Robert Hurley. London: Penguin, 1981.

Fraiman, Susan. *Unbecoming Women: British Women Writers and the Novel of Development*. New York: Columbia University Press, 1993.

Fraser, Rebecca. *Charlotte Brontë*. London: Methuen, 1988.

Frawley, Maria H. *Anne Brontë*. English Authors Series. New York: Twayne, 1996.

Freeman, Janet H. "Telling over Agnes Grey." *Cahiers Victoriens et Edourdiens* 34 (1991): 109–26.

———. "Unity and Diversity in *Shirley*." *Journal of English and Germanic Philology* 87 (1988): 558–75.

Fry, Christopher. "Genius, Talent and Failure: The Brontës." Adam Lecture 1986. King's College, London, 1987.

Gallagher, Catherine. *The Industrial Reformation of English Fiction: Social Discourse and Narrative Form, 1832–1867*. Chicago: University of Chicago Press, 1985.

Gardiner, Juliet. *The Brontës at Haworth: The World Within*. New York: Collins & Brown, 1992.

Gates, Barbara Timm, ed. *Critical Essays on Charlotte Brontë*. Boston: G. K. Hall, 1990.

Gérin, Winifred. *Anne Brontë*. London: Thomas Nelson & Sons, 1959.

———. *Branwell Brontë*. London: Thomas Nelson & Sons, 1961.

———. *The Brontës: The Formative Years*. Harlow: Longman, 1973.

———. *Charlotte Brontë: The Evolution of Genius*. Oxford: Clarendon Press, 1967.

———. *Emily Brontë: A Biography*. Oxford: Clarendon Press, 1971.

———. Introduction to *The Tenant of Wildfell Hall*. London: Penguin, 1979.

Gilbert, Sandra M., and Susan Gubar. *The Madwoman in the Attic: The Woman Writer and the Nineteenth-Century Literary Imagination*. New Haven: Yale University Press, 1979.

Gilmour, Robin. *The Novel in the Victorian Age: A Modern Introduction*. London: Edward Arnold, 1986.
Glen, Heather. Introduction to *The Professor*. London: Penguin, 1989.
Goetz, William R. "Genealogy and Incest in *Wuthering Heights*." *Studies in the Novel* 14 (1982): 359–76.
Goodman, Charlotte. "The Lost Brother, The Twin: Women Novelists and the Male-Female Double Bildungsroman." *Novel* 17 (1983): 28–43.
Gordon, Felicia. *A Preface to the Brontës*. London: Longman, 1989.
Gordon, Jan B. "Gossip, Diary, Letter, Text: Anne Brontë's Narrative Tenant and the Problematic of the Gothic Sequel." *English Literary History* 5 (1984): 719–45.
Gordon, Lyndall. *Charlotte Brontë: A Passionate Life*. New York: Norton, 1996.
Gruner, Elisabeth Rose. "'Loving Difference': Sisters and Brothers from Frances Burney to Emily Brontë." In *The Significance of Sibling Relationships in Literature*, edited by JoAnna Stephens Mink and Janet Doubler Ward, 32–46. Bowling Green, Ohio: Bowling Green State University Popular Press, 1993.
Hall, Kate. "Maternal Influence on Charlotte Brontë." *Brontë Society Transactions* 21 (1993): 3–7.
Harris, C. C. *The Family and Industrial Society*. Studies in Sociology, no. 13. London: George Allen & Unwin, 1983.
Hawkes, Terence. *Metaphor*. Critical Idiom Series. London: Methuen, 1972.
Heilman, Robert B. "Charlotte Brontë, Reason and the Moon." *Nineteenth-Century Fiction* 14 (1960): 283–302.
Helsinger, Elizabeth K., Robin Lauterbach Sheets, and William Veeder. *The Woman Question: Society and Literature in Britain and America, 1837–1883*. 3 vols. Chicago: University of Chicago Press, 1983.
Hirsch, Marianne. *The Mother/Daughter Plot: Narrative, Psychoanalysis, Feminism*. Bloomington: Indiana University Press, 1989.
Holstein, Suzy Clarkson. "A 'Root Deeper than All Change': The Daughter's Longing in the Victorian Novel." *Victorian Newsletter* 75 (1989): 20–28.
Homans, Margaret. *Bearing the Word: Language and Female Experience in Nineteenth-Century Women's Writing*. Chicago: University of Chicago Press, 1986.
———. "Dreaming of Children: Literalization in *Jane Eyre* and *Wuthering Heights*." In *The Female Gothic*, edited by Juliann E. Fleenor, 257–79. Montreal: Eden, 1983.

Hook, Andrew, and Judith Hook. Introduction to *Shirley*. London: Penguin, 1974.

Horn, Pamela. "The Victorian Governess." *History of Education* 18 (1989): 333-44.

Houghton, Walter E. *The Victorian Frame of Mind, 1830-1870*. New Haven: Yale University Press, 1957.

Hudson, Glenda A. *Sibling Love and Incest in Jane Austen's Fiction*. Basingstoke: Macmillan, 1992.

Hughes, Kathryn. *The Victorian Governess*. London: Hambledon Press, 1993.

Ingham, Patricia. *The Language of Gender and Class: Transformation in the Victorian Novel*. London: Routledge, 1996.

Ittman, Karl. *Work, Gender and Family in Victorian England*. Basingstoke: Macmillan, 1995.

Jacobus, Mary. "The Buried Letter: *Villette*." In *Reading Woman: Essays in Feminist Criticism*, 41-61. London: Methuen, 1986.

———. "The Question of Language: Men of Maxims and *The Mill on the Floss*." *Critical Inquiry* 8 (1981): 207-22.

Jalland, Pat. *Death in the Victorian Family*. Oxford: Oxford University Press, 1996.

Jay, Elisabeth. *The Religion of the Heart: Anglican Evangelicalism and the Nineteenth-Century Novel*. Oxford: Clarendon Press, 1979.

Kane, Penny. *Victorian Families in Fact and Fiction*. Basingstoke: Macmillan, 1995.

Karl, Frederick R. "The Brontës: The Self Defined, Redefined and Refined." In *The Victorian Experience: The Novelists*, edited by Richard A. Levine, 121-50. Columbus: Ohio University Press, 1976.

Kavanagh, James H. *Emily Brontë*. Rereading Literature Series. Oxford: Basil Blackwell, 1985.

Keefe, Robert. *Charlotte Brontë's World of Death*. Austin: University of Texas Press, 1979.

Kelly, Mary Ann. "Paralysis and the Circular Nature of Memory in *Villette*." *Journal of English and Germanic Philology* 90 (July 1991): 342-60.

Kern, Stephen. "Explosive Intimacy: Psychodynamics of the Victorian Family." *History of Childhood Quarterly* 1 (1974): 437-61.

Kestner, Joseph. *Protest and Reform: The British Social Narrative by Women, 1827-1867*. Madison: University of Wisconsin Press, 1985.

Kettle, Arnold. *An Introduction to the English Novel*. 2 vols. London: Hutchinson, 1951.

Knapp, Bettina L. *The Brontës: Branwell, Anne, Emily, Charlotte.* New York: Continuum Press, 1991.
Knies, Earl A. "Art, Death, and the Composition of *Shirley.*" *Victorian Newsletter* 28 (1965): 22–24.
Knoepflmacher, U. C. *Emily Brontë: Wuthering Heights.* Cambridge: Cambridge University Press, 1989.
Korg, Jacob. "The Problem of Unity in *Shirley.*" *Nineteenth-Century Fiction* 12 (1957): 125–36.
Kucich, John. "Passionate Reserve and Reserved Passion in the Works of Charlotte Brontë." *English Literary History* 52 (1985): 913–37.
Lamb, Michael E., and Brian Sutton-Smith, eds. *Sibling Relationships: Their Nature and Significance across the Lifespan.* Hillsdale, N.J.: Lawrence Erlbaum, 1982.
Langer, Gary F. *The Coming of Age of Political Economy, 1815–1825.* New York: Greenwood Press, 1987.
Langland, Elizabeth. *Anne Brontë: The Other One.* Women Writers Series. Basingstoke: Macmillan Educational, 1989.
———. *Nobody's Angels: Middle-Class Women and Domestic Ideology in Victorian Culture.* Ithaca: Cornell University Press, 1995.
———. "The Voicing of Feminine Desire in Anne Brontë's *The Tenant of Wildfell Hall.*" In *Gender and Discourse in Victorian Literature and Art,* edited by Antony H. Harrison and Beverly Taylor, 111–23. DeKalb: Northern Illinois University Press, 1992.
———. "Women's Writing and the Domestic Sphere." In *Women and Literature in Britain, 1800–1900,* edited by Joanne Shattock, 119–41. Cambridge: Cambridge University Press, 2001.
Lasch, Christopher. *Haven in a Heartless World: The Family Besieged.* 1977. New York: Norton, 1995.
Laslett, Peter, and Richard Wall. *Household and Family in Past Time.* Cambridge: Cambridge University Press, 1972.
Lawrence, Karen. "The Cypher: Disclosure and Reticence in *Villette.*" *Nineteenth-Century Literature* 42 (1988): 448–66.
Leavis, Q. D. "A Fresh Approach to *Wuthering Heights.*" In *Lectures in America,* 83–152. New York: Pantheon Press, 1969.
Lee, Hsiao-Hung. *"Possibilities of Hidden Things": Narrative Transgression in Victorian Fictional Autobiographies.* New York: Peter Lang, 1996.
Levin, Amy K. *The Suppressed Sister: A Relationship in Novels by Nineteenth- and Twentieth-Century British Women.* London and Toronto: Associated University Presses, 1992.
Levy, Anita. "Blood, Kinship, and Gender." *Genders* 5 (1989): 70–85.

Liddell, Robert. *Twin Spirits: The Novels of Emily and Anne Brontë.* London: Peter Owen, 1990.
Lloyd Evans, Barbara, and Gareth Lloyd Evans. *Everyman's Companion to the Brontës.* London: J. M. Dent & Sons, 1982.
Lock, John, and Canon W. T. Dixon. *A Man of Sorrow: The Life, Letters and Times of the Rev. Patrick Brontë, 1777–1861.* London: Thomas Nelson & Sons, 1965.
Longford, Elizabeth. *Eminent Victorian Women.* New York: Knopf, 1981.
MacFarlane, Alan. *Marriage and Love in England: Modes of Reproduction, 1300–1840.* Oxford: Basil Blackwell, 1986.
MacKay, Angus M. *The Brontës: Fact and Fiction.* London: Service & Paton, 1897.
McKnight, Natalie J. *Suffering Mothers in Mid-Victorian Novels.* New York: St. Martin's Press, 1997.
McMaster, Juliet. "'Imbecile Laughter' and 'Desperate Earnest' in *The Tenant of Wildfell Hall.*" *Modern Language Quarterly* 43 (1982): 352–68.
McNees, Eleanor, ed. *The Brontë Sisters: Critical Assessments.* 4 vols. The Banks, Mountfield: Helm Information, 1996.
Malone, Catherine. "Charlotte Brontë: Gothic Autobiographies." Ph.D. diss., Oxford University, 1993.
———. "'We Have Learnt to Love Her More than Her Books': The Critical Reception of Brontë's *Professor.*" *Review of English Studies,* ns 47 (1996): 175–87.
Martin, Robert. *The Accents of Persuasion: Charlotte Brontë's Novels.* London: Faber, 1966.
Marxist-Feminist Literature Collective. "Women's Writing: *Jane Eyre, Shirley, Villette, Aurora Leigh.*" In *The Sociology of Literature: 1848,* edited by Francis Barker et al., 185–206. Colchester: University of Essex Press, 1978.
Mason, Michael. Introduction to *Jane Eyre.* London: Penguin, 1996.
May, Leila Silvana. "Relatively Speaking: Representations of Siblings in Nineteenth-Century British Literature." Ph.D. diss., University of California, Berkeley, 1994.
Maynard, John. *Charlotte Brontë and Sexuality.* Cambridge: Cambridge University Press, 1984.
Mellor, Anne K. *Romanticism and Gender.* New York: Routledge, 1993.
Michie, Elsie B. *Outside the Pale: Cultural Exclusion, Gender Difference, and the Victorian Woman Writer.* Ithaca: Cornell University Press, 1993.

Michie, Helena. *Sororophobia: Differences among Women in Literature and Culture*. New York: Oxford University Press, 1992.

Miller, J. Hillis. *The Disappearance of God: Five Nineteenth-Century Writers*. Cambridge: Harvard University Press, 1963.

———. *Fiction and Repetition: Seven English Novels*. Oxford: Basil Blackwell, 1982.

Miller, Lucasta. *The Brontë Myth*. London: Jonathan Cape, 2001.

Mink, JoAnna Stephens, and Janet Doubler Ward. Introduction to *The Significance of Sibling Relationships in Literature*. Bowling Green, Ohio: Bowling Green State University Popular Press, 1993.

Mintz, Steven. *A Prison of Expectations: The Family in Victorian Culture*. New York: New York University Press, 1983.

Mitchell, Juliet. *Women: The Longest Revolution*. London: Virago, 1984.

Moers, Ellen. *Literary Women*. London: W. H. Allen, 1977.

Moglen, Helene. *Charlotte Brontë: The Self Conceived*. Madison: University of Wisconsin Press, 1984.

———. "The Double Vision of *Wuthering Heights*: A Clarifying View of Female Development." *Centennial Review* 15 (1971): 391–405.

Moore, George. *Conversations in Ebury Street*. New York: Boni & Liveright, 1924.

Murray, Janet Horowitz. Introduction to *Miss Miles, or A Tale of Yorkshire Life Sixty Years Ago*, by Mary Taylor. New York: Oxford University Press, 1990.

Murry, Janet Horowitz, ed. *Strong-Minded Women and Other Lost Voices from Nineteenth-Century England*. Harmondsworth: Penguin, 1984.

Nelson, Claudia. *Boys Will Be Girls: The Feminine Ethic and British Children's Fiction, 1857–1917*. New Brunswick: Rutgers University Press, 1991.

Nestor, Pauline. *Charlotte Brontë*. Women Writers Series. Basingstoke: Macmillan Educational, 1987.

———. *Female Friendships and Communities: Charlotte Brontë, George Eliot, Elizabeth Gaskell*. Oxford: Clarendon Press, 1985.

Neufeldt, Victor A., ed. *A Bibliography of the Manuscripts of Patrick Branwell Brontë*. New York: Garland Press, 1993.

Oliphant, Margaret. "The Sisters Brontë." In *Women Novelists of Queen Victoria's Reign: A Book of Appreciations*. By Oliphant, Eliza Lynn Linton, et al., 1–60. London: Hurst & Blackett, 1897.

O'Neill, Jane. *The World of the Brontës: The Lives, Times, and Works of Charlotte, Emily and Anne Brontë*. London: Carlton Press, 1997.

Paden, W. D. *An Investigation of Gondal*. New York: Bookman, 1958.

Paige, Lori A. "Helen's Diary Freshly Considered." *Brontë Society Transactions* 20 (1991): 225–27.

Parker, Patricia. "The (Self-)Identity of the Literary Text: Property, Proper Place, and Proper Name in *Wuthering Heights*." In *Literary Fat Ladies: Rhetoric, Gender, Property*, 155–77. London: Methuen, 1987.

Payne, Susan. "The Strange within the Real: Mimesis and Fantasy in Charlotte Brontë's *Villette*." In *The Strange within the Real: The Function of Fantasy in Austen, Brontë and Eliot*, 61–122. N.p.: Bulzoni Editore, 1992.

Peer, Larry H. *Beyond Haworth: Essays on the Brontës in European Literature*. Provo: Brigham Young University Press, 1984.

Perkin, Joan. *Women and Marriage in Nineteenth-Century England*. Chicago: Lyceum Press, 1989.

Perry, Ruth. "Women in Families: The Great Disinheritance." In *Women and Literature in Britain, 1700–1800*, edited by Vivien Jones, 111–31. Cambridge: Cambridge University Press, 2000.

Peterson, M. Jeanne. "The Victorian Governess: Status Incongruence in Family and Society." In *Suffer and Be Still: Women in the Victorian Age*, edited by Martha Vicinus, 3–19. Bloomington: Indiana University Press, 1972.

Phillips, Marion J. "Charlotte Brontë's Favourite Preacher: Frederick Denison John Maurice (1805–1872)." *Brontë Society Transactions* 20 (1990): 77–87.

Pike, E. Holly. *Family and Society in the Works of Elizabeth Gaskell*. American University Series. New York: Peter Lang, 1995.

Pinion, F. B. *A Brontë Companion: Literary Assessment, Background and Reference*. Basingstoke: Macmillan, 1975.

Poovey, Mary. *Uneven Developments: The Ideological Work of Gender in Mid-Victorian England*. London: Virago, 1989.

Prentis, Barbara. *The Brontë Sisters and George Eliot: A Unity of Difference*. Basingstoke: Macmillan, 1988.

Pykett, Lyn. *Emily Brontë*. Basingstoke: Macmillan, 1989.

Qualls, Barry V. *The Secular Pilgrims of Victorian Fiction: The Novel as Book of Life*. Cambridge: Cambridge University Press, 1982.

Rabinowitz, Nancy Sorkin. "'Faithful Narrator' or 'Partial Eulogist': First-Person Narration in Brontë's *Villette*." *Journal of Narrative Technique* 15 (1985): 244–55.

Raphael, D. D. "Adam Smith." In *Three Great Economists: Smith, Malthus*,

Keynes, 6–104. Past Masters Series, edited by Keith Thomas. Oxford: Oxford University Press, 1997.
Ratchford, Fannie Elizabeth. *The Brontës' Web of Childhood*. New York: Russell & Russell, 1964.
Ratchford, Fannie Elizabeth, ed. *Gondal's Queen: A Novel in Verse by Emily Jane Brontë*. Austin: Universtiy of Texas Press, 1955.
Ricardo, David. *The Principles of Political Economy and Taxation*. 1817. London: J. M. Dent & Sons, 1973.
Rich, Adrienne. "*Jane Eyre:* The Temptations of a Motherless Woman." In *On Lies, Secrets and Silence, Selected Prose 1966–1978*, 89–106. New York: Norton, 1979.
Robbins, Ruth, and Julian Wolfreys, eds. *Victorian Identities: Social and Cultural Formations in Nineteenth-Century Literature*. Basingstoke: Macmillan, 1996.
Rodolff, Rebecca. "From the Ending of *The Professor* to the Conception of *Jane Eyre*." *Philological Quarterly* 61 (1982): 71–89.
Rose, Phyllis. *Parallel Lives: Five Victorian Marriages*. New York: Vintage, 1994.
Rosengarten, Herbert J. "Charlotte Brontë's *Shirley* and the *Leeds Mercury*." *Studies in English Literature, 1500–1900* 16 (1976): 591–600.
Sadoff, Dianne F. *Monsters of Affection: Dickens, Eliot and Brontë on Fatherhood*. Baltimore: Johns Hopkins University Press, 1982.
Sanger, C. P. *The Structure of Wuthering Heights*. Hogarth Essays, no. 19. London: Hogarth Press, 1926.
Schor, Esther. *Bearing the Dead: The British Culture of Mourning from the Enlightenment to Victoria*. Princeton: Princeton University Press, 1994.
Scott, P. J. M. *Anne Brontë: A New Critical Assessment*. New York: Barnes & Noble, 1983.
Senf, Carol A. "Emily Brontë's Version of Feminist History: *Wuthering Heights*." *Essays in Literature* 12 (1985): 201–14.
Shapiro, Arnold. "Public Themes and Private Lives: Social Criticism in *Shirley*." *Papers on Language and Literature* 4 (1968): 74–84.
Showalter, Elaine. *A Literature of Their Own from Charlotte Brontë to Doris Lessing*. London: Virago, 1982.
Shuttleworth, Sally. *Charlotte Brontë and Victorian Psychology*. Cambridge: Cambridge University Press, 1996.
Silver, Brenda R. "The Reflecting Reader in *Villette*." In *The Voyage In: Fictions of Female Development*, edited by Elizabeth Abel, Marianne

Hirsch, and Elizabeth Langland, 90–111. Hanover, N.H.: University Press of New England, 1983.
Sinclair, May. *The Three Brontës*. London: Hutchinson, [1912?].
Slinn, E. Warwick. *The Discourse of Self in Victorian Poetry*. Basingstoke: Macmillan, 1991.
Smith, Margaret. Introduction to *Jane Eyre*. Oxford: Oxford University Press, 1993.
Solomon, Eric. "The Incest Theme in *Wuthering Heights*." *Nineteenth-Century Fiction* 14 (1959): 80–83.
Spivak, Gayatri Chakravorty. "Three Women's Texts and a Critique of Imperialism." *Critical Inquiry* 12 (1985): 243–61.
Stevenson, W. H. "*Wuthering Heights*: The Facts." *Essays in Criticism* 35 (1985): 149–66.
Stewart, Garrett. "A Valediction for Bidding Mourning: Death and the Narratee in Brontë's *Villette*." In *Death and Representation*, edited by Sarah Webster Goodwin and Elisabeth Bronfen, 51–79. Baltimore: Johns Hopkins University Press, 1993.
Stone, Donald D. *The Romantic Impulse in Victorian Fiction*. Cambridge: Harvard University Press, 1980.
Stone, Lawrence. *The Family, Sex and Marriage in England, 1500–1800*. Abr. ed. New York: Harper & Row, 1979.
Stoneman, Patsy. "The Brontës and Death: Alternatives to Revolution." In *The Sociology of Literature: 1848*, edited by Francis Barker et al., 79–96. Colchester: University of Essex Press, 1978.
———. "Catherine Earnshaw's Journey to Her Home among the Dead: Fresh Thoughts on *Wuthering Heights* and 'Epipsychidion.'" *Review of English Studies*, ns 47 (1996): 521–33.
———. Introduction to *Wuthering Heights*. Oxford: Oxford University Press, 1995.
Sussman, Herbert. *Victorian Masculinities: Manhood and Masculine Politics in Early Victorian Literature and Art*. Cambridge: Cambridge University Press, 1995.
Sutherland, Kathryn. "*Jane Eyre*'s Literary History: The Case for *Mansfield Park*." *English Literary History* 59 (1992): 409–40.
———. "Writings on Education and Conduct: Arguments for Female Improvement." In *Women and Literature in Britain, 1700–1800*, edited by Vivien Jones, 25–45. Cambridge: Cambridge University Press, 2000.
Swindells, Julia. *Victorian Writing and Working Women: The Other Side of Silence*. Oxford: Basil Blackwell, 1985.
Tanner, Tony. Introduction to *Villette*. London: Penguin, 1979.

Tayler, Irene. *Holy Ghosts: The Male Muses of Emily and Charlotte Brontë.* New York: Columbia University Press, 1990.
Taylor, Charles. *Sources of the Self: The Making of Modern Identity.* Cambridge: Cambridge University Press, 1989.
Thompson, Nicola. "The Many Faces of *Wuthering Heights*: 1847–1997." *Brontë Society Transactions* 23 (1998): 31–45.
Thompson, Wade. "Infanticide and Sadism in *Wuthering Heights*." *Publications of the Modern Language Association* 78 (1963): 69–74.
Thomson, Patricia. *The Victorian Heroine: A Changing Ideal, 1837–1873.* London: Oxford University Press, 1956.
Thormählen, Marianne. *The Brontës and Religion.* Cambridge: Cambridge University Press, 1999.
———. "The Brontë Pseudonyms." *English Studies: A Journal of English Language and Literature* 75 (1994): 246–55.
Tillotson, Kathleen. *Novels of the 1840s.* Oxford: Clarendon Press, 1954.
Tosh, John. *A Man's Place: Masculinity and the Middle-Class Home in Victorian England.* New Haven: Yale University Press, 1999.
Tromly, Annette. *The Cover of the Mask: The Autobiographers in Charlotte Brontë's Fiction.* English Literary Studies Monograph Series. Victoria, B.C.: University of Victoria Press, 1982.
Trumbach, Randolph. *The Rise of the Egalitarian Family: Aristocratic Kinship and Domestic Relations in Eighteenth-Century England.* New York: Academic Press, 1978.
Van Boheemen, Christine. *The Novel as Family Romance: Language, Gender, and Authority from Fielding to Joyce.* Ithaca: Cornell University Press, 1987.
Vicinus, Martha, ed. *Suffer and Be Still: Women in the Victorian Age.* Bloomington: Indiana University Press, 1972.
Vine, Steven. "'When I Am Not': Mourning and Identity in *Wuthering Heights*." Paper presented at conference, The Legacy of the Brontës, 1847–1997, School of English, University of Leeds, April 1997.
———. "The Wuther of the Other in *Wuthering Heights*." *Nineteenth-Century Fiction* 49 (1994): 339–59.
Waddell, Julia. "Women Writers as Little Sisters in Victorian Society: *The Mill on the Floss* and the Case of George Eliot." In *The Significance of Sibling Relationships in Literature*, edited by JoAnna Stephens Mink and Janet Doubler Ward, 47–57. Bowling Green: Bowling Green State University Popular Press, 1993.
Waters, Catherine. *Dickens and the Politics of the Family.* Cambridge: Cambridge University Press, 1997.

Webb, Igor. *From Custom to Capital: The English Novel and the Industrial Revolution*. Ithaca: Cornell University Press, 1981.
Weeks, Jeffrey. *Sex, Politics and Society: the Regulation of Sexuality since 1800*. 2d ed. London: Longman, 1989.
Wheat, Patricia H. *The Adytum of the Heart: The Literary Criticism of Charlotte Brontë*. London and Toronto: Associated University Presses, 1992.
Wheeler, Michael. *Death and the Future Life in Victorian Literature and Theology*. Cambridge: Cambridge University Press, 1990.
Williams, Judith. *Perception and Expression in the Novels of Charlotte Brontë*. Ann Arbor: UMI Research Press, 1988.
Williams, Raymond. *The English Novel: From Dickens to Lawrence*. London: Hogarth Press, 1984.
———. *Keywords: A Vocabulary of Culture and Society*. London: Fontana Press, 1988.
Winnifrith, Tom. *The Brontës and Their Background: Romance and Reality*. Basingstoke: Macmillan, 1973.
———. Introduction to *Charlotte Brontë: Unfinished Novels*. Stroud: Alan Sutton in Association with the Brontë Society, 1993.
———. *A New Life of Charlotte Brontë*. Basingstoke: Macmillan, 1988.
Wohl, Anthony S. *The Victorian Family: Structure and Stresses*. New York: St. Martin's Press, 1978.
Wolff, Robert Lee. *Gains and Losses: Novels of Faith and Doubt in Victorian England*. London: John Murray, 1977.
Woodward, Llewellyn. *The Age of Reform, 1815–1870*. 2d ed. Oxford: Oxford University Press, 1992.
Wyatt, Jean. "A Patriarch of One's Own: *Jane Eyre* and Romantic Love." *Tulsa Studies in Women's Literature* 4 (1985): 199–216.
Yaeger, Patricia. "Violence in the Sitting Room: *Wuthering Heights* and the Woman's Novel." *Genre* 21 (1988): 203–29.

INDEX

A. G. A (Augusta Geraldine Almeda), 42, 57, 59–60, 111. *See also* Gondal
Agnes Grey (Anne Brontë): as domestic improving literature, 8; Patrick Brontë's influence on, 8; concern with family's formative role in, 8, 18, 119–20, 123–24; criticism of restrictive education in, 33–34, 131–33; use of governess to criticize family in, 120, 122, 124–28; and status incongruence of governess, 121–22, 127; class criticism in, 122–23; consumption of alcohol in, 125; education of Tom Bloomfield in, 125–26; Mrs. Murray's maternal failings in, 126–28; Rosalie Murray's marriage to Sir Thomas Ashby in, 128–30; criticism of female redemptive potential in, 129; Rosalie Murray Ashby's maternal failings in, 130–31
Aimé-Martin, Louis, 13, 17
Angria (Charlotte and Branwell's imaginary world): writing motivated by sibling rivalry, 42; sibling rivalry in content of stories, 42–43, 44–46; Northangerland's Byronic influence on Zamorna, 46–48; Mina Laury as typical of Charlotte's heroines, 47–48, 51–52. *See also Henry Hastings*; Juvenilia; *Spell, The*
"AS to GS" (Emily Brontë), 60–61
Aykroyd, Tabitha (Brontës' domestic servant), 11

Barker, Juliet (biographer), 1, 2, 19, 63
Bell, Currer, Ellis, and Acton (Brontë pseudonyms), 6, 62
Bildungsroman: pattern of novels, 7; *Jane Eyre* as, 67, 85–86; *Agnes Grey* as, 132–33; *Shirley* as failed, 215n9
"Biographical Notice of Ellis and Acton Bell" (Charlotte Brontë), 36, 64, 65–66, 118, 136
Blackwood's Edinburgh Magazine, 17, 27–28, 44
Bodichon, Barbara Leigh Smith, 141–42
Branwell, "Aunt," 11, 18, 20, 24
Brontë, Anne: knowledge of Latin, 24; as governess, 38, 122; loss of intimacy with Emily, 58; defends separate authorial identity, 64–65; as characterized by Charlotte in "Biographical Notice," 65–66, 118; literary reputation, 118; literary differences compared with Charlotte and Emily, 118–19; comparisons with Patrick Brontë's writing, 119; and Branwell's affair with Mrs. Robinson, 136; death of, 182
Brontë, Branwell. *See* Brontë, Patrick Branwell
Brontë, Charlotte: writes to Robert Southey, 25–26; as feminist, 29, 31–32, 34–35, 171–72, 173; rejects Henry Nussey, 38; as governess, 38, 122; encourages sisters to publish, 62–63; defends separate authorial identity, 64, 65–66; reveals Ellis and Acton Bell, 65–66; views on Chartism, 163; and death of siblings, 179, 180, 183–85, 196–98; and Branwell's death, 181–82; and Anne's death, 182; and Emily's death, 182; marriage to Arthur Bell Nicholls, 210–12
Brontë, Emily: knowledge of Latin, 24; as feminist, 30–31; at Roe Head, 38;

255

views of Haworth, 38; defends separate authorial identity, 65; as characterized by Charlotte in "Biographical Notice," 65–66; death of, 182
Brontë, Maria (mother): death of, 11; relationship with Patrick Brontë, 19
Brontë, Maria and Elizabeth (sisters), 22, 23
Brontë, Patrick (father): enabled daughters' literary achievements, 2, 21; as educator, 18; Elizabeth Gaskell's portrait of, 18–19; as example of self-improvement, 20; views on female nature and education, 20, 22–23; as educator of Branwell, 20, 24–25; views on education, 21; tests children behind mask, 22; as example of patriarchy with Robert Southey, 26
Brontë, Patrick Branwell (brother): enabled sisters' literary achievements, 2; as leader in juvenilia, 6, 43, 44; educational regime, 24; demise of, 24–25; as caricatured by Charlotte in juvenilia, 41; as portrait painter, 52–53; affair with Mrs. Robinson, 136; death of, 181–82
Brontë family: as typically Victorian, 19; gender differences in, 20; sisters' home education in, 23–24; as portrayed in *Jane Eyre*, 88–89. *See also* Family as context of Brontës' writing
Brother: brotherhood forsaken in *The Professor* and *Shirley*, 9, 148, 155, 163; Branwell caricatured as, 41; as rivals in Charlotte's fiction, 42–43; twin brothers in *The Spell*, 48–50; Henry Hastings as, 52–54, 55–56; Hareton Earnshaw as brother figure, 112; in *The Professor*, 155–57; in "The Story of Willie Ellin," 209

Captain Henry Hastings. See Henry Hastings
Carlyle, Thomas: *Chartism* and *Past and Present* provide industrial context for *Shirley*, 151–52; influences Dickens's and Gaskell's industrial novels, 151–52; uses sibling rivalry to describe social relations, 153–54
Chartism, 162–63
Childhood, Evangelical notions of, 14–15
Collaboration, of Brontë siblings, 6, 30–31, 57–58, 62–63, 188, 212. *See also* Juvenilia
Cousins: in Brontë fiction, 112; Robert Moore and Caroline Helstone as, 173
Cowan Bridge (Clergy Daughters' School), 15, 23

Death rate in Haworth, 15, 180
Dickens, Charles: challenges domestic ideology, 5; Wemmick's view of home in *Great Expectations*, 12; *Hard Times* as influenced by Carlyle, 151, 153; Gradgrind family in *Hard Times*, 155
Domestic ideology: promoted in guidebooks, 4; Brontës debate in fiction, 5–6; Evangelical influences, 6; "separate spheres," 11; "home virtues" in, 12, 14, 17. *See also* Family, Victorian views of

Education: Patrick Brontë's views on female education, 22–23; of Brontë sisters, 23–24; of Branwell Brontë, 24–25; Victorian views of female education, 32; Brontës as advocates for broader female education, 33–35
Eliot, George: challenges domestic ideology, 5; gendered education in *The Mill on the Floss*, 16; childhood in *The Mill on the Floss*, 111
Ellis, Sarah Stickney: *Women of England*, 5, 26, 95; reviews Charlotte Brontë's novels, 28; criticizes male selfishness, 138; uses sibling rivalry to describe social relations, 153–54; view of woman's redemptive potential, 154; Charlotte challenges her view of woman's redemptive potential, 155, 157–58
"Emma" (Charlotte Brontë): 209–10
Enclosure, theme of: in Brontës' fiction, 3; containment of women in the home, 17–18, 96; in the parsonage, 37–38; in *Wuthering Heights*, 96, 106–7
Engels, Friedrich, 12

Family: formative role, 4, 6; changing definitions of, 10–11; nuclear model of, 11; role in instilling gender differences, 15–16; disciplinary function of, 16–17; Brontës as typical Victorian family, 19
Family, Victorian views of: formative role,

4, 6, 13–14; as haven from workplace, 12, 152–53; as model for social relations, 13; role in instilling gender differences, 15–16; disciplinary function of, 16–17; mother's educative role, 17; containment of women in, 17–18; female education in, 32; death in, 180–81. *See also* Domestic ideology

Family as content in Brontës' fiction: as "defining community," 1, 6, 7; as site of fulfillment, 3, 35; complexities of, 3, 212; formative role of, 5–6; role in bildungsroman pattern of novels, 7

Family as context of Brontës' writing: environment at Haworth, 1–2, 37–39; collaborative efforts, 6, 30–31, 62–63, 188, 212; sisters defend separate identities in public sphere, 37, 62, 63–65; homesickness affects literary output, 38

Father: Arthur Huntingdon as, 9, 144–45; call to fathers in *Shirley*, 34, 164–65, 174; Earnshaw's transgressions as, 97–98; William Crimsworth as, 160–62; William Farren as, 167–68; Hiram Yorke as, 168

Female role in family: as "relative creature," 5, 95; Patrick Brontë's views of, 20, 22–23; conflicting views of, 26–27; inheritance of property, 114, 115–116; redemptive potential, 129, 140–41, 157–58; "oneness" in marriage, 141–42. *See also* Woman question

Feminism: Brontë sisters as feminists, 2–3, 30–31; Charlotte Brontë as feminist, 29, 31–32, 34–35, 171–72; feminist protests in novels, 31; Brontës advocate female "independency," 33; in *Shirley*, 178

Gaskell, Elizabeth: challenges domestic ideology, 5; *Life of Charlotte Brontë*, 19, 63; *Mary Barton*, 151, 163, 167; *North and South*, 151–52, 166; Charlotte's correspondence with, 180, 184; Charlotte visits, 184

Gérin, Winifred (biographer), 20, 24, 136, 142

Gilbert, Sandra M. and Susan Gubar (*The Madwoman in the Attic*), 2, 36, 37, 68, 72, 83–84, 99, 164, 188, 189

Gondal (Emily and Anne's imaginary world): founding of, 42; nature of collaboration, 57–58; as sibling dialogue, 58–61. *See also* Juvenilia

Gordon, Lyndall (biographer), 2, 207, 210

Governesses: Charlotte and Anne as, 38, 122; status incongruence in Victorian society, 121–22; challenge to maternal responsibilities, 127. *See also Agnes Grey*

Heger, Constantin, 188, 208
Hemans, Felicia, 10, 17
Henry Hastings: Elizabeth Hastings as forerunner to Jane Eyre, 52, 56; as critique of Charlotte's relationship with Branwell, 52–53, 56–57; Elizabeth Hastings's parallels with Charlotte Brontë, 53–54; parallels with Scott's *The Heart of Midlothian*, 54; sibling rescue plot of, 55–56

Infant Custody Bill, 31, 144
In Memoriam (Alfred Tennyson), 183, 207

Jameson, Anna, 173–74
Jane Eyre (Charlotte Brontë): Reed family as defining community in, 7–8, 69–75, 77–78, 81–82; "poor orphan child" motif in, 8, 67–68, 74; search for kinship in, 8, 67–68, 78; role of God in, 8, 68, 69; as female bildungsroman, 67, 85–86; references to *Pilgrim's Progress* in, 68, 84, 85, 86; Jane's economic identity in, 71–72, 74–75, 81, 83, 90; Jane's understanding of God in, 73–74, 77, 86–88, 94; Lowood as defining community in, 76, 77–78; Helen Burns as "poor orphan child" in, 76, 77; role of primogeniture in, 78–79; kinship with Rochester in, 79–80, 82; Ingram family as defining community in, 80–81; Jane's affinities with Bertha Mason in, 83–84; Jane's dreams of self-dependency in, 84–85; Christian topography of, 85; role of Mother Nature in, 86; providential ontology of, 87–88, 92–94; kinship with Diana and Mary Rivers in, 88–89; Rivers family parallels with Reed family in, 90; St. John Rivers's marriage proposal in, 90–91; Rochester's conversion in, 92–93

Juvenilia: emulates *Blackwood's Edinburgh Magazine*, 27–28, 44; origins of, 39; Patrick Brontë's role in, 39–40; as compensation for loss of mother and sisters, 40; Brontës' identification with characters in, 40–41; division into two imaginary worlds, 41–42; Branwell's formative influence on, 43, 44; Charlotte's reliance on male narrators in, 43–44. *See also* Angria; Family as context of Brontës' writing; Gondal; *Henry Hastings*; *Spell, The*

Lady's Magazine, 27–28
Lamb, Ann Richelieu (*Can Woman Regenerate Society?*), 26, 95, 136–37
Laury, Mina (Charlotte Brontë's juvenile heroine), 47–48, 51–52
Lewis, Sarah (*Woman's Mission*), 16, 26, 126–27, 138, 143

Married Women's Property Acts, 31
Martineau, Harriet (*Household Education*), 18, 32–33, 123, 173, 174
Maurice, F. D., 183
Maurice, Mary, 121, 127
Moglen, Helene, 19, 96, 156, 168, 178, 189
More, Hannah, 16, 21, 23, 24
Mother: educative role in family, 17–18, 126–27, 137; Helen Huntingdon as, 18, 143–46; role of Mother Nature in *Jane Eyre*, 86; and governess, 121–22, 127; maternal failings in *Agnes Grey*, 126–28, 130–31; criticism of Mrs. Markham as, in *The Tenant of Wildfell Hall*, 137–38; Mrs. Pryor as in *Shirley*, 174–75

Nicholls, Arthur Bell, 210–12
Northangerland (Branwell's juvenile hero). *See* Angria
"North Wind, The" (Anne Brontë), 59–60
Norton, Caroline, 144
Nussey, Ellen, 1, 22, 38, 54, 58, 89, 122, 150, 180, 182, 184–85
Nussey, Henry, 38

Oliphant, Margaret, 31, 43, 118
Orphans, in Brontës' fiction, 11, 72. *See also Jane Eyre*; "Orphan's Lament, An"

"Orphan's Lament, An" (Anne Brontë), 60–61

Pensionnat Heger (Brussels), 24
Pilgrim's Progress: in *Jane Eyre*, 68, 84, 85, 86; in *Villette*, 191, 200
Poems by Currer, Ellis, and Acton Bell, 62
Poor Law Amendment Act, 13, 150
Primogeniture, 71, 78–79
Professor, The (Charlotte Brontë): sibling rivalry in, 9, 148, 154–58; Reuter's objection to female literary ambition in, 26; publishing history of, 63, 187–88; corruption of family relations and values by industrialization in, 147–49; self-help in, 149–50; female redemptive potential in, 157–58; role of Hunsden Yorke in, 157, 160, 162; class conflict in, 158–59; parallels with *Jane Eyre*, 158–60, 162; William Crimsworth's portrayal of Frances in, 160; William as father in, 160–62
Pseudonyms. *See* Bell, Currer, Ellis, and Acton

Reading, Brontës': theological, 21; books loaned by Smith, Elder, 28–29; of Jane Austen, 29
Reid, Mrs. Hugo (*Plea for Women*), 26–27
"Relative creatures" (Sarah Ellis, *The Women of England*), 5, 31, 95. *See also Wuthering Heights*
"Reminiscences of Charlotte Brontë" (Ellen Nussey), 1, 150
Richmond, Rev. Legh: *Domestic Portraiture*, 14–15, 17, 21–22; similarities with Patrick Brontë, 21–22
Rigby, Elizabeth (review of *Jane Eyre*), 31
Roe Head (Margaret Wooler's school), 21, 24, 38
"Roe Head Journal," 38
Rousseau, Jean-Jacques (*Émile*), 21, 23
Ruskin, John, 13, 147

"Self-Communion" (Anne Brontë), 58
Shirley (Charlotte Brontë): corruption of family relations and values by industrialization in, 9, 147–49; sibling rivalry in, 9, 148, 154–55, 172; rejection of Patrick Brontë's sexism in, 20–21; paternalism in (call to fathers), 34, 164–

65, 174; Rose Yorke's protest in, 34–35, 169, 178; oppression of women and workers in, 148–49, 163–64, 167, 170, 174; Yorkshire industrial background to, 150, 162; Chartism in, 162–63; criticism of Robert Moore as millowner in, 163, 165–66; role of Hiram Yorke in, 165, 168; Robert Moore's views of family in, 166, 177; role of William Farren in, 167–68; Yorke family in, 168–69, 177; Robert Moore's views of marriage in, 169–70; Caroline Helstone's unrequited love in, 170–71; Caroline's desire for employment in, 171–72; Caroline's relationship with Shirley in, 172–73; demand for female education and employment in, 173–74, 178; role of Mrs. Pryor in, 174–75; Shirley's views of marriage in, 175–76; Robert Moore's reformation in, 176–77; ambiguous ending of, 177–78; portrayal of death in, 186–87
Sibling rivalry: as context of juvenile writing, 39; as content in Charlotte and Branwell's juvenile writing, 42–43, 44–46; in *The Spell*, 48–51; in *Wuthering Heights*, 97–101; in *Shirley*, 148, 154–55; in *The Professor*, 148, 154–58; used by Carlyle and Ellis to describe social relations, 153–54; in "The Story of Willie Ellin," 209
Sinclair, May, 144
Sister: Elizabeth Hastings as, 52–54, 55–56; sister-savior motif in Victorian fiction, 55; in "AS to GS," 61; Rivers sisters in *Jane Eyre*, 89; Caroline's sisterhood with Shirley, 172
Smiles, Samuel (*Self-Help*), 123–24, 150
Smith, Adam, 149
Smith, George, 28, 180, 188, 201, 208
Southey, Robert, 25–26
Spell, The, 48–51
Sybil, or Two Nations (Benjamin Disraeli), 163

Taylor, James, 186, 208
Taylor, Mary: criticism of Charlotte Brontë's feminism, 29–30, 171–72; "The First Duty of Women," 30; *Miss Miles*, 30; represented in Rose Yorke in *Shirley*, 168; and dream of Charlotte's elder sisters, 197
Tenant of Wildfell Hall, The (Anne Brontë): Patrick Brontë's influences on, 8, 119, 140; Helen Huntingdon as "saving angel" in, 9, 18, 139–41, 142–43; criticism of "gendered" morality in, 16, 134–35, 136–38; concern with family's formative role in, 119–20, 143; critical condemnation of, 133–34; Branwell Brontë's influences on, 135–36, 182; consumption of alcohol in, 138; criticism of male indulgence in, 138–39; criticism of "oneness" in marriage in, 141–42; diary format of, 142–43, 145–46; Helen prioritizes motherhood over wifehood in, 143–46
Thackeray, William Makepeace, 24, 184, 211
"To a Wreath of Snow by A G Almeda," (Emily Brontë), 59–60

Villette (Charlotte Brontë): and deaths of Branwell, Emily, and Anne, 9, 179, 185–86, 187–88; open-ended fate of M. Paul in, 49, 179, 193, 205–7; Lucy's family's death as metaphorical shipwreck in, 179–80, 189–94; parallels between Charlotte Brontë and Lucy Snowe in, 179–80, 185, 188–90, 197–98, 201; Lucy Snowe exercises narrative control in, 179–80, 189–90, 193–94, 205–7; influence of M. Heger on, 188; Bretton family as haven in, 190–91, 199–200; allusions to *Pilgrim's Progress* in, 191, 200; M. Paul as "Emmanuel" in, 191, 207, 209; Lucy as "anesthetized survivor" of family death, 194–96; ghostly nun in, 195–96, 204–5; Lucy's dreams during long vacation in, 196–99; Graham Bretton's letters in, 200–202; M. Paul asserts kinship with Lucy in, 202–3; Paul's family seeks to keep Lucy and Paul apart in, 203–5

Whately, Mrs. Elizabeth, 121
Williams, W. S.: as correspondent with Thackeray on *Jane Eyre*, 24; as correspondent with Charlotte on the "woman question," 27; as correspon-

dent with Charlotte on Sarah Ellis, 28; Charlotte's advice on educating daughters, 34; as correspondent with Charlotte on "Ellis Bell," 65; views on Chartism, 163; as correspondent during illnesses and deaths of Brontë siblings, 180–86

Wilson, Rev. Carus (founder of Clergy Daughters' School), 15

Wollstonecraft, Mary, 32

Woman question, 26–27. *See also* Female role in family

Woolf, Virginia, 26

Wuthering Heights (Emily Brontë): as tragedy of Catherine Earnshaw, 8; "relative creature" motif in, 8, 96, 113; female role in inheritance of property in, 8, 114, 115–16; female movement in, 16, 95–96, 104, 106–7; Heathcliff's "birth" into Earnshaw family in, 72, 97–98; Catherine's protest against her "relativity" in, 96, 108–9; Earnshaw family as defining community in, 97; Nelly Dean's role in sibling rivalry at the Heights in, 98–99; Nelly's bond with Hindley in, 99–100; Hindley's rivalry with Heathcliff in, 100–101; Catherine's identification with Heathcliff in, 101–4, 111, 113; Catherine's relationship with Edgar and Heathcliff in, 105–6, 107–9; Isabella's escape in, 109–10; Catherine's delirious return to childhood in, 110–12; parallels with childhood in *The Mill on the Floss*, 111; younger Cathy's marriage to Hareton in, 112, 117; Catherine's names on the windowsill in, 112–13; Heathcliff substitutes property gain for Catherine in, 114, 116–17

Zamorna (Charlotte's juvenile hero). *See* Angria